Enjoy! Melissa Foster

Searching for
LOVE

The Bradens & Montgomerys
(Pleasant Hill – Oak Falls)

Love in Bloom Series

Melissa Foster

ISBN-13: 978-1948868488
ISBN-10: 1948868482

Cover Design: Elizabeth Mackey Designs
Cover Photography: Sara Eirew

WORLD LITERARY PRESS
PRINTED IN THE UNITED STATES OF AMERICA

A Note to Readers

If this is your first Love in Bloom book, all of my love stories are written to stand alone, so dive right in and enjoy the fun, sexy ride! I have been wanting to write Zev Braden and Carly Dylan's story for years. Theirs is a second-chance love story like no other. But in order to have a future, they must first come to grips with their tragic pasts and the way it has changed them. I hope you laugh, cry, and fall hard for Zev and Carly, just like I have.

You will find a Braden family tree included in the front matter of this book.

The best way to keep up to date with new releases, sales, and exclusive content is to sign up for my newsletter or download my free app.
www.MelissaFoster.com/news
www.MelissaFoster.com/app

About the Love in Bloom Big-Family Romance Collection

The Bradens & Montgomerys is just one of the series in the Love in Bloom big-family romance collection. Each Love in Bloom book is written to be enjoyed as a stand-alone novel or as part of the larger series, and characters from each series make appearances in future books, so you never miss an engagement, wedding, or birth. A complete list of all series titles is included at the end of this book, along with previews of upcoming publications.

Download Free First-in-Series eBooks
melissafoster.com/free-ebooks

See the Entire Love in Bloom Collection
melissafoster.com/love-bloom-series

Download Series Checklists, Family Trees, and Publication Schedules
melissafoster.com/reader-goodies

BRADEN FAMILY TREE

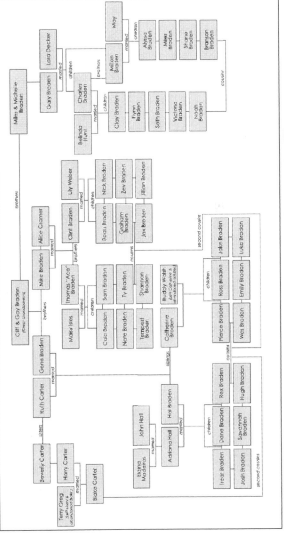

MELISSA FOSTER

Chapter One

ZEV BRADEN DIDN'T know which was worse, seeing the woman who had captured his heart in second grade with another man or knowing his family had betrayed him by leaving him in the dark about her attending his oldest brother's wedding. Beau had gone all out to give his new bride, Charlotte, a fairy-tale wedding at Sterling House, the Colorado Mountain inn she'd inherited. He'd built a wedding tent that brought the enchanted forest indoors, with miles of white silk draped over an artfully built frame of tangled branches and decorated with tiny white lights and strings of faux pearls. A crystal chandelier hung from an ornate iron tree in the center of the tent, and flowers spilled out of lush centerpieces. It was an intimate setting for their large family and close-knit friends. But at that moment Zev didn't feel quite as close to his beloved family as he normally did. He and his five siblings enjoyed giving each other a hard time, but they had *always* had each other's backs.

Until now.

He took another swig of tequila, chewing on that thought.

He *should* be celebrating the discovery of a lifetime this weekend. He had spent the last several years, and tens of thousands of dollars, searching for the wreckage of pirate

Garrick "One-Leg" Clegg's ship, the *Pride*, which sank off the coast of Silver Island in 1716. Two days ago Zev had discovered three concretions—hard masses that develop when metals start to disintegrate and combine with salts present in ocean water, forming a conglomerate that cements rock, sand, clay, and any nearby artifacts—at the site where he believed the ship had gone down. An X-ray of the masses had shown what appeared to be iron and silver artifacts and coins. Zev had given the largest concretion, which weighed nearly one hundred pounds, and the supporting X-rays and documentations to his attorney to begin the legal process of having the vessel arrested, which would hopefully grant him exclusive salvage rights to the sunken ship and all artifacts he hoped to find. But instead of celebrating his history-making discovery, he was downing tequila to dull the ache of seeing Carly Dylan again.

The *Pride* was supposed to be *their* discovery. They'd become obsessed with the sunken ship when they'd seen a documentary about it in third grade, and their interest had only grown over the years. They'd even made plans to spend the summer after their freshman year in college searching for the wreckage. When they were kids, Carly had been his fellow adventurer, troublemaking cohort, and best friend, and as they'd matured, she'd also become his lover and, he'd thought, his *future*.

But that was before...

Zev spotted Beau and their brothers Nick and Graham heading his way. *Traitors.* He stared them down as they approached. He and his brothers were all tall, broad shouldered, and athletic, but Zev and Beau had something else in common—the torturous past that had changed both of their lives.

Goddamn Beau. If they weren't at his wedding reception,

Zev would be tempted to knock the big-ass grins off each of their faces.

"I know you're celebrating your discovery, but if you keep sucking down that tequila, it'll be the *only* thing leaving you flat on your back tonight," Graham said with a smirk. He was the youngest of Zev's siblings. Graham and their brother Jax could be Beau's doppelgängers, with short brown hair, meticulously manicured scruff, and serious eyes, while Zev and his older brother Nick wore their hair longer, and Zev let his scruff go long stretches without a thought, much less a trim.

Zev offered the bottle of tequila to Graham, chewing over the fact that he'd had to learn about Carly's living there, her close friendship with Beau and Charlotte, *and* the fact that she'd catered desserts for the wedding secondhand when he'd overheard a conversation during the reception.

"No thanks, man. The only thing I want knocking me on my back is my beautiful Sunshine." Graham glanced across the lawn, where their twin siblings Jax and Jillian were chatting with Graham's wife, Morgyn, aka Sunshine.

Zev's attention was quickly drawn past Morgyn and the others to the woman who had haunted his thoughts and starred in his every fantasy for as long as he could remember. When he'd first seen Carly before the ceremony, stunning in a sexy peach dress that showed off her long legs and slim waist, their eyes had connected with the heat of summer lightning, and *Carls* had slipped from his lips like a secret just as *Zevy* had fallen from hers. Hearing her sweet, breathless voice after nearly a decade had left him momentarily numb. She'd been carrying a tray of chocolate desserts, following Cutter Long, a real-life fucking cowboy who Zev knew was one of Charlotte's closest friends. Cutter had barely left Carly's side since the ceremony, and now Carly was holding his arm, laughing at something he'd said. Zev had once been the guy by her side. They'd even attended the same college. But that was a long time ago.

He couldn't look away from her. She was even more beautiful than he had remembered. Her hair was a lighter blond now, but even after all this time he could still feel the silky strands trailing through his fingers. He could still see her big blue eyes sparking with heat and playfulness as they rolled around in the grass or treaded water in the ocean.

He gritted his teeth, struggling to push away the happier memories he'd held on to like lifelines since the day he'd broken up with her and left their hometown of Pleasant Hill, Maryland, two days after her best friend, and Beau's then-girlfriend, Tory Raznick, had been killed in a car accident. Tory had been visiting a girlfriend and she'd flown home early without telling anyone. She'd wanted to surprise Beau, but Zev had taken him out to a party. When she'd texted from the airport, they'd been drinking, and Beau hadn't heard the phone. She'd called several other people looking for a ride home, but in the end, she'd taken a cab. It was a stormy night, and the driver lost control of the car less than three miles from the airport. Zev knew it wasn't his fault Tory had been killed, but guilt from taking Beau out that night, and the realization that someone they loved could be torn from their lives at any second, had tipped an iceberg that had crushed him.

Nick nudged Zev's arm, jerking him from his thoughts, and said, "Dude, Carly's looking hotter than ever. If I'd known she was into cowboys—"

"Shut the fuck up." Zev took another swig of tequila.

Nick chuckled and tipped his hat. He was a horse trainer with a body built for a fight and an attitude that always seemed to be begging for one.

Zev had seen Nick knock a man out with a single punch, but that wouldn't stop Zev from going after him if he continued pushing his buttons. He might be leaner than his massive brother, but his nomadic treasure-hunting lifestyle had also made him quicker. *Fearless* and *fast* was a dangerous combination when frustrations burned through Zev's veins, as they were now. But he didn't give Nick a chance to get any deeper under his skin. Instead, he set an angry stare on Beau and said, "Why didn't you tell me she was coming?" He eyed his other brothers. "You *all* knew she lived here, and *nobody* clued me in. What the hell is up with that?"

Beau rolled his shoulders back and said, "The last time I brought up Carly, you said you'd slaughter me if I ever mentioned her name again."

"You did, bro," Graham agreed. "Remember? We were at Mom and Dad's last Fourth of July, when Beau and Char got engaged."

How could he ever forget the day he'd never seen coming?

After Tory died, the pain and guilt had been so overwhelming that Zev and Beau had both needed to get the hell away from Pleasant Hill. Beau hadn't been able to even be in the same room with his childhood best friend, Tory's older brother, Duncan, without wanting to tear something apart. Although Zev had rarely returned home, he'd kept up with his family and had known about the ever-growing rift between Beau and Duncan. Which was why when Duncan had walked into their parents' house the night Beau had gotten engaged, Zev had been ready to take him down—until he'd learned that Beau had found a way to move past Tory's death and had made amends with Duncan.

That was the day that had made Zev wonder if he could find a way to move past all that had happened, too. But the only person he wanted to move forward with was Carly, and before the wedding, he'd seen her only once since they'd broken up, and she'd made it clear she was over him.

"I know what I said." Zev leveled Beau with a serious stare and said, "But come on, man. You couldn't have warned me? You and Char are close to her. You *knew* she'd be here with Cutter. What the *hell?*"

"Hey, I have no idea what's up with her and Cutter." Beau glanced at Charlotte, heading their way with Morgyn and her toughest sister, Sable, just one of the many Montgomery siblings who had made it to the wedding, and said, "But please tell me you're not going to back out of watching the animals for us while we're on our honeymoon." He had surprised Charlotte with a weeklong honeymoon to the small village in France where her maternal grandparents had lived.

Zev had agreed to stay at the inn and watch their chickens and thief of a dog, Bandit, *prior* to his epic discovery because none of his siblings had been able to commit. Last night he'd arranged for the remaining, smaller concretions he'd found to be sent to his cousin Noah's marine biology laboratory on the outskirts of town, where he could work on extracting the treasures while he was watching the inn. He'd spent every minute since wondering which sibling he could wrangle into taking his place. But now that he knew Carly lived there, he didn't know what the hell he wanted.

"The horses are at Hal's ranch, so you won't have to muck the stalls," Beau said, as if it were a selling point. "I know you've got a lot going on right now, but nobody else can do it."

"Yeah, dude, I definitely can't stick around to take care of their animals," Nick said. "I'm heading to Virginia to buy a couple of horses at the end of the week."

"Morgyn and I are leaving tomorrow for two weeks in Seattle, and everyone else is taking off first thing tomorrow, too," Graham added. "Jilly and Jax have a big-city fashion show and will be gone for two weeks, and Mom and Dad have a meeting about the winery expansion." Their mother's family owned a chain of wineries called Hilltop Vineyards, and their father, an engineer, was helping with the designs. "Sorry, Zev, but it's all on you."

Charlotte came to Beau's side, looking gorgeous in her fairy-tale-style wedding gown, which Jillian and Jax, both fashion designers, had made for her. Beau put his arm around her and leaned in for a kiss. Seeing his brother happy and so in love again brought warm memories of how it felt to *be* with the person he loved. Zev stole another glance at the only woman who had ever made him feel damn near *anything*. He may not know what he wanted, but one thing was certain: Leaving was no longer his highest priority.

"Don't worry," Zev said. "I'd never leave you hanging."

"Bet you say that to all the girls, *Foreplay*," Sable said with a raise of her brows, earning chuckles from his brothers.

"Wouldn't you like to know?" Zev countered. Morgyn had come up with the nickname Foreplay, which she claimed meant he was the guy women sought for a good time but never for anything long term. As far as Zev was concerned, that was pretty damn accurate.

"You've been staring at Cutter and Carly for so long, I'm starting to wonder which one you're into," Morgyn teased.

"You know I don't swing that way, Sunshine. But if I did, it wouldn't be with *that* cowboy." Zev took another swig of tequila, his gaze shifting to Carly again. Jillian and Jax had joined her and Cutter, and it looked like they were all having a great damn time.

"Funny, I was thinking a cowboy was exactly what I needed." Sable flipped her thick mane over her shoulder and turned her attention to Nick. "What do you say, burly boy? Can all those muscles move on the dance floor, or are they only good for toiling away on your ranch?"

"Baby, there's nothing this body can't do." Nick put a hand on Sable's lower back, leading her toward the makeshift dance floor.

"I want to dance!" Morgyn exclaimed. She grabbed Graham's hand, and they followed Nick and Sable.

Charlotte took Beau's hand and said, "They're playing *our* song, hubby. We should dance, too." She stepped closer to Zev and lowered her voice to say, "Carly doesn't bite, you know."

"Well, that's a damn shame, cutes," Zev said with a grin. "I always loved the way she used that sexy mouth of hers."

Charlotte gave a happy little squeal and said, "I bet she'd bite if you asked her to!"

"Come on, beautiful. I'm sure Zev doesn't need any help in that department." Beau led her away, leaving Zev alone with his dirty thoughts of Carly and her talented mouth.

No one knew Zev had run into Carly in Mexico when she was on spring break the year after Tory's death. He'd just finished a diving expedition, and he was having a drink in a bar when he'd heard her infectious laugh. He'd thought he'd imagined it, but then he'd seen her across the room, stunningly beautiful and enticingly familiar. The second their eyes had connected, an inferno had blazed between them, and the all-consuming emotions he'd been trying to forget had nearly swallowed him whole. Their connection had always been so strong they'd never needed many words to convey their thoughts, and that night had been no different. They hadn't talked about losing Tory, or his leaving Pleasant Hill. In fact, they hadn't talked much at all, except for Zev to say he was in no position to make any promises, to which Carly had said, *I don't want promises. I only want tonight.* They'd spent one incredible night in each other's arms. Zev had known then that he'd made a mistake leaving the way he had, and he'd thought—*hoped*—they might be able to find their way back into each other's lives. But when he'd woken up the next morning, Carly was gone without a trace, leaving him confused, hurt, angry, and fiercely determined *never* to feel that way again.

As he looked at her now, flashing her radiant smile at that fucking cowboy, he accepted the truth he'd spent years trying to deny. Carly Dylan hadn't just captured his heart when they were kids. She'd claimed his entire being—mind, body, and soul—and she'd *own* them until long after the day he took his last breath.

CARLY HAD BEEN given months to prepare for seeing Zev again, and she'd used her time wisely, coming up with a solid plan where she'd act confident and unfazed by his presence. A plan that would allow her to make it through the evening with her self-respect intact and her panties in place. She'd practiced with her employee and bestie, Birdie Whiskey, until small talk and confident mannerisms were rote. She'd trained herself *not* to play with her earring, which Zev had always called her *tell* because she only did it when she was skating around the truth. She'd even dressed the part in a peach wraparound dress Birdie had helped her pick out. Birdie said it exuded class and sophistication with just enough sex appeal to make any man lose his mind. But Carly's carefully constructed plan had gone to shit when she'd walked around the corner of the inn and had come face-to-face with the man whose younger self had been her first *everything*—crush, kiss, intimate touch…The man she'd once planned to marry.

The man who shredded my heart into a million pieces.
Twice.

The second time had been unknowingly, but still…

Cutter nudged Carly's arm, jerking her from her thoughts. She must have zoned out while Jax and Jillian were talking because they were all looking at her expectantly, and she had no idea what she'd missed.

"You holding up okay?" Cutter asked.

She had known the cocky cowboy for years. Cutter was the barn manager for the Woodlands dude ranch, owned by Wes Braden and Chip Shelton, two of their friends. She'd met them all through Treat Braden, a real estate mogul who she'd later learned was a second cousin to Zev. Treat and his now-wife, Max, had wandered into her aunt's chocolate shop in Allure, Colorado, when Carly had been working. Once she'd connected the familial dots, she was glad she'd never said anything to him about having dated Zev. Outside of her friends and family in Pleasant Hill, she'd never confided in anyone but Birdie, Charlotte, and Cutter about her history with Zev after her best friend, Tory, had been killed. And other than confiding in a therapist, she'd *never* said a word to anyone about having run into him in Mexico. She'd been lucky to have been embraced by so many wonderful people when she'd moved to Colorado the summer after their encounter in Mexico. It had made her painful transition a little easier, even though it had taken a long time before she'd found her footing and had truly begun building a life there.

"She's *fine*. She's just in shock from seeing my brother again," Jillian said. Tory and Carly had been like sisters to Jillian, and she'd been torn up by Tory's death and Carly and Zev's breakup, too.

Zev's family had tried their best to help Carly through the tragic loss of her best friend and the breakup, but it had been too painful to be near them, and she'd eventually pulled away. She hadn't seen them in years, and then last summer she'd run into Beau and Charlotte when she was home visiting her parents, and they'd realized they didn't live far from each other in Colorado. It had been weird at first, seeing Beau so in love with someone other than Tory, but Carly had really liked Charlotte, and she'd pushed those memories away for fear that they might hinder their friendship. They'd become close friends, and she was happy for them. Even though she was nervous about seeing Zev, when they had asked her to cater the wedding, there was no way she was going to let them down.

Now, with her stomach in knots, she was questioning that decision.

Jillian waggled her brows and said, "Or maybe Carly's day-dreaming about Zev." She was just as feisty and pushy as always.

"I am *not*," Carly insisted, despite the fact that her body had been humming since she'd first seen him, and she could barely look at him without going weak in the knees.

Jax, the most even-keeled of Zev's brothers, said, "That's his loss, Carly. I'm sorry for what he put you through."

"Thanks, Jax."

"I'm sorry for what happened, too," Jillian said. "That was a horrible time for everyone, but it was a long time ago. Zev is a different person now, and you guys were great together." She tucked her burgundy hair behind her ear, gazing across the tent at Zev. "Just look at him. He doesn't even look like he did when you two were together. He has an edge to him now. I think his longer hair fits his mysterious image. Don't you think, Car?"

Like metal to magnet, Carly's eyes found Zev. She'd been stealing glances at him throughout the evening, trying to puzzle together the lanky teen she'd known with the gorgeous man before her, sporting chiseled, rugged features and thick scruff.

"*Yes*," Carly said too breathily, and quickly schooled her tone. "I mean, it's *fine*. Whatever. He always had good hair." Even as a kid he'd worn his hair shaggier than his brothers. She used to love to run her fingers through it. Her hands itched with the desire to touch it again, and frustration stacked up inside her. "Why are you pushing him on me, Jilly? You *know* how he hurt me."

"I'm sorry. I can't help it," Jillian said. "You two are like two sides of the same coin."

"I'm *over* him. Tell her, Cutter. Tell her I'm over him."

Cutter put his arm around Carly and said, "She swears she's over him."

"Seriously?" Carly glowered at him. "After *all* the times I've had your back, that's how you're going to play this?"

Jillian answered before Cutter could. "It doesn't matter what you've told him. The electricity zinging between you two could light this tent on fire."

"She's right, Carly, but you know I've got your back." Cutter looked at Jax and Jillian and said, "I know Zev's your brother, but if he stirs up trouble with Carly, he'll have me to deal with." He glanced in Zev's direction and said, "Although he looks nice enough."

He looks like the guy who ruined years of my life, and still manages to make my stupid heart race.

"He's more than *nice enough*," Jillian said protectively. "Zev's a good person."

"I didn't say he's not. I said he'd have me to deal with if he messes with Carly," Cutter clarified.

"While you two debate the values of Zev, *this* good guy is going to grab one of Morgyn's hot sisters for a dance. It looks like Pepper and Amber are free." Jax looked at Cutter and said, "What do you say? You want to ask one of them to dance?"

"I'm always up for dancing with a fine woman," Cutter said with a smirk.

Carly rolled her eyes.

"Wait," Jillian said. "The only single guys here that I'm not related to are Cutter and Duncan, and I'm *not* dancing with Duncan." She took Cutter's hand, and Cutter looked at her lasciviously. "Get those dirty thoughts out of your head, cowboy. You're getting to dance with me, and that's *it*."

"Stronger women than you have said the same thing and ended up warming my mattress," Cutter said.

"That stops now, cowboy," Jax warned as they walked away, leaving Carly alone.

The Bradens had a huge extended family, with cousins in several states, and many of them were there celebrating. Carly was literally surrounded by throngs of hot single men, and she couldn't stop thinking about the only one she *shouldn't* want. She fought the urge to steal another glance at Zev, but the pull was too strong, and her eyes darted in his direction.

Her breath caught in her throat. Zev was looking right at her as he set a bottle on a table and headed her way.

Shitshitshit.

She frantically looked around for someplace to hide or a group to get lost in. But her head was spinning, and almost everyone was dancing, so she made a beeline for her safety zone—the dessert table—the one place that could always occupy her mind. She had been catering desserts for events like this for years. She knew how to look busy. But as she stood before the table staring at the chocolate treats she'd made, the only things in her mind were the echo of her heart pounding against her ribs and the mantra *breathe, breathe, breathe.*

She felt Zev's presence before he stepped beside her. It had always been that way. He was an enigma, a force in and of himself that made the air sizzle and the universe seem to hold its breath. She stared straight ahead as he came to her side, sending goose bumps chasing up her flesh. *Breathe, breathe, breathe.* Holy cow, breathing was a bad idea. He smelled musky and rugged, not so different than he had as a teenager, but definitely more *potent.*

He plucked a chocolate truffle from the table, and his sleeve inched up his arm, revealing several braided and beaded leather bracelets. Why did that make him even hotter?

"Too bad they don't have boxes of sugary cereals, huh, Carls?"

His rich, deep voice sent rivers of heat through her, but it was his mentioning their shared love of cereal that had her heart softening. That was one of their *things*, mixing boxes of cereal and taking them to one of their special places to eat dinner. They'd had so many *things*. They used to make up stories in response to each other's questions and sneak out at night to make out, make love, or go on adventures. They'd had their songs, their dreams, and their dares. She'd really loved their silly dares.

She inhaled deeply, steeling herself against the years they'd spent as a couple and reminding herself of her plan. She could do this. She *would* do this. Even if she couldn't look at him.

She stood up a little straighter, pretending to look over the desserts, and in her most confident voice, she said, "I haven't had cereal since I was a teenager."

"Aw, come on. You'd never give up Lucky Charms or Froot Loops."

Her stomach knotted with memories of her and Zev collecting the plastic prizes they'd found in the cereal boxes and trading them like gold. Her favorites had been a pink plastic ring with a star on top and a yellow plastic treasure chest she'd traded him for spinning tops. A few weeks later he'd asked her to be his girlfriend, and she'd given him her answer the next night. She'd written *yes* on a piece of paper, put it in the treasure chest, and had left it on his windowsill. When he'd found it, he'd said to keep the ring safe because one day he would give it to her while he was down on one knee. It had all seemed so real in seventh grade. She'd been heartbroken years later when she'd looked for the ring and realized she'd lost it. On the heels of that memory came another, of planning their matching tattoos of the Lucky Charms marshmallows when they were in college. They were supposed to get them the summer after their freshman year, right before they were supposed to leave together for a trip to Silver Island, where they were going to rent a cottage and a boat to search for Garrick "One-Leg" Clegg's ship, the *Pride*. They'd had so many dreams for their future, including living out of a van with so few worldly possessions they could fit them in backpacks.

But when Tory was killed, Carly had lost both of her best friends and all of their shared dreams.

She shoved those thoughts down deep and said, "Actually, I *have* given them up. There's a lot you don't know about me. I'm not the same girl I used to be." She risked a glance, and Zev's lips curved up in the charming, seductive smile that had always reeled her in. Her stomach flip-flopped.

No!

No flip-flopping!

His eyes slid down her length, leaving a titillating trail of pinpricks in its wake. Damn him.

"You're right, Carls. There's nothing *girlish* about you anymore. You're *all* woman, and you are exquisite." He popped the truffle in his mouth, eating it slowly, his eyes never leaving hers. "This chocolate is amazing, but I still don't believe you gave up cereal."

She nervously crossed and uncrossed her arms. "Believe it. I'm into chocolate now. I run a chocolate shop in Allure called Divine Intervention. I made that truffle you just ate."

"Really? Your aunt's place?"

She couldn't believe he remembered. She used to visit her aunt Marie in the summers. Marie wasn't a blood relative. She had been Carly's mother's best friend since childhood, but to Carly she'd always been *Aunt Marie*.

"Yes, Marie's place," she said.

"Cool. And I see you're into cowboys these days."

Cowboys? Oh my gosh. Cutter! In a split second she decided to use his misunderstanding to her advantage. "Yup. Cutter's my boyfriend. He's great, super nice, and he *loves* chocolate." *Ramble much? He loves chocolate? Ugh...*

Zev's eyes shifted to the side of her head, his lips curving up in a knowing grin. She realized she was playing with her earring and quickly dropped her hand, silently chiding herself. *So much for practice makes perfect.*

"You might want to rein in your boyfriend before Sable has her way with him." He snagged another chocolate and popped it into his mouth.

She looked at the dance floor. Cutter was dirty dancing with Sable. Where the hell was Jillian? Thinking fast, she said, "We have an open relationship. He's just *one* of my boyfriends."

Zev arched a brow. "Is that right?"

"Yes." She lifted her hand toward her earring and quickly dropped it again. Why did he make her so nervous? She squared her shoulders and said, "I told you I've changed."

"I guess that means your evenings are spoken for?"

"Definitely. For *weeks*," she added for good measure, but the lie was accompanied by a pang of heartache. Her evenings were mostly spent watching documentaries about marine and land archaeology, the things she loved but had given up. But she wasn't about to let him know that. "I'm busy *all* the time. Out practically every night. You know me, Good-Time Carly."

Zev stepped closer, stealing the oxygen from the entire tent. "That's too bad, Carls. I'm staying at the inn for a week, watching the animals for Beau, and I was hoping we might be able to catch up."

She swallowed hard. The last time they'd *caught up*, she'd ended up with a lot more than just a broken heart.

"Maybe I should dare you to get out of one of those dates so we can spend time together." He leaned in so close she could smell the alcohol on his breath as he said, "You never were able to resist a dare."

She put her hand on the table to combat her weakening knees.

Zev glanced at her hand on the table, and a slow grin curved his lips. His dark eyes met hers, and he said, "Maybe that adventurous girl is still in there after all."

He leaned closer, his chest pressing against her as he whispered in her ear, "I know I hurt you, and I'm sorry. I hurt me, too." He touched his lips to her cheek in a tender kiss, then turned and walked away, leaving her with a bone-deep ache as she fought the urge to run after him.

Chapter Two

LATER THAT EVENING, twinkling lights and the flames from the bonfire illuminated the patio of the inn. The reception had ended more than an hour ago and most of the guests had left, but Zev's family, along with the Montgomerys and a few of Charlotte's closest girlfriends, were staying at the inn and leaving in the morning. They'd changed out of their dress clothes, and several of them were hanging out by the fire. The din of laughter and voices hung in the air, but thanks to heartbreakingly beautiful Carly, Zev was so fucking confused, he needed a few minutes alone to try to clear his head.

He paced the lawn, unable to stop thinking about her. After they'd talked at the dessert table, she'd avoided him for the rest of the reception and then she'd left with Cutter as soon as the cake was cut. Despite her play-with-her-earring fibs and that strong facade she'd put on, he'd *seen* the truth. With a cowboy by her side or not, the sparks between them were still there, and they were hotter than ever. In those short minutes they'd talked, desire and memories had blazed through him, unearthing the well of emotions he'd spent years burying. It had taken all of his control not to sweep her into his arms, kiss that sexy spray of freckles across her nose like he used to, and then take her in the kiss he'd longed for since he'd left Pleasant Hill and try to erase their years apart.

As teenagers they'd been able to overcome just about any obstacle. But curfews, fights with parents, and boredom were nothing compared to the tragedy that had turned their lives upside down. He'd believed leaving town would save Carly from being sucked into the depths of guilt and despair that had consumed him after Tory's death. After years spent wondering if he'd made a mistake, he needed to find out once and for all if she still felt for him what he'd never stopped feeling for her.

"Come on, Zev!" Jillian waved him over to the bonfire. "We're toasting Knox and Aubrey's engagement!" Graham's business partner, Knox Bentley, had proposed to his girlfriend, Charlotte's best friend, Aubrey Stewart, only moments before the beginning of Beau and Charlotte's wedding.

Zev knew Jillian would pester him until he joined them, so he tried to push thoughts of Carly away and headed over to the patio as his brothers opened bottles of champagne. Cheers rang out as they filled glasses and passed them out. Rather than joining Jillian and his boisterous brothers, who had been needling him about Carly all evening, Zev hung back by Pepper, Sable's sweet fraternal twin. Pepper handed him a glass of champagne, looking beautiful in a pair of jeans and a cute blue top.

"Thanks, Pep," Zev said as Charlotte began a toast.

"Everyone knows that Aubrey and I grew up together in Port Hudson." Charlotte beamed at Aubrey, who was as tall and blond as Charlotte was petite and brunette, and said, "Aubrey knows *all* my secrets."

"Including the juiciest ones!" Aubrey chimed in, making everyone laugh.

"That is *true*," Charlotte said. "Aubrey, you were the first person I told about my feelings for Beau, and you helped me so much in those early days, pushing me in your not-so-gentle way to just go for it when I was scared to death. Nothing could make me happier than knowing my best friend and her charming, handsome man have been touched by the magic of the inn just as Beau and I have. Here's to Aubrey and Knox, who I hope will have a long, happy life together!"

Everyone cheered, and Jillian hollered, "Maybe you could toss some of your inn's magic my way!" causing another round of laughter.

Zev tapped his glass unceremoniously to Pepper's. She looked at him curiously and said, "You're usually in the middle of all the action. You okay?"

"Yeah. Work's just got me sidetracked." It wasn't a total lie. Between seeing Carly and being on the cusp of making the biggest discovery of his life, he didn't know which way was up.

"Jilly didn't give me any specifics, but she said that you found something off Silver Island. When I was developing the seizure alert necklace, it was all I could think about. You must be itching to get back out on the water." Pepper was a brilliant scientist. Her sister Amber had epilepsy, and when Pepper was in graduate school, she'd developed a seizure alert necklace that she'd since patented and now sold all over the country.

Zev downed the champagne and set his glass on a table. "If it were any other night, I'd be on my boat with my team, pumped to get back in the water and see what other pieces of history we could unearth." As Jilly sidled up to him, he said, "But I'm here for the next week, watching Beau and Char's animals."

"I've heard all about the *Chickendales*," Pepper said softly.

"Leave it to a romance writer to name her chickens after hot actors." Charlotte had named her chickens after the actors in *Magic Mike*.

"When Zev's not chasing chickens, he'll be getting reacquainted with *Carly*," Jillian said in a low, teasing voice.

Zev shook his head, though if he had it his way, he'd be doing exactly that.

"I did hear something about you and Carly having once been an item," Pepper said inquisitively.

"It was a long time ago—" As Zev spoke, Bandit darted around the side of the house with something in his mouth, followed by Trace Jericho, Pepper's brother-in-law, who was carrying his baby girl like a football against his chest.

"Take Emma Lou!" Trace hollered, barely slowing down enough to pass his tiny bundle to Zev. "Bandit's got Brindle's breast pump!" He took off after the dog.

A cacophony of noise erupted as several of their friends and family ran after them, calling out, "Bandit!" Zev's parents were doubled over in laughter as Bandit barreled around the yard, darting between trees, leading everyone in a zigzag chase.

Zev held the adorable baby with both hands wrapped around her rib cage, his arms straight out in front of him. Emma Lou's lips curved into a frown. Her eyes slammed shut, and a shrill wail spewed from her tiny lips.

"*No, no, no*, baby. Don't cry," he pleaded, which only made her cry louder. "It's okay. *Shit*. Uh…Pep? Little help?"

Pepper set down her glass and reached for the baby. "And here I thought you'd be a natural."

"*Nope*. I don't do babies." He picked up *her* glass and downed the champagne. When he and Carly were together, they'd talked about having kids and raising them to be little adventurers. But Tory's death had changed his view on many things, including having a family. Why bring something beautiful into a world where tragedy could strike at any time and cripple everyone it touched?

"That's a shame," Pepper said, cradling the baby. She bounced her a little, calming her into silence. "There's nothing more attractive than a cute guy with a baby in his arms."

"I get by all right without the extra appendage," Zev said. "I don't see you rushing to have babies. Why didn't you bring a date to the wedding?"

Pepper caressed the baby's cheek and said, "Because I don't have a man in my life who I want my family pushing me to marry."

He knew the feeling. "But there *is* someone keeping your bed warm?" Her sisters claimed she never dated, but Pepper was too smart, pretty, and kind for him to buy it.

Her cheeks pinked up. "I'm not Sable. I don't talk about my personal life."

"Should I take that as a *no?*"

"I didn't say that," she said uneasily, gazing out at the yard, where Beau and Trace were trying to corner Bandit and her sisters were hollering directions on how to do it more effectively.

"You didn't have to. That's cool, Pep. I'm picky, too."

"I got him!" Beau hollered, hanging on to his big, black, spoiled dog's collar. Bandit dropped the breast pump, and *whoops* and cheers rang out. Everyone headed back toward the patio.

"My sisters call you *Foreplay,*" Pepper said, looking at Zev with a serious expression. "I highly doubt your definition of picky is the same as mine."

"Clue me in to your definition."

Pepper gave him a scrutinizing look. "I think a man needs to treat a woman like a diamond before he's treated like he's worth a penny."

"Ouch. That's harsh." He chuckled.

"Told you we were different," Pepper said. "What's your definition of picky?"

"Let's just say, every gem is worth a look, some are even worth polishing, but there's only one Holy Grail."

The others arrived at the patio at once, out of breath and talking over each other, bringing an end to Pepper and Zev's conversation.

"That was crazy!" Brindle reached for her baby and said, "Thanks for watching her, Auntie Pepper. Looks like I'll be buying a new breast pump tomorrow."

Zev stepped away to let the girls talk.

Sable jogged over to him and said, "Hey, Foreplay, we're heading inside to play quarters. Want to come?"

"Sure. I'll be right there." He pulled out his phone, navigated to the internet, and began thumbing out *Divine Intervention*.

A heavy hand landed on his shoulder. There was no mistaking his father's aftershave. He'd worn the same scent for as long as Zev could remember. While their mother was the glue that held their family together, always reaching out to touch base with each of their six children and the significant others of those who had them, their father was the solid foundation on which their family relied. Clint Braden had always been meticulous, careful, and *steady*. He could weather a storm without yielding to the wind and carry the weight of his entire family on his back without his legs buckling.

"How's my boy?" his father asked.

"Great, Dad. You?" Zev pocketed his phone.

"My son just married the woman who brought him back to us. I'd say life is pretty damn good." Before meeting Charlotte, Beau had spent almost as much time traveling as Zev did, and he had been days away from taking a job in California that would have kept him away from Pleasant Hill for most of the year. Charlotte pulled him out of the dark place in which he'd buried himself and taught him how to live and love again. Now they split their time between Colorado and Maryland, and Zev's parents couldn't be happier to have their son back.

His father motioned toward the lake and said, "Walk with me. It's been a while since we've had any time alone."

Usually when his father wanted to talk, it was about getting Zev to visit more often. A couple one- or two-day visits a year weren't enough for his family, but it was about all Zev could handle before guilt swamped him.

As they walked across the lawn, his father made small talk about the wedding and how happy his mother was to have another daughter-in-law. They talked about half a dozen other things as they made their way along the water's edge. Eventually his father brought up Zev's work, which was probably where the conversation was headed the whole time.

"When will you hear back from the attorney?" his father asked.

"Hopefully by the end of the week."

"I hope that goes smoothly for you." His father slid a hand into the pocket of his slacks and said, "I always thought it was odd that the courts treated shipwrecks like criminals. Arresting the vessel is such an odd way of looking at things. I mean, you can't really put a sunken ship under arrest, and you haven't even found the ship, so there's nothing to arrest."

"There's no doubt that admiralty law is an oddity, but it's a necessity. I've got enough historical and scientific documentation showing the changing shoreline and pinpointing where the ship was believed to go down to prove that what remains of the ship is probably buried within a four- or five-mile radius of the vicinity of where I found the concretions. The concretions and the X-rays also support that data."

"I guess they have to start somewhere."

"Absolutely. Can you imagine the chaos that would ensue if word got out that a shipwreck worth millions was found and there were no laws of ownership in place? That kind of money brings all sorts of crazies out of the woodwork. Without the laws, anyone could dive for the treasure, and I'd imagine, people would kill for it."

"You're probably right," his father said. "This must be hard for you, being here for so long after the discovery you've made."

"Yeah. A week feels like a month."

"It always has with you. You live more life in a day than many people live in a week. I've always admired that about you. What's your plan while you're here? And is this another five-year project like the one with Luis?"

Shortly after Zev's hookup with Carly in Mexico, he'd joined an expedition with another treasure hunter, Luis Rojas. They'd hit it off, and then they'd hit it big when they'd discovered the wreckage of the *Black Widow*, a sunken pirate ship, in international waters between the United States, the Bahamas, and Cuba. They'd spent five and a half years there unearthing millions of dollars in jewels, coins, and other treasures. Once they'd found the bulk of the known artifacts, Zev had taken his millions and gone out on his own to look for the only treasure that really mattered to him, the *Pride*.

"While I'm here, I'll be working at Noah's lab to extract the artifacts from the smaller concretions I shipped. But as far as timing goes for the expedition, that'll depend on what we find when we get back in the water and how fast we find it. It could take eight to ten years, or much longer, to find the bulk of the treasure, assuming it's there. Luis's team will be searching the *Black Widow* site for another two decades, until it's bled dry. And you know how New England winters are. We'll take advantage of all the weather windows, but it's hard to estimate timing for a month, much less a decade."

His father stopped walking and gazed out at the moonlight shimmering off the inky water with a troubled expression. "Ten years? You'll be almost forty."

"Your point?" Zev had never been someone who worried about getting older. He welcomed it. It was far better than the alternative.

"I'm not sure I have one," he said lightly. "I was just thinking that when I was forty, I had six kids and a chaotic, fulfilling life."

"If you're pushing for grandkids, you're barking up the wrong tree. You should be taking a walk with Beau or Graham."

"I'm not vying for grandchildren, although I'd surely welcome them. I miss having little ones around. Brindle and Trace's baby sure is darlin'."

"She's cute, but *loud*."

A single deep laugh fell from his father's lips. "Everyone's loud, son. But some of the loudest voices are the ones only a parent can hear." He met Zev's gaze and said, "I guess I do have a point to this talk."

"You usually do."

"It's no secret that your mother and I worry about you."

"I know you do, and just in case I ever forget, Jilly reminds me every time we video chat." He pushed a hand through his hair, turned toward the lake to avoid his father's keen eyes, and said, "I'm fine, Dad."

"Yeah, I know you are. We're blessed that our children can handle themselves in this world. But parenting is an endless job. I'll worry until the day you bury me six feet under."

He glanced at his father and said, "How about we hold off on that for a while?"

"Fine by me." He studied Zev for a moment before saying, "Remember when you made your first big discovery with Luis?"

"Best day of my life." That wasn't the truth, but it was the only one he could voice. He'd had many even better *best* days, but they all involved Carly.

"Do you remember what you said to me?" He didn't give Zev a chance to answer. "You told me that was what you were meant to do, and I believed you, son."

The way he said it gave Zev pause. "You have doubts now?"

"Not really. But sometimes people are meant to do more than one thing with their lives. I saw you talking with Carly at the reception, and I have to tell you, Zev. I don't think I've ever seen the light that she brings out in you shining as bright from *anything* else, including that discovery."

He hadn't expected his father to bring up Carly. His chest felt too tight, and he tried to fill his lungs with the crisp evening air. It burned all the way in. "Yeah, well, we have a lot of history."

"You have a lot of *love*," his father countered.

Zev bent to pick up a rock, and threw it across the lake, wrestling with his father's words. "Someone should have told me she lived here and that she'd be at the wedding. I was blindsided."

"Sometimes being surprised is better than having time to try to figure out how to handle things. Your mother claims so, at least, and she's a smart woman."

"Yes, she is."

"So, you and Carly? Did you tell her you've found the ship you two had planned on searching for?"

Zev scoffed. "No, Dad. We've got a lot to deal with before I throw that out there. It would feel like bragging. According to Carly, I don't know who she is anymore." But just like when he'd seen her in Mexico, the second their eyes had connected, he'd felt that hook she'd always had in him digging beneath his skin and reeling him in. He'd suffer a thousand hooks if she were at the other end of the line.

"There's probably some truth to that. Tragedies change people. *Life* changes people."

"I don't know, Dad. Sometimes I think I'm the same stupid kid I was before I left home, just a whole lot richer. But other times I can't remember who that kid was."

"Maybe you're not meant to figure all that out by yourself." His father kicked at a quarter-size stone and bent to pick it up. He studied it, turning it over in his hand as he said, "You know, you can unearth treasures until the day you die, and I'll support your every endeavor."

He always had. When Zev had left home to travel, he'd taken a backpack full of his belongings and the money he'd saved while working through high school and his first year of college. When he'd contacted his father to get some engineering advice about an apparatus he and Luis wanted to build in order to clear away sand on the seabed, his parents had helped fund the project by giving him the money they'd saved for his college education. If it weren't for those funds, he and Luis might never have found their way to the wreckage.

"I appreciate that, Dad."

"This is the only time you'll ever hear me say this." His father's expression turned thoughtful, and he said, "You've been searching for a very long time, and I'm proud of everything you've accomplished and of the man you've become. But I'm not sure you'll ever find what you're looking for, and I'd hate for you to end your life with your pockets full of money and an empty heart."

"That's deep, old man." And scarily spot-on for how Zev had felt when he'd woken up to an empty bed in Mexico and reluctantly let Carly slip away. He'd believed it was for the best because it was what she'd wanted. But it had damn near killed him, and every time he thought about it, it drove that knife deeper.

"Sometimes you have to turn those searches inward and dig deep to find what you're really looking for. I thought you might need a nudge." He picked up another stone and said, "Forgiveness starts from within, but I think that's only half the battle you're fighting."

Zev gritted his teeth against his father's ability to see right through him.

"You *are* worthy of her forgiveness, Zev. Give yourself the chance to prove it to her."

"Dad, I left—"

"Don't bother telling me. I know what you did, and I believe I know what *you* think you did, too. I've never been a meddling parent, but I'll fight you on this one, son. You need to do this, if only so you're able to move on without regrets. I see it in your eyes, and when you were with Carly today, I believe I saw it in hers, too."

Zev ground out a curse and turned away.

"Love's a wicked bitch, Zev, but the best kind of bitch," his father said, picking up a few more stones. "Once she sinks her claws in, you don't have a chance in hell of escaping."

Zev's blood pounded through his veins. He didn't want to escape. He wanted to drive to Carly's house and make her talk to him. But from what he knew about Carly, there was no *making her* do anything. "Considering the indifference she tried to portray this afternoon, I have a feeling I'm the *last* person she wants to hear from, much less let into her life."

"And what do you think about that?" his father asked.

He paced, trying to quell the ache inside him and stop the truth from coming out. But if Carly had unearthed his long-ago-buried emotions, his father had just shoveled them onto the shore, and his words burst free. "I think it's *bullshit*. She's scared. Hell, I'm fucking scared. I came here wondering who I could get to watch Beau's animals so I could take off and get back to hunting. But I *can't* do it, Dad. I can't walk away from her again. Not without knowing for sure if what we had, what I still fucking feel *today*, can be salvaged."

"Believe it or not, I'm glad to hear that, son. Sounds to me like you're ready to embark on your most important expedition yet."

Damn right he was. But this was an expedition unlike any other. Zev had thought he'd always known who he was and what he'd accept to make a happy life, even if it wasn't what he'd truly wanted. But he was wrong. There were stakes at play with Carly that he'd *never* expected.

"And if I fail?" As the words left Zev's lips, he realized he

31

had no idea who he'd be if she looked him in his eyes and said she was done with him.

"Then you're fucked, son," his father said far too blatantly. "But I have faith in you." He handed Zev the stones and said, "Drop those in your pockets."

"Why?"

His father slung an arm over his shoulder as Zev pocketed the stones and said, "The right woman will distract you from everything else. This way you won't be swapping an empty heart for empty pockets."

Chapter Three

CHOCOLATE HAD SAVED Carly once, and with any luck it would pull her through this week and help her forget Zev Braden and his charming ways. Hopefully it would erase his sinful voice, too, which had taunted her throughout her sleepless night. Even as a young girl she'd been drawn to his voice. Back then it had been raspier and more interesting than other boys' their age. But now his voice was rich and manly with a hint of gruffness. She knew plenty of men, and *none* had a voice that made her body heat up like Zev's had yesterday. But she knew it was more than just his voice that had done her in. It was the confident yet casual way he carried himself, the spark of intrigue in his eyes, his familiarity, his playfulness, the way he looked at her, their history. It was *everything* about him. Why had she wasted her time practicing small talk and feigned confidence when what she really needed was blackout glasses and a noise-control headset? Who was she kidding? It wouldn't have mattered if she'd been encased in lead. Their connection was potent enough to melt even *that* off her body.

Ugh...

She set a tray of chocolate hearts on the counter between the chocolate-covered pretzels she was packaging and the chocolate-peppermint bars she was cutting to sell in the shop. On Sundays Divine Intervention was open only from ten to three, and Carly usually went on a horseback ride before coming in. She'd been too keyed up to sit still and had skipped it, and had come to work at five a.m. hoping to lose herself in the world of temptation that had always done the trick before. But as she took in the plethora of specialty treats littering the counters—more than she could sell in a day—her mind trickled back to Zev. Unfortunately, even after all these years, it never wandered far.

She hadn't allowed herself to search for him online after he'd left Pleasant Hill. It would have been too painful if she'd found evidence of him having a blast while she was trying to remember how to breathe. But after Mexico, she'd broken down and searched. It was like he'd dropped off the face of the earth—and she'd been so messed up, she'd felt like she'd been dropped on her head. She could have asked his family for his whereabouts, but then she would have had to admit that she'd done something just as bad to him as he'd done to her. They were both guilty of walking away. She'd sworn off searching for him ever since. She hadn't even given in to the urge to see his face when she'd heard he'd hit it big a number of years ago. She'd come to rely on playing head games with herself to keep from giving in to her heart, which desperately wanted to find its way back to him.

Until Charlotte asked her to cater desserts for her wedding.

That was when she'd finally allowed herself to search for images of Zev online. She hadn't been surprised that he wasn't on social media. He'd never been interested in showing off. But she'd seen a few pictures of him on some of his siblings' social pages, although his face was obscured in most and she had a feeling that was purposeful. He was mentioned in articles about his discovery in international waters off the coast of the Bahamas, but he wasn't pictured. Carly had kept herself out of the Bradens' lives for so long, she'd never known the details of that multimillion-dollar discovery until she'd read about it in the weeks before the wedding. But even that hadn't surprised her. She'd always believed Zev would find anything he looked for—which was another reason she'd been so heartbroken.

He had never come looking for *her*.

She went back to packaging chocolate-covered pretzels for the gift baskets. As she scooped them up and poured them into cellophane bags, Zev's voice whispered through her mind. *Maybe that adventurous girl is still in there after all.* His younger voice followed the manly one, traipsing through her head like a ghost—*Come on an adventure, Carls. You're the only one who can keep up with me.*

Zev's voice wasn't the only thing that had set him apart from other boys when they were growing up. He'd had an edge to him even then, a *restlessness*. A need to do more, *see* more, and *understand* more than other kids. They'd known each other their whole lives, and to this day Carly's mother swore Carly had crushed on Zev from the time she was in second grade, when their entire class had raced in the schoolyard. She and Zev had beaten every other kid to the finish line, and the two of them had tied. She'd insisted on a rematch, and they'd tied again. The third and final time they'd raced had also resulted in a tie. She'd challenged Zev to a race every day for the next three weeks, each one ending in a tie. She'd finally stopped challenging him, in lieu of practicing with the hopes of winning the next time she went up against him. But a week later he'd knocked on her front door and asked if she could come out to play. He'd carried a walking stick that he'd carved and painted with his father's help over one shoulder with a pillowcase tied to the end of it, packed full of supplies for their *expedition*. She'd thought he'd looked like a *real* explorer standing on her front porch, his shaggy hair hanging in his eyes, worn jeans with a hole in the knee, and hiking boots that were too big because he'd outgrown his own and borrowed Beau's. And in that raspy voice, he'd said, *Come on an adventure, Carls. You're the only one who can keep up with me.* Her mother was right. Even the memory of that day made her heart feel heavy and full.

The bells above the front door to the shop jangled, drawing Carly from her thoughts.

"Carly? I'm sorry I'm late!" Birdie called out as she rushed through the shop toward the kitchen, stopping to peek at herself in a mirror on the wall.

Birdie was Carly's right hand in all things chocolate-shop related, including managing Quinn Finney, who worked part time. Her mind moved in seventeen directions at once, which might drive some people crazy, but Carly loved that about her. Birdie's brilliant mind worked wonders, coming up with social media posts and holiday events that lured in throngs of customers. Carly used to be that fast-thinking, up-for-anything girl. She had been the spontaneous, pushy, *yang* to Tory's careful, organized *yin*. It never failed to boggle her mind how much she'd changed since Tory's death. She'd become the careful, organized *yin*, and she felt lucky to have Birdie, her rambunctious, ever-energetic *yang*.

"I went to the Roadhouse last night with Quinn and Sasha, and you know how it is once I get on that mechanical bull," Birdie called out from within the shop, turning her head this way and that as she looked in the mirror. Sasha was her older sister, and the Roadhouse was a biker bar where their family hung out. "I know you're an only-Wednesday-night girl, but you would have had so much fun last night!" she called out as she leaned closer to inspect her eyes in the mirror. Carly went to the Roadhouse every Wednesday night to spend time with Birdie's family.

Birdie flitted into the kitchen carrying a number of shopping bags in each hand, her wild dark hair flying over her bare shoulders. She stopped abruptly. "*Whoa*. Did we get orders I don't know about?"

Carly twisted a gold tie around a bag of chocolate-covered pretzels and said, "Nope. What's in the bags?"

"Oh, these?" She held them up, grinning as she sauntered through the kitchen. "We went by Karma's boutique before going to the bar, and I picked up the cutest thank-you cards to send to the people who take the class tonight. We have five spots filled, by the way, but I have a good feeling that we'll fill the sixth today." They held monthly chocolatier classes, and Birdie was always picking up little extras for the participants. "Anyway, I *had* to get *you* a few cute outfits since if I don't give you three weeks' notice and mark a spot on your carefully planned schedule, you refuse to pry yourself away from those mind-numbing documentaries to go shopping. Wait until you see what I got you! I'll show you after I help get all this food under control."

If it weren't for Birdie, Carly would live in her Divine Intervention shirts and Daisy Dukes all summer, like the ones she was currently wearing. Birdie had a fashion sense all her own, as proven by the circa 1980s off-the-shoulder ruffled dress she had on, but she was usually careful to choose less outlandish outfits for Carly.

Carly watched with amusement as Birdie carried the bags

into the office, rambling about riding the mechanical bull longer than any of the guys at the bar.

Five, four, three, two—

"The wedding!" Birdie exclaimed, running out of the office. "Oh my gosh! How was it? All this chocolate either means you had out-of-this-world sex with Zev or something bad. *Really* bad." She hurried over to Carly, took her by the wrist, and dragged her away from the counter. "Spill, woman!"

Carly tried to assemble her thoughts. "It was—"

"Tell me *everything*. From the first second you saw him right down to the last! Did you do our plan? Did it work? You wore the dress, right?"

"Can I talk now?" Carly teased.

"Yes! Go! Sorry..." Birdie huffed out a breath and said, *"Everything."*

Carly laughed. "I wore the dress, but when I saw him..." A shiver of heat darted through her, and she felt her cheeks burn.

Birdie squealed.

"Don't get too excited. I basically told him I was a slut." Carly walked back to the counter with Birdie on her heels.

"What? *Why?* You're the farthest thing from a slut. You're a nun without a habit. You're the girl my brothers all wish I were. You're the—"

"That was the plan, remember? Confident? Popular? Unaffected by him?"

Birdie snagged a chocolate pretzel and bit into it. "Yes, but where in all of that do you hear the word *slut?*"

"I didn't call myself that. But I told him I have *lots* of boyfriends, including Cutter." She shifted her eyes away and said, "And that we have an open relationship."

"Oh my God, girl! *Cutter?*" Birdie laughed. "You'd never go out with Cutter. My brothers can attest to the fact that you don't like big, burly ranchers." The Whiskeys owned Redemption Ranch, and most of Birdie's family worked there.

"Hopefully Zev doesn't know that." She began assembling a gift basket and said, "I didn't mean to take it so far. I was just going to say Cutter was my boyfriend, but then Cutter was dirty dancing with someone else and I had to come up with a cover story. I couldn't help it. It was really hard seeing Zev again. I was lucky to be coherent enough to string words together to form a sentence. You should have seen the way he looked at me. Birdie, I actually got weak in the knees! Who does that? I still can't believe it happened."

"*Damn.*" Birdie put her arms around Carly and patted her back, whispering, "I knew you were still hooked on him."

Carly pushed out of her embrace. "I'm *not*, and even if I was, I'd never act on it. I have a business to run and a life to live. Festival on the Green is only a week away, and you know that's one of my favorite events of the year. It's always so much fun. I have no room in my life for heartache." Festival on the Green was a weeklong event with sidewalk sales, live music in the park, and a sea of tents. One of Carly's favorite local artists, Kaylie Crew, was booked to sing at the event, along with several other bands, and Carly couldn't wait to see her perform. She'd never forget how she'd fangirled when Treat and his wife, Max, had walked into the chocolate shop with Kaylie and her husband, Chaz, years earlier. She'd nearly lost her mind when she'd learned that Kaylie and Max were besties. Kaylie had become a regular customer, and Carly still got butterflies when she saw her.

The bell over the door chimed as a couple walked into the shop. Carly called out one of her standard greetings. "I'll be right with you. Please don't rob us. I'm too tired to chase you down the block."

The couple laughed.

Birdie lowered her voice and said, "What happened after you told him about you and your harem of men?"

"We talked for a minute, and then I avoided him until I could leave."

"I *knew* I should have gone with you. Then I could have gotten a read on the situation. So, is he gone? Back to his life of treasure hunting? Is that why you're making enough chocolate to feed everyone in the state?" She waved at the goodies Carly had made and said, "You know this screams of sexual frustration, right?"

"I *am* sexually frustrated," she whispered harshly. "Zevy is potent enough that I'll probably be frustrated long after he leaves town next week."

"Wait! He's still here? For a week?" Birdie rubbed her hands together and said, "Where is he staying?"

"Do *not* even think about it." Carly turned her by the shoulders and gave her a gentle shove toward the door. "Go help our customers."

BIRDIE WORKED HER social media magic, putting the word out that they had gone *chocolate happy* and were having a ten-percent-off sale. By a little before three o'clock, they had sold most of the goodies Carly had made, and she was packaging the rest in a gift box for one of Birdie's older brothers, Callahan, who went by the nickname Cowboy. He'd stopped by to pick up an order of truffles and tarts for a movie night the ranch was hosting for a group of Boy Scouts.

Carly tied a ribbon around the gift box and said, "How many kids are you expecting tonight?"

"Thirty or so. Two Scout troops." Cowboy was about six four with bulbous muscles, hair the color of wheat, and a beard that was a shade darker.

"That's great. I'm sure they'll have fun. Are you guys ready for Festival on the Green?" Redemption Ranch always had a booth at the event to raise awareness for their services and collect donations. Since the ranch didn't close for the event, they had a host of volunteers to help with the festival.

"We're about as ready as we'll ever be. I *know* you're ready. You run this place like a well-oiled machine." He glanced into the shop at his sister and said, "Did Birdie tell you about a hot yoga class she's going to?"

"Mm-hmm. Why?"

"There's a dude instructor. Do you know anything about him? Are you going to the class?"

"I'm teaching a chocolate class at three thirty, so no yoga for me. But it's a *yoga* class, Cowboy. I don't think Birdie's virtue will be in danger." Carly set the gift box in a larger box with the truffles and tarts. She heard the bells over the door ring and glanced at the clock, glad she still had plenty of time to get ready for her class.

Cowboy scowled and said, "Would you go to that yoga class if you weren't busy?"

"I'm not really into yoga. I like to hike and do things outdoors, but the idea of getting sweaty inside doesn't make much sense to me." She swore she heard Zev's voice, and just as it registered, memories of her and Zev rolling around naked and sweaty in his hotel room in Mexico came rushing back, making her hot all over. She turned away, hoping Cowboy didn't notice.

"Should I pretend you're *not* blushing a red streak?"

"Yes, *please*." She heard what sounded like Zev's voice again. Praying she'd made it up in her head, she peered into the shop—and nearly choked. Zev was standing at the counter talking with Birdie. Carly flattened her back against the wall next to the doorway, as nervous to see him as she was elated. She quickly realized how *bad* that was. She couldn't afford to be flustered when she taught her class. "Tell me I'm seeing things. Is there a really good-looking guy out there with longish hair? Please say no. He can't be here."

Cowboy's expression turned serious. His eyes narrowed and he looked into the shop. "That guy stalking you or something? Need me to take care of him?"

"No. He's fine. He's…" *Making my heart race.* "I used to go out with him. Let's just get your stuff and get moving. My class starts soon."

"An ex, huh?" Cowboy got a rascally look in his eyes. "I've got your back, Carly. Don't sweat it." He picked up the boxes in one arm and hooked his other arm over her shoulder.

"No, really, Cowboy, I'm—" She stopped talking as he led her into the shop and Zev and Birdie looked over.

Zev's eyes caught Carly's, and her stomach tumbled. He looked delicious in a dark T-shirt and faded jeans. His gaze shifted to Cowboy, and his jaw clenched. Cowboy cocked an arrogant grin. Birdie looked baffled, and Carly was too flustered to think straight.

"We've filled the sixth slot for the class!" Birdie exclaimed. "He's signing up right now." She slapped a paper on the counter and handed Zev a pen. "What did you say your name was?"

"Zev Braden," he said, eyes locked on Carly.

Lordy, that voice…

Birdie's eyes widened. "You're *Zev*?"

"The one and only," Zev said with an air of authority.

"Thanks for the little extra gift, darlin'." Cowboy kissed Carly's cheek and swatted her ass.

Carly let out a surprised *squeak*. Birdie giggled, and Zev's eyes narrowed.

Cowboy nodded at Zev in that manly way men had when they were sizing each other up and claiming alpha status. Zev was a formidable guy, but Cowboy rivaled Nick Braden in size, and when he puffed out his chest, not many men could match his breadth.

Zev lifted his chin and threw his shoulders back, nodding curtly in return. Zev had never been one to back down from a challenge, and it was thrilling to see that hadn't changed.

Cowboy looked at Carly and said, "Why don't I hang around for class, darlin'? Make sure things don't get out of hand."

"No!" Carly and Birdie said at once.

Birdie grabbed her purse and hurried around the counter toward them. She took Cowboy by the arm and dragged him toward the door. "Come on, Cowboy. I need your help with my car."

She pulled open the door, and Cowboy stilled, an immovable mountain. He looked Carly dead in the eyes and said, "You sure you've got this?"

"Yes, thank you," she said far more confidently than she felt. Her eyes drifted to Zev, and a smug grin spread across his face.

She realized she was playing with her stupid earring again and dropped her hand, wishing she could tie it down.

"Let's go, Cowboy," Birdie said loudly. "Damsel in distress here. My car needs fixing." She moved behind him and *shoved* him out the door, calling over her shoulder, "Class list is in the drawer. See you tomorrow. Have fun!"

"Your taste in men sure has changed," Zev said with a playful look in his eyes, closing the distance between them. "Do you have an open relationship with him, too?"

Carly struggled to keep a straight face. "Why would I limit myself to just one boyfriend when there are so many buff cowboys around here?"

"What'd you do, put out an ad in the local newspaper?"

Without thinking, she fell back on their storytelling days. "Actually, he rescued me. My car broke down, and suddenly there he was, sitting on a big, beautiful white horse. He fixed my car just like that." She snapped her fingers. "He followed me home, and I climbed onto his horse, and we rode off into the sunset. The rest is history."

Zev stepped closer, electricity sparking between them. Her breathing quickened, and she tried to reel it in. But she missed this. She missed *him*. She wanted to keep up the storytelling, to build a tale they both wanted to continue, like old times. But that was dangerous. The line between *playing* and *touching* had always blurred fast for them, like wicks of dynamite igniting, unstoppable and explosive.

"It's hard to believe the woman who used to get jealous if a girl asked me for a ride home would have an open relationship with any man, much less *two*." He paused just long enough for that truth to make her chest ache.

Was there anything he didn't remember about her?

"That makes about as much sense as the woman who despises milk chocolate working in a chocolate shop, Carls."

His tone was warm, as if basking in good memories. She hadn't always despised milk chocolate. When they were in fourth grade, they'd stolen and eaten an entire bag of chocolate bars from her parents' pantry, and she was sick all night. He'd begged his parents to let him spend the night so he could help her feel better. But since they'd stolen the chocolates, his parents must have known the worst punishment was keeping them apart, and they hadn't allowed him to stay over. Carly hadn't been able to stand the taste of milk chocolate ever since. Why did knowing he remembered that make keeping her distance even more difficult?

Trying to climb out from underneath that memory, she forced herself to redirect to the present and said, "I don't just work here—I *own* the shop—and I need to get ready for my class. You should get going."

"That cute little brunette already took my money for the class. Besides, you, me, and melted chocolate? That has *fun* written all over it. You might not like milk chocolate, but you *know* I love it. And on you...?" He leaned in, his eyes darkening as he said, "I could eat *that* all night long."

She inhaled shakily just as the door to the shop opened and a young couple who had signed up for the class last week walked in. They'd been so touchy-feely, they'd reminded Carly of how close she and Zev used to be. She hadn't thought much about it at the time—there was always *something* reminding her of Zev—but now that he was standing right in front of her, it brought those memories rushing in, making her even more nervous.

She forced her attention to the couple and said, "The class is starting in fifteen minutes. Feel free to look around." Lowering her voice, she said to Zev, "I have to get ready, and if you're staying, you'll need to keep your chocolate fantasies to yourself."

"I never said anything about *fantasies*." His lips quirked up. "But it's good to know where your thoughts have gone."

The heat in his voice seeped beneath her skin, unearthing all those dark fantasies she pretended didn't exist. He licked his lips, as if he knew exactly what he was doing to her. She struggled to ignore the desire bubbling up inside her, but it was like trying to keep a wave from crashing over the shore.

He leaned impossibly closer and whispered, "They must be good. You're blushing."

With a frustrated groan, she spun on her heel and stalked toward the kitchen. It was going to be a *very* long night.

Chapter Four

ZEV WAS MEZMERIZED. The last forty minutes had been bittersweet, watching the girl he'd loved as the professional woman she'd become. Carly moved confidently around the kitchen of the chocolate shop looking hot as sin in denim shorts and a red T-shirt that had SURRENDER TO DIVINE INTERVENTION printed across the chest in brown swirly letters. If he were a man of faith, he might take that shirt as a sign, or at least try to convince Carly of it. But this was her domain, and as much as he wanted to explore the fantasies he'd seen simmering in her eyes earlier, he was enjoying seeing this side of her. She talked as much about the history of chocolatiering as she did about the recipe for the white-chocolate almond-butter cups they were making. She handled the class with humor, grace, and a certain level of authority, making her even more impressive. Everyone was having a good time, although Carly was giving the others one-on-one attention and pointedly not getting too close to Zev. But that didn't stop him from catching every one of her stolen glances.

He didn't blame Carly for keeping her distance. Despite the indifference she was trying to portray, there was no escaping their intense connection.

"Zev, you're going to burn the chocolate," Miranda, the flirtatious blonde working beside him at the stove, whispered. She had been trying to get his attention since the class began. "You're supposed to take it off the double boiler and scoop half of the white chocolate into a bowl so you can mix in the matcha."

"Right. Thanks." Zev tore his eyes away from Carly, who was praising a couple's efforts, and picked up the pot of white chocolate. "Excuse me, Teach?" he called out.

Carly turned his way, and in her beautiful blue eyes he saw the walls she'd been erecting since the class started. The walls he was determined to take down.

"I think I need a little *hands-on* attention over here," he said coyly.

"I'll help you!" Miranda exclaimed.

That wasn't the attention he was looking for, but as Miranda showed him how to sprinkle in the matcha, there was no hiding the jealousy wafting off Carly like a breeze. This would probably earn him a solid place in hell, but he decided to use it to his advantage, turning all of his attention to Miranda.

"Thanks, sweetheart," he said. "You're *very* good with your hands."

"You have *no* idea how good. Have you taken her classes before?" Miranda whispered. "I don't think she likes you very much."

"No? I thought she really dug me."

Miranda shook her head. "It sounds like you need a few lessons in the ways of women." Her eyes drifted down his chest, and she said, "I can help you with that, too."

"I bet you can." He snuck a glance at Carly, who practically had fumes coming out her ears as she strode to the front of the room.

"You're all doing great." Her eyes found Zev's, the jealousy of moments ago morphing to a look as icy as winter wind. "I'm sure you don't want to be here all night, so let's keep moving along." She shifted her gaze away and said, "Put a teaspoon of white chocolate into each mini muffin cup and then we'll get them into the fridge to chill and start to tidy up our workspaces before we add the almond butter and the final layer of white chocolate."

Miranda spent the rest of class brushing against Zev every chance she got and whispering double entendres, while Carly avoided him completely. Zev kept his eyes on Carly and his ears open as she talked about chocolate being *her life* and long hours spent in the shop. He took it all in, trying to unravel his thoughts and figure out hers. Aside from trying to avoid what was so clearly still between them, she was impressively comfortable and in control in that kitchen. He was having trouble reconciling the girl who had dreamed of being a world-traveling archaeologist and had hated the confinement of working retail when they were in high school with the woman who appeared to be living a life that was primarily indoors.

By the time they finished making their white-chocolate almond-butter cups and cleaning up their workstations, Zev had come to the conclusion that there was probably a modicum of truth to his not knowing who Carly was anymore, at least on the surface. But while she might have changed directions, he had a feeling that the dreamer in her wasn't gone for good. She'd poked her pretty mischievous head out with the story she'd told about being rescued by that fricking cowboy. And the jealousy that had simmered in Carly's eyes had *definitely* belonged to the girl he'd fallen in love with.

Carly handed out boxes for them to take their chocolates home and made her way around the room praising each person's efforts and thanking them for coming. Zev took his time putting his treats into the box. He had no plans of leaving without getting a few minutes alone to talk with Carly. He wanted to clear the air, to figure out if their breakup was the reason she'd stopped pursuing her dreams. They'd started college together, and he'd always assumed she'd gone on to get her archaeology degree. How did she end up in Colorado? How long had she been there? Hell, he wanted to know everything about her. Including how much she hated him for leaving.

Unfortunately, Miranda was packing up just as slowly as he was. She eyed his chocolates, which didn't look great, and said, "I still don't understand why yours are so uneven."

I was too busy watching Carly to worry about how much chocolate I was pouring into the cups. "I guess I was sidetracked."

Miranda touched his arm and said, "I can't say I'm sorry for sidetracking you."

Zev glanced at Carly, who had fire in her eyes.

"That's one of the hazards of flirting in the kitchen," Carly said sharply. "You got lucky. Usually someone gets *burned.*"

Zev's chest constricted, and he shifted his arm out of Miranda's reach.

"I guess we'll have to stay out of the kitchen from now on." Miranda giggled.

"I need to be out of here in a few minutes, so if you two could wrap it up, that would be great." Carly gave Zev a scathing look and said, "I've got to do something in my office. I hope you don't mind showing yourselves out."

Fuck. He'd meant to get Carly jealous, not to piss her off.

"Thank you!" Miranda called after her. She turned to Zev

and said, "Want to hit the bar down the street?"

"I can't, thanks. I have to meet an old friend."

"Oh," she said with a frown. "Well, do you want to exchange numbers? Get together another time?"

"Actually, I'm not in town for very long. But I'll walk out with you." He picked up his box and they walked through the shop. As he opened the door, he said, "Thanks for helping me in class."

"It was fun. You sure you don't want my number?"

"You're a beautiful woman, Miranda. But I gave my heart away years ago, and trust me, I'm not worth your time."

Her brow wrinkled. "How do you know I'm not just looking for one night of fun?"

"Even if you were, I'm not. Take care, Miranda. I just realized I left something in the kitchen."

He closed and locked the door and headed back toward Carly's office.

She was standing by the sink in the kitchen when he walked in. He tossed the box on the counter, startling her. Carly dropped the pan she was holding, and her hand flew to her chest. "You scared the life out of me."

"I'd rather scare the pants off of you," he said as he came around the counter.

Her eyes narrowed. "Where's your *girlfriend?*"

"I've only had *one* girlfriend in my life." He closed the gap between them, enjoying the flare of heat in her eyes, and said, "And I'm looking at an older, more beautiful version of her."

"*Zev.*" The warning came out breathy.

His dreams couldn't compare to that sound. "Say it again."

She shook her head, looking sultry and hauntingly beautiful.

He caressed her cheek, and longing rose in her eyes. "Your

skin is still as soft as velvet." He brushed his thumb over the seam of her sweetly bowed lips, and they both sighed.

"*Zevy,*" she whispered, full of desire. "What are you doing?"

"I don't know," he said, surprised by his honesty, but there was no stopping it now. "I've missed you, Carls." He ran his fingers up her arm and threaded them into her hair. His entire body exhaled, as if he'd been waiting his whole life for that simple touch. "God, Carls, I've even missed your fucking hair." The urge to kiss her was overwhelming. She licked her lips, and he felt himself leaning closer. "Tell me you haven't thought of me, you haven't missed me, and I'll walk out that door."

"No you won't," she said with a slow shake of her head and a plea in her eyes. "You can't."

"You're right, I can't. But if you had said it, I wouldn't do this."

He lowered his lips to hers, praying she wouldn't push him away. Their first touch was electrifying. He kissed her rough and greedy, devouring her sweet, sinful taste like a starving man at a buffet. He'd wondered if she would react differently to him after all this time. If she would be as eager as she had always been, battling for control and giving in to submission in equal measure. But she was right there with him, just as she always had been. She rose up on her toes, making hungry noises as she grabbed his head with both hands and opened her mouth wider. He'd missed her so fucking much, he grabbed her ass and held *tight.* He was hard, and she was soft and perfect. Years of repressed desire surged through his veins, and a growl roared out as he hoisted her onto the counter and recaptured her mouth. He hauled her to the edge, wedging himself between her legs, grinding against her. He wanted to strip her naked, relearn all the dips and curves of her body, pleasure every inch of her until they were too worn out to speak. Somewhere in the back of his head he knew they needed to talk, but he was *lost* in her. In *his* Carly. His thoughts fractured, and the world faded away, until there was only the feel of her body pressing against his, her hot, willing mouth kissing him back, and her intoxicatingly familiar taste. He didn't know if he was dreaming, awake, or stuck in some alternate forgiving universe, but he never wanted to leave.

Then he felt what he feared most. Her hesitation. The gears in his head started churning again as she slowed her efforts, pulling back the slightest bit. He fought the urge to deepen the kiss, to try to get her to fly away with him for just a little longer. He reluctantly drew back and touched his forehead to hers, wishing he'd never have to let go. She clung to his back, her nails digging through his shirt. They'd never needed words, but he felt them climbing out of his heart, clawing up his throat, and tumbling from his lips. "I'm sorry, Carls. I'm so sorry."

"I can't," she said in a strangled voice, and pressed her hands to his chest. "I can't do this with you. I can't fall in love with you again."

He didn't move with the force of her hand, keeping her close as he said, "You don't have to. You never fell out of love with me. I feel it, Carls."

She looked away, and in a thin voice she said, "Just go."

"Carly—"

She met his gaze, and the anguish in her eyes had him reaching for her again. But she leaned away and said, "Please go, Zevy. I need you to leave."

She'd let him in, even if only briefly, giving him hope despite her words. He gritted his teeth, wanting to demand she let him stay, or plead if that's what it took, and knowing he couldn't do either. "I'll go," he relented. "But we're not done, Carly. You know we're not done."

Chapter Five

CARLY FLEW OUT of her pickup truck Monday morning and bolted through the doors of Divine Intervention more than an hour late. She must have forgotten her phone at work last night, which meant she'd had no alarm this morning.

"Good morning!" she said as she darted past Birdie and a customer and headed into the kitchen. She didn't slow down until she reached her office, where she dropped her bag on the desk and turned on her computer. She was supposed to turn in an order last night, and she'd completely forgotten. Now she'd have to work some kind of magic to have the products shipped in time to make the specialty order for her customer's baby shower this weekend. She also needed to order supplies for the festival.

She hated to be rushed. She'd run the chocolate shop without so much as a hiccup for years, and in *one* evening Zev Braden managed to turn her calm, cool, ultra-organized life upside down. She'd almost forgotten the *true* power of his ravenous and *magnificent* mouth. It had always been her biggest pleasure—from the things he said, to his kisses, and the way he'd used it in places that made her toes curl.

She flopped into her chair, cursing herself for kissing him

last night and knowing she'd do it all over again no matter what the stakes. He was the *king* of kisses. Even her favorite documentaries hadn't taken her mind off them last night.

Her fingers flew across the keyboard as she typed an email to the supplier of the European chocolate her client preferred. She wiggled in her seat, trying to get used to the thong she'd been forced to wear. She hated thongs. Sunday night was her laundry night, and she'd been so flustered after kissing Zev, she had completely forgotten about that, too. If not for Birdie's shopping trip, she would've had to wear dirty shorts. It was times like these when she wished she were a clothes hoarder like most women. But Carly had never been big on owning *too much* of anything. Birdie was forever teasing her about being the only woman business owner who was proud of being able to fit all of her clothes in one suitcase, and still fit in her clothes from when she was twenty. Carly still had T-shirts from every concert she and Zev had attended, and according to Birdie, she wore them all too often. She'd always been a utilitarian. It was one of the first things she and Zev had realized they had in common. They used to dream about living in a van and being able to pick up and travel on a whim.

But there were no whims in the world of a chocolatier.

She glanced at her to-do lists and the calendar sitting beside her computer, as if she needed proof that her business revolved around plans, not whims. Her week was outlined by task, day, and hour on the master list hanging behind her desk. Two more detailed lists itemized the lesser duties that had to be carried out on a daily or weekly basis, and those resided on her desk. All of the bigger events and orders for the summer were highlighted in pink on her calendar, proof of how far she'd come and how well she ran the business.

Carly had been slightly jealous when Marie had first told her of her plans to go *adventuring*. But that jealousy had been accompanied by thoughts of Zev, and Carly had pushed it aside and thrown all of her energy into the business. Marie had enjoyed her downtime as much as her time at work and had earned a steady stream of income that she'd been happy with. She hadn't had aspirations to take the business to the next level. But when she gave the business to Carly, Carly had different plans. She wanted to prove to her aunt that she was worthy of her trust, but she also needed to prove to herself that she didn't *need* the dreams she'd left behind. She'd outlined goals of taking on more events each year and had strategized new marketing plans, which Birdie had since tweaked and perfected. She'd dedicated herself to the business, putting in long hours seven days a week, and had far surpassed her goals.

She wasn't about to let all that fall apart because of Zev *Kisser Extraordinaire* Braden.

Trying to ignore the hitch in her chest, she finished typing an apologetic and slightly pleading email requesting a rush delivery for the chocolate. Before ordering supplies for the festival, she double-checked inventory and previously placed orders. Once that was taken care of, she worked through the rest of her emails, returned phone calls, and *finally* she searched her office top to bottom for her phone. Coming up empty, she looked high and low in the kitchen, relieved to see Birdie had made their special Monday truffles and treats. Maybe showing up late wouldn't make for a crazy day after all. If only she could find her phone...

She made her way up front. The shop was quiet, which was unusual for a Monday, but Carly was thankful to have a moment to breathe. "Sorry I was so late. I can't find my phone anywhere, so I had no alarm."

Birdie opened a drawer and pulled out Carly's phone. "I found it in the pantry."

"The pantry?" Carly took it, trying to remember when she might have put it in the pantry. Most of the night was a blur of her heart racing while trying to teach the class and then of Zev gazing into her eyes, when her brain had failed to function and she'd given in to those sinfully delicious kisses…

"Someone left their chocolates here last night," Birdie said, snapping her out of her reverie. "So…I started putting the pieces together. You *never* lose your phone, which means you were supremely distracted last night, and based on the fact that you're uncharacteristically late today and the state of that *messy* bun you have going on, I'd say it's safe to assume you and Zev got *reacquainted* last night."

Carly shoved the phone into the back pocket of the denim shorts with lace trim that Birdie had given her and said, "Don't ask." She turned away, pretending to straighten up the shelves of wooden blocks with a saying about chocolate printed on them.

"Oh, *I'm* asking!" Birdie hurried out from behind the register in a cute blue-and-white polka-dot minidress that matched her headband and said, "You're wearing the outfit I bought you, too! I knew that burgundy tank would look great on you. The pink lace bralette and the leather necklaces are perfect touches. Did Zev like them this morning? I noticed last night that he was wearing leather bracelets."

"I wouldn't know. I told him to leave last night." She tried to move around her friend, but Birdie blocked her way, grinning like the pesty-but-lovable bestie she was.

"Did he leave last night, or in the wee hours of the morning? I assume it was *after* the great sex?"

"We *didn't* have great sex," Carly snapped, hating herself for taking her frustrations out on Birdie.

Birdie's smile faded. "Bummer. Zev sucks in bed? I wouldn't expect that from the way he looks."

"*No.* I don't know! He didn't suck when we were together." Carly groaned and pushed past Birdie's all-too-exuberant self. "Maybe he does suck now, but I doubt it. He sure knew what he was doing when he kissed me."

Birdie let out her signature squeal and followed Carly around the store as Carly pretended to straighten bags of candies and other goodies. "You *totally* owe me one for last night, by the way. I went to the ranch after my yoga class and Cowboy was getting ready to come back *here*. He was worried about you. He said when you saw Zev, you totally freaked out. But don't worry, I told him it was the *good* kind of freak-out, not the bad one."

"Yeah, well, now you know what being with Zev does to me. He makes me forget who I am and turns me into an unorganized mess who can't sleep. He occupies every iota of my brain so I can't think of anything but the way he kissed me and how his hands felt in my hair and—*ugh! See?*" She stomped across the store.

Birdie put her hand on her hip, speaking sarcastically. "God forbid your perfect world gets upended by a hot guy who looks at you in ways I've *never* seen a man look at a woman."

There was no denying the way Zev looked at her like she was the only thing he saw. But she'd *been* his and he'd left her behind. And she'd done the same to him in Mexico. But that had been her survival instincts kicking in. She didn't know if she could walk away again.

"I can't be with him, Birdie. He hurt me."

"You were teenagers. Everyone knows teenagers are stupid, and you had both lost someone you loved, Carly. You told me how close you and Tory were and that you guys double dated all the time. Losing a friend like that would be a lot for *anyone* to handle, much less a guy who's got hormones and nineteen-year-old stupidity messing with his head."

"But he *never* called, and he *never* came back for me. You're supposed to be on *my* side, aren't you?" She felt like she might cry for no good reason, just like she had last night while she'd consumed almost the entire box of Lucky Charms she'd bought on her way home after class.

Birdie's expression softened. "I am *always* on your side, no matter what. But he must have come back here last night, which means he wanted to see you again. This was taped to the door this morning." She reached into the pocket of her dress and handed an envelope to Carly.

Her pulse quickened at the sight of *Carls* written in Zev's messy handwriting across the front of the envelope. His penmanship hadn't changed a bit.

"He's the only person I've ever known to call you Carls," Birdie said.

A lump swelled in Carly's throat. "Yeah," she said just above a whisper and slipped the envelope into her back pocket with her phone.

Birdie looked at her wide-eyed. "You're not going to open it?"

"I can't right now. If it's goodbye, I'll be sad. If it's not, I'll be confused. There's no good outcome."

"I swear, you have been out of the dating game for way too long."

"I date," she insisted.

"Two or three times a year does *not* count as dating. If you relied on men to sustain yourself, you'd be emaciated. Carly, come on. Don't you believe in destiny?"

Carly fought a wave of sadness. "Fate took my best friend's life, and then it stole my boyfriend away from me, so I don't really buy into all that mumbo jumbo about things being written in the stars."

"It's true that fate took Tory, and I know that must have been horrible. But Zev's leaving wasn't fate. It was destiny. Fate is that which can't be changed. Destiny is what comes through actively making decisions and committing to a path of changing, learning, and growing. When you came to Colorado, you took responsibility for your life *and* your destiny. You took a leap of faith and look what it's done for you."

"That wasn't me taking responsibility. I was just trying to survive a broken heart," Carly corrected her.

"That's what I'm saying. You made a conscious decision to make changes and survive what you'd gone through. Don't you think Zev could have been doing the same thing when he left Pleasant Hill? Trying to survive in the only way he knew how? You said Beau stayed away from home, too."

"Beau lost his girlfriend. Zev *didn't*. I was right there with him. He's the one who ran away. I lost *him*."

"I know, and that's got to hurt more than I could ever imagine. But maybe that envelope tells you why. Or maybe it's an apology since you sent him away last night. You'll never know unless you open it. But that's all I'll say on the subject. Promise." She walked toward the counter and stopped before she reached it. "I think you should open it."

"You just broke your promise," Carly teased.

"At least *think* about it," Birdie urged. "He seemed really nice. Before I knew who he was, I was all geared up to give him my come-on-big-boy lines."

"You and probably every other woman who has ever met him. Miranda hit on him in class last night, and he ate it up." A wave of jealousy moved through her.

"She's female, so that's no surprise," Birdie said lightly.

"I thought you weren't going to say anything else about him."

"I'm not." Birdie knitted her brow and pressed her lips together, looking like she was going to burst.

Carly threw her hands up and said, "Just say it already. Get it all out so I can go make—and *eat*—a white-chocolate cheesecake."

"*Please* open it!" Birdie exclaimed. "I'm dying to know what it says."

"*Birdie*. You know where I'll be if you need me." She headed for the kitchen.

As she set out the ingredients for the cheesecake, the envelope burned a hole through her pocket with the same insistence her body had craved Zev last night. She looked at the counter where they'd made out, and shivers of heat skated through her. She closed her eyes, but that was even worse. She could still feel his hands in her hair and his hard length grinding against her center. Her eyes flew open, but she didn't try to push away the lust pooling low in her belly as Zev's voice trampled through her mind. *I'm sorry, Carls. I'm so sorry.* She'd thought he was apologizing for kissing her, but now that she was thinking about that moment more specifically, he *had* seemed like he'd wanted to say more.

Her nerves prickled as she pulled the envelope from her

pocket and stared at her name, remembering the notes he used to leave in her car, in her locker at school, and taped to the outside of her bedroom window. She felt herself smiling with the memories, her pulse spiking as she ran her finger beneath the flap to open the envelope. But fear of the worst stole her smile, and she froze.

What if it is goodbye?

Inhaling deeply, she thought, *What if it's not?*

She didn't know what to hope for. She felt the same way she had when she'd left for college at the end of the summer after Zev had gone away. She'd been afraid to leave in case he came back, and at the same time, she'd been afraid to stay in case he didn't.

She refused to be that lost girl again, stuck in a middle ground. She tore open the envelope and unfolded the paper, needing to know one way or the other. Her eyes fell to the middle of the page, where Zev had written, *Hey there, beautiful. I dare you to sing our song.*

Like magic, the twangy fast beat of "Life Is a Highway" by Rascal Flatts played in her head. He'd drawn an arrow along the bottom of the paper all the way to the edge. She turned the paper over and read what he'd written. *You're in my blood, you're all around. Sing it, baby. I love that sound. Z*

Happiness bubbled up inside her, despite all that lay in their pasts.

Leaving the envelope taped to the door, the dare, and the cheesy rhyme born from their song was all quintessential *Zev*. They'd always taken lyrics and twisted them into their own. She set the paper aside, humming the song as she preheated the oven and began mixing the ingredients for the crust of the cheese-cake. It had been forever since she'd thought of their song. It felt so good, she began swinging her hips and whispering the lyrics. She pressed the crumble crust into the pie pan, washed her hands, and queued up "Life Is a Highway" on her phone. She turned it on repeat and began combining the ingredients for the cheesecake.

By the time she poured the batter into the crust, she was full-on dancing, adding in a spin every few lines. The chorus rang out after she put the cheesecake in the oven, and she grabbed the spatula, using it as a microphone, dancing across the kitchen singing and whipping her hair from side to side. She belted out the lyrics and twirled around—stopping cold at the sight of Birdie in the doorway watching her, holding an enormous gift basket full of sugar-cereal boxes. Carly's heart skipped. There was only one person who would send a basket of cereal.

"Who *are* you?" Birdie asked with a laugh. "If *this* is what kissing Zev Braden does to a girl, then let *me* in on that action."

Carly pointed the spatula at her and said, "Back off, Birdie. I'm not afraid to use this thing."

"Let's just hope you'll let *him* use his *thing*, because if his kisses put you in this kind of mood, imagine what docking his boat in your harbor will do." Birdie set the basket on the counter and plucked an envelope from between two boxes of cereal. "I think treasure boy has struck again."

Carly knew exactly what making love with Zev would do to her. There would be no going back. Reality rolled in. She wouldn't want to walk away again, and she wouldn't survive making love to him and then watching him walk away, either. She turned off the music, disappointed in herself. She'd totally lost her mind over a *dare* and a *song*.

She tossed the spatula in the sink and said, "What am I

doing, Birdie? I can't fall for Zevy again."

"You're not *falling*. You're dancing, having fun." Birdie went to her and said, "Carly, I've known you since you moved here, when you were so sad I wanted my mom to wrap you in her arms and not let go until you were better. I've watched you become an amazingly strong woman. You've taught me so much about being resilient and standing on my own two feet. You're my best friend, and I love you. You taught me everything I know about this business and what it takes to run it. You should be proud of everything you've accomplished. Especially with the shop."

"*We've* accomplished, Birdie. We did it together."

"I followed *your* lead. I love who you are every day, Carly, but I've never seen you look or sound as happy as you did when I walked into the kitchen just now. I think Zev might be good for you despite all the darkness."

Carly sighed. "We were good together, but he's the one who broke me."

"I know you think that. I'd say that maybe he's the only one who can unbreak you, but that sounds bad, because you're *not* broken. But I've never seen that girl I just saw, so maybe he's the only one who can find that secret part of you again. That part that makes you dance and sing." She handed Carly the envelope from the basket and said, "I want to know why he thinks you need four boxes of cereal. Is that a sex thing I don't know about?"

Carly laughed. "No, but it was our thing. We never slowed down when we were together, not even to eat. Cereal was portable. We could munch on it while we hiked, or sailed, or hung out on the beach."

"You were a cheap date, *and* it sounds like you guys had

tons of fun. That's it—I need a Zev in my life."

"I was never bored or hungry or anything but happy when I was with Zevy. We just clicked, you know? That's why I was so devastated when he left." Carly opened the envelope and withdrew a folded paper. A phone number was written across the flap. She and Birdie exchanged a curious glance as she unfolded the note and read the handwritten message. *I dare you to sext me a picture.*

Carly's jaw hung open. "I am *not* doing that."

"Oh, yes you are!"

"*No.* Kissing him is one thing, but I don't send dirty selfies to *anyone.* Who knows where those things could end up? No way."

Birdie giggled. "This is going to be so funny!" She took Carly by the wrist, pulling her over to a chair, and shoved her into it. "Give me your bra."

"I will *not.*"

"You're such a prude. Lucky for you, so are Sasha and I." Birdie turned around and said, "Unzip me. Quick, before a customer comes in."

"No. You're nuts."

Birdie made a frustrated sound, trying to reach her zipper.

"Fine, geez." Carly unzipped her dress. "How did you get it zipped up, anyway?"

"I have a zipper pull." Birdie proceeded to take her arms out of her dress and remove her bra. She put her dress back on, leaving it unzipped, and placed the cups of her bra over Carly's knees, hooking it behind them. "I can't believe you've never done this. You're not *that* much older than me."

Carly had about five years on her. "I don't even know what you're doing. He's going to know they're my knees!"

"Trust me, sweetpea, I learned from the best." She snagged Carly's phone from the counter and moved behind the chair. "Okay, knees together, tuck your legs back." She leaned over Carly's shoulder and took a few pictures. "Sasha knows all the tricks. All you have to do is take it really close up. She once sent a shot like this to a guy, and he started sending her pictures of him jerking off to it!"

"Gross!"

"He was *big*, too." Birdie drew out the word *big*. "When Sasha told him he'd jerked off to her *knees*, he got *so* mad. It was freaking hilarious. But then my brothers found out. I've never heard them so mad at her." She gave a little shrug and showed Carly the picture.

Sure enough, Birdie's black lace bra cupping Carly's knees looked just like cleavage. "Birdie, this is *awesome*."

"Right?" she said proudly. "Your guy gets his jollies, and nobody has blackmail pictures of your body."

"This feels wrong on so many levels, but I kind of love it." Carly gave Birdie her bra and thumbed out a text to Zev while her friend put herself back together.

THE LABORATORY WHERE Zev was going to work on the concretions was part of the Real DEAL (Discover, Experience, Appreciate, Learn), a total immersion exploratory park for kids that included educational exhibits and hands-on activities, located on the border of Weston and Allure. The park, which was still under construction, was the brainchild of Zev's cousin Dane, a shark tagger and the founder of the Brave Foundation, which used education and innovative advocacy programs to protect sharks, and in a broader sense, the world's oceans. After living on a boat for years, Dane had moved his wife and son back to Weston, Colorado, to be closer to their families. Dane's brother Hugh, a professional race car driver, and their brother-in-law, Jack Remington, a survivalist, had both jumped on board with the endeavor, just as Noah had, greatly expanding Dane's original vision from the exploration of marine life to include several other disciplines.

Noah was giving Zev—and Bandit—a tour of the facility. Zev wasn't used to having a dog at his heels, but Beau had asked him to bring Bandit on as many outings as he could to keep the dog from getting lonely. Bandit had a history of stealing things when he was left alone, and Zev had experienced his thievery firsthand that morning when Bandit had stolen his towel while he was showering, leaving him to dry himself off with a frilly little hand towel.

"This place is going to be incredible," Zev said as they left the building that would house the aquarium and headed into the survivalist area. "Thanks for letting me bring Bandit." Bandit, with his thick black fur and ever-present red bandanna tied around his neck, trotted happily beside him, looking up every few steps. He had a white stripe down the center of his snout, and Zev had to admit, he was a damn cute thief.

Noah ruffled Bandit's fur and said, "Bandit and I are good buddies. Beau brings him everywhere." Noah was a few years younger than Zev. As a marine biologist, he spent his time at sea or in a laboratory. He sported a year-round tan and his sandy-brown hair always looked windswept, as if he'd just stepped off his boat. As they walked into another building, he said, "Jack is going to have interactive survivalist exhibits here, and that hallway connects us to the mini racetrack that Hugh is setting up."

Zev followed him down the hallway. From what Zev had already seen, he was sure the Real DEAL was going to be something people came from all over to experience. "It's hard to believe all of this started with Dane and Lacy's idea to build a small aquarium and a few educational exhibits."

"When have you ever known a Braden project to stay small? Dane and I worked together on a number of expeditions these last few years. When he mentioned the idea of the park, I jumped at the chance to join him. I figured it was a great use of my inheritance. I'm pumped that I'll be educating kids about marine life, and I'm working on collaborating with a local college for use of our lab. They want me to hold lectures and that kind of thing."

"That's great. I know you said you'll be teaching kids about marine life, but have you considered marine and land archaeo-logical exhibits? When I was a kid, we went to an archaeological museum, and that's when I knew I wanted to explore. I was so pumped about the idea of *finding* history, I used to dream about it."

"Used to?" Noah arched a brow. "Dude, you told me that you've wanted to find the *Pride* since you were a kid."

"You got me there." Although his dreams of exploring had been pushed to the side the day he'd left Pleasant Hill, and he'd replaced them with dreams about Carly. Thoughts of her had only increased his desire to find *their* ship. "I saw a documentary about it when I was in third grade. We were studying pirates, and that stuck with me." He and Carly had been in the same class, and from that moment on, the *Pride* had gone to the top of their *one-day* list—the list of things they wanted to do together, like a bucket list. They'd later added other places they wanted to explore and things they wanted to do, like getting matching tattoos, cliff diving, surfing, and dozens of other things.

"Sounds to me like maybe you should think about partnering with us. You could teach kids about shipwrecks and treasure hunting, what happens to things when they get lost at sea." Noah nudged his arm and said, "You could spark interest for future treasure hunters."

Zev shook his head. "I don't know, man. I'm not great at staying in one place, and hopefully I'll be unearthing treasures from the *Pride* for years to come. But I really appreciate you letting me work here this week."

"I'm happy to. I'll be in and out during the day doing some research now that my lab is up and running. It'll be nice to have company."

Bandit trotted happily next to Zev as they made their way through more buildings.

When they headed across the grounds toward the laboratory, Zev said, "How are you handling being landlocked?" Like Zev, Noah was usually on the move. They had connected a few times during their travels over the years, and Zev had never pegged him for the kind of guy to settle down in one place.

"It's taken some getting used to, but I'm not done with the sea. That'd be like being done with women." Noah cocked a grin. "I saw you talking to the cute blonde who catered the desserts at the wedding. Anything happening there? If not, I heard she's got a chocolate shop in Allure. I might have to wander over there for a *taste*."

"Her name's Carly. She and I have a lot of history, so how about you dip your banana in someone else's chocolate?" Zev had been reliving Carly's kisses, the sound of her voice, the feel of her hands since he'd left last night. If he had it his way, soon they'd be enjoying a lot more than just kisses, and his would be the only lips doing any tasting.

Noah clapped Zev on the back as they entered the laboratory and said, "Sure thing, dude. Come on. I'll show you where I put your tools."

Zev followed him past an impressive array of marine tanks and work areas to two basins in which the two concretions were stored in a caustic solution to keep them from drying out and to protect the artifacts. Marine concretions formed in all shapes and sizes, ranging from minuscule to weighing several tons. These concretions were roughly twelve and eighteen inches in length and weighed about fifteen and thirty pounds. The tools Zev had shipped were set up on a worktable just to the left. "This is perfect. Thanks, man."

His phone vibrated. He pulled it out of his pocket and saw Carly's name in a message bubble. When they were younger, Carly would never have sent an X-rated selfie. He didn't think that had changed, but he'd had to push her buttons and remind her of all the fun they'd had together, because despite her refusal to send dirty selfies, he knew she'd loved getting the request as much as he'd enjoyed getting a rise out of her.

He opened the message, and his body heated up at the cleavage shot she'd sent.

Noah glanced over Zev's shoulder and whistled. "*Damn*. Is that from Carly?"

As Zev said, "Yeah, back off," he recognized a tiny scar that he knew was located just above her left knee and stifled a laugh. *That's my clever girl. Good to see you're not completely done with me.* He'd never forget the night she'd gotten that scar. They'd been in the Pleasant Hill Archaeology Club together throughout middle and high school. The summer between their junior and senior year, they'd gone on a weeklong dig with the club and had snuck out of their tents to hook up by the river. They'd been taking off their clothes when Carly's foot had gotten caught in her pants. She'd fallen and landed on a rock, slicing into her leg so deep, she'd needed stitches. He'd felt terrible about her getting hurt, but nothing could have stopped them from seeing each other every minute they were able, and the next night, when he'd snuck out to see her, he'd held on to her every second.

"Chicks usually wait weeks before sending body shots," Noah said, pulling Zev from his thoughts. "You move fast, dude."

Zev didn't have much time before he was heading back out to sea, and he wasn't wasting a second of it tiptoeing around the woman he'd once thought he could get over. Not only was there no getting over Carly Dylan, but he had no fucking idea how he'd leave at the end of the week and go on with his life if she couldn't open her heart to him again.

He pocketed his phone and said, "Only with her, man. Only with her."

Chapter Six

BIRDIE HELD THE basket of cereal as Carly locked the shop Monday night. Her stomach had been in knots all day. After she'd sent the text to Zev with the fake cleavage shot, he'd messaged, *I'd know those legs anywhere.* It had taken only a minute of looking more closely at the picture for her to see the scar and realize her mistake. She'd already texted to thank him for the basket of cereal, to which he'd responded, *I dare you to take a bite.* He'd added a devil emoji and then texted, *Now I've got your number* with a winking emoji. He was so sneaky!

"Have you heard from Zev since he outed you on the picture?" Birdie asked.

Carly took the basket from her and said, "Nope."

"That's a lot of disappointment in one little word. This doesn't have to be the end of your sexy-texty game. You could text him, you know. Flirting is not a one-way street."

"There's a lot more to it, Birdie. I am disappointed, but I'm also mad at myself for *being* disappointed, which makes me royally confused. Why can't I just leave well enough alone? You hear about people saying they're over their exes all the time. Why can't *I* be one of them?"

"Because you're not over him."

"I *am*." The words tasted bitter and untrue.

"I'm not buying it, Carly."

"*Fine.* Maybe I'm not over him, but I know where we'll end up if I text him. I'll just get hurt. His life isn't here, Birdie. It's out at sea or exploring some distant land. He's never going to stay put, and I'm not the same girl I was. I don't want that anymore."

Birdie put her hand on her hip and said, "You don't want *what*? That life? Or *him*? Because you were *singing* into a *spatula* a few hours ago, and now you look like you want to crawl under a blanket and eat a pound of ice cream. I don't think you know what you want."

"I hate that I can't pull the wool over your eyes."

"You can't pull it over your own eyes, either." Birdie fished in her purse for her car keys and said, "Look, you told me how in love you two used to be, and yeah, he broke your heart. But you said you haven't seen him since he broke up with you a hundred years ago. Aren't you at all curious about what could happen between you? Or about what he's been up to? Don't you want to give him hell for breaking up with you? I mean, if I were you, I would want to do all of those things *and* kiss him some more. *Definitely* kiss him. A lot."

Carly huffed out a breath. "Don't you think I *want* to kiss him? I want to do all those things you mentioned. But it's hard, and it's scary, and I know what'll be between us. Last night when we kissed…" She sighed and looked up at the sky, shaking her head. "Those were the best kisses I've ever had. Even better than when we were young, which I didn't think could ever be surpassed."

"Then you should have *kept* kissing and let this thing play out. Who cares if it's scary? It's better than letting him leave town and not having said your piece. My mom always says that unspoken words can kill a relationship faster than the skeletons they might let out of the closet." Birdie's mother, Wynnie, was Marie's sister. She was a licensed psychologist and she'd helped Carly through the worst of times when she'd first moved to Colorado.

"I love your mom, but why can't shrinks ever say anything like *Let it be?*"

"What fun would that be? Want to know what *I* say?"

Carly shrugged. "Sure."

"That man knows you in ways I doubt anyone else does, and you know where he's staying. Go see him. And don't sweat it if you're late in the morning. I'll come in early *just in case.*" Birdie looked at the basket of cereal and said, "And if it doesn't go well, you can drown your sorrows in Lucky Charms and Froot Loops." She giggled and said, "I love you, and I will always have your back. I'll celebrate your happiness or pull you out of your sadness." She walked backward toward her car and said, "But for the record, I'm pulling for a little under-the-covers treasure hunting!"

Me too.

But wanting and doing are two very different things.

Carly stood in front of the shop remembering all of the things she'd thought about saying to Zev if she ever got the chance. Maybe Birdie had a point. He *was* staying at the inn, which wasn't that far from Allure, and she knew the inn was closed until Beau and Charlotte returned from their honeymoon. Charlotte had told her that Zev's family had only planned on staying until Sunday morning, and that Zev had been the only one who had time to watch the animals for them. *Zev*, the guy who almost *never* went home to visit, had agreed to give up a week of his time for Beau.

I guess guilt is a powerful motivator.

She always wondered if he'd felt guilty for taking Beau out and getting drunk with him the night Tory had been killed. Memories of the next evening and their painful breakup came rushing back. Zev had paced like a caged animal, hands fisted, anger and sadness warring in his eyes, his every word spat like a curse. *Tory's death fucked me up and I can't deal with it. How can I expect you to?* He'd been so unlike the carefree Zev she'd known, hollering about being guilty and broken, hardened to her every plea. They'd argued for what had felt like an hour, but in reality had been much less. She'd said she'd deal with anything for him, but he'd looked her dead in the eyes, with tears in his own, muscles corded, the veins in his neck plumped like snakes, as he'd said, *That's why I'm leaving, because you shouldn't have to.* As he'd walked away, her pleas to take her with him fell on deaf ears. She'd felt her heart shatter as her last words tumbled from her mouth, tears flooding her cheeks. *Zevy! If you can walk away from me, then you never loved me.* He'd turned with tears in his eyes and said, *You're wrong, Carls. I'm walking away because I love you.* She'd never seen anyone so anxious, angry, and sad all at once, until the next morning when she'd found the note taped to her window. *You are and will always be the very air that I breathe, the only treasure to my empty chest. Forever yours, Z.* She'd run the three blocks to his house, but in her heart she'd known he'd already left, and when she'd gotten there, her worst fears confirmed, she'd collapsed to her knees in the Bradens' yard.

Tears welled in her eyes with the memory. She swiped them away, wondering if he'd ever felt guilty for leaving *her.* She doubted it, since he'd never reached out to her, which hurt and pissed her off even more. He *should* feel guilty. He should kiss her freaking *feet* for breaking her heart the way he had.

She strode toward her truck. She was going to see him at the inn, and she would tell him *exactly* how she felt.

There was an envelope stuck under the windshield wiper. She set the basket on the hood and snagged the envelope, silently chastising her stupid heart for hoping it was from Zev as she tore it open and read it. *I dare you to meet me tonight. If you don't show up by eight o'clock, I'll take the hint and leave you be.*

He'd drawn a map with no street names, only landmarks, like they used to draw. There was a giant *X* at the end of the line. At the bottom of the paper was an arrow. She quickly flipped it over and read the back.

> *We both know I won't leave you be. But I know we need to talk and I promise to adhere to our five-foot rule. No touching, no kissing. Just talking (if that's what you want).*
> *Z*

She and Zev had come up with the idea of staying five feet apart when they were teenagers and their connection had been so fierce they'd ended up making out every time one of them wanted to talk. She put the basket of cereal on the bench seat and settled in behind the wheel of her aunt's old pickup truck, and she realized Zev's note had washed away her steely resolve to give him hell.

A girl could get whiplash from this roller coaster of emotions.

She started the engine, and as she drove out of the parking lot, she knew it wouldn't matter if she was smiling over his note or not; the hurt he'd caused had come out last night when they were kissing. It would definitely show up again. She just had to give it the chance and face him.

ZEV HAD TRAVELED the world with little more than a backpack. He'd sailed through treacherous storms and come across more dangerous situations than any one man ever should. And yet, as he paced beneath the umbrella of a large tree in Serenity Park, he could remember only a handful of times when he'd been even close to this nervous, each of them revolving around Carly. The first time he'd kissed her, he'd worried he was doing it wrong. The first time he'd felt her up, he'd been afraid she'd swat him away. The first time they'd had sex, he'd been so nervous he could barely breathe. But until now, nothing had come close to the crushing anxiety he'd felt after Tory's death, when he'd known he needed to get away from her, from Pleasant Hill. Hell, from himself if that were possible.

Trepidation stacked up inside him. What if she didn't show? What if he'd come across as too cocky by asking for that sexy text? What if their instant and intense connection when they'd kissed had scared her off? What if she'd expected him to act more remorseful from the get-go? *Fuck.* He'd tried to find a balance in those moments before he'd first approached her, but there was no balance without forgiveness. There was only survival or falling to his knees, and he wasn't going to make a scene at the wedding. When he'd gone to her shop to apologize and had seen her with another fucking cowboy, jealousy had taken hold, and he'd wanted only to win her back.

He glanced at the blanket beneath the tree, on which he'd set a loaf of French bread, a box of saltines, and a bottle of wine from Hilltop Vineyards. It was exactly what they'd had the first night Carly had ever gotten drunk. They'd stolen the bottle from his parents' stash. He'd thought it was romantic to re-create that night, but now his gut clenched with worry. What if the reminders of what they'd had didn't conjure the same warm feelings for her as they did for him? What if they reminded her of losing Tory and of his leaving?

He caught movement out of his peripheral vision, and his heart nearly stopped. There she was, walking across the grass like an angel illuminated by the setting sun. She slowed, looking over at the blanket, and stopped about ten feet away. Zev held his breath, sure she was going to turn and leave. He'd give anything to get her to stay long enough to talk, to just let him explain himself.

She looked from the blanket to the ground between them. Her hair curtained her face as she shook her head.

He lowered his eyes for a second, trying to calm his nerves, but it was a futile effort. "Just hear me out," he pleaded.

"Really, Zevy? Is that Hilltop wine?" She lifted her face, a half smile curving her lips.

Relief swept through him. "Stolen from Beau and Char's wine cellar."

"Zinfandel?" she asked nervously.

"Is there any other kind?"

When he stepped forward, she met him halfway and said, "You're playing dirty." Thankfully she sounded amused, not angry.

He turned his palm up and said, "Cards on the table, Carls. We're *really* good at playing dirty."

She laughed softly again, balm to his fractured heart, and said, "I'm surprised you didn't bring Bandit. Did Beau forget to warn you about Bandit stealing and hiding things when he's left alone?"

"I've experienced his thievery. I had to use a flimsy hand towel with lace on the edges and a pink heart sewn into it to dry off after my shower this morning. I know Beau and Bandit are a pack, but I'm not used to having a sidekick. I think it's worth the risk of him stealing something tonight. I wanted to be able to give you my full attention."

He reached for her hand, but she shook her head and said, "Five-foot rule."

"Right, sorry." He waved to the blanket. "Sit and drink, or walk and talk?"

She looked around them. He'd wanted to find someplace neutral, open, where she wouldn't feel like he was pushing her to kiss him again...or do more. He'd thought about meeting her at the park down the street from her shop, but that didn't feel neutral enough. Serenity Park was halfway between the inn and Divine Intervention.

"Walk and talk," she said. "Bring the bottle."

He grabbed the bottle and said, "It's probably better if we walk. There are more bushes for you to puke in near the water."

"*Ha ha*," she said sarcastically. "I was *thirteen*, and I wanted to impress you. It was the first time I'd ever drank alcohol."

"You impressed me all right, all over my sneakers."

That soft laugh escaped again, and he took that as a good sign. As they walked toward the lake, he said, "We've shared a lot of firsts, haven't we?"

"Yeah."

"First girlfriend/boyfriend," he said, hoping to keep things light for just a little while before he said what he'd come to say. "First kiss. It was a good one, remember?"

"I remember being really nervous, and then the second our lips touched, like magic, all my worries fell away."

"It's still magic," he said, bringing her eyes to his. She quickly looked away, but not before he saw longing and sadness in her eyes. *Too much too soon.* They needed to talk about that sadness, but he knew it might be the end of their night, and he wasn't ready for that. He scrambled for something else to say, but between his nerves and that look, he couldn't think straight, so he said, "What do you remember most about our first kiss?"

"The way I felt like I was floating on air until you slipped your tongue into my mouth, which totally freaked me out."

He laughed, relieved by her levity. "Come on. You had to expect it. You had been asking me when I was going to kiss you for a week."

"Yeah, but it was still invasive, and thrilling, in a nerve-racking way. I'm sure you could tell I got flustered."

"Why do you think I put my hand on the back of your head? I wasn't about to let you get away. Nick taught me that trick."

Her jaw dropped. "You talked to *Nick* about kissing me? Do you have any idea how embarrassing that is?"

"Do you know how embarrassing it was to have to go to him in the first place for pointers? I figured I had one shot with you, and I wasn't about to blow it. God, I was so nervous."

"I could tell you were," she said softly.

"You could *not*."

"I could tell a *lot* of things that night. Like how you pulled your T-shirt down to hide your hard-on."

"I think I need a drink for this." He opened the wine and took a swig, then handed her the bottle. "You were my first grope, you know. You were so soft and perfect. I was sure you'd been put on this earth just to make me happy."

"And you were so *hard*. I remember thinking it had to hurt."

They both laughed.

She took a drink and said, "We sure fumbled through our firsts."

"We might have fumbled at the beginning, but we got the hang of things. I know we were just kids, but I've never experienced anything even close to what we had."

Her eyes looked troubled again as she tipped the bottle up to her lips. She was quiet for a minute, and then she said, "I remember how you looked at me *after* our first kiss. It was the same way you looked at me after the first time we had sex, like I was your earth, sun, moon, stars, and sea all in one."

"You were, Carls." *You still are.* "You turned my world upside down every day from the moment we first started hanging out together until the day I left." He wondered if the regret in his voice was as loud in her ears as it was in his. They walked in silence along the edge of the lake for a few minutes. Zev wrestled with bringing up the reasons why he'd left. But he wasn't ready to give up this happier place yet. It felt good to be with Carly, to see her smile and hear her voice as they relived happy memories. "Remember when we decided we should be more than friends?"

"You mean when you asked me to be your girlfriend in a note that you taped to my bedroom window?"

"Yes." Another nervous night.

After sneaking out together, they'd said good night through that window. And after their last kiss, when she'd closed the window, they'd used their breath to fog it up and wrote messages as fast as they could before the fog faded. They'd become so adept at writing backward, they could do it as quickly as they wrote forward. They'd said good night by that window hundreds of times, and every time was as heart-wrenching as the last. The hours between good night and school the next morning seemed to go on forever. But now he knew what forever really felt like.

"I still have that note," she admitted. "And all the others."

His gut twisted. Had she kept the note he'd taped to her window the morning he'd left town? He bit the bullet and said, "I wasn't sure you'd show up tonight, but I'm glad you did. I'm sorry for the way I left, Carly. It wasn't fair, and I've always regretted it."

She stopped walking, turning her beautiful, troubled eyes on him. Her breathing quickened, and she said, "That was really messed up."

She clenched her mouth shut like she was holding back, and it made him feel even worse because they'd always said what they'd felt, and he deserved whatever she was trying not to say. "I know, and I'm sorry, Carls."

"You broke my heart." *Heart* came out cracked and shaky, her lower lip trembling. "No," she panted out, her voice escalating. "You did *worse* than that. You fucking *destroyed* me," she seethed, every word hitting him like a knife to the chest. "I lost my best friend when Tory died, and then you *abandoned* me! You were my *life* for six years, Zev. Six *years*. I couldn't imagine a day without you, and then suddenly there I was, completely and utterly *alone*. I didn't know how to live in a world without you and Tory in it. I could barely get out of bed. I thought I'd die from grief. How could you do that to me?" Tears spilled from her eyes as she shouted, her words fast and venomous. "Do you have *any* idea what that was like? You never even explained why or gave me a chance to go with you. You said you had to leave, and then you were gone. Who *does* that?"

"Someone who was fucked up," he snapped, angrier at himself than she could ever be, deserving of her every accusation. Struggling to rein in his anger, he gritted out, "Tory was like a sister to me, too. Her death messed me up on so many levels, I didn't know how to climb out of the darkness that had consumed me. It was *me* who dragged Beau out to the party that night. *I* was the one who got him too drunk to drive, and when we found out about Tory, he dropped to his *knees*." His gut seized with the memory. He paced as the long-held hurt tumbled out. "He just fucking collapsed. The guy I idolized, the brother who could take on the world, just fucking lost it. Then you—the girl I *loved*, the person I *lived* for—you were *so* broken, and I felt like that was on *me*, too. I was so mad at myself, so full of grief, I became a hateful, angry monster overnight. I couldn't think straight. I couldn't see anything but devastation around me, and yeah, I know Tory's death wasn't my fault, or Beau's fault. We didn't cause the accident, and who the hell knows what would have happened if Beau had picked her up from the airport that night. We might have lost them both. But she was the love of his life, and in the blink of an eye she was *gone*." His hands fisted and he closed the distance between them, needing her to hear the rest of his confession. "All I could think about from that second on was who I'd be and how I'd survive if I lost *you*, and I couldn't fucking handle it."

"But you *walked out* on me!" she yelled as tears streaked her cheeks. "You made *sure* you lost me."

"I *had* to," he said through clenched teeth, sadness and anger pounding inside him. "Goddamn it, Carly, don't you see?

I was so fucking scared, and I hated myself so much, I would have *destroyed* us. That carefree kid was *gone*. Every time I looked at you, all I could think about was losing you the way Beau had lost Tory, and I knew that if he couldn't survive it, there was no way I could. You were my other half, the fucking blood that pumped through my veins." Carly's shoulders shook with sobs, but Zev couldn't stop the truth from finally coming out. "We wouldn't have survived Tory's death as a couple because I couldn't look at you without hearing a fucking voice in my head telling me that I could lose you at any second. I couldn't *stop* hearing it. I was filled with *rage* and *fear* and I knew you'd hate who I'd become. I hated myself, Carly. I would've ruined *you*, and I couldn't have lived with that."

She dropped the wine bottle to the grass and shoved at his chest, pushing him away, then stalking forward and hollering in his face. "So you left to save yourself, and to hell with what it did to me?"

"*No*," he said vehemently. "I thought you'd be better off without me."

"Oh, *right*." She scoffed through her tears. "Like I could ever be better off without the guy I'd loved my whole life?" She shoved him again, seething. "I waited for you to come back! I stared out my bedroom window night after night, *sure* you'd be back for me."

His chest was so tight, he could only choke out, "Carly..."

"You said Beau collapsed? Well, guess what? So did I, on your parents' front lawn. I ran to your house the next day, hoping and praying I could change your mind, but you were *gone*. You left me behind," she choked out.

"I *had* to, bab—"

"Don't!" She shook her head, tears flooding her cheeks.

"You *always* asked what I needed. *Always!*" Sobs stole her voice, and he reached for her again, but she jerked back and said, "But not that night. You just walked away like I meant nothing to you."

"I walked away *because* you meant *everything* to me!" He didn't mean to yell, but her pain, and her venom-laced words, cut him to his core. He ground out a curse, trying to reel in his emotions, but it was like trying to stop a tsunami. "I didn't ask you because I thought I knew what you needed, and that was for me to leave. Do you think it was easy for me to walk away from you? The only person I wanted to be with? To leave my home? My family? It was the hardest thing I'd *ever* done. I've thought about you every second of every damn day of my life. When I close my eyes, I see your face. When I see a blonde on the street, my heart fucking beats faster with unstoppable desperation to see you, which is followed by the debilitating reality of knowing I should keep my distance. I physically *ached* at the sight of you in Mexico. I knew I'd made a mistake by leaving, and I thought maybe we could find our way back into each other's lives. But by then you were *done* with me." He lowered his voice as the crushing pain of waking up alone returned. He lifted his eyes to hers and said, "At least I had the guts to say goodbye."

She turned away, shaking her head and swiping at her eyes, her voice cracking as she said, "I couldn't take a chance that you'd leave me first."

"I wouldn't have," he confessed, but he had no idea if she'd heard him. He walked around her, giving her no choice but to look at him. She lifted her tear-streaked face, looking deflated, like she had nothing left to give. "I get it, Carly. You were in survival mode. That's why I didn't go after you. I knew I was selfish when I broke up with you and left home, and I've regretted it every day of my life. I was a broken, stupid kid who loved you too much to understand how to deal with it. I *am* sorry, Carly. I'm so fucking sorry for the way I hurt you, the way I hurt everyone. I don't blame you for wanting to hurt me back."

"It was stupid of me to leave. I was still so in love with you, I cried the entire plane ride home the next day, and then…" She turned away again, and Zev moved with her.

"And then *what*? Talk to me, Carls. Let's just get it all out, right here, right now." He cradled her face in both hands and wiped her tears with the pads of his thumbs. How was it possible to look so sad and so beautiful at once? He didn't let go of her face; he couldn't. He might never get another chance to hold it. "I thought I was doing the right thing by not going after you in Mexico. I didn't want to make it any harder for you."

"I wish you *had* come after me." More tears streamed down her cheeks, wetting his hands. "I needed you," she said shakily. "I needed you so badly."

He pulled her into his arms, holding her as she cried. "I'm so damn sorry. I didn't know. I took off, angry and hurt and blaming myself all over again. I didn't mean to hurt you by not coming after you."

"It doesn't matter," she said a little sharply.

He drew back, gazing deeply into her eyes. He saw her walls going up again and said, "It *does* matter, Carly. Everything that has ever happened between us matters. It's shaped who we are and how we feel. I've lived a hundred years in the last decade, every minute wishing I could go back in time and start over. I should have walked out of that bar in Mexico and never looked back. I should have let you live your life without any further pain. But I couldn't. I loved you too much."

She tilted her head, a small smile on her lips despite her tears. "I *wanted* that night with you. So much had happened in the time since you'd left Pleasant Hill. I finally felt like I could breathe again, and then I saw you and my heart beat like it only ever had when we were together. No one else has *ever* made me feel that way, and I'd almost forgotten the difference between merely surviving and really living. If Tory's death taught me one thing, it was the importance of spending time with the people I love. I *wanted* you that night, but in the predawn hours, I thought about how you'd never come back for me after Tory died, and all that old pain swamped me again. I thought hurting you would give me closure. But it only made me sadder. And then…" She swallowed hard and lowered her eyes.

"And then what, Carls?"

CARLY HAD IMAGINED having this conversation with Zev so many times, but even after all these years, she was terrified. She lifted her eyes, but not her face, looking at him from behind her hair—hiding from the truth that had once torn her apart as badly as when Zev had left Pleasant Hill. She inhaled a shaky breath, mustering all of her courage, and said, "Then I found out I was pregnant."

The air rushed from Zev's lungs. "Preg…*pregnant?*"

She nodded. "I found out six weeks after we were together in Mexico."

"You have a kid? *We* have a kid?" Confusion rose in his eyes. "How can I not know this? Does my family know? I don't…I don't understand."

She shook her head. "We don't, Zev. I miscarried a few weeks after I found out."

"Oh, *shit*, babe…" Tears glistened in his eyes. He looked as wrecked as she felt, and *she'd* had a decade to get over the pain. He pulled her into his arms and said, "You should have had someone track me down. I would have come back to be with you."

His heart slammed against her cheek. "I hated the way I left you in Mexico and the way you left after Tory died. I was so confused. I didn't know what to do. I didn't tell anyone."

He drew back, gazing into her eyes, and said, "*Jesus*. I should have been more careful. I always got so carried away with you."

"Don't do that. It was *both* of our faults. I never blamed you."

"Then why didn't you tell me?"

"At first I didn't know if I should even tell you I was pregnant, because I didn't want you to come back for a child if you didn't want *me*."

"I *wanted* you, Carly! I fucking wanted you so badly. But I thought you were done with me."

Tears blurred her eyes, and she swiped at them with a shaky hand. "I know that *now*. But Tory was gone; you were gone. I had nobody to talk to. I was all alone at school." Her chest constricted. "I was a mess for weeks while I tried to figure out what to do. When I was finally able to think clearly enough to make a decision, I realized how much I wanted the baby. I was worried that if I'd tracked you down, it would seem like a ploy, something out of a bad movie where the ex comes up pregnant and tries to trap a guy."

"I'd never think that of you."

"I know! But I was hurt. It took me a minute to figure that out. When I finally came to that realization, I was going to try to track you down, but then I miscarried. I don't know if it was stress or just not meant to be, but it doesn't matter why it happened."

"*Christ,*" he ground out between gritted teeth, and hauled her into his arms again. "I should have been there."

"None of that matters now."

"It *all* matters. You must have told your parents. Did they help you through it?"

"I went home when school was over, but I never told anyone. It was too painful to talk about, and I knew everyone would blame you, and that would have been wrong." She looked up at him, still in the circle of his arms, and said, "We were both there that night, and *I'm* the one who left without a word."

"You didn't have to protect me. All these years, you've carried that burden alone?"

"I've never told my friends or my parents, but eventually I talked to a therapist, and that helped a lot."

He sighed, clearly relieved. "Good. I'm glad. But I still wish you had told me, even after the fact."

"Every time I thought about finding you, it was just too much, too sad. I didn't want to do that to you because nothing could change the outcome. Nothing good could have come from it."

"I could have been there to help you through it. I would have come back. You shouldn't have had to go through that alone."

The regret and sincerity in his voice told her it was true. He would have come back. She believed that now with her whole heart, but it didn't change what she believed *then*. She pushed from his arms as more hurtful truths spilled out. "How could I have known that? You'd let me suffer alone before."

Anguish rose in his eyes. "I thought I was saving you from *more* heartache when I left. I fucked up. I get it, and I will forever regret it. But tonight, when I told you that I knew in Mexico I had made a mistake and I wanted to try again, I *meant* it. You don't have to believe me when I say I would have come back, and I don't blame you for not trusting me to be there for you back then. I'm a lot of things, Carly, and I've made big mistakes in my life, but I have *never* lied to you."

Their painful past swept in like a vulture, digging its talons in. She lifted her chin as fresh tears slid down her cheeks and said, "You once told me you'd love me forever."

"That was *not* a lie," he said adamantly. "I have loved you since we were kids, and I will love you until the day I die. I have never felt anything even remotely close to what I feel for you for anyone else." His chest rose with his deep inhalation, anguish rising in his eyes, as real as the ground beneath his feet. "How could I, when I left my heart in your hands? I have nothing left to give. Except to you, Carly. *Only* to you."

Years of heartache from feeling lost, from convincing herself he didn't love her, telling herself she hated him for leaving when her love had never dimmed, crashed over her, drawing fresh sobs.

"I'm sorry," he choked out. "Damn it, Carls. I'm so fucking sorry."

He gathered her in his arms, and she went willingly, burying her face in his chest as her tears fell.

He kissed her forehead, holding her tighter. "I wish I'd done things differently. I wish so many things. God, can you ever forgive me?" He stroked her back, whispering apologies, the sorrow in his voice drawing more tears. "I'm sorry for how I left, for not coming back for you, for Mexico, for the baby we lost…the years we lost."

His heartfelt words went on and on as they stood beneath the stars, letting it all go. He didn't rush her, didn't make her feel bad for falling apart, because he was falling apart, too, pouring his heart out in supportive, loving words. She had no idea how long they stood there, but he held her until he had no more words to say and she had no more tears to cry.

Eventually they threw out the wine bottle and made their way back to the blanket. Zev kept his arm around her. Even after everything they'd gone through, he still felt more like *home* than any person, place, or thing, ever had.

He kept her close when they sat on the blanket, running his hand down her back, threading his fingers through her hair, and kissing her temple, all the while apologizing and making promises in the dark—not to hurt her again, to make it up to her, to earn her forgiveness. Every word healed an ache, filled an empty spot. When they fell silent, letting the cool evening air wash away all the years of sadness, Carly realized why she'd never told anyone close to her about being with Zev in Mexico, or about the pregnancy. Zev was the only one she needed to tell. He was the salve to her wounds, the love that filled her lonely heart.

He was the only person who could make her feel whole again.

He brushed his lips over her temple and said, "I feel like I've been gutted, learning about what you went through after Mexico, and I'm sure what I'm feeling isn't even half as awful as it was for you when it happened. I wish I could take all your pain away."

"You are taking it away." She rested her head on his shoulder and closed her eyes, soaking in his support. "I've held that secret for so long, I didn't realize how much it was weighing on me. I feel a lot better having told you. I hated keeping a secret from you, and I know that's crazy after all that we've been through, but it's the truth. I know now that what happened was probably for the best. I was in no position to raise a child, and I doubt you were, either."

"That's probably true, but I still wish I could have been there for you."

She studied his face for a quiet moment, and it was all there looking back at her. The truth of how tortured he'd been by leaving, how much more he wanted in Mexico, and even the love he still had for her. "Knowing what I do now about how you felt in Mexico, I wish you had been, too. We've both made big mistakes."

"I feel like I've lived a lifetime in the last two hours."

"Is that good or bad?" *Please say good.*

"It's good, Carls." He caressed her cheek, pressed a kiss to the freckles on the bridge of her nose. "I've been wanting to do that since the wedding."

When they were younger, she was insecure about those freckles, but he'd always loved them. She wanted to climb into his arms and let him kiss her worries away, but she was still confused, wanting to let him in and scared to do it.

"Where do we go from here, Zevy?"

"I don't have all the answers," he said softly. "But does that mean you want there to be a *we*?"

She smiled. "You say that like I have a choice."

"You always have a choice, Carls."

She shook her head. "Not when it comes to you."

"Am I allowed to gloat over that?" He laughed softly, hugging her against his side, and said, "I'm only here until Sunday. We've got six days to figure out what this is. I know I've made bad decisions in the past, but I will do everything within my power not to hurt you again. You said you've changed, and I want to learn about all those changes. I want to get to know the person you've become, and I'd like for you to get to know the man I've become. What do you say? Will you give us a shot?"

Her heart said *yes!* but she'd learned to listen to her head. "I'm scared to spend time with you. I already feel myself falling back into us. I really loved us."

"I loved us, too," he said tenderly.

That made her tear up again, but these were happy tears. She blinked rapidly to keep them at bay and said, "Honestly, I think I'm more scared of *not* spending time with you. I know what life is like without you, and no matter how far I've come or how many friends I make, something's always missing."

"Thank God," he whispered, full of relief. "I have always felt that way. That's the power of us, Carls. You've always been the treasure, and without you I'm just an empty chest, hoping for a shot at more. We've got six days, babe."

"My life is here; yours isn't. Six days can only lead to heartache."

"We can't know that. I'm not that broken, stupid kid anymore, Carly. Believe it or not, I'm a pretty smart guy with a much clearer perspective on life than I had back then."

That's the problem. It's too easy to fall in love with grown-up you.

"We can figure this out. It doesn't have to be an all-or-nothing scenario, does it?" He caressed her cheek and said, "Where's the spontaneous always-up-for-an-adventure girl I fell for all those years ago?"

She shrugged, unsure if that girl still existed and trying to rein in her hopes that six days could really lead to more.

"That girl showed up here tonight, Carly. She's in there somewhere, stuck beneath the hurt and worries of our pasts." He brushed his thumb lightly over her lips, spreading heat through her like wildfire. "Six days could set her free."

Oh, how she wanted to believe him!

She clung to his words like a lifeline, and later that evening, after he walked her to her truck and kissed her so tenderly it felt like the first time, only better, she drove home and curled up beneath her blankets feeling a little less lonely as she let his words carry her off to sleep.

Chapter Seven

THE COUNTER CUT *into the backs of Carly's knees, but the pain only added to the pleasure as Zev pounded into her. Afternoon sunlight flooded the kitchen, and the devilish grin on his face made her want him even more desperately. She should have shut the kitchen door to the shop, but when his mouth hit hers, she hadn't thought of anything but wanting more. Thank goodness Birdie was busy with customers. He thrust harder, faster, and she fisted her hands in his hair, guiding his mouth to her neck. His teeth grazed her as he sucked her flesh. She gritted her teeth to keep from moaning as pleasure stacked up inside. Zev hauled her just over the edge of the counter, holding her ass with both hands, his hips jackhammering, burying himself so deep she could feel him in her throat. Every stroke of his cock sent her closer to the edge. The bells over the front door chimed, and panic gripped her. She tore her mouth away.* "Hurry!" *Zev crushed his mouth to hers just as Cutter's voice rang out.* "Carly?"

Shit! Her eyes slammed shut, and Cutter called her name again, his voice closing in on them just as the orgasm crashed over her, and she screamed, "I'm *coming!*"

She bolted upright, gasping for air. Her heart thundered as she looked frantically around her bedroom. *Holy shit.* Her nightshirt was sweaty, her sex pulsing and wet. She pressed her hand to her heart and closed her eyes, trying to process the fact that she'd just orgasmed from a *dream*. Where the hell had that come from? Her traitorous brain needed to calm the hell down.

She climbed out of bed on shaky legs and padded into the kitchen for a glass of water. Last night's talk with Zev had been as *difficult* as it was cathartic, and it had made her feel freer than she'd felt in years. She'd held on to the hurt and anger from his leaving, and the guilt for sneaking away in Mexico, for so long that she felt like a different person without it, but *this* was ridiculous and a little scary.

It hadn't been *easy* to bare their souls and move past the hurt, but once they'd cleared the air, it hadn't been all that difficult to feel like *Carls and Zevy* again.

She looked at the glass in her hand. Water wasn't the kind of drink she needed to calm her nerves. She used the bathroom and went back to bed, reliving and picking apart every word they'd said. Her mind kept circling back to one thought. If one night of clearing the air had this effect on her, what would six days do to her?

She lay there for a while longer, her pulse sprinting, her mind running in circles. Was she being silly? Six days was still *only* six days. The dream had just been a dream. *A fantasy.* That didn't quite fit, because fantasies didn't often come true, and she had no doubt that if she and Zev were alone, he'd end up buried eight inches deep. "Oh God…" Even her fantasies were reckless with him.

Zev's devilish grin sailed into her mind, and she threw her covers off. If she stayed in bed, she'd probably end up having three more orgasms. As much as she needed them, she was not going to feed those fantasies. She needed to remember to protect her heart, which had spent most of her life either loving him or pretending not to. She forced herself out of bed, got ready for the day, and headed into the shop.

After an hour of checking emails, bookkeeping, and organizing specials for the next several days, Carly's mind was still toying with her, drawing her into the world of *what ifs*, the world of her and Zev that she'd denied for so long. She dragged her chair into the closet in her office and climbed up so she could see the top shelf. Reaching behind the boxes of holiday decorations and office supplies, she retrieved a large box she'd cleverly marked RECEIPTS. She blew the dust off the top of the box and climbed off the chair. She pulled the chair back to her desk and sat down with the box in her lap. Her nerves prickled just thinking about the memories of her and Zev it held. All of their remember-when pictures: pictures they'd taken to commemorate their adventures and times with friends. She remembered all of their *remember whens*. When she'd first moved to Colorado, she couldn't bear the thought of leaving them behind. But it was too hard to resist falling back into the memories, and she'd asked Marie if she could store them somewhere. Marie had put them in her attic, and when Marie sold her house, Carly had been doing so well, she feared if she brought the pictures into her house, she'd end up going through them again and slipping back into that dark place of wanting answers she might never get. She'd hidden them here in the supply closet and had never once looked in the box.

But now she had the answers she'd always wanted.

She lifted the lid with a shaky hand, and her eyes sailed over several pictures of her and Zev as kids playing in a sprinkler, climbing the side of a hill with Beau and Nick, and riding their bikes in front of Zev's parents' house. A lump formed in her throat, and she closed her eyes as memories flooded her. Her phone vibrated in her pocket, startling her. She quickly put the top back on the box, pulled her phone from her pocket, and saw Marie's name on the screen. Marie had texted last week from Venezuela to say she was leaving in a few days to go to Nassau to stay in one of Treat Braden's resorts.

Carly opened the text, feeling like she'd been caught with her hand in a cookie jar. A picture of Marie's feet in the sand, with the ocean in the background, popped up with the message *Loving Nassau! I think I might stay for a week or two. Taking my morning walk and thinking of you. How was the wedding?* She hadn't wanted to worry Marie, so she'd played it cool and hadn't let on that she was nervous about possibly seeing Zev.

She thumbed out, *The wedding was great! Everyone loved the chocolates.*

Marie responded with, *Of course they did! Anything interesting you want to talk about?*

Carly knew she was fishing for news about Zev. She didn't want to open that can of worms, so she typed, *Not unless you want a blow-by-blow of Cutter dirty dancing with every girl in the place.*

Her phone vibrated a second later with Marie's text. *I hope you got pictures! Guess where I'm going tonight?*

Relieved Marie didn't push, Carly typed, *A luau?*

Her phone vibrated seconds later. Zev's name appeared in a message, and a nest of bees took flight in Carly's stomach. She stared at his name, wide-eyed. It was barely six o'clock in the morning, but he'd always been an early riser. With her heart in her throat, she opened and read the message. *Morning gorgeous. What's your address? I'll bring over milk to go with your Lucky Charms. We can ring in the new day together.*

Her body came alive in celebration with no cognitive effort. She was far too excited about the idea of ringing in a new day with him and was surprised to find herself actually considering it. She could spare an hour. Couldn't she? An hour alone with Zev at her house to…Her mind went *straight* to the bedroom.

This was not good.

Well, it would probably be *sinfully good*, but watching a sunrise with Zev would not be conducive to protecting her heart. She needed her house to remain a safe haven, someplace that held *no* physical memories of Zev. There was no way she would let him get his enticing scent all over her furniture or her *sheets*, which she had a feeling was where they'd end up if he came over.

Before she could respond, a text from Marie rolled in. *A coconut bar on the beach! They serve all drinks in coconuts. I'm going to have breakfast with friends. Love you!*

Leave it to Marie to have already found a group of friends. Carly imagined a handful of fiftysomething women talking about how much they don't need men.

And neither do I.

It was true. Carly didn't need a man. But there was no denying that she *wanted* Zev.

Six days means five potentially steamy nights…

She rolled her eyes at herself and typed, *My house is a no-Zev zone, and I need to keep it that way.*

His reply came quickly. *I'm in you, Carls, and you're in me. I've been there with you all along.*

The bells above the front door chimed, and Birdie's voice rang out. "I'm here, and you're supposed to be mattress dancing with Zev!"

Shit! Carly grabbed the box and hurried into the closet to hide it. Then she went to greet Birdie and bury herself in work.

&

CARLY'S NERVOUS ENERGY came in handy. By early afternoon she had accomplished twice as much as usual. Birdie was in rare form, rambling on about social media, the upcoming festival, happenings at the ranch, and about a dozen other things. Carly kept up pretty well, at least until another text from Zev rolled in, which had stopped her cold, turning Birdie and the customers to white noise.

The bells on the door chimed and the shop went quiet. "I'm thinking of sleeping with Cutter," Birdie said, heading toward the kitchen.

"Mm-hm." Carly didn't look up from her phone, where her eyes were still glued to the text from Zev. *Take a leap of faith with me. Meet me at Silk Hollow at 2.*

Birdie was rambling about something, but Carly's mind was running in circles. Silk Hollow was a swimming hole surrounded by granite cliffs and fed by a small waterfall. It wasn't far from the Sterling House, and it was known as the best cliff-diving spot around. It was also one of the places she and Zev had put on their one-day list when they were in middle school. His family had been visiting his cousins in Weston, Colorado. Dane had gone to Silk Hollow with his friends, and Zev had been too young to tag along. Dane had come back with exciting stories of the fun they'd had, and after Zev had come home, he'd told Carly all about it. They'd vowed to go cliff diving there together one day and have their own fun.

"Or maybe Beau," Birdie said as she walked past Carly.

"Okay," she said absently, mentally arguing with herself about wanting to go see Zev.

Birdie continued talking, her voice fading back to white noise as she walked away from Carly, then becoming louder as she approached from behind.

"Stand back, everyone! I've got this!" Birdie hollered.

Carly whipped her head around and found Birdie wearing safety goggles and looking adorably ridiculous in her crop top and high-waisted shorts, holding a fire extinguisher that was as big as her torso. "*What* are you doing?"

"I have been telling you my plans to sleep with different guys all morning, including the UPS guy, the dude at the coffee shop who we think is hot, *Cutter*, and even *Beau*, and you have approved of every one of them! That can only mean that your brain is fried. I'm going to put out the fire."

"Birdie!" Carly pocketed her phone and tried to take the extinguisher from her hands, but Birdie pulled it away.

"Don't you *Birdie* me. I can't afford for you to have burn-out brain. You're my guiding light, my mentor, and at the moment, I'm living vicariously through you and really getting tired of waiting for you to do all the dirty things with Zev that I want to!"

"Oh my *God*. You're *so* fired!"

Birdie set the extinguisher down and pulled off her goggles. "No I'm not. You love me, and you know I'm right. Now, hand over your phone. I need to see what's got you so mind-boggled that you'd say *okay* to me sleeping with Beau."

"I'm not giving you my phone. I'm sorry I've been out of it today. It's a weird time right now."

"Clearly." She waved to Carly's shorts and faded concert T-shirt and said, "You're wearing *that* shirt and UGGS. *News flash!*

Nobody listens to Journey anymore. And *UGGs*, Carly? It's *summertime*."

"They're like comfort food. I just needed them today."

"But *why*? You said last night was good, that you talked and cleared the air. Why aren't you dressing slutty and walking on air?"

"Because Zev makes me want to be the girl I used to be—which was never slutty, by the way—and that's dangerous. He wants me to meet him at Silk Hollow at two o'clock, and I know that means he'll want me to cliff dive with him."

Birdie's face contorted with confusion. "No, he won't. He probably wants you to meet him for a picnic so you can get past talking and do more kissing."

"Trust me. He wants us to dive. Zev has always been a thrill seeker."

"Then I'm totally confused. You once told me that he knew you better than anyone, but I can't even get you to ride the mechanical bull because you're afraid you'll get hurt."

"I know, but I wasn't always that way. Remember when we first met and I told you I used to be adventurous?"

Birdie wrinkled her nose. "I've got to be honest. I thought you'd exaggerated. You were having such a hard time, I thought you were just trying to make yourself seem more...I don't know. *Fearless?*"

"I didn't exaggerate. I was a thrill seeker, too. But with Zev nothing seemed scary. He was full of confidence and always watching out for me, and that made *me* feel indestructible. But after Tory died and he left, I found out I wasn't."

A familiar wave of sadness moved through her. It had gotten far less painful over the years, but until now it had still possessed the power to drag her under. When that awful feeling didn't come, she realized it was because she and Zev had finally confessed all of their heartaches and fears, their secrets and regrets, and their disappointments in themselves and in each other. She didn't know if he was right or wrong thinking that she might have ended up hating who he was and changing who she was because of it if he had stayed in Pleasant Hill. They would never know for sure. But at least now she understood that he thought he'd been protecting her, and even though it hurt, that was who he'd always been. In fact, it was who they'd always been. Wasn't that why she'd never tracked him down after the miscarriage? To protect him from pain that couldn't change the outcome? With those realizations came a renewed sense of freedom. This time she didn't feel as confused as she had just hours earlier. She felt an increased sense of *wellness* that she hadn't known she was missing.

Were there other things she was missing that she wasn't aware of? She thought about what Zev had said about the adventure seeker in her showing up last night at the park, and she wondered if he was right.

"Birdie, do you think it's possible that I still have that thrill seeker in me?"

Birdie tapped the top of the extinguisher and said, "That's a tough question, because a true thrill seeker would have been playing hide-and-seek between the sheets this morning with that gorgeous man who is doing everything possible to get your attention."

Carly couldn't stop a soft laugh from coming out and shook her head. "I'm being serious."

"So was I," Birdie exclaimed.

"Birdie!"

"Okay, *fine*. Did you really used to do all the things you

told me you did when we first met?"

"Yes, and more. We went cliff diving, skydiving, parasailing…" Long-forgotten excitement bubbled up inside her as she rattled off the things she and Zev had done together. "We skied, hiked, camped out. We had bonfires on the beach and made up warrior dances in the moonlight. We were *crazy*." She laughed and said, "There wasn't much we didn't do. During the summers we went on archaeological digs with the archaeology club to Mexico, Spain, Canada…"

"Wow, and I thought the days you wore your hair down instead of in braids or a ponytail, you were being adventurous." Birdie waggled her finger and said, "Actually, you've worn your hair down for two days in a row. *Yeah*, I think you do have an adventurous spirit buried deep inside you somewhere. But listen, if you don't want to go to the falls with Zev, I totally have your back. I'll grab my bikini and take your place."

"Can you stop, please?"

Birdie giggled. "But it's so fun to tease you. You're always so in control and organized. I like seeing you a little bit more of a hot mess like me. You should go to the falls. Have fun. Quinn will be here at five, so we've got the place covered."

"Really?" She was getting more excited, and nervous, by the second. "There's one other thing that worries me. Two, actually. You know how when you were a kid, you felt indestructible?"

"No, because I always had my brothers hovering over me like I'd break if someone looked at me wrong."

"Well, I never had that, but I'm almost *thirty*, and I know the truth. No one is indestructible. I've kept up my deep-sea diving skills when I go home to visit in the warmer months, but—"

"You *have*? Well, thanks for cluing in your bestie. Maybe I would have liked to try that with you one day. Oh *wait*," she said sarcastically. "I couldn't have because I didn't *know* you had those skills."

"I'm sorry. It's not like I was trying to hide it. I don't go out on group dives or anything. It's just something I do for myself." *A way of holding on to my memories with Zev.* Whoa. That came as a surprise, but she realized it was true. She and Zev really had opened some sort of vortex to her inner being.

"You're forgiven. Go on, Little Miss Secret Keeper. I'm listening," Birdie teased.

"Jumping off a cliff is different from deep-sea diving. I haven't done it since I was a teenager, and it's scarier now. Accidents happen all the time."

"You sound like Doc. He's always warning me about the dangers *that surround us.* He's such a weirdo. He thinks I'll get hurt crossing the street." Birdie's oldest brother, Seeley, went by the nickname Doc. He was a veterinarian, and though he was overprotective of Birdie, he was no less rambunctious than his brothers. "What are you *really* afraid of? Jumping or jumping and Zev not being there for you if you hit rock bottom?"

Carly froze. Way to bring her fear right up to the surface. She didn't want to believe he'd do that to her again after everything they'd said last night, but how could she not worry about it? Protecting her heart had to be her number one priority. But part of that was getting more clarity. Gaining peace of mind by really getting to know him again so she could figure out if Zev would be true to his word and either put that worry to rest or put them to rest.

"Guess I hit that nail on the head," Birdie said cheerily.

"I kind of hate you right now." Carly grabbed the fire extinguisher and headed into the kitchen with Birdie trailing behind her. She put the fire extinguisher back in its place and headed into her office. Could she see him and still protect herself? She'd like to believe she could, but if her dream was any indication of what they were both capable of, she needed to keep a clear head. She needed guidelines, to establish rules of engagement. It was a good thing she'd become a planner, because if ever there was a time to plan, it was now.

"So…should I go home and grab my bikini, or are you going to throw caution to the wind and meet Zev?"

Carly snagged her bag from behind her door and walked past Birdie, back into the shop. "I'm going to meet him. But there will be no caution throwing today." She stopped in the middle of the store. "Shoot. I just remembered I promised to get an estimate to the Rolfs for their daughter's birthday."

"I'll do it! Don't worry about anything. I'll go through each of your lists and make sure everything is done. I promise. It makes me so happy that you're going! You should wear your blue bikini, or the *green* one. *Oh…I love* that one." Birdie crossed her arms, her brow furrowing in concentration. She pointed at Carly and said, "You know what? I have a *good* feeling about this. You should definitely wear the green bikini because green is the color of a four-leaf clover, which is good luck, and he sent you Lucky Charms *and* you got that email about the chocolate arriving on time to prep for the baby shower. That's super lucky."

Carly chuckled at Birdie's ramblings. "I'm going now."

"Okay! Green bikini! I'm counting on Zev charming you, you throwing caution to the wind, and you getting lucky!"

ON THE WAY to meet Zev, Carly devised her plan. Sure, the plan at the wedding hadn't gone very well, but this was different. That initial shock of seeing him had worn off. Now the path was clear. Okay, not *clear*, clear. It was clouded with lust and about a million other emotions. But this time her plan was foolproof.

Zev was leaning against the side of Beau's truck, looking through a magazine, when Carly arrived. He was shirtless, wearing only hiking boots and black swim trunks. He looked up, flashing his knee-weakening grin. Zev Braden fully dressed and flashing that grin was a force to be reckoned with. But shirtless, with all that tanned, toned flesh on display?

Hello, Wind, meet Caution.

He tossed the magazine in the truck, slung a backpack over his shoulder, and headed her way. "Hey, babe. I'm glad you made it," he said, helping her out of her truck. He leaned in and kissed her cheek. "Mm. My favorite scent."

"Nervousness?" she said teasingly.

"No. *Carly Joanna Dylan*. Nothing else comes close." He swept one arm around her waist, pulling her against him, and *Lord have mercy*, he felt too good for words. "You've always smelled like summer sunshine and winter rain with a hint of lemons. The best of everything."

"And you smell like trouble waiting to happen."

"We like trouble. Remember?"

He dipped his head and kissed her neck, sending thrills skittering through her. It took everything she had to step from his arms. She put a hand on his chest to keep her distance, but he felt so good, she instantly regretted it. His wolfish smile told her he'd read her mind. She dropped her hand and said, "I have a feeling this is going to be a very trying day, so I need to set a few things straight."

"Go for it. You've got my undivided attention. But before you ask about Bandit. I thought about bringing him, but I worried he'd run off while we're cliff diving."

"That was probably smart, but I could have watched him. I'm not diving."

Confusion rose in his eyes. "What? You're my dive partner. This was on our one-day list. I can't dive without you."

Her heart stumbled, but she'd promised herself she'd stick to her plan, so she said, "I haven't jumped off a cliff since the last time we did it together. And FYI"—she poked his hard chest as she said each letter—"There will be no free falling into *you* today, either. I'm taking these six days as a gift. Six days for us to reminisce and have fun together with no expectations."

"No expectations?"

"That's right. I'm not putting my heart out there to get broken. I can't, Zevy, and I know you can't see it, but I'm fully prepared and wearing my virtual safety harness."

He lowered his voice and said, "Is that code for chastity belt?"

She was fully aware of his uncanny ability to turn her on or completely disarm her in equal measure, and she loved that about him, which was why her answer came as easily as it did honestly. "I haven't decided yet."

He stepped closer, his body heat soaking through her clothes as he said, "As you wish, Carls."

He reached for her hand, and when she took it, the content-ed look in his eyes felt like a sigh of relief. His hand was strong, his skin rough, making her acutely aware of the differences between the teen he'd been and the man he was. She stole a glance, admiring all his *other* manly parts, like his powerful biceps and thick, muscular thighs straining against the thin fabric of his swim trunks as they headed across the parking lot to the trailhead.

"You really aren't going to jump with me?" he asked.

"We'll see," she said.

"You know I'll never pressure you into doing anything you don't want to." A devilish spark glimmered in his eyes, and he said, "That was always your job. Maybe *I'm* the one who needs the chastity belt."

"Shut up!" She bumped him with her shoulder, and he laughed so loud it made her laugh, too. Her cheeks burned with the memories of the first time they'd talked about having sex. She'd been the one to initiate it.

He leaned against her as they followed the narrow dirt trail up the hill and said, "I was so innocent. You corrupted me."

"I did *not*." They'd been in tenth grade, and they'd been going to third base for weeks. Every time they made out, they'd ended up rolling around, grinding against each other. She'd stroked him through his jeans, and one night she'd gotten the courage to give him a hand job. The pleasure in his eyes, the way his entire body flexed and shook, and the sounds he'd made were like a drug. From that moment on, going further was *all* she'd thought about. She'd even confided in Tory, who had been going all the way with Beau for months. Tory had shared with her other things she and Beau had done, and Carly had wanted to try it all. She wanted to *taste* him, to have him *inside* her, to have *him* taste *her*. One night when they were getting hot and heavy, she'd blurted out, *Let's do it.* He'd gone stock-still, a mixture of excitement and trepidation in his eyes. He'd asked her a hundred times if she was sure, and she'd loved that about him. They hadn't had protection that night, and they'd had to wait a few days until he could steal a condom from Beau's stash, but it had *definitely* been at her urging.

"Okay, we'll pretend you didn't push me into giving up my virginity," he teased.

"You're such a pain."

"Yeah, but a good pain, right? Kind of like a great stretch after a long, hard night."

She couldn't help saying, "We had many long, *hard* nights."

"I thought we weren't talking about you taking advantage of me."

She tried to glare at him, but they both laughed.

"All right, enough about you and your wicked ways." Still holding her hand, he waved his other hand around them and said, "Look at this gorgeous place. You've got mountains and meadows and the clear blue sky. The air is so crisp and comfortable. It's wild that you and Beau both ended up here. I don't know if Beau ever mentioned this, but when he came here to help Char with the inn, he was about to move to LA. Char helped him heal, and the strange thing is, from what Char says, she came to Colorado to heal, too, after losing her parents. I'm starting to think that Colorado is like rehab. How did you end up here?"

"You have no idea how accurate your thoughts are. I never went back to college after I had the miscarriage. I was depressed and kind of lost. My aunt suggested I come here and help her in the chocolate shop, and my parents supported the idea. There were too many memories back home and at school, so I came out here and stayed with Marie. But it turned out that she and my mother had very specific plans for me, which I didn't know about until I got here." She gazed out at the trail before them, remembering how often she'd hiked there in the first few months after moving to Colorado, when she'd needed a place to clear her head. Though she'd never swam or dived at Silk Hollow, she knew the way by heart. The trail wound through tall grasses and over a hill, following a creek for about a mile before they'd come to the swimming hole.

"You're smiling, so I take it they were good plans?"

Her smile was caused by how easy and nice it was to be with Zev more than the plans they were talking about. But she kept that little tidbit to herself and said, "Scary, but good. The weekend I arrived, Marie took me to Redemption Ranch, which is owned by Birdie's parents, Tiny and Wynnie Whiskey. I'm not sure if you remember, but Marie isn't my real aunt."

"I remember. She was your mom's best friend, right?"

"Yes." She loved that he remembered. "Marie is Wynnie's sister, which is how I met Birdie. She was only fourteen at the time, and I was nineteen. I know that seems like a big age gap, but she was so full of life and I was so down. She was a godsend."

"She's pretty chipper."

"She's a hot mess sometimes, but she's brilliant, and one of the best, most caring people I've ever known. Tiny was one of the founders of the Colorado chapter of the Dark Knights motorcycle club, and all of her brothers are members. They're tough, and some of them look rough, but they've got hearts of gold. Her family and the people at the ranch helped me tremendously. You met one of Birdie's brothers, Callahan, *Cowboy*, at my shop the other night. He's like a brother to me. All of the Whiskeys have become like family."

"Hey, I'm not judging you or anything, but it's kind of gross to have an open relationship with someone you consider a brother." He squeezed her hand and winked.

"I've missed your sense of humor. It's still so easy to talk to you."

"I'm glad. I've missed everything about you." He lifted her hand and kissed the back of it as they made their way around a boulder. "Tell me more about how they helped you."

"They did so much. Redemption Ranch doesn't just rescue horses; they also help people. Wynnie is a licensed psychologist. She and a team of other medical professionals, mostly comprised of Dark Knights and their family members, work at the ranch and hold daily therapy sessions for groups and individuals. They hire ex-cons, recovering drug addicts, and people with social and emotional issues to work on the ranch, and through the work they do, and therapy, they help them heal, find their purpose, and get back on their feet. The first three months I was in Colorado, I worked at the ranch and went through therapy during the week, and I worked at my aunt's shop on the weekends. There was always someone at the ranch to talk to who had been through worse things than I had, who had suffered losses and knew how to help me through my grief. Working with the horses gave me something to focus on and a physical outlet for some of my frustrations. Therapy gave me the tools and knowledge I needed to heal, and the Whiskeys gave me a family of friends, which I desperately needed for a hundred different reasons."

"I'm so glad you had them," Zev said as they made their way up a steep incline. "But now I feel like a dick for wanting to kill Cowboy."

She laughed softly.

"Seriously, though, I'm glad you have people who have your back. Is Wynnie the therapist you mentioned last night?"

"Yes. I told her about us, and she's the only person besides you who knows about Mexico and the miscarriage. She helped me realize that so much had happened all at once with losing Tory and our breakup that I had never fully grieved losing either of you. Then leaving you the way I did in Mexico and the miscarriage just piled on guilt and more grief."

She stopped walking and faced him as things became clearer to her. "Zevy, I grieved for all of those losses a long time ago. I think most of last night's tears were from finally being able to get it all out to the right person. Some were also for *you*, since it was the first you'd heard about the pregnancy. But I'm sorry I yelled and that I shoved you. I didn't realize how much was trapped inside me until it started coming out like Mount Saint Helens."

He smiled, but it wasn't a humorous smile; it was a thoughtful one, the type that urged her to hear his next words. "I'm sorry, too. My anger wasn't directed at you. It was all at me, but I never should have raised my voice."

"I know it was hard for both of us, but I'm glad we got it out. I feel better than I have in a long time."

"I do, too, but I'll always regret hurting you."

"Then we're even, because of the way I left you in Mexico. But I'm not still grieving those things. It's all in the past. Now I know *why* you left, and you know why I left in Mexico. Wynnie, Marie, and the Whiskeys showed me I *could* move on, and I know we can, too. I really want to put all that behind us and enjoy this time together."

"I'd like nothing more," he said softly, as if it took a lot to get the words out.

As another weight lifted from her shoulders, their eyes locked, turning that relief to something much hotter. His chest expanded with a deep inhalation, his muscles cording with restraint. It was good to know she wasn't treading alone in the well of their desires. She wanted to bridge the gap, to seal their words with a kiss, but she knew where that would lead, and she wasn't quite ready for that just yet. He must have seen that in her eyes, because without a word, he took a step, bringing her with him along the trail. *Thank you, Zevy.*

"I'm trying here, Carls," he said, holding her hand tight as a vise. "But you better talk before I give in and kiss you."

She wrestled with the desire to lean in and kiss *him*, but before she could make up her mind, he looked at her out of the corner of his eye and said, "You're making this *very* hard."

A giggle bubbled out, breaking her spell.

"If you don't start talking, we're not going to make it to the cliffs. I'll haul your gorgeous ass over my shoulder and carry you off to a cave."

"Oh my…That does *not* sound so bad."

"*Carls*," he growled, making her laugh again. "As much as I want you, I'm not doing that to us. I won't do anything that you might regret later. *Please*, cut me a break and talk about something that can't be taken sexually."

"That's hard to do with you."

He glared at her. She realized what she'd said and laughed hysterically, earning more stern looks, which only made her laugh harder.

"I'm *sorry*," she said, trying to tamp down her laughter, scrambling for something to talk about. "Okay. Let's see. I told you I never finished college, but I went back to school to become a chocolatier, and it was a good thing, because a few years ago my aunt sold her house and most of her belongings, packed a couple of suitcases, and said she was going off to see the world." She noticed his grip on her hand had eased and stole a glance at him. He was breathing a little easier. "Marie was the most independent woman I'd ever met. She's never been married, never had a long-term relationship as far as I know, and she owned her own business. But she'd never gone *anywhere*. She said if she didn't do it then, she might never get the chance. She signed the business over to me, and I've been running it ever since. How bizarre is that?"

"I think it's pretty awesome. It sounds like it was just what you needed."

"Yeah, I think it was the right thing at the right time, like last night."

He pulled her closer, guiding her around a rock in the trail, and said, "What's your life like now?"

"It isn't very adventurous anymore, and that's okay. I have little adventures. Between festivals and concerts, there's always something going on around here. Next week is Festival on the Green, one of my favorite events, and of course working with Birdie is *always* an adventure," she joked. "I have a good life here, and I think we've talked about it enough. I want to know what *you've* been doing all these years. I'm sure your life is a million times more exciting than mine."

"You've overcome so much. You've become a chocolatier and you run a business that you never planned to run. I'd say that's a hell of an adventurous life."

"That's sweet, and maybe kind of true. I haven't ever thought about it that way." She pointed to her sneakers and said, "But these feet have not left the ground in years. Please tell me about your life so I can live vicariously through your stories.

I want to hear it all. Except about the women. You can leave them out the same way I left out the men in mine."

He scowled, but his eyes gave his joke away as he said, "You mean there've been other men in your life?"

"So, *so* many," she said with a dramatic roll of her eyes. "Between my open relationships with cowboys and my dozens of other rough and rugged boyfriends, it's hard to keep track." She loved playing games with Zev, but she wanted him to know the truth about who she was, so she said, "There haven't been that many men in my life, but there have been enough. I'm sure you haven't been a saint for all these years while you've been out on your *Pirates of the Caribbean* adventures."

"I haven't been a saint, but nothing's ever *clicked*."

"For me, either." Their eyes met, and they both slowed their pace, the air between them thickening at the speed of light. Her pulse quickened as voices cut through the air, jerking her back to reality. It was just the distraction she needed. Silk Hollow was right around the other side of the boulder. She started jogging up the hill, tugging him behind her, and said, "Tell me about your adventures, *Captain Jack!*"

"I don't look like Captain Jack. He's got really long hair," he said as they rounded the boulder and Silk Hollow came into view.

Tufts of lush grass poked out from the rocky landscape. People shouted as they jumped from various boulders surrounding the deep end of the gorge, serenaded by cheers from their friends below as they plunged into the water. A group of twentysomethings were sitting on the rocky dirt shore, listening to music and hollering to a group of people who had just started the trek up the boulders toward the dive spots.

"Captain Jack is *old*, and his body kind of sucks," Zev said with an arrogant grin.

She laughed, loving his cockiness. "But Johnny Depp is still *hot*." She let go of his hand and ran down the incline toward the water. "Come on, *Johnny!*"

He took off after her and hollered, "Call me Johnny again, Carly Dylan, and you'll pay for it."

She dropped her backpack on the rocks, squealing as he caught her by the waist and spun her around. "Can I call you *Captain?*" she shouted.

"Only if I can call you *mine.*"

Her heart said *yes!* and she wished it were that easy. But worry crept in, and she knew she needed to be smarter this time. To learn about his situation, just as he'd learned hers.

"You *wish*, Captain Jack!" she said playfully, and wiggled free from his grasp. She stripped off her clothes, nearly igniting from the flames in his eyes, and yelled, "Race ya!" as she ran into the water.

Chapter Eight

ZEV DROPPED HIS backpack and took off after Carly hoping for icy water, because *damn*…She had curves that could make a dead man weep and the last thing he needed was to be sporting wood around all those other people. They splashed through the cold water, laughing like old times. When they hit the deep end, he dove for her, taking her under with him, and guided her slippery body back up to the surface. She gasped, laughing as he swept her into his arms, holding her soft wet body against him and kicking to keep them both afloat.

"It's so cold!" she said, pushing her hair from her eyes with one hand, her arm hooked around his neck.

"I can help with that." He leaned in for a kiss, but she wiggled free and dove beneath the surface.

He took the hint—*too much, too fast*—but he still went after her. They splashed and laughed, swimming around the basin, careful to steer clear of the divers plunging around them. Carly went under, and he lost sight of her. He spun around just as she broke the surface, splashed him in the face, and swam away. He snagged her around the waist and lifted her into the air. She squealed, arms and feet flailing as he tossed her into the deeper water.

Carly shrieked, *"Zevy Braden!"* in midair and plunged beneath the surface.

She was the only person who called him Zevy, and he'd always loved the way she said it like he was all *hers*. Even as a kid she'd said it with authority and ownership. Other girls were *silly*, but Carly had always been different. She was funny and playful but so smart. Way smarter than him.

He swam underwater, snagging her around the waist again, sparking more giggles. She sounded just like she had years ago, bringing a flood of memories of swimming together as kids back home, and later as teenagers, when the sight of her in a bathing suit made him hard as stone and the feel of her slippery body squirming against his was too much to take. He remembered them mastering how to kiss underwater and sneaking away from their families at the beach to make out. Memories came one right after another just as they had when they were hiking up the hill to get there. He remembered their youthful treks, hobo stick in hand, cereal in their backpacks. Even then his pulse beat faster around her. He hadn't realized until years later that those pulse-racing, secret-keeping moments were woven into the fabric of falling in love with her. He'd thought of her every damn day and missed her with every iota of his being, and still he hadn't realized exactly how *much* until now, when she was finally within reach.

She put her arms around him, out of breath and smiling, and exclaimed, "This is so fun! I want to hear all about your adventures. Every single one of them."

"Nah, come on. They weren't that great." He wanted to keep playing around, holding her, watching her walls come down one laugh at a time.

"Stop being humble. You live the life we dreamed of, and I

want to hear about how wonderful it is."

His gut twisted with regret. "*Carls.*"

"I'm not *sad* or begrudging you for all you've done, Zev." She was beaming at him without an ounce of negativity. "We were put on separate paths, and you've heard all about mine. I want to hear about yours."

Carly had never been one to hold a grudge, but he was surprised that it still held true when he'd set off to live a life without walls or boundaries. A life that he had hoped he could get so lost in, he might be able to forget the hurt he'd caused without forgetting anything about the love they'd shared, even if it hadn't turned out that way.

She pushed out of his arms, swimming around him, and said, "The last time I did anything with archaeology was my second year of college. I interned for two semesters doing conservatory work and extracting items from concretions for a marine study. I've kept up my deep-sea diving skills, and I've gone on a couple of land-based archaeological getaways, but they weren't anything like what we talked about." Her expression turned sheepish. "I looked you up online after I saw you in Mexico, but I couldn't find anything on you. I never looked again until Beau and Char hired me to cater their reception. For some reason, I still couldn't find pictures of you, but I read about you finding a shipwreck with another guy."

"I didn't let them photograph me for the articles about our discovery because people are batshit crazy when it comes to money. I'd rather be the grungy guy with the backpack that people give space to than the rich guy who found the sunken ship who becomes the target of every scam out there."

"I don't blame you for that. But you've done *amazing* things, and I want to hear about them."

"None of it was romantic, like we imagined." They'd dreamed of spending nights in cabanas and making love on boats beneath he stars. But what teenagers would let bugs and snakes into their dreams of makeshift tents or life-threatening squalls that left them praying for their lives and shaking with cold dampen their fantasies?

She splashed him and said, "Let me be the judge of that. I forced myself *not* to think about you for so long, now that we've cleared the air, I kind of like thinking of you out there in the wild."

He swam underwater to her, guiding her to waist-deep water out of the shadows of the boulders, far away from the divers.

"Tell me *everything*," she said, sunlight twinkling in her eyes.

He didn't want to tell her about the lonely, painful months following his leaving Pleasant Hill, when it had taken everything he had just to make it through the day, forcing himself to get as far from home as quickly as possible for fear of turning back. So he began with their last encounter. "The day after we hooked up in Mexico, I went to a bar to drown my sorrows, and that's when I met Luis Rojas—"

"The guy you found that ship with off the coast of the Bahamas?"

"Yeah," he said as a group of teenagers bounded into the water. He put an arm protectively around Carly and said, "Want to sit in the sun a bit?"

She nodded, and they made their way back to their belongings. They spread towels on the ground beside the rocks, and as they sat down, Carly said, "Tell me about Luis."

"You'd like him. He's an old-school kind of guy who

doesn't mince words and looks like an aging pirate. In fact, *he's* got Captain Jack hair with some gray in it, a bushy beard, and eyes like my father's that see *everything*. He's very wise, and an underwater archaeologist. He'd just turned fifty-five when we met, and he'd been trying to find the wreckage from the *Black Widow* pirate ship for more than twenty years. We hit it off right away. Anyway, he was leaving the next day to head down the coast, and he hired me on. He became my mentor, my best friend, and if you ask him, he'd probably tell you that he was my therapist, too. We've had a lot of great conversations over the years. Not a day passes that I don't miss working with him. And by the way, he often gave me hell for the way I left you." Luis hadn't known Carly, Tory, or Beau, which had made him safe for Zev to talk with about everything that had happened without seeing the devastation in his eyes that Zev had seen in everyone else's. And even though Luis had given him a hard time about the way he'd left Carly, talking with Luis had also allowed him to revel in the sweetness of what he and Carly had once had.

"He was right," Zev said. "I should have stuck around so we could have tried to work through things together, but I was too immature to realize it. Nothing has ever felt right without you, Carls. Something was always missing. Like I said, I knew in Mexico that I'd made a mistake by leaving, but what I didn't understand until I saw you at the wedding, was that nothing would ever feel right because you were the *something* that was missing. I've been lonely for *us*. For all the little things we had, for our friendship as much as our love. I missed the way we used to look at each other and know what the other was thinking, our inside jokes, our stories, the way we could lie beneath the stars without saying a word and be happy. When I was busting my ass to make ends meet, I knew if you were there, we'd be having fun even in the most awful, exhausting times." He exhaled a long breath, feeling like he'd held that in forever, despite their talk last night. "I missed that spark that makes your blue eyes even bluer the first time you see something. And yes, I had *moments* of greatness in the discoveries I made, but I was always *pushing* through, trying to forget what I'd done to you. Only I never could, because you were—you *are*—a part of me. Hurting you means hurting myself."

She lifted her chin almost defiantly and said, "I agonized over the idea of you *not* missing me. So, as awful as it sounds, I'm glad to hear that you were tortured by it, too. You thought I'd hate you if you stayed. I have to believe you knew what you were doing, and I think hating you would have been worse than being left behind. Hate eats away at you. Hurt makes you stronger." She leaned back on her elbows and closed her eyes, tipping her face up toward the sun. "At least that's the way I'm looking at it. But I don't want to dwell on the past, so tell me something I *don't* know. I want to hear about all the good stuff."

Needing to be closer to her, he moved from his towel to hers and lay beside her, propped up on one elbow.

Turning smiling eyes to him, she said, "What are you doing?"

"Proving I'm not that stupid kid anymore."

"By squishing onto my towel?"

He put his arm around her waist, tugging her closer, and said, "By not letting you get away."

"Okay, Casanova. Woo me with your stories."

He told her about how he and Luis had gone over Luis's calculations, worked through maps and historical data, and Zev had found an error in Luis's calculations, which had put him too far east to find the wreckage. Over the next year and a half, they searched a five-mile area around the new coordinates. "In addition to the treasures the *Black Widow* was known to have on board, it had eight cannons. We used a proton magnetometer to detect metal beneath the seafloor. The magnetometer can't detect gold and silver, but it'll pick up the ships' anchors, magnetite ballast stones, cannons...When it picked up an enormous mass, we were pretty sure we'd found the site. But we had to dig farther beneath the ocean's floor—"

"Without harming any buried artifacts," she said excitedly.

"Exactly. Luis had heard about a guy who had built an apparatus that would fit over his ship's twin diesel propellers to direct the prop wash down to blast the sand away without harming potential artifacts. I called my father to ask his advice on the best way to build it. He ended up helping fund the project and hooked us up with an engineering buddy of his who was able to connect us with a team to build the equipment faster than I ever thought possible." He told her about living on Luis's boat and years of unearthing treasures, describing the process from start to finish, and she was as mesmerized as she used to get when they'd watch archaeological documentaries. "We spent every second we could at that site for just over five years, until it became clear that anything more to be found would be few and far between. There was a bunch of legal hoopla to go through, and we'd ended up getting only a portion of what the treasures were worth, which was still more than either of us could ever spend. But I'd have done it for free. The thrill of discovery was fucking amazing."

"A moment of greatness." She lifted up on her elbow with stars in her eyes. "Tell me more."

"Luis is semiretired now. He no longer dives, but he oversees a team of divers who still dive a few months out of the year. He said he'd found his treasure and it was high time he tried to find a good woman to keep him warm at night. Guess he was tired of the likes of me."

"I guess so," she teased. "If you were lonely, then I'm sure he was, too. Did he have women friends, or anyone special to keep him company?"

"We didn't bring women on the boat, if that's what you're asking. He'd hook up with women when we were inland, but our lives weren't focused on finding long-term relationships. He just scratched the occasional itch. But treasure hunting is *not* an easy life, and by then he was nearing sixty. He'd had enough, and he had more money than he could ever spend. He wanted to settle down, enjoy creature comforts, fall in love…"

Their eyes connected, and he saw that she was struggling with the desire brimming in hers. He couldn't resist coaxing her along and reached over, gently touching her side. When she didn't swat him away, he ran his fingers lightly along the dip at her waist and over the swell of her hip, drawing out the moment before sharing news of his latest discovery of what he hoped were artifacts from *their* ship.

Goose bumps chased his fingers, and she rocked forward with a giggle. "You're tickling me."

He'd like to tickle that bathing suit right off her. Instead, he moved his hand to the space between them.

"I'm *waiting*," she said melodically. "What have you been doing since Luis retired?"

"Remember the *Pride*?"

"How could I ever forget? We did our senior career-day presentation on it and aced it. *Two Treasure Hunters, One Ship.*

Modern-Day Goonies Hunt for the Pride. God, we really believed in ourselves, didn't we?"

"We sure did. I never stopped researching it, but I didn't have the capital, or the know-how, to really go after it until I'd worked with Luis and we made our discovery. I've spent the last several summers searching off the coast of Silver Island for the wreckage."

She sat up, eyes wide. "You *have*? That's awesome! Have you found anything? Were our calculations close?"

"We were close." He pushed himself up beside her. "We thought it was—"

"Eleven miles offshore," they said at the same time, and they laughed.

"But I believe the site is only about six miles offshore and spans about four or five miles from the island's westernmost coast. But I have no doubt that if you and I had gone out there together, we wouldn't have given up until we found it." He paused before telling her his news, wanting to capture her moment of elation. "Two days before the wedding, I found concretions from what's got to be *our* ship."

"You did *not*! Oh my God! *Zevy!* Tell me. Tell me everything! How did you find them? What was it like when you first realized what they were? How did it feel? What's the site like? How big are the concretions? How many did you find? Did you have them X-rayed? Is anyone working on them yet?"

And there it was, even more magnificent than he'd remembered. Man, he missed sharing his life with her. He told her about the years he'd spent narrowing down the location of the wreckage, the exploratory dives and digs, the multitude of findings that were false alarms rather than valuable artifacts. He described using the magnetometer, and the test holes they'd dug, and the ones they'd blasted using an apparatus like the one he and Luis had commissioned, and how that had led to the discovery of the concretions. As he spoke, he decided to surprise her with the concretions that he'd shipped there rather than telling her about them.

"I wish you could have been there to experience it. I got this feeling in the pit of my stomach when I found the first concretion. That was *our* moment of greatness, babe. When I realized what I'd found, my first thought was *This one's for you, Carls.*"

"It was not," she said disbelievingly.

"Not only was it my first thought, but when I got back up to the boat, I actually hollered it up at the sky. I guess I thought you might get one of those chills down your back or something and think of me. Clearly I was delirious."

"Oh my gosh, *Zevy!*" Her wide, beautiful eyes danced with joy. "I can't believe you found the *Pride.*"

"I don't have solid proof yet, but I'd bet my life on it. We dug down about ten feet below the ocean floor to reach the concretions, but I found them so late in the day I didn't have a chance to sweep the crater with the magnetometer again and see if it picked up on more metal buried even deeper. I had to give the largest one to my attorney so he could work on arresting the vessel." His attorney, Jeremy Ryder, was one of the best admiralty and maritime lawyers in Boston.

"There's *got* to be more down there."

"I know there is. I can feel it my bones, Carls. I was really close to backing out of attending the wedding so I could go diving, but I couldn't do that to Beau. I'm so damn glad I didn't back out." That earned him a slightly shy smile, which tugged at something deep inside him.

"Me too," she said softly. "But you must be dying to get back."

"I'll be out on the water first thing Monday morning with the mag, and with any luck, it'll light up like the Fourth of July. But we researched the process as kids—you know how it goes. My attorney needs to get the vessel arrested and the substitute custodian paperwork formalized; the artifacts need to be extracted from the concretions and proven to be from the *Pride*, if possible. Even then there are other pieces that have to fall into place after the vessel is arrested."

The US Marshal Service served as custodian of all arrested vessels, though they don't have the manpower to take on the responsibilities and often a substitute custodian stood in its place. It was the custodian's job to look after the wreck, make sure it wasn't damaged and was properly documented by underwater archaeologists, and ensure the treasures and artifacts were brought back to shore, preserved, and accounted for. Hopefully that would go fairly smoothly, but an announcement about the discovery would be placed in a local newspaper, and from there, who knew how many people would come out of the woodwork claiming they'd already discovered the wreckage. If that happened, Zev could face insurance issues and legal battles. It was all stressful, but he wasn't going to let that get the better of him. He was focusing on the here and now.

On *Carly*.

"I'm on pins and needles and it's not even my discovery," she said excitedly. "I know there's a process, and it'll take time, but *still*. I can't believe you're doing it, Zevy. How long can you dive there? What will you do over the winter?"

"I'll dive until it's too cold or the water's too treacherous to continue. Usually when the weather gets too cold, I take off.

I've been all over the world, hiking, surfing, diving, cliff diving. You name it, I've done it. Before I had any money, I'd sleep in hostels, camp, you know the drill. I've been to Thailand, New Zealand, Costa Rica, Australia, Spain, and a hundred other places. If any of my relatives are traveling and I can make it work, I try to connect with them. I met up with Graham, Morgyn, and Knox in Belize."

"You've gone to so many of our *one day* places," she said with admiration.

"*Yes*. But like I said, it wasn't all that we'd hoped, because you weren't there. It sounds far more glamorous than it was."

"Well, I'm here *now*. Feel this." She grabbed his hand and pressed it over her racing heart. "I've been living in my safe little mecca for so long, I'd forgotten what excitement felt like."

He held her gaze, tracing the dip of her cleavage with his fingertip, loving the darkening of her eyes and the way she breathed a little harder as he said, "Feels pretty damn amazing to me."

ALL OF CARLY'S lady parts were chanting *Kiss him! Kiss him!* She'd been fighting the urge all day. But Zev made her want more than she had in what felt like forever, and she could handle only one dangerous leap at a time. If she was going to find the part of herself she'd locked down tight, she needed her legs to function, and kissing Zev would pretty much guarantee that they wouldn't.

She popped up to her feet, pulling Zev up with her, and said, "Come on. I want to do it."

"*Here?* In front of all these people?" he said, drawing her into his strong arms.

His skin was hot, his eyes hungry, and when he dipped his head and kissed her neck, dragging his tongue along her heated flesh, lust pooled deep in her belly.

"I don't think that's the smartest move," he said huskily. "But I spotted a cave we can swim to."

The thought of having Zev buried deep inside her made her lady parts do much more than chant. She was *this close* to giving in to her desires and letting Zev explore *her* cave. But while getting down and dirty in a cave with Zev would be the *ultimate* adventure, she already knew that sexually attracted part of her was still alive and kicking. She needed to know if the adventurous thrill-seeking girl she'd once been still existed, or if it was just wishful thinking. She forced herself to step out of his arms.

He snagged her hand, giving her a wanting, knee-weakening look.

Buck up, knees! You have a job to do.

"Dream on, Captain Jack," she said. "I want to climb the rocks and take *that* leap with you."

"Make no mistake, babe, my *dreams* turned to dark-and-dirty *fantasies* about you a long time ago."

The air rushed from her lungs at his lustful, inviting tone.

He palmed her ass, sending more thrills darting through her, and said, "Are we jumping or what?"

Between the *Kiss him! Kiss him!*, the *fantasies* comment, and the feel of his hot hand on her ass, all she could manage was "Uh-huh."

He drew her close again, and she felt his arousal pressing into her belly. He squeezed her bottom and said, "Let's go, babe, before it gets too hard for me to walk."

With those words in her ear, Carly had no idea how she made it up the hill and over the boulders to the top of the cliff, but with Zev anything was possible. God, she'd missed that feeling. She looked down, and her heart beat so fast she thought she might pass out. She tightened her grip on Zev's hand.

"What do you need, Carls?"

With her hand in his and the warm summer sun kissing her skin, there was only one thing she needed. "A little more courage."

"I've got enough for both of us. But do you want to start lower?"

"*Yes!*" she exclaimed, holding on to his hand like a lifeline. "But there's no way I'm going back down." She inched out to the edge of the cliff and curled her toes around it. "If I'm going to do this, I'm jumping in with both feet." Did he know she was talking about much more than the jump? "At least if I die, it'll be with you."

"'Goonies never say die,'" he said, squeezing her hand. "Do you want to count us down?"

She nodded, a rush of nervous energy bubbling up inside her. "One!" Zev gripped her hand tighter. "Two!" She looked at him and *knew* she could do this. "*Three!*"

As they leapt off the rocks, she could feel the chains that had bound her to years of hurt breaking free. She flew through the air toward the freedom and happiness she'd forgotten existed. Zev never let go as they plunged into the cold, deep water and swam up to the surface. They both *whoop*ed. Throwing her arms around his neck and pressing her lips to his was as natural as holding her breath as they sank below the surface again, their mouths still connected. Just like they used to.

He held her tight as they resurfaced, laughing and kissing.

Kissing Zev was better than sugary cereal, better than sunshine and sandy beaches. Kissing Zev, being with him, and breaking the tethers to her past brought back the Carly she knew. The Carly she'd lost—and only now realized she'd *missed* like a severed limb.

"Again!" she yelled, and he kissed her. She'd been talking about jumping, but the kiss was just as nice.

They swam to the shore, and then they jumped, flipped, dove, laughed, and kissed so many times it felt like the whole world had gone still and they were the only things moving. Carly had good, close friends that she loved. But in all the time she'd known them, she'd never felt this invigorated and alive. Zev's voice whispered through her mind. *That's the power of us, Carls. You've always been the treasure, and without you I'm just an empty chest, hoping for a shot at more.* He was wrong. *She'd* been the empty chest, and he'd been her treasure.

She splashed him and swam away underwater. She watched him turning, looking for her. She surfaced behind him and threw her arms around his neck, clinging to his back like a monkey to a tree. "Take me for a ride!"

His hearty laughter rang out seconds before he dove under the water like he used to, carrying her on his back as he swam this way and that, breaking the surface for breaths, then diving back under, drenching her in happy memories she'd spent years repressing.

When they broke the surface, she felt his heart racing through his back. She rested her head on his shoulder, soaking in the feel of him. How could she have thought she could control her feelings for him over the next several days? And why had she wanted to? The only thing she needed to control in order to protect her heart were her expectations. This time together was a gift, and she intended to enjoy every blessed minute as if it were the last they'd ever get.

She had her doubts about being able to keep her expectations in line, but she was no longer a young girl pinning her hopes on the man of her dreams. She knew the realities of their lives, and believed the happiness consuming her would be worth every ounce of heartache if their time together didn't lead to more.

"Climb up top, sugarbum." He reached behind him, grabbing her ass.

She squealed, sounding so much like Birdie it gave her a second's pause, but it didn't last long because she used to be that carefree girl and it felt *great* to feel that way again. She pushed Zev's hair out of the way to climb onto his shoulders— and went stock-still at the sight of a Lucky Charms tattoo down the center of the back of his neck. Emotions clogged her throat as she took in the shapes, all black with the exception of the last: A star, *the power to fly beyond jumping off cliffs or skydiving.* A rainbow, *the power to travel.* A heart, *the power of life. We called it the power of love.* A four-leaf clover, *the power of luck.* Her heart felt like it might burst when she reached the last shape—a treasure chest full of coins, tattooed in gold, *the power of us.*

"Zevy…you got our tattoo," she said with disbelief.

He reached behind him again, hooked his fingers around her waist, and shifted her around to his front, guiding her legs around him. The longing in his eyes brought another rush of emotions.

"Those are *our* shapes. They're *our* story," he said earnestly. "I left thinking I was saving you from my grief, but that didn't mean I left all we had behind. I never had any intention of forgetting anything about us, or you, Carls."

She felt like she might cry as she leaned back in his arms, looking down at their connected bodies, and pulled down the left side of her bikini bottom just enough to reveal her matching tattoo. The only difference between the two was that in addition to the gold being inked in color, she'd had the treasure chest inked in gold with black straps. "I didn't want to get it on my neck where other people would ask about it. Answering questions would have been too painful."

"*Christ*, Carly. My heart is going to explode."

She wrapped her arms around him, feeling the same, and said, "Then you'd better kiss me one more time before that happens."

Their mouths crashed together fierce and urgent. She didn't hold back as their teeth gnashed and their tongues battled. She wanted his passion, craved the scratch of his whiskers, the burn of his smoldering heat. Her senses reeled. She pushed her hands into his hair, taking as much as she gave. Each swipe of their tongues coaxed her deeper into his *taste*, his *smell*, the lust and greed pulsing between them. He groped her ass with one hand, his other crushing her chest to his. Somewhere in her periphery she heard splashes and voices, and in a far-off part of her mind, she knew they needed privacy, but she didn't *care*. Zev was here and she was in his arms, filling up all her empty spaces. She never wanted this moment to end. How was it possible to feel so much, to *want* so greedily?

He tore his mouth away, scanning their surroundings with ravenous eyes, and growled, "Not here." He plowed through the water, into the cavernous mouth of the rocks. Shrouded by darkness, he reclaimed her lips, still trudging deeper into the cave, out of sight of the other swimmers. She tightened her thighs around him, pawing at his muscular arms and back, and wanting so much more. He stopped walking and broke their kisses again, his eyes searching the darkness.

They were alone. *Thank freaking God.*

"Kiss me," she said breathlessly, tugging his mouth back to hers.

Their bodies ground together, pushing him forward. His arm hit the rocks behind her, buffering her from their sharpness as they devoured each other. His other hand moved beneath her ass, so close to her center, she whimpered needily. She loosened her thighs around him, hinting at the approval she knew he sought. He stroked her through the thin material of her bikini, drawing more desperate sounds. He pushed his thick, rough fingers into her bikini bottom, teasing over her center, and intensified their kisses. His finger thrust inside her, sending scintillating pleasures through her. He zeroed in on the magical spot he'd been the first to discover, alighting flames along her skin despite the cold water.

"Fuck, baby," he gritted out. "You feel so good."

The hunger in his voice was an aphrodisiac all its own. He sealed his mouth over her neck, sucking and kissing as she rode his fingers. He was lost in a sea of sensations. Her head fell back, and a long surrendering moan escaped.

"I need your mouth," he demanded.

She scrambled to make her brain function, and he crushed his mouth to hers. He sucked her tongue, a trick he'd learned when they were younger, driving her out of her flipping mind. He sucked hard, pain and pleasure coursing through her. Just when she thought she couldn't take any more, he eased his efforts, kissing her so slowly and thoroughly her thoughts fell away. He kissed and touched, teased, and made the most enticing, hungry sounds, taking her right up to the edge of madness. She was caught in a web of arousal, her entire body trembling. Lust prickled her limbs. Desires pounded through her until every breath felt like it might be her last, and she finally, *gloriously*, shattered into a million blinding pieces. Her body bucked and quivered as she rode the waves of their passion. Just when she started to catch her breath, he intensified his efforts. His fingers were relentless, every stroke sending her higher. She wanted to hunker down with his talented mouth for a long, delicious winter and feast on it morning, noon, and night, like she was doing now, as she gave herself over to him, and he completely, *blissfully* unraveled her once again.

"Oh *God*" rushed from her lungs. "I *need* you, Zevy. All of you."

His face was a mask of restraint. "I need you, too, but I don't want to make a mistake."

"I'm protected. I promise."

His lips curved up, and he kissed her again, deep and tender. "I wasn't talking about that kind of mistake. There's nothing I want more than to make love to you right this second, and doing it *here*, with all those people out there?" He tightened his grip on her. "That's *us*, Carly, and I want it so badly I can taste it. But I promised I wouldn't hurt you, and I intend to keep that promise. I don't want you to regret anything we do."

Her cheeks burned and she buried her face in his neck. "Oh my gosh. *What* have you done to me?" She lifted her head, meeting his serious eyes, and said, "I haven't done anything reckless since Mexico, and here I was ready to—"

He silenced her with a deep, sensual kiss, leaving her too light-headed to be embarrassed.

"This is who we *are*, Carls. What we have is so much bigger than us. It takes over, and yes, sometimes we're reckless because we're usually powerless to stop our momentum. But this time you can count on me to make sure we're smarter about *when* and *how* we're reckless." He brushed his lips over hers and said, "No embarrassment. Okay, babe? I love the power of us, and I hope we never lose it."

She nodded, full of too many emotions to speak.

A devilish glimmer rose in his eyes, and he said, "But I am only human, and you are the woman I have fantasized about since I was old enough to have dirty thoughts, so if I have any hope of remaining in control, you need to peel your gorgeous body off me."

She giggled as she lowered her legs. "This is a first. I don't think I can remember a time that you ever asked me to back off. Oh wait, *yes* I do. On the hike up here. I could get a complex from this behavior, you know."

He pulled her in for another kiss, his arousal pressing into her, and said, "I think we need the five-foot rule for a few minutes. I want to take you someplace and show you something, but walking out of here sporting a baseball bat might turn a few heads."

They lingered in the cool water. Remembering how much fun it was to taunt him, she said, "Did I mention that I'm thinking about taking up baseball? I love running the bases, but there's nothing quite like getting a good grip on that wood."

He gave her a deadpan look, the muscles in his jaw bunching. She giggled and splashed him. He shoved his hands along the surface of the water, shooting water straight into her face, and she dove away. He went after her. They made their way out of the cave laughing and splashing, and swam into deeper water.

When they finally settled down, treading water in the warm sun, Carly thanked him for slowing them down. "My brain was fuzzy. You always know the right thing to say. Then again, your mouth has always made me happy."

He looked at her out of the corner of his eye.

She couldn't resist adding, "And your tongue. I *really* like your tongue."

He lunged, catching her around the waist. She shrieked as he hauled her against him with a fierce and sinful look in his eyes and said, "You keep talking like that and you'll make a liar out of me."

"We wouldn't want that, now, would we?" she said flirtatiously. She knew she shouldn't push it, especially after he was strong enough to slow them down and do right by her. But she'd missed this playful banter so much, she couldn't get enough of it, and she might only have a few days to get her fill.

"*Carly,*" he warned. "I'm really trying to do the right thing here."

"Okay. You're right. I'm sorry." She pushed out of his arms and said, "So where is this place you want to *take* me?"

"Hey, didn't I just say—"

Laughter bubbled out before she could stop it.

"That's it!" He grabbed her and tossed her over his shoulder. "You're nothing but trouble."

"I'm sorry!" she said, laughing hysterically as he carried her out of the water. "I couldn't help it!"

He set her down on her feet and tossed her a towel. "Wrap yourself up in that before I lose my mind."

This was *too* much fun! She turned around and bent at the waist to dry her legs, giving him a great view of her ass.

"*Carly,*" he growled.

She turned wide, innocent eyes on him. "What? I'm *just* drying off. You don't want me to be *wet* all day, do you?"

He chuckled, shaking his head as he reached for his towel. "I can see this is going to be a *long, hard* day."

"Only if I'm lucky," she teased.

He hauled her into his arms again and said, "I'm done being good."

"Gee, I hope not. I'm sort of counting on all your goodness lasting for, *oh*, say…six days."

"Damn, I've missed us," he said heatedly. As he lowered his lips to hers, she hoped it was a very *long* day, because she never wanted it to end.

They dressed and hiked back down to the parking lot. As she opened the door to her truck, he said, "I like your wheels."

"It was my aunt's. Where are we going, anyway?"

"It's a surprise. Follow me to the inn. We can leave your truck there and take mine."

She glanced at Beau's truck and said, "Don't you mean your brother's truck?"

"Yes. My van is on Silver Island."

"Your van?" *Of course you have a van.* Teenage memories pummeled her. *One day it'll be just you and me, Carls. We'll park our van at the beach and watch the sunset, or at the top of a mountain and rock each other's worlds beneath the stars.*

"It's nothing fancy, but when I'm not sleeping on my boat, I live in my van. This winter I'll store the boat on the island and travel in the van." He slipped a hand to the nape of her neck, drawing her into another enticing kiss, and said, "Follow me, beautiful."

As she watched him walk away, she realized her virtual safety harness had been about as useless as her and Birdie's plan for the wedding.

Maybe she needed that chastity belt after all.

Chapter Nine

"WOULD YOU MIND if I change out of my bathing suit before we go wherever you're taking me?" Carly asked as she grabbed her backpack and hopped out of her truck.

She looked like an angel with her hair half-dry, golden tendrils framing her face, her sun-kissed cheeks a little pink. He could look at her all day and never get his fill. He was dying to tell her about the concretions, but he held back, wanting to see the spark of excitement in her eyes when he surprised her with them.

He took her backpack, carrying it along with his own, and reached for her hand as they walked up to the entrance of the inn. He kissed her hand, and she glanced at him a little bashfully. He loved that she was still as sweet as she was sultry and that their breakup hadn't hardened her.

As he unlocked the door, Carly said, "Did you know Char swears the inn works some sort of magic that makes people fall in love?"

He waggled his brows and said, "Maybe I should hold you hostage here for the week so you have no choice but to fall for me." He pushed open the door and Bandit barreled out, tail wagging. The happy pooch went paws-up on Zev's legs, and

Zev loved him up. "Hey, buddy. Did you miss me?"

Bandit barked and went to greet Carly, licking her leg.

"Hi, sweetie. Is Uncle Zevy being good to you?" She crouched, letting Bandit lick her face. "I missed you, too."

The way she said *Uncle Zevy* made him wish he was an uncle just so he could hear her say it more often. "I've got to admit, I'm a little jealous of that dog right now."

Bandit bounded down the steps and into the yard as Carly rose to her feet, slowly dragging her eyes down Zev's body, heating him up from the inside out. "You're the one who wanted to behave."

Fuck behaving. He took her in a rough, demanding kiss, struggling to hold back all that he wanted to give but unwilling to be toyed with anymore. When their lips parted, he kept her body flush with his, her heart pounding against him, and he gritted out, "I was giving you time to be sure you wanted to go further before I unleashed all my hotness on you." He paused to let his words sink in, enjoying the need simmering in her eyes. "But the hell with being chivalrous."

He sealed his mouth over her neck the way he knew she loved. She grabbed his arms, rising on her toes as he dragged his tongue all the way up her neck to her ear, and said, "I don't want to fuck this up, Carls, but don't take that to mean I don't want to fuck *you* six ways to Sunday. I have wanted you in my bed every day of my goddamn life."

She made a hauntingly sexy sound and said, "I forgot about your dirty talk."

"No you didn't," he challenged, holding her gaze. "You haven't forgotten a damn thing about us. You just buried who you used to be the same way I buried the boy I was." Her eyes narrowed slightly, the confirmation clear. "The question is, my beautiful adventurer, can we find a way to blend the people we've become with the kids who fell so deeply in love they refuse to stay hidden?" He knew he was coming on strong, but he didn't want to leave any room for misunderstanding. The adventurous Carly had only begun climbing out from under her careful facade, but he was beginning to wonder if her cautiousness wasn't a facade after all, but rather the traits of the stronger woman she'd had to become because of him. He was more careful, too, which was why he'd slowed them down in the cave.

She swallowed hard and said, "That's a big question."

"A question we might not be ready to ask ourselves." They'd both grown up, and being cautious was just one of many changes that had come from what they'd been through. But one thing definitely *hadn't* changed. The desire in her eyes wasn't thwarted by his pushy question. He kissed her softly, feeling her restraint, needing to see where she really stood, because he truly did not want to mess this up. "So I'll ask you this question instead. Do you remember all the dirty things I loved doing to you?"

"*Zevy.*" Her eyes flamed, but in the next second, control overtook the heat, giving him more silent answers even before she said, "Wouldn't you like to know? But speaking of *dirty*, I really should rinse off if we're going somewhere."

Talk about conflicting messages, my sweet girl. Was that an invitation or a statement? There was only one way to find out. "Sounds good to me." He ran his hand down her hip, earning another flare of desire. "I'll wash all your good parts."

His cell phone rang, and Bandit bolted up the steps, banging against Carly's legs on his way inside. She wobbled, and Zev caught her around her waist.

"Geez! What is he, your wingman?" she teased as his phone

rang again. "Don't you want to get that?"

She might be speaking more sassily, but the desire in her eyes remained, and he wasn't ready to let that go yet, so he said, "Not as badly as I want to get *this*." He squeezed her ass and nipped at her lower lip, earning an even *hotter* look. But as she'd done moments before, she instantly regained control. She stepped from his arms just as his phone rang again.

She took her backpack from his shoulder with a sexy smirk and said, "I need to shower, and *you* need to get that call."

He pulled his phone from his backpack and saw his sister's name on the screen. "Even after all these years, Jilly's still cockblocking us." When they were younger, Jillian always seemed to wander into the yard or the room where they were making out. She and his other siblings called him often enough to keep tabs on him. He put the phone to his ear as they headed inside and said, "Hold on, Jilly."

"Just point me in the direction of a *cold* shower," Carly said.

He led her to the grand staircase, and as they headed up to the second floor with Bandit on their heels, he said, "I'm in the Peter Pan suite." Charlotte loved fairy tales, and while she and Beau lived in a house on the property that her great-grandfather had renovated to replicate Snow White's house, Beau had transformed each of the inn's suites to have fairy-tale themes.

"Guess that makes me *Wendy*," Carly said.

"Hey, it's better than where they wanted to put me—in the Rapunzel suite." He pointed to his hair.

"Your hair isn't even that long, and I like it," she said as he opened the door to the suite. "Don't forget Jilly's on the phone."

"Shoot. Thanks. I'll grab a fresh towel for you. Bandit likes to steal them." Zev put the phone to his ear and headed down the hall to the linen closet. "Hey, Jilly, sorry about that. What's up?"

"Was that *Carly*?" she asked enthusiastically.

"Who else would it be?" He pulled the phone away from his ear as she shrieked with delight.

"Does this mean you guys are back together? Did you guys finally talk after we left? How was it? Are you...?"

He chuckled as she shot off a half dozen questions. He grabbed a couple of towels from the linen closet and realized that Carly was getting *naked* right down the hall and he was on the phone with his sister. What the hell?

He stalked back down the hall, heating up at the thought of Carly stripping off her bikini, and said, "Jilly, I'm sorry, but I can't really talk right now. Did you need something?"

"No! *Go.* I'm so excited for you guys. I have to call Char!"

He was about to remind her that Char was on her honeymoon as he entered the suite, but the bathroom door was ajar and he heard the shower running. All his thoughts turned to Carly. He ended the call, set his phone on the dresser, and knocked on the bathroom door, the force pushing it open. Steam billowed out from above the glass doors, behind which Carly stood with her face tipped up toward the shower spray. His gaze moved down the length of her, and his heart turned over in his chest when he came to *I'm sure* written in the steam on the glass.

He dropped the towels and pulled off his shirt. *The hell with the concretions.*

Carly turned, and their eyes locked through the hazy glass as he pulled off his boots. She slid the door open, watching as he finished undressing. She beckoned him with a crook of her finger and a sultry look in her eyes, sexier than any fantasy he'd ever conjured. She fucking owned him. No fantasy could come close to the woman he adored giving herself freely to him.

He stepped into the shower, gathering her slick body in his arms. "*Carls,*" he whispered as he lowered his mouth to hers.

Heat rocketed through him as her soft body conformed to his hard frame, and he intensified the kiss. Their bodies slithered, grinding and rocking as they feasted on each other's mouths. Their hands were everywhere at once. He loved the way she touched him, grabbing his ass, clawing at his back. Her back hit the wall, but they didn't slow down. He couldn't get enough of her as he groped her breasts, ground his cock against her center. Desire pounded through him, and he tore his mouth away with a curse.

"I want all of you at once," he growled.

"Take me, Zevy. All of me."

He crushed his mouth to hers, making love to it like he wanted to make love to her—deep and possessive. He wanted to kiss her for hours, but there was no slowing down the greedy desire pulsing through him. He tasted his way down her body, nipping and sucking, earning one sinful sound after another, every moan making him ache. He palmed her breasts, taking one in his mouth, sucking hard, making her cry out with pleasure, and then easing his efforts, licking and teasing her nipple. He grazed the sensitive peak with his teeth, squeezing her other nipple between his finger and thumb.

"Oh, yes!" she cried.

Her hips rocked, and he reached up with one hand, sliding two fingers over her lips, and said, "Suck them."

She opened her mouth, and her lips closed around his fingers. She sucked and teased, taking them in and out as if they were his cock as he loved her breasts, earning one greedy noise after another. When she fisted her hands in his hair, pleading, "Don't stop," he thought he was going to lose his mind. She held his mouth to her breast. He withdrew his fingers from her mouth with the need to touch more of her and sucked harder, grabbing her ass with both hands and earning a sharp inhalation.

She clutched his ass and he rose up, reclaiming her hot, willing mouth. *Fucking heaven.* He trapped her lower lip between his teeth, tugging it gently, then peppered her mouth with tender kisses. He kissed her cheek, her shoulder, her neck, anywhere he could reach. He wanted *all* of her, heart and soul.

"This....*you*..." he panted out. "You're all there is for me, baby. You're all there's ever been."

He took her in another smoldering kiss, and then he blazed a path down the center of her body, kissing her breasts, sucking her smooth belly, nipping her hips, and dragging his tongue in and around her belly button until she was trembling all over. He moved lower, dragging his tongue around her sex and inner thighs as he nudged her legs open wider. Warm water rained down his back as he teased her sweetest spots with his hands and mouth. Her essence spread over his tongue, and he couldn't hold back his moans of pleasure. She tasted sweeter than sunshine and hotter than sin, familiar and somehow also thrillingly new.

Perfect.

He dipped two fingers inside her and lowered his mouth to the apex of her sex, sucking and licking her most sensitive nerves. She bowed off the wall, clawing at his shoulders, her hips rocking.

"Oh *God*—" she cried out in desperation. "Zevy, *please*..."

"I've got you, baby. I've always got you."

He quickened his efforts, fucking her with his fingers as he feasted and teased. He brought his other hand to her ass, caressing the soft globes, then teasing his fingers between them.

"Oh *Lord…Don't stop!*"

She panted and whimpered, riding his hand, her thighs flexing and shaking as he sucked her clit and teased her bottom, sending her shooting for the stars. She fisted her hands in his hair as her climax consumed her. He reveled in the sweet sounds of surrender streaming from her lips, and when she started drifting back down to earth, he moved his mouth between her legs, taking her up to the peak again. He stayed with her until she slumped, spent and sated, against the wall. Only then did he kiss his way up her body, slowing to love her breasts again, earning full-body shivers.

He took her face between his hands, and she stared hazily, *hungrily*, into his eyes. God, he loved her. "Still with me, baby?"

"*So* with you."

"You're protected, Carls? You sure?"

"*Yes.*"

He angled her mouth beneath his, slicking his tongue along her lower lip. She grabbed his arms, arching into him, her tongue reaching for his. She was killing him one sexy whimper at a time. He traced her lower lip with his thumb, and she licked it, desire simmering in her eyes. She was so *wanting* and willing, so sweet and delicious, he couldn't stop his dirty demands from spilling out. "I need to fuck your mouth, baby, and then I want to fuck you."

"*Mm, yes.*" Her hands moved down his chest as she sank to her knees.

Every touch of her lips, every slick of her tongue branded him as *hers*, just as they always had. When she wrapped her hand around his erection, his hips thrust instinctively. Her big blue eyes flicked up with the sweetness of an angel and the wickedness of a vixen. Warm water rained over her as she licked him from base to tip, sending fire through his veins. As she took him in her mouth, she held his gaze, loving him the way she used to, only it felt different now, more intense.

"God, I've missed your mouth, baby."

She smiled around his cock and did something incredible with her tongue along the head. *Christ almighty.* He sank back against the cold, wet tiles, moaning loudly. He tangled his hands in her wet hair, and it took all of his control not to drive his cock down her throat. But he let her set their pace. She took him deep and agonizingly *slowly*, sucking so hard he swore she'd suck the marrow from his bones.

"*Jesus*, Carls…"

A spark of victory shone in her eyes, and she withdrew his cock from her mouth, making a dramatic, and fucking-*hot*, show of stroking him with her hand as she dipped lower and licked his balls. She squeezed him tighter, worked him faster. He gritted his teeth against the fire throbbing through his veins.

"*Fuck.* I need you, baby."

Hauling her up to her feet, he captured her mouth and lifted her into his arms. She sank down onto his shaft, tight as a vise. They both moaned, and he ground out "*Fucking hell*" as she said "*Ohmygod.*"

Their eyes locked, and in the space of a few silent seconds, a world of hopes and dreams for *more* were conveyed. Hopes he'd thought about a million times and pushed away a million more and dreams he'd never dared allow to consume him after he left her. But now his hopes and dreams clung to the ones in her eyes, daring to rise to the surface. He vowed never to push those dreams away again. As their mouths came together, they found their rhythm in love so all-consuming, and everything else fell away. There was only the two of them, the sounds of their lovemaking, the feel of finally coming home, the fusing of their hearts. Did she feel it, too, or was he alone in a fantasy that felt real?

She dragged her nails down his back, the titillating pain snapping him from his trance.

"Come *with* me," she demanded, eliciting zings of electricity that had him thrusting faster, taking her deeper. "Ah, ah, *ah!*"

He'd never tire of hearing her needy sounds. Her nails cut into his flesh, the pain and pleasure sending lust coursing down his spine. He buried his face in her neck as her body clenched around him, drawing him closer to the edge with every pump of his hips. Her back hit the wall again, and they used it for leverage, catapulting them into a torrent of moans and pleas, thrusting, and grinding as their climaxes consumed them. The pleasure went on and on, until Zev was barely breathing, every thrust driven from his soul, bleeding him dry. Carly went boneless in his arms, their bodies jolting with aftershocks.

Zev closed his eyes, reveling in the feel of her, her sweet sighs of satisfaction sailing into his ear. He kissed her lips, her cheek, and when her eyes opened, he wanted to burn the loving look in them into his mind so he could revel in it for hours.

"*Zev,*" slipped from her lips like a secret.

But there were no secrets left to unveil. There was only the truth that the love that had bound them together for so long, the love he didn't know how to exist without, was still there. Neither one might be ready to address it yet, but it was as real as the water raining down on them.

He kissed her softly. "I know, babe. I feel it, too. I'm going to take my time bathing every inch of you, and then I'm going to carry you to my bed and get you dirty all over again, because we're not done, Carly. We'll never be done."

A LONG WHILE later, they lay on their backs on a bed on the porch of the Peter Pan suite, their hands touching between them as they tried to catch their breath. Carly's gaze moved beyond the sheers surrounding the bed Beau had built out of knotty wood and elegantly twisted iron to the rustic lanterns hanging from gnarled branches along the ceiling and the plants billowing out of giant pots, which gave the sleeping porch a jungle-like feel. The cool early-evening air brushed over their bodies, still damp from their lovemaking. Carly had seen all of the renovations Char and Beau had made, but the porch looked completely different—*better*, more *romantic*—with Zev lying next to her naked and sated. Then again, everything looked different after the incredible way he'd explored and ravaged her. She was sure *she* looked different, too.

"I think you've ruined me for all of mankind," she said. "The bionic man couldn't live up to *that*."

"*Exactly.*" Zev squeezed her hand.

"That was your goal, huh? Ruin me for all other men."

"Babe, if you're still thinking about other men, then I did something wrong."

"Trust me, you didn't do *anything* wrong. I feel like a teenager again. Like we're back down by the creek in Pleasant Hill with a blanket and our mix CDs." She sighed. "I didn't think we could ever top those times. Remember how we used to go at it for *hours?*"

"What do you think kept me going all these years?" He rolled onto his side and kissed her. His expression had gone from a ravenous beast to a sated lion. His gaze moved appreciatively over her face and down her naked body as he traced her curves, as if he were trying to memorize her.

She'd dreamed of how she'd feel if she and Zev ever ended up in each other's arms again, but now she couldn't even remember what she thought she'd feel, because this was unlike anything she'd ever imagined or experienced. She felt transformed into a younger version of herself, a girl who didn't overthink and hold back. It felt so good, she was tempted to peer into the future, but reminded herself that expectations led to heartbreak. She didn't want to think about the fact that they had only six days together, or that one of those days was already more than half over, but she forced herself to. It was a good reminder that this time together was temporary, nothing more, and for now it was okay to be the old Carly and enjoy every minute for the gift it was.

Zev was still drinking her in. He'd always enjoyed her body, and she'd always loved the way it felt to be admired by him, but this, too, felt different. She'd never been self-conscious about being naked around him, and she knew it had a lot to do with the fact that they'd dared each other to skinny-dip so often when they were young, it had become natural. He'd seen her body developing just as she'd seen his. When they were younger, they'd been each other's first and only lovers. But now he was a *man* studying a *woman*, and she wondered what he was thinking. Was he comparing her to other women? Or thinking about how she'd changed and whether she lived up to the image he'd held in his head? She didn't love the insecurities those thoughts stirred, but she *was* curious, so she said, "Why are you looking at me like that?"

"I was just thinking about how lucky I am. I can't believe you're still single." His eyes met hers as a caress. "You're still the sweet, sexy, fun girl I knew, but now you're even more beautiful, you're stronger, you're *careful*, protective of yourself. I know that last part is my fault, but damn, baby, you're one impressive woman."

"You're making me blush."

"Just being honest. While we were apart, I thought about you every day, but there were certain things I never let myself consider. Like if you were with someone else, if you were engaged, married, having babies. I had made it clear early on to my family not to bring your name up, because even though I left so you could move on, it would have crushed me to hear you had." His expression turned apologetic. "I know that's selfish, but I was so fucking lonely away from you and my family, our memories were all I had to pull me through."

The part of her that had been so hurt when he'd left wanted to do a little happy dance that he'd paid some sort of penance, but at the same time, thinking of Zev being lonely made her unbelievably sad. She'd known he was devastated when he'd left, but she'd always thought he'd found his way back to being the same worry-free person he'd been when they were together. He'd been so full of life and filled with hope and fathomless dreams, he was like his own brand of magic. As if he could make *anything* come true.

"I think sometimes we have to be selfish in order to survive. I did the same thing," she confessed. "But then I learned how important it was to make every moment count with the people I love while they're in my life."

"Which is why you agreed to spend this time with me, isn't it?" he asked with a grin that conveyed, *You still love me. You know you do.*

Warning bells went off in her head. Apparently he was still excellent at asking questions that would bring broader answers than one might think, so she answered carefully. "Like I said, these six days are a gift, and I want to enjoy them. I still can't believe we're *here* together, and we...*wow.*"

He kissed her softly and said, "You're great for my ego."

"I won't tell you what part of me you're great for. I'm sure I'll be sore in places I never realized I could be sore."

"Then I guess I should temper my thoughts about what I want to do to you later."

She feigned a scowl and said, "You'd better *not* temper them."

"I *love* that you have not changed in that regard."

"I thought I had; then you went and proved me wrong. But if this *ruining* is going to continue, then I need food to replenish my energy." She sat up, pulling the sheet over her chest. The descending sun cast a romantic glow over the porch. "I thought Beau and Char had put you in the Peter Pan room because they thought you refused to grow up. You know, always dreaming of finding treasures. But I think it was because of this sleeping porch, wasn't it?"

"Sure was. I don't do well sleeping indoors." He stepped from the bed, reaching for her in all his naked glory, and said, "Come on, beautiful. Let's get cleaned up and forage for food."

Chapter Ten

AFTER A QUICK and handsy shower, Carly pulled on her underwear and shorts and looked around for her shirt. Zev stepped into his shorts *commando*. As if she wouldn't think about *that* for the rest of the afternoon. *Sheesh.* The man was a walking billboard for sex on legs. She forced herself to stop looking at him and focused on searching for her shirt. She emptied her backpack and realized she'd forgotten to pack a bra, but she *had* worn a tank top over her bathing suit, and it was nowhere to be found.

"Zev, did you move my shirt when I was in the shower?" She turned and found him watching her intently. Her lion was obviously getting hungry again. A shiver of heat trickled down her spine. Her stomach growled, reminding her she needed to eat. She crossed her hands over her breasts and said, "*Zevy…*"

He scrubbed a hand down his face and said, "Sorry, but *look* at you. Covering up or not, you're *fantastic.*" He leaned in for a kiss, staying close for several more.

She could get used to this.

No, no, no. No getting used to anything.

"I didn't move your shirt. But if it's missing, I know who stole it." He hollered out the bathroom door, "*Bandit!*"

"You think he stole my *shirt?*"

Bandit trotted into the bathroom, tail wagging.

"This innocent-looking dog has already stolen my towel, socks, one of my notebooks, which I still haven't found, and my binoculars. When I was collecting eggs from the chickens this morning, he ran off with the bucket. I think we can add your shirt to this scavenger's list." Zev loved up Bandit. "Hey there, thief. Did you take my girl's shirt?"

My girl. Carly tried to quell the giddiness bubbling up inside her.

Bandit cocked his head and licked Zev's cheek.

"I'm taking that as a *yes.*" He ruffled the dog's head and stood. "I'll give you one of mine."

He took her hand, leading her into the bedroom. She had forgotten how much of a hand holder he was. She'd missed it.

Char and Beau had done a great job of decorating to bring out the elegance of the Darlings' London home. A crystal chandelier hung in the center of the room, and just beyond was a sleek and intricately carved mahogany canopy bed, as rich and luxurious as it was romantic. On the far wall was a hand-painted mural of the London cityscape with silhouettes of Peter Pan, Wendy, and her brothers flying in front of Big Ben in the moonlight. A shadow of Peter Pan peeked out from behind the closet door, and there were lanterns as bedside lights and pristine hardwood floors with a plush and elegant area rug.

Zev fished around in a duffel bag and held up a faded Maroon 5 T-shirt. "Remember this one?"

"I can't believe you still have it." She snagged the shirt they'd bought at a concert together and put it on. It was soft as butter and smelled like Zev.

"I guess you got rid of yours?" There was an arc of disappointment in his voice.

"No freaking way."

"*Ah*, see, Carls?" he said as he gathered her in his arms. "The T-shirts, the tattoos. They're signs that we were always supposed to find each other again. We're finally exactly where we're supposed to be."

He touched his lips to hers, and it felt so good, she put her arms around him, going up on her toes for more. He wanted more—she had felt it in his touch—and he was telling her now. It was so easy to be in the moment with him, she felt herself free falling into them.

She pushed away gently, though she remained in his arms, and said, "Zevy, you can't do this."

"What's that?" He rubbed his nose along her cheek and pressed a kiss there.

"Make me want more than the six days we have. It's not fair."

He met her gaze, confusion written in his wrinkled brow. "Why not? I want more, and it feels like you do, too."

His optimism was like a drug, and she desperately wanted to overdose on it, but she knew where that could lead, so she said, "Because your life is out in the wild, and mine is here."

"So what? Life isn't black-and-white, babe. There's a world of ways we can make this work." He kissed her softly. "You're fooling yourself if you think this is all there is between us, but we don't have to go there yet. I don't want your cautious mind dragging you away from me out of fear."

"I'm not going to pull away, but I can't afford to be hurt again."

He took her hand, leading her out of the suite and into the hall. "Then don't shut me out when this week is over. We both like to travel. I'll come see you, you'll come see me."

She sighed. "You still make everything seem easy and possible."

"Because it is if we want it to be. We have already lost too many years, and that's on me. I was messed up, but I've learned and grown. I won't hurt you again, Carls." He squinted at something on the floor at the top of the stairs and peered over the railing, uttering a curse.

"What's wrong?" She looked over the railing and saw postcards littering the staircase and the floor below.

"Bandit is at it again. He stole my postcards. *Damn it.* How does Beau put up with this?"

They picked up postcards on their way downstairs, and they found dozens more scattered farther from the stairs. There must have been a hundred or more postcards dating back to two years after Zev had left home, all addressed to him in care of post offices around the world, and they were all from Graham. Some of the messages were short, like, *Thinking of you* and *Send me the last-time-we pic*, while others gave brief updates on the goings-on of their family members. A few were cutting, like, *That was a dick move, missing Mom's birthday. Good thing we love you. Come back soon.* and *Answer Jilly's calls. She's worried about you.*

"What's a last-time-we picture?" Carly asked as she picked up another postcard.

Zev's expression turned thoughtful. "After Tory died, I stopped saying goodbye. It felt too final. And after you and I broke up, I stopped taking remember-when pictures, because those were *ours.* Now I take last-time-we pictures before I leave my family...in case it's the last time we see each other."

That was such a big-hearted Zev thing to do, tears dampened her eyes. He had always loved his family so much, it was one of the reasons she'd thought he might come back to Pleasant Hill. But now she knew he'd thought he was too angry, too jaded, and might ruin anyone he loved.

She regained control of her emotions as they picked up the last of the postcards.

"These are *all* from Graham. He's been writing to you all this time?" she asked, following him into the enormous farmhouse-style kitchen with Bandit on their heels.

They put the postcards on the table, and Bandit went to lie down beneath it.

"Yeah," Zev said. "I keep up with everyone else by phone, but Graham has this thing about mail."

"I love that he wrote to you. I can't tell you the last time I got a letter or a postcard in the mail. Why does he have a thing about mail?"

Zev shrugged and said, "What are you hungry for? I can throw some meat on the grill."

"*Zevy...?*" she said, wondering why he was avoiding the question.

He wrapped his arms around her and kissed her neck.

"That's not going to sidetrack me, even if I enjoy it. If the reason is private, you don't have to tell me."

"It's not private. I just didn't want to think about it. For some weird reason, Graham's old-fashioned. He sends postcards because he thinks it makes every place I go feel like home."

That didn't surprise her. The Bradens were always watching out for each other. "Did it?"

"No, but I like getting mail from him. It gives me some-thing to look forward to, but nothing feels like home. You've always been missing." He kissed the bridge of her nose and said, "Right now this kitchen feels like home, and before this the sleeping porch felt like home, and the shower, and Silk Hollow."

She melted a little at the sweetness of his words and the warmth in his voice, wishing she'd never snuck away in Mexico. Maybe they would have made up sooner, had a family, and built a life together. But those were dangerous thoughts that could only bring sadness for the years they'd lost, so she forced them away, concentrating instead on the gift they'd been given and not whether it would last for six days, six years, or an eternity. They had *now*, and that was wonderful.

"I speak the truth, even if it sounds cheesy," he said. "But I think Graham sends postcards more for his peace of mind than anything else. I think he likes being able to pinpoint my whereabouts to be sure he could find me pretty quickly if he needed to."

"That makes sense, but it also makes sense that Graham would want to help you feel less alone." She picked up the card that said Jilly was losing her mind and waved it. "Although it looks like he gave you a hard time from afar, too."

He chuckled. "Yeah, you know that Braden family creed? *Family knows no boundaries?* Well, that goes for every aspect of our lives. But I deserved it. There were times when I couldn't take the reminders that being home brought, so I just went radio silent. It wasn't fair to my family, but survival instincts are pretty tough to fight."

"I went through that for a while," she admitted.

"Yeah, it sucked. There were so many times that I wanted to come back and see if you and I could work things out. But I was afraid of screwing you up even more."

Even though she wouldn't wish suffering on anyone, there was something cathartic about hearing that he'd struggled in order to stay away and allow her to heal. He was still the same big-hearted Zev he'd always been, but even that brought questions. She didn't want to take away from their easy conversation, so she asked her question playfully.

She ran her finger down his chest and said, "Then why did you just fuck my brains out?"

"Careful, babe, or your dirty mouth will get us in trouble again."

"Good to know. That skill might come in handy later. But I'm serious. What changed your mind about screwing me up?"

"I didn't know you were going to be at the wedding. Nobody warned me. I didn't even know you and Char were friends." He shrugged, but the depth of emotion in his eyes told her the answer he was about to give wasn't cavalier. "Once I saw you, I didn't have a choice. There was no turning back. If you'd shut me down, or if I'd seen hate in your eyes instead of what we both know we have, then maybe I would have tried to walk away. But I can't even say I would have done it, because I feel like this is where we're supposed to be. I know you're not ready to commit to anything more than this week, and I get that. I don't blame you. I know I need to earn back your trust on all levels, not just in the bedroom, and only *you* can decide if and when you'll ever be ready to risk your heart again. But I know where mine stands, Carly, and that's in your hands. It always has been."

She was glad that he wasn't brushing their past under the carpet even though she'd said she didn't want to dwell on it. "Thank you for understanding. I know I have to earn back your trust, too, because of how I turned my back on you in Mexico. If you're as thorough on all other levels as you are in the bedroom, maybe the risk will be worth the reward."

"Right back at ya, beautiful, only there's no maybe about it on my side." A wolfish grin spread across his face.

"That's a pretty cocky smile."

"I'm a *cocky* guy, as you recently found out."

She rolled her eyes. "Let's see if you're as good in the kitchen as you are in the bedroom. I have a hankering for cereal."

"Baby, I'll never let you down again." He threw open a pantry where six boxes of her—their—favorite cereals were lined up on the top shelf. "I'll even give you all of my clover marshmallows from the Lucky Charms." He winked and said, "You know, to increase your chances of getting lucky. Next test?"

They both laughed as they filled two bowls with a mix of all three cereals and went outside to eat on the balcony. Bandit followed them out and plopped his furry body down beside Zev's chair for a nap. They ate as the sun descended behind the mountains, spreading ribbons of pinks and purples across the evening sky.

"Why is the wedding tent still up?" Carly asked. "I thought Char said it was being taken down Sunday night."

He shrugged. "They came and took the tables and chairs but never came back to take the tent down."

"That's weird. Did you call them?"

"Of course. They're coming tomorrow afternoon. Tell me something I don't know about you, Carls. What was it like taking over your aunt's business?"

"Oh gosh. I guess it was scary, but also exciting. You know how I always loved a challenge." She told him about the way she'd grown the business by adding classes, selling shirts and other Divine Intervention merchandise, and working with Birdie to create an online presence.

"Does Marie keep in touch?"

"Yeah. She texts mostly. She comes back from time to time for visits, but she's out there traveling the world and living her best life, and I'm here living mine."

"Do you ever regret not going into archaeology full time and missing out on all the travel you wanted to do?"

"It comes and goes. Sometimes I miss it, but then I think about all I have here, with the shop and my friends. I have a good life." As she said it, she heard her younger self saying *I don't want a good life. I want a great life*, which was what she and Zev used to tell everyone. The chocolate shop was her safe haven. She'd thrown herself into it, and in return it had given her stability and sanity. But the truth was, the dreams she'd left behind lingered in the back of her mind. She tried not to dwell on them because all of those thoughts led to Zev, and without him, those dreams didn't feel worth chasing.

"What would make your life here *great*?" he asked.

Her answer came as easily as it did honestly. "More days like today."

Happiness rose in his eyes. "I've got that covered. All I need is for you to agree to give me all of your free time until I leave."

"*All* of my free time?" Not that she had much on any given day, but *wow* she was a little nervous at how much the idea excited her. Yes, it made her nervous, too, but she *wanted* time with him. She wanted to enjoy every second of it so when he left she'd have no regrets.

"Six days is not much time, and we're almost down to five," he urged. "What's your schedule like this week?"

"I usually work from about six or seven in the morning until six or seven in the evening."

"Whoa, Carls. Really? How many days a week?"

"It depends. Most days, but not all day on Sundays. The shop is only open from ten to six except on Sundays, when it's open from ten to three."

His brows knitted. "Why don't you hire more help?"

"I don't need more help right now. I don't have to stay late *every* night; I choose to. Birdie works full time, and a girl named Quinn has worked for me part time for a few years now, helping out in the evenings and on weekends. She works at a bank and hates it. She's always willing to take on more hours for me, but I like being kept busy."

"You were never someone who needed to be *kept busy*. You were always thinking up things to do. You had lists, remember?"

She pushed a Froot Loop through the milk in her bowl and said, "I still have lists. They're just different types of lists, like inventory, orders, and schedules. I love the work I do. I get to meet all sorts of people. I have regular customers who stop by to talk, and I cater events. A customer is having an elaborate baby shower on Sunday, and I'm really looking forward to making the treats for it on Saturday." She loved baby showers the most, because making baby-themed chocolates for other people's miracles gave her hope of what she might one day have.

His expression turned thoughtful. "It's not hard for you, making desserts for baby showers?"

"Making the sweet little confections shaped like pacifiers and rattles gave me a pang at first," she said, loving that he thought to ask. "The miscarriage was horrible, and I don't want to demean that at all, but I think what threw me over the edge was that it was such a tumultuous time all around, because of what I'd done to you in Mexico. It felt like I'd lost the last piece of you I would ever have, and it kind of felt like losing you all over again, which made it harder."

He reached over and squeezed her hand. "I'm sorry. If I'd known…"

"I know. I've accepted that it wasn't meant to be at that point in our lives, and therapy helped me put things into perspective. Now I *love* baby showers and children's birthday parties because they give me hope of what I might have someday. But I rarely go to those events unless they're really big deals. Usually I just make the treats and the customers pick them up at the shop, like next weekend."

"So you *do* still want to have kids?"

She nodded eagerly. "Yes. Don't you?" Their dreams had always included three children who they'd wanted to name Journey, Scout, and Chance, regardless of their genders.

"I didn't think I did," he said with a shake of his head. "I was pretty fucked up after Tory died. I couldn't imagine bringing a helpless child into a world where I couldn't always protect them. But then you told me about what happened, and I would have wanted that baby, *our* baby, and I would have protected it, and you, with my life. So maybe my view on having a family is changing because of us."

"It's weird how events have domino effects, isn't it? I'm sorry you felt that way, but I do understand it. Tory's death kicked the legs out from beneath our whole community. It's scary to think how fast things can change, which goes right back to my belief of enjoying time with the people we care about so we don't miss the chance. It makes me happy to know you would have wanted our child. You'll be a great dad if you ever choose to be one, but you have so much on your plate right now with the *Pride*, I can't imagine fitting anything else in." Although he was here now, with her, taking care of Bandit for his brother.

He was looking at her intently again, and she liked this new Zev who thought before he spoke as much as she'd liked the teenager on the cusp of manhood that he'd been.

"You're making me rethink a lot of things about myself, Carls."

"Good, because you're making me think a lot, too."

"I want to do a lot more than make you *think*," he said, lightening the mood again. "So, when do I get time with you? I'll take whatever time I can get. Should I plan for after seven o'clock?" He ate a spoonful of cereal, his eyes locked on her.

She didn't want that little time with Zev. She wanted *more* time, especially after the amazing day they'd had. "Not necessarily. I can make arrangements to get off earlier."

"That would be great, but I don't want to screw up your schedule."

She ate a bite of cereal, thinking about it, and said, "You sure about that?"

"Unfortunately, yes. I promised myself I wouldn't do anything that could screw up your life. Do I *want* more time with you? *Absolutely*. Twenty-four-seven if I can have it. But not if it messes you up in any way. You tell me when I can see you and I'll deal with it."

"Aren't you accommodating?" she said playfully.

"I aim to please, and based on your reactions earlier, I'd say I *pleased* multiple times."

She felt her cheeks burn, and she remembered how they'd ended up at the inn today. "Didn't you say you wanted to show me something when we were at Silk Hollow?" She narrowed her eyes and said, "Or was that just a ploy to get me into your bed?"

"As I recall, *you* distracted *me* from our mission with your need to *rinse off*."

"Right," she whispered, grinning like a fool. "I can't say I'm sorry about that."

"Then that makes two of us." They finished their cereal, and he said, "I do have someplace I want to take you, but now I'm in a quandary because it's a little late to go there, and I have something *else* I was hoping to do with you tonight."

"Does it have anything to do with getting me upstairs in your bedroom again?" she asked with a shameful amount of hope.

"If it were up to me, I'd sweep you away to Neverland forevermore, but I can't just let you use me for my body all week, or you won't get to enjoy the whole *Zev* experience and realize how much you want more than six days with me." He leaned in for a long, slow, sugary kiss and remained close as he said, "What I have in mind doesn't end in the bedroom, but if you say you'll hang out with me for a few more hours, I promise you won't be disappointed."

More time with Zev? *Yes, please.* That little warning voice in her head was drowned out by the pure enjoyment of being with him. "Now you've piqued my curiosity."

"Say you'll stay and hang out with me, Carls. Give us a chance."

He said it so earnestly, she wanted to blurt out, *I'll stay!* But she fell back into one of their games, because she missed those, too, and they had always made her happy, just like Zev. "Milk race? If you win, I'll stay." When they were younger, they'd race to see who could drink the milk from their cereal bowls the fastest, and Zev *always* won.

"You're on."

They picked up their bowls, and she said, "One." Zev said, "Two," and they both said, "Three," and lifted their bowls to their lips, guzzling the sugary milk. Milk dripped down their chins, and Zev finished in seconds. He pushed to his feet and hollered, "Yes!" causing Bandit to jump up and bark.

Carly put her bowl on the table, and Zev swept her into his arms, kissing her hard, milk mustache and all. "You're *mine* tonight, baby!"

"Oh, *darn*. Guess I have no choice but to endure a few more hours with you."

"You played me like a fiddle, and it makes you even *hotter*. Come on, beautiful," he said as he grabbed the bowls. "Let's clean up these dishes, check on the chickens, and then I'll show you your surprise."

"Surprise? So, we're going where you wanted to take me earlier?"

"Nope. We'll have to do that tomorrow," he said as they headed inside.

They washed the bowls and then they headed out to check on the chickens. Bandit led them down a path through the woods. The scents of pine and fresh earth hung in the air. They joked around and talked, sharing so many delicious kisses, Carly wanted to skip the surprise and drag him up to the suite. But at the same time, she was loving every second of just being with Zev. He was interesting and funny, telling her stories about his travels and about searching for the *Pride*. His passionate descriptions made her feel like she was right there with him, hiking, surfing, and diving in the deep blue sea.

They headed back through the woods to the inn, and when a flock of birds took flight from the tops of the trees, Bandit bolted ahead.

Zev slung an arm over Carly's shoulder and said, "It feels kind of like old times, only better."

"Because we've cleared the air?"

"Probably. Guilt is a ravenous beast."

"So are you," she said softly.

A low laugh rumbled out of his lips as he pushed a branch out of the way so she could pass through to the grassy field in front of the Sterling House. Three gorgeous stories of glass, stone, and cedar and grand terraces made the stately inn look rustic and elegant at once.

"This place is so pretty. Everyone in town is thrilled that Char and Beau are reopening the inn."

"Is this what you'd like to have one day? Land, animals? A peaceful life in the mountains?"

It was a good question. "To be honest, I haven't thought in terms of *one day* for a very long time."

"I can't imagine that. You were such a dreamer. Your dreams fed mine."

"Funny, I always thought yours fed mine."

"Maybe it was both, and maybe you *should* think about what you want out of life," he said lightly.

Asking herself that question would be anything *but* light. All she'd ever wanted when they were together was to travel the world with him, going from one adventure to the next, discovering things about each other and different cultures along the way. Did she still want that? She certainly still wanted *him*.

"What do you want, Zev?" she asked as they walked around the side of the inn. "Are you happy traveling and living in your van or on your boat? Not having one place to call home?"

"That's a loaded question. You know what home feels like to me."

Remembering his sweet words, she said, "*Me*."

"Exactly. I love seeing the world and not knowing what

tomorrow will hold. I love the thrill of trying to find what other people think is lost forever and getting up one morning and reading about something across the country and then getting on a plane and going to see it, just so I don't miss out. I love the work I do, babe, just like you do."

"I can hear that."

"I don't know if I could ever do what you did and stay in one place for very long. I mean, look at where I'm sleeping. I get restless if I'm confined. You of all people know that. Hell, you used to be that way, too."

Even when they'd gone off to college and could sleep in each other's dorm rooms, they'd still go on midnight adventures. The outdoors had been such a huge draw to both of them, it wasn't unusual for one of them to wake up the other at two in the morning and say, *Let's go explore.* Goose bumps rose on Carly's arms. She missed those times. But they couldn't have stayed like that forever. Eventually real life would have gotten in the way. At least that's what she'd told herself on the rare occasion she'd allowed herself to think about what their lives would be like together.

"That's true," she said. "But after Mexico, the safety of knowing what tomorrow held was what saved me."

"I can see that," he said as they came to the backyard. "I'm sorry, but I can't wrap my head around you not craving the excitement or the unstoppable need to explore. It seemed like it ran through your veins, like it does mine. You really don't miss lying beneath the stars planning trips to all the places you want to see?"

Hearing the enthusiasm in the voice of the man with whom she'd wanted those things made the longing she'd spent a decade repressing force itself up to the surface.

"I'd be lying if I said I don't miss it sometimes. I just don't think about it because I don't think I'd give up my life here for it. This is my home now." As she said it, worry trampled through her. Was she driving a stake between them? Even if she was, he needed to know that she wasn't the dreamer she'd once been. She might be jumping in with both feet to this gift of a week and rediscovering parts of herself she'd missed, but she still had to maintain a foothold in reality. Their lives were in very different places now. At the end of their time together, Zev would go back to his life, and she'd have to shuck the rediscovered pieces of herself like old husks and fall back into her overly scheduled, though enjoyable, safe life once again.

"And it's a beautiful place to call home," he said, snapping her from her thoughts. He waved at the majestic mountains, the glistening lake, and the wedding tent, which looked even prettier in the starlight. Suddenly he laughed and splayed his hands up toward the sky. "I finally get it!"

"Get what?"

"I have been wondering why the universe chose *now* to bring us back together, and I think I just figured it out," he said excitedly. "You *need* me."

She rolled her eyes. "As if I didn't need you all those years ago?"

"That was a different type of need. I think the universe knew what we didn't. We both needed to grow up in order to heal and become the adults we were meant to be. And yeah, it sucked to be apart. It was excruciating, but I know I'm a better person for it. I think before I act, and I'm aware of *all* of my faults, of which there are many. And you're stronger and even more self-confident. You're smarter than I'll ever be, Carls, and you've proven that you don't need me in the way we used to need each other."

"But you *just* said I need you *now*."

"You do, but in a different way. And I need you, too, but not in that old way, either. You've started seeing life as this regimented, clearly defined, black-and-white element, and I'm here to remind you that the life you've created is *not* at risk of falling apart if you add a little glow and color outside the lines sometimes."

"Okay. I can see that," she admitted. "But you're living our dream. Why would *you* need *me* right now?"

He took her hand, leading her toward the tent, and said, "I don't have that answer yet beyond the obvious, that I have loved you forever and my life is a lonely, *half*-fulfilling dream without you in it. But we've got this week to figure it out, and I'm sure the answer will become clear. Starting with a little reminder about where it all began." He stopped at the entrance to the tent, which was dark, and pulled his phone from his pocket. "Bear with me a sec." He did something on his phone, uttered a curse, then said, "Got it!"

He tapped something on the screen, and all of the sparkling lights inside the tent lit up. Carly's heart nearly stopped at the sight of Charlotte's enormous round wicker daybed covered with blankets and several big, fluffy pillows in the middle of the tent and an enormous movie screen where the dance floor had been. Beside the bed, a projector and a laptop sat atop a table. An old-fashioned popcorn machine and a variety of fruits, nuts, candies, and granola bars—all the things Carly and Zev used to munch on while watching movies—sat atop a large table off to the side. Bottles of water, juice, and champagne bobbed in a cooler full of water.

"*Zevy...?*" she said breathlessly. "This is amazing. I thought you said they didn't come to take down the tent."

"That wasn't exactly true. They did, but I asked them to leave it up. I wanted to surprise you." He put a hand on her lower back, leading her into the tent.

"You definitely succeeded at that. I'm *awestruck*. When did you have time to do all of this?"

"Nick helped me set it up after everyone went to sleep Saturday night."

"Nick?" Remembering that it was Nick who had given Zev advice about kissing her, she said, "He must think all we ever do is make out."

"Actually, he gave me a hard time, just like he did the first time I went to him. He lectured me about treating you right and told me that I'd better not hurt you this time, or I'd have *him* to deal with."

"Wow, really? He comes across as such a player. I wouldn't think he'd care so much."

Zev shook his head. "I'm sure Nick does his fair share of *playing*, but he's always watched out for you. I never told you about how he caught me stealing Beau's condoms the first time you and I wanted to hook up."

"No way!" she said with a laugh.

"Oh *yes*. He took the ones I stole and gave me a lecture about what it means to have sex with a girl. He told me not to be a dick afterward or to run my mouth about it, that kind of thing. And then he told me that if I was mature enough to have sex with a girl, I was old enough to buy my own condoms to protect her."

"Seriously?"

"Yup. And that's not all. He wanted me to take *complete* responsibility, so he drove me to the drugstore to make sure I didn't take the 'pussy way out' and order them online."

"Oh my gosh. Are you kidding?" She laughed. "I guess I owe Nick a thank-you, too." She hooked her fingers into his belt loops and said, "Thank you for doing all of that and for going to all of this trouble for us." She glanced at the movie screen, and then it dawned on her *when* he'd set it up. "Wait a second. You did this *Saturday* night? After the wedding?"

"Yeah. Everyone left Sunday morning, and I didn't want the others to know and make a big deal out of it in case you blew me off. Beau knew I wanted to borrow the movie projector and screen, but he never asked why."

She took a step back and said, "That's very presumptuous, to think I'd jump into bed with you."

"First of all, I didn't do it so we could have sex. There's a whole inn for that. I did it so we could watch *The Goonies* and *Indiana Jones*, your two favorite movies. I thought it would be cool to hang out like old times."

"Oh," she whispered, feeling silly.

He grabbed her shirt, tugging her slowly into his arms, and said, "*You*, my sexy seductress, are the one who got *me* naked this afternoon, remember?"

"Who, me?" she said, feigning innocence.

He kissed her softly. "Don't even pretend that you didn't want to tear my clothes off when you saw me at the wedding. We practically combusted the second we saw each other."

"Oh, you think so, do you?" she said sassily.

"Hell yes. There was no hiding the lust in your eyes."

"Dream on, Braden—"

He grabbed her ribs, tickling her. She shrieked.

"Stop!" she said through her giggles.

"Admit it!" *Tickle, tickle.* "You wanted me!"

She twisted free and ran away laughing. "I did *not* want you!"

"You wanted every inch of me!" he countered, chasing her around the daybed. He caught her around the middle and tackled her onto the mattress, tickling her into hysterical giggles. "Admit it!"

"No!" She tried to roll away, but he trapped her hands, pressing them into the mattress, straddling her waist.

"Admit it," he said with a wicked glimmer in his eyes.

She shook her head, trying not to laugh.

He dipped his head, brushing his nose over hers, and said, "You wanted me then, and you want me now." He trailed kisses across her cheek to her ear and slicked his tongue along the shell.

The air left her lungs in a rush.

"I can feel it even if you don't say it," he said huskily into her ear.

He kissed her earlobe, then nipped it just hard enough to send pinpricks of pleasure rippling down her body.

"*Zevy*," she pleaded, their eyes locking. "*Kiss me.*"

As he lowered his lips toward hers, he whispered, "Say you want me."

He didn't give her time to answer. The press of his lips was surprisingly gentle, a caress of a kiss, with long, slow sweeps of his tongue. It was the type of kiss grandmothers reminisced about and young girls dreamed of. A kiss that transported them to far-off places with white knights and glamorous castles. Carly had never dreamed of white knights. She'd dreamed of Zevy in hiking boots or a wet suit, and the closest her dreams came to castles were the old and ivy-covered ones, empty save for ghosts of years past, where she and Zev could explore. He was a master explorer, as proven by the way he was currently exploring her mouth, his tongue running over the smooth ridges of her teeth. He drew out their pleasure, releasing her hands and cradling her beneath him, kissing her so exquisitely, the voice in her head whispered, *Be careful,* but her heart pounded out a much louder message, *Let go...*

And she did, abandoning all thought and letting his kisses carry her to those far-off places full of colors and lights, deserts and oceans. A world full of hopes and possibilities. When their lips finally parted, she instantly mourned the loss, leaning up for more.

"Tell me, Carls," he whispered. "I need to hear it."

She tried to remember the last thing they'd said. It wasn't the words that came back to her first, but the imploring, loving look in his eyes, the same one that was gazing down at her now, and his words followed, *Say you want me.* Her heart was beating so fast, there was no holding back the truth. "I never stopped wanting you."

His head dropped beside hers, as if the words had offered the relief he needed. He kissed her cheek, then gazed into her eyes again and said, "Say you'll stay with me tonight."

"There's no place I'd rather be."

Chapter Eleven

ZEV HAD WOKEN to the sounds of the sea and colorful sunrises in exotic locations all over the world, but none compared to waking up to the crow of the roosters while lying in a simple wedding tent with Carly Dylan sleeping naked and safe in his arms. He'd been awake for hours reveling in their closeness. They'd slept together nearly every night their first year of college, and he'd thought he'd never be able to sleep without her again. He'd run himself ragged in his travels, chasing fatigue, but no matter how exhausted he was, the minute he'd closed his eyes, Carly was front and center in his dreams. But last night he'd slept harder in the few hours after they'd made love than he ever had before, and while Carly was still the star of his every thought, she was also finally his reality.

They had five more days together. He had four more nights to hold her, love her, and to try to earn her trust. She loved him. He was certain of that, even if she was holding the words in. But he understood her worries. He just needed to figure out what to do about them.

The *Pride* was supposed to be *their* discovery, and even though he'd been elated with what he hoped would prove to be a history-making find, he'd been honest when he'd said he wasn't fulfilled. But he couldn't be a white-picket fence guy any more than Carly could give up the life she'd worked so hard to create. He needed answers that could only come with time. He just hoped five days was enough to show her that they were worth holding on to until they figured it out.

Bandit, asleep on the ground beside the daybed, lifted his head from his paws, his ears standing up. He'd woken with the roosters, too, and he'd gone to check things out, ambling back into the tent a long while later and falling right back to sleep. Zev was getting used to having Bandit following him around like a shadow, checking on the chickens, and jumping into the truck whenever he opened the door. But he didn't think he'd ever get used to having his shit stolen.

"Hey, buddy, what's the matter?" Zev whispered. He didn't dare reach out to pet him for fear of waking Carly.

Bandit jumped to his feet and ran out of the tent, probably in search of more stuff to steal. At least he couldn't get into any of Zev's things since the doors to the inn were closed. That reminded him that Bandit had stolen Carly's shirt, and he made a mental note to look for it.

Bandit barked in the distance, rousing Carly, who snuggled into his side. She made a sleepy sound and pressed a sweet kiss to his chest. She lifted her face, a sleepy smile curving her lips.

"Morning, babe." Zev kissed her.

He ran his hand down her back, resting it on the curve at the base of her spine. Last night he'd given that sexy spot extra-special attention. She'd always been ticklish there, and he'd enjoyed making her squirm almost as much as he'd enjoyed loving his way up her spine, kissing every vertebra, and lavishing the back of her shoulders and neck with openmouthed kisses as she writhed beneath him, rubbing her ass against his cock. He was getting hard just thinking about how she'd risen on her hands and knees and he'd loved her from behind until they'd collapsed into each other's arms.

"Mm. Good morning to you, too." She wrapped her hand around his erection, heat rising in her eyes.

She stroked him tight and slow, licking his nipple. Holy fucking hell, she remembered all of her little tricks.

"Come here, beautiful." He rolled her onto her back and moved over her, kissing her as she spread her legs wider and he aligned their bodies.

"A girl could get used to this."

"I'm counting on it." As he lowered his mouth to hers, Bandit barreled into the tent.

"Carly?" a male voice called out.

Zev rose on his palms just as Cutter walked into the tent. Zev lowered himself to cover Carly's naked body and said, "Dude!"

"*Cutter!*" Carly scrambled to cover up, pushing Zev's chest. "*Move!*"

Cutter looked confused as Zev shifted off Carly, quickly covering her with a sheet, and said, "Dude, *turn around.*"

"Oh *shit*. Sorry!" Cutter turned his back to them and said, "Guess Zev rescued you from the Island of Denial."

"Shut up! What time is it? Why are you here?" Carly snapped.

"It's eight thirty," Cutter said. "Birdie called me. She's been texting you all night and got worried about y—"

"*Eight thirty?*" Carly hollered, clutching the sheet to her chest. "What day is it?" She shook her head as if she was trying to rattle her brain into submission. "I need to go! Where are my clothes? I have to call Birdie!" She looked frantically around them. "Where's my phone?"

"Your phone is still in the house," Zev reminded her. "Cutter, how'd you know we were out here?" He scanned the ground for Carly's clothes, but saw only his shorts by the entrance to the tent. *Goddamn dog.*

"I went by Carly's place first. She *never* stays out all night, but since you're here, I figured I'd check the inn, and followed Bandit back here."

Zev looked at Carly, who was frantically searching through the blankets, and said, "*He* knows where you live, but you can't tell me?"

"*He* won't leave his scent on my sheets." She stomped off the bed, holding the sheet around her as she scanned the ground. "*Where* are my clothes, Zev? I have to go!"

She was so frantic, he scrambled for a way to help her calm down—for her own sanity *and* to keep her from thinking their night together was a mistake simply because they'd overslept.

"I think Bandit took them," he said as he stepped from the bed, naked. He didn't care that Cutter was there. He was solely focused on helping Carly calm down and pulled her into a kiss. She stood rigid in his arms. He held her tighter, kissing her deeper, until she gave in to her own desires, melting against him. He continued kissing her, hoping to replace any remaining panic with something much more comforting, and when she made a soft, pleasure-filled sound, he knew she was okay.

She sighed as their lips parted, looking at him a little hazy-eyed.

"Thank you for yesterday," he said for her ears only. "And for trusting me enough to stay last night. Take a shirt and a pair of my compression shorts from my backpack. The shorts should fit. I'll try to find your missing clothes. I need to talk to Cutter, but I'll call you about getting together later, and I promise to set an alarm from now on."

Her eyes widened, as if she just realized she was late. "Okay! I gotta go!"

She went up on her toes, giving him a chaste kiss, and then she gathered the sheet around her legs and ran out of the tent. The sheet parted, giving both Zev and Cutter a great view of her ass. Bandit bolted after her.

Zev snagged his shorts from the ground and stepped into them, glancing at Cutter, who was still watching Carly. "You want to take a picture of her ass or what?"

Cutter's gaze shot to Zev, his jaw tense.

"What's the deal with you two?" Zev crossed his arms, staring him down. Cutter was a big dude, and he was giving Zev the same scrutinizing once-over Zev was giving him. *Go ahead, dude, check me out, because I'm the one she digs.*

"I should be asking you the same question." Cutter matched Zev's stance, arms crossed, chin held high, and said, "You show up here after all these years and get her into bed. What's your plan, Zev? Carly's like family to a lot of us around here. I know what you did to her, and if you fuck her over again, you won't get off scot-free this time."

Zev scoffed at that. "There's no such thing as scot-free." Carly had said she hadn't told anyone about the miscarriage, and he believed her. Which meant Cutter probably knew only about what had transpired when Zev left Pleasant Hill, but that was enough for him to realize Cutter was important to her. He pushed past the jealousy riding his shoulders and realized that the big-ass cowboy had been there for Carly when he hadn't. As painful as it was to admit his own faults to Cutter, if he was ever going to be the man Carly needed, the man she *wanted* in her future, then he had to do the right thing by her on all levels.

Including this one.

"I'm glad you've got her back," Zev said, uncrossing his arms. "I never meant to fuck her over. I thought I was protecting her by leaving. But that's a long story. All you need to know is that I have no intention of hurting her ever again."

The scowl on Cutter's face remained in place. "Good."

"Listen, man, I know all you see is some guy who hurt your friend and has no ties to anyone or anyplace. But looks can be deceiving. Carly and I have years of history and ties that bind us together in ways that no space of time or distance could ever erase. *She's* my person, and wherever she is, is my place."

"Does that mean you're sticking around after Beau gets back?" Cutter asked with a skeptical lilt to his voice.

"That's for me and Carly to work out. But I would like to get to know you and her other friends better. Maybe we can go for a drink one night?"

"Are you coming to the Roadhouse with Carly tonight?"

"The Roadhouse?"

"It's a bar where we all hang out Wednesday nights. No matter how busy she is, she never misses it."

"Oh yeah, we'll be there." Zev tried to play it cool, like he knew about her plans, though he wondered why she hadn't mentioned them. "We might be a little late. We have something to do first." He was excited to show Carly the concretions, but he didn't want to cause her to miss a weekly get-together with her friends.

Unless she didn't want him to go with her and that was why she hadn't mentioned it.

Well, hell.

"Cool." Cutter looked around the tent and said, "Did you

set all of this up for Carly?"

"Yeah. Tents and movies were two of our *things* when we were younger."

"Seriously? I can't imagine her sleeping in a tent, but uh…I guess I don't have to *imagine* it now."

Zev shot him a warning glare.

Cutter held his hands up and said, "It was a joke. But for what it's worth, I have no idea who that woman was that ran out of this tent with her ass showing. The Carly I know is up with the sun, at the shop by seven, and her idea of a wild time is riding horses at Redemption Ranch on Sunday mornings."

"Really?" Zev wondered why Carly hadn't mentioned that to him, either. They'd ridden horses when they were younger, but it had never been one of their things. He wondered what else had become *her* thing. He remembered the story she'd told him about the other guy, Callahan, who had acted like her boyfriend rescuing her when her car had broken down. Had she made that up, or was it true after all? Was horseback riding her and *that* guy's thing? She'd said he was like a brother to her, and Zev definitely didn't want to impede on that time if it was their thing. He clearly had a lot to learn about Carly's life.

"Do you know her friend Callahan? I think his family owns that ranch you mentioned."

"*Cowboy?* Sure. Everyone knows the Whiskeys. Why?"

"Think you can get him to meet us at the bar? I'd like to get to know him, too." Bandit bounded toward them carrying something in his mouth.

"Trust me, once I get the word out that you two will be there, they'll all be waiting to meet you."

"You make it sound like I'm walking into an ambush."

Cutter grinned. "Don't be silly. Nobody's going to be hiding in the bushes."

Zev chuckled, crouching as Bandit came to his side. "Give it here, boy." Bandit dropped Carly's green bikini bottom at his feet. Zev picked it up and checked it for holes.

"Guess you and Carly went swimming."

"Cliff diving," Zev said, pocketing her bikini bottom. Cutter's brow wrinkled with disbelief. "Looks like there's a lot we both don't know about Carly. Have you got someplace to go? Because I could use a little help moving things back where they belong after I feed the chickens. We can head inside, grab a cup of coffee, and talk while we work."

"I can stick around for a bit," Cutter said, and they headed for the inn. "I don't know how much time you've spent with Char, but let me give you a little advice. Don't let her hear you call the chickens anything but *Chickendales*."

"Yeah, Beau told me."

Cutter said, "And don't let Carly hear you call her *Carls*. She hates that name."

He fucking *loved* knowing that—and staking claim. "That's because it's my name for her."

"No shit?"

"No shit. You know she hates milk chocolate, right?"

"She's allergic," Cutter said.

Zev laughed and clapped a hand on Cutter's shoulder. "I think it's going to be an interesting morning, my friend."

BY THE TIME Carly got to the shop, it was almost ten o'clock, which should have thrown off her entire morning, but Birdie had saved the day by coming in early and making all the specials. Carly had surprised them both. Despite starting out behind schedule and volleying Birdie's forty-minute interrogation about her night with Zev, Carly was in the *best* mood and more inspired than ever. She'd not only caught up on all her normal tasks quickly, but she'd also come up with a surprise for Zev—a chocolate treasure chest—that she could make for special orders, too. She'd spent the afternoon listening to the mix CDs Zev had made for her their senior year of high school while mixing, baking, and painting molds, creating just the right elements for his surprise.

The kitchen counters were littered with chocolates in various stages of completion. She was making heart-shaped and coin-shaped chocolate truffles with a gold luster coating, chocolate-covered cake balls dipped in sprinkles, white- and milk-chocolate beads, which she was currently stringing together like necklaces, chocolate and candied jewel-shaped treats, and the element she was most proud of, a chocolate treasure chest complete with gold buckles and black straps.

Quinn had stopped in for a quick visit during her lunch break at the bank, and she'd been quizzing Carly about her night with Zev and taste-testing *everything*. With Quinn's hourglass figure, Carly swore the calories went straight to her hips and boobs. She looked like a sexy librarian, sitting across from Carly in her pencil skirt and fancy blouse, her long legs crossed, one high heel bouncing up and down as she eyed the chocolates through her black-framed eyeglasses. She tucked her chestnut hair behind her ear and said, "I think you're nuts. You should let Zev see your place. Any man who can make you forget what day it is deserves a standing ovation in my book."

Quinn had been there when Zev had texted about their date

tonight. They were meeting at four o'clock, but he wanted to pick her up at her place, and Carly still wasn't quite ready for that.

Carly shook her head. "I can't. Once he's there, I can forget having a place where I won't think of him. He's got *that* much of a hold on my heart."

"That's all the more reason to let him in." Quinn plucked another chocolate bead from the tray and ate it.

Carly pointed the needle she was using to thread the chocolate beads onto string and said, "Quinn Finney, if you eat one more bead, I'll thread your fingers onto this string."

Quinn's shoulders sagged. "*Fine.* One day you're going to hire me to work here full time and I'll make them myself."

"Eating the profits. I'll keep that in mind," Carly teased. "Speaking of working here, thank you again for taking next week off from the bank to work the festival. You were such a big help last year. We couldn't do it without you."

"You're very welcome. I'll be here bright and early Sunday morning to help make all the goodies, and I promise not to eat too many."

Carly smiled. "It's okay, Quinn. I just want enough for Zev's surprise."

"I know. Like I said, someday you'll realize I belong here full time."

"You know I want to hire you full time one day. I just don't have the need right now." She heard the bells chime over the door and wondered if customers were coming or going. It had been a madhouse all morning.

Birdie hurried into the kitchen looking eighteen in her purple overall shorts with her hair piled on her head in a messy bun. "*What* is going on today? It's like Grand Central out there.

I swear festivalgoers must be arriving a week early." She tapped on the counter and said, "What did I miss?"

"I was just telling Carly she needed to hire me full time." Quinn pointed to a chocolate truffle and looked inquisitively at Carly, who nodded. "Thank you!" She popped the truffle into her mouth and said, "And one day one of Birdie's fine-ass brothers is going to sweep me off my feet and marry me."

Birdie laughed. "I'm sure any one of them would be happy to sweep you into their *beds*. But I don't want to think about that. *Ew*. I can't unsee that image." She closed her eyes and pressed her fingers to her temples. "*Quinn and Cutter, Quinn and Cutter, Quinn and Cutter.*" Her eyes flew open. "That's better! Let's talk about what Carly's orgasm master has done to her. Look at all this magnificent stuff!"

"Magnificent *and* delicious," Quinn said, eyeing the beads. "You really need to make those beads for the shop. I'd eat them by the bag."

"You can have *two* more," Carly said, earning a cheer from Quinn. She pushed another bead onto the needle. "But I need the rest for Zev. I cannot wait to surprise him."

"Surprise him by letting him in *your* bed," Quinn said with a waggle of her finely manicured brows.

Birdie shot a knowing look at Carly. She and Carly had already had this conversation. Carly shook her head and said, "You don't understand. It's not that simple."

"What's not to understand?" Quinn asked. "You're banging your hot ex, who according to Birdie is sexy as *fudge* and put you in such a deep orgasm coma you couldn't even answer your phone. I'd let a man like that in my bed any day of the week."

"Zev and I have a lot of history. We had a really bad breakup, and now we're figuring out if we can make things work again."

"And he's *madly* in love with her. I could see it in his eyes," Birdie said. "Cutter caught them knocking boots this morning in the wedding tent."

"Birdie! We were *not* knocking boots."

"*Damn.*" Quinn leaned across the counter and said, "My prim-and-proper boss caught *almost* screwing the hottie? Do tell!"

"Coma Girl hasn't stopped smiling since she got here," Birdie said.

Carly rolled her eyes, but the truth was, she hadn't stopped smiling since she'd put on Zev's compression shorts earlier that morning. It was ridiculous that at just shy of thirty years old she'd not only been caught almost having sex, but she'd also done a *sprint of shame* while wrapped in a sheet.

"When do I get to meet the OM?" Quinn asked. "At the bar tonight?"

"OM?" Carly asked.

Quinn whispered, "Orgasm master."

Carly couldn't help but laugh right along with them. "Actually, he's taking me someplace special tonight, so I don't think I'll be there." She said it with a pang of regret. Other than when she was out of town, this would be the first Wednesday night she'd missed with her friends in years, but she and Zev had only five more days, and she didn't want to miss a second of it.

"I don't blame you," Birdie said. "If I had that man in my bed, I wouldn't be leaving it, either."

The bells above the door chimed, and Birdie said, "Duty calls," and headed into the shop.

"I'd better get back to work, too." Quinn pushed from the stool where she was sitting and said, "I'll be back at four to work." She stole a cake ball and hurried out of the kitchen.

Carly loved Quinn and considered herself lucky to have Quinn and Birdie as friends *and* employees. They were smart, reliable, easy to get along with, and courteous to customers. Marie had worked by herself, except during festivals and events when she'd hired friends to help her. During her first few years of business, the people she'd hired had ended up being less than dependable. She'd told Carly that it was easier to offer less and enjoy her job more than to be stressed and babysitting employees.

Carly finished stringing one beaded necklace and had started the next when Birdie peeked into the kitchen, excitement dancing in her eyes.

"Hottie McOrgasm is here to see you," she said in a hushed voice.

"Zev's *here?*" She tried to temper her giddiness.

"Yes, and Quinny took a nice long look at him on her way out. You'll be glad to know she fully approves. I'll keep him busy while you get ready."

"Oh *no* you won't, little Miss Flirt Bunny." The heels of Carly's strappy sandals *clicked* on the floor as she strode past Birdie into the shop.

"You look *hot!*" Birdie whisper-cheered.

Carly didn't often wear sandals with heels, but she'd been in such a good mood that morning, she'd taken a little extra care when choosing her outfit, pairing them with a cute floral miniskirt Birdie had given her last Christmas and a flowy white spaghetti-strap top. Her entire body did a double take as Zev strode toward her in a pair of cargo shorts and a tight T-shirt. She loved that he came to see her in the middle of the day, and she was glad for the extra height from the heels. It put her closer to his mouth.

"Wow, babe. You look gorgeous." He leaned in for a kiss, but the soft press of his lips felt different, *restrained*. "Do you have a minute to talk?"

Her stomach clenched.

He lowered his voice and said, "In private?"

In the space of a second, several heart-wrenching thoughts pummeled her. Had the vessel been arrested and he'd decided to make other arrangements for the animals so he could get back out on the water? Had he decided their lives were too far apart and it was better to end things now? Had Cutter gotten overprotective and started an argument this morning? She swallowed hard, not wanting to believe Zev would cut their time together short, much less end it completely. But the unease in his voice couldn't be ignored.

"Sure, let's take a walk outside." She led him out the front door so he wouldn't see the surprise she was making. As they descended the steps, she said, "Is everything okay?"

"Yeah, there's just something that's been eating away at me all day."

"What is it?" She tried to concentrate on the warm sun kissing her cheeks, the FESTIVAL ON THE GREEN banner hanging across the road, and the colorful decorations on the ornate iron fences and old-fashioned streetlights that lined the brick-paved road, instead of the knots tightening inside her as she waited for him to say more.

"I know I came on strong with you, Carls, and I asked for all of your free time. But I realize now that was selfish. I don't want to impede in your life and make you miss out on the time with your friends, or—"

"Or *what*, Zevy? What are you trying to say?" She felt like she was going to cry. *Great job of managing your expectations, Carly.* Was this the end?

He stopped walking, turning troubled eyes to her. "Babe, Cutter asked if I was coming with you to the Roadhouse tonight. He said you go every week. I don't want to sound like a jealous prick, but if there's some other guy, or parts of your life you don't want me involved in, then we should talk about it."

"What?" She was confused by his question, and her words came out angrily. "I told you there were no other guys."

"Then why didn't you tell me about the Roadhouse?" he asked carefully, not accusatorily. "Is it because you're not sure about us and you want to keep that part of your life separate until you're sure? It's okay if it is. I just want to understand where you're coming from."

"*No*, that's not it at all." She pressed her hand to her chest, trying to calm herself down. "*God*, I thought you didn't want to keep seeing me, or you decided to leave early."

"Aw, shit. Hell no, babe. I'm sorry." He gathered her in his arms and said, "I just don't want to mess this up, and if that means backing off, I'll do it. If you need time with your friends, *take* it. You've got a life, and I want to *add* to it, not make you miss out on it."

"Oh, *Zevy*," she said softly, wanting to bottle up his vulnerability. He was so virile, and he'd been pouring his heart out so openly, it was easy to forget that *he* was risking his heart, too. "Remember how I said that if I learned one thing from Tory's death, it was to spend time with the people I care about while I have the chance?"

"Yes, of course."

"Birdie's family, the Whiskeys, hang out at the Roadhouse. I go Wednesday nights to spend time with them. I didn't tell you because *you're* special to me, too, and selfishly I wanted time alone with you. I wanted to see what you had in store for us tonight. That's all."

A nearly silent laugh fell from his lips. "Really?"

"Yes, really."

"*Christ*, I'm an idiot." He shifted his eyes away.

"No. You're *communicating*, and that's a good thing. It's so much better than taking off and thinking you're doing the right thing when you're not." She took his hand and said, "I'm scared about how all of this will end up, but I don't want to hide you, Zevy. I guess I just wanted to hide *with* you." The relief rolled off him as he pulled her into his arms and told her how much he needed to hear that.

"I want to hide with you, too." He pushed his hands into her hair and pressed his lips to hers, soothing all of her frazzled pieces and lingering as if it were soothing his, too. He kept her close after the kiss, like he'd been doing, and said, "But as much as I want you all to myself, the Whiskeys are important to you, and that makes them important to me. I want to get to know the people who helped you and care about you."

"You do?" She felt teary again. What was going on with her?

"I do, babe. You didn't just lose me when I left. You drifted away from my family, too, and they'd been your family since we were kids. I can't stop thinking about how much worse I made things for you. The last thing I want to do is take you away from the people you love like family. I'd really like to try to work it all in tonight if you don't mind. I'll take you to the place I wanted to surprise you with last night, and afterward we can head over to the Roadhouse." He kissed her softly and said, "And then we'll hide away for the rest of the night. Just the two of us."

191

"That sounds perfect."

"Good. But I still need your address," he said playfully, lightening the mood. "I promise not to leave my scent on your sheets." He flashed a cocky grin and said, "But I make no guarantees about your couch, table, chair…"

She grabbed the front of his shirt, pulling him closer, and said, "In your dreams, Braden." She went up on her toes and kissed him, and then she snuggled against his side as they walked back toward the shop. "I'll meet you at the inn at four o'clock."

"One day you'll realize there are *no* Zev-free zones in your life."

He had no idea how right he was.

"Bring extra clothes so you can stay over. I promise not to let Bandit steal them."

She glanced at him and said, "They're already packed and in my truck."

"Aw, babe," he said happily, and hauled her against him, kissing her slow and sweet, and oh so deliciously. "Thank you."

"I'll have a surprise for you tonight, too," she said.

His brows lifted. "Your address?"

"No," she said with a laugh.

"Sexy lingerie?"

She shook her head. "You'll never guess."

They came to her shop, and he drew her into his arms again, touching his forehead to hers, and said, "Every minute I get with you is a gift. I don't need anything else." He brushed his lips over hers with a twinkle of a tease in his smile and said, "Except maybe your address."

Chapter Twelve

CARLY PULLED UP to the inn at four o'clock on the dot. She'd had butterflies in her stomach all afternoon. She'd seen Zev only five hours ago and she was already bursting to see him again. She felt like a breathless girl of seventeen waiting for him to pick her up for school or seeing him coming toward her in the school hallway, looking at her like the hungry wolf he'd been. She'd felt lucky that of all the girls their age, *wildcat Zev*, the guy so many girls had drooled over, had chosen *her*. But Zev had argued the opposite, that *he* was the lucky one and *she* was his treasure.

As she climbed from her truck, she saw Zev and Bandit sprinting around the side of the inn, but in her mind, she saw him moving in slow motion, his wavy hair bouncing with every powerful step, his muscular arms and legs pumping. He was one heck of a big, beautiful man, and he was all hers. *At least for now.* The thought felt wrong, tumbling through her mind like cold, rough stones. Seeing his vulnerable side earlier and knowing he wanted to meet the people who had become like family to her had touched her just as deeply as the tears, laughter, and toe-curling kisses of the last few days had healed her. A kernel of hope had taken root inside her that maybe this wasn't just a here-and-now thing between them. She *wanted* to hope, to stop forcing herself to think about these six days as temporary, because *temporary* was the last thing she wanted.

An irresistibly devastating grin broke out on Zev's face, and he swept her off her feet, spinning her around as he kissed her, sending Bandit into a barking frenzy.

"I missed you!" Zev said, kissing her again. His eyes gleamed with excitement as he set her feet on the ground. "Are you ready to go? I can't wait to show you your surprise."

"Yes! But one second. I made you something." She ducked into the car, and he ran his palm over her ass. "*Zevy...*" she said, secretly loving that he couldn't get enough of her. She grabbed the bakery box with the surprise she'd worked on all day. She'd never been prouder of something she'd made, and she hoped he liked it.

As she handed it to him, he said, "*Mm.* Goodies made by my chocolate goddess? Thank you." He kissed her again, and then he lifted the top, his expression morphing to one of disbelief. His gaze moved over the chocolate treasure chest with its intricately detailed gold buckles and black straps, filled with chocolate jewels painted in various colors, gold-dusted truffles, chocolate rocks painted to look marbled, and gold and silver bars. The white- and milk-chocolate beaded necklaces she'd made spilled over the sides of the chest, and she'd scattered silver and gold coins along the tray on which the treasure chest sat, which was covered with a mix of ground almonds and brown sugar to look like sand.

"Carls, you *made* this?"

"Just for you!" she said as he set the box on the hood of the truck.

"This is phenomenal." He opened the sides of the box and

pressed them flat, admiring his gift from all angles. "Gold bars, jewels, pearl necklaces…This is a fucking masterpiece, babe. I always knew you were good with your hands, but I had no idea you were so talented with chocolate. Is the sand edible, too?"

"Yes. It's made from almonds and brown sugar," she said, but he was already dabbing his finger in it and licking the mixture off.

"*Mm.* Baby, this is the coolest thing I've ever been given. Thank you." He leaned in for another kiss, and she soaked in his praise.

"I'm so glad you like it. Birdie took a million pictures. We're going to offer a smaller version as a specialty item." She told him about how much fun she'd had making it for him, and about Quinn stealing the beads.

"Someone is as passionate in the kitchen as she is in the bedroom." He drew her into his arms and kissed her jaw. "You're an artist." His eyes heated, and he said, "I want to create body art with those chocolates and eat them off you."

Her body hummed to life as he lowered his lips to hers in another lust-inducing kiss. "Zevy," she whispered. "We can't do this."

"Nobody's here to stop us," he said, kissing her neck.

His whiskers tickled oh so *good.* She'd joked with the girls about doing sexy things with chocolate, but she'd never actually done it. She wanted to give in, to run inside and strip off her clothes for him to ravage her as he wished. But she knew they'd never leave the inn if she did. As he kissed a seriously toe-curling and convincing path up her neck, she forced herself to lean back and said, "Hold that thought."

"I want to hold much more than a thought," he said gruffly, pulling her closer.

His eyes were dark as night, the wicked look in them *almost* too enticing to deny. "This is how we got distracted last night. We both know if we go inside with that on our minds, we're not going to leave until morning. And I'm curious about where you want to take me."

"Sexy girl, I want to *take* you on the table, the stairs, the counters, and everyplace in between, and then I want you to ride me like I'm your stallion, because, baby, I *am*."

Her ability to speak got lost in a sea of desire, and a needy sound fell from her lips. She held on to him, feeling lightheaded as visions of Zev taking her in all those places took hold.

He brushed his scruff over her cheek, sending white-hot sparks rippling down the length of her, and said, "But I'm excited to show you your surprise, too, so we'll just have to rein in our desires until after we meet your friends tonight." He pressed a kiss beside her ear and said, "You'd better stay out here while I put that in the fridge, because I definitely cannot be trusted to keep my hands off you."

Holy moly...

The next few minutes were a blur as Zev took his gift inside and Carly tried to push away the dirty thoughts burning through her mind.

When Zev came back outside, he slapped her butt, jerking her back into reality, and said, "Let's go, hot stuff. Your surprise awaits you." He opened the passenger door and leaned in close, whispering, "Unless you need to change your panties first?"

"Zev!" She swatted him, making him laugh as he scooted out of reach.

He was still chuckling as he went around to the driver's side and opened the door. Bandit bounded onto the seat between them, and Zev climbed in after him.

The drive down the windy mountain roads was a pretty one, filled with gorgeous trees, lush bushes, and wildflowers. As they drove through town, Carly asked where they were going, but Zev just shrugged and sang along to the radio. She gazed out the window lost in her thoughts until the song "Shallow" came on and Zev belted it out at the top of his lungs. He bobbed his head, pretending to sing into a microphone with one hand, the other holding the steering wheel. His voice cracked when he sang along with Lady Gaga, making Carly crack up. When he aimed his fake microphone at her and said, "Sing with me," she belted out the lyrics off-key, too. In their years apart, she'd pretty much convinced herself that she'd romanticized the joy they brought each other, but there was no denying it.

Jillian was right, they were two sides to the same coin.

As the town fell away behind them, the complex where the Real DEAL was being built came into view. Carly thought he'd drive past it, but he turned into the lot and parked beside a Jeep. Construction workers were loading up their trucks at the other side of the lot.

"What are we doing here?"

"You'll see," he said coyly.

"Isn't this owned by your cousins? Treat's brothers?" The construction of the Real DEAL had been front-page news, and the communities of Weston and Allure had rallied behind Dane Braden and his business partners.

"Yeah, it's owned by Dane and Hugh, their brother-in-law, Jack, and our cousin Noah. How do you know Treat?"

Treat Braden was gorgeous at six six with black hair and sharp dark eyes. He was hard to miss, and he exuded an air of authority. But even the self-made billionaire didn't hold a candle to Zev.

"He and Max are two of my favorite customers. I met them when I first came to Colorado and was working for my aunt, before they were married. But *everyone* around here knows Treat. He's done a lot for the community. I was surprised he didn't have his fingers in *this* pot."

Zev cut the engine and said, "I was surprised, too. Did you tell him about us?"

She shook her head. "I didn't even know his first name until he'd been in the shop several times, and I found out he was your cousin weeks later and I was trying to get over you, so…" She shrugged like it was no big deal, but she'd never forget how seeing the love between Treat and Max had sent her thoughts right back to Zev. Their happiness had *almost* made her want to try to find him, which would have been an impossible task.

Zev squeezed her hand, nodding solemnly. "Young and stupid is no excuse, but I am sorry."

"You know what? I didn't realize this before, but now that there has been a little time since our talk at the park, I can see that all the bad feelings I'd been harboring had clouded my vision in another way. I needed the therapy I went through for more than just the breakup and the miscarriage. I needed time to grieve for Tory and time to figure out who I was without *her*. If you had stayed, I might have thrown myself into us and buried some of the grief and rediscovery that I needed."

"I think I needed to deal with Tory's death, too, and Beau's loss of Tory."

She sighed, feeling another level of relief that she hadn't realized she needed. She leaned across the seat, and Bandit licked her arm as she tugged Zev into a kiss and said, "I'm glad you're here. I thought I'd healed, but I think I needed you for that."

"That makes two of us." He stole another kiss before climbing out of the truck.

Bandit leapt out after him, and Carly opened her door as Zev came around to her side of the truck. She took his hand as she stepped out and said, "Are we allowed to be here while it's under construction?"

"Yes." He pointed past the main building and said, "We're going to the third building on the left." He whistled to Bandit, who was sniffing the grass at the edge of the parking lot. "Come on, boy."

Bandit trotted happily beside them as they made their way past the main building.

"Bandit seems like he's been here before."

"He has. This is where we've been spending time when I'm not with you. I'm getting used to having the little thief around. Which reminds me," he said as they passed the second building. "I have your bikini bottom at the inn."

"I wondered where it went."

"Our four-legged thief took it." He ruffled Bandit's fur. "I haven't found your other clothes yet, or my Maroon 5 shirt, but I'll buy you new ones."

"It's fine. I'm sure they'll turn up."

As they passed each of the buildings, Zev told her about the tour Noah had given him and all the cool things that were going to be offered. Most of the information had been noted in the articles she'd read online, but hearing Zev talk about it made it even more exciting.

"Kind of makes you want to borrow a kid or two and bring them here when it's open, huh?" she teased.

"Forget the kid. I'd like to do all of this stuff with you." He pulled open the door to a building. As they made their way down a hall toward a set of double doors, Zev draped an arm around her and said, "Maybe it's time to start a new *one-day* list."

She wanted to whip out her phone and start the list right then. But even though she wanted to hope for more, there was no silencing that little reality-reminding voice in her head, which she'd lived by for so many years. "That's awfully tempting, but we don't even know what's going to happen after this week."

"Sure we do." He winked and hugged her against his side as he said, "We're going to color outside the lines and find a way to make it work."

He sounded so sure of himself, she *wanted* to believe him. A second chance at forever with the man she couldn't help but love was the *only* thing she truly wanted. But they still had obstacles to overcome, and she couldn't just brush those under the carpet. She wanted to believe that she could count on him to stick around if they experienced another devastating blow, but how could she know for sure? What if she just needed him, not because of a dire circumstance, but just *because*? Would he be able to drop everything to be there for her? Could *she* leave her business at the drop of a hat to be there for him? She didn't want to give up what she had there in Colorado, and she definitely didn't want him to give up the life he loved. But at the same time, she *wanted* Zev.

Whoa. What am I doing? She was getting way ahead of herself for a woman who was supposed to be tempering her expectations.

One of the double doors swung open, and a tall, handsome man who looked a lot like Zev but with shorter hair barreled out and said, "Hey, Zev. I was just on my way out. I thought I was going to miss you." Bandit barked and pushed his way between them, wanting all of the guy's attention, which he was happy to give.

"I'm glad you didn't. I wanted you to meet Carly." Zev put a hand on her lower back and said, "Carly, this is my cousin Noah. He's a marine biologist and one of the partners here."

"Hi. It's nice to meet you." Carly extended her hand as Noah came in for a hug, and it turned into an awkward but funny embrace.

Noah clapped Zev on the shoulder and said, "This guy's been talking about you so much, I feel like I already know you."

"I hope that's a good thing," she said, realizing she had no idea what Zev had been doing there.

"It's a very good thing, and I'm hoping it's *enough* of a good thing to convince him to join us in this endeavor. He's got some great ideas about shipwreck exhibits for kids, and he can't dive in New England in the winter. Seems like a match made in heaven, if you ask me. Maybe you can talk some sense into him."

"I told you I'd think about it," Zev said.

Noah scoffed. "We all know what that means."

"I don't understand," Carly said. "You want him to be part of the Real DEAL?"

"Yes. To create exhibits, give talks, workshops for kids," Noah explained. "The possibilities are endless. Listen, I've got to run. I have a meeting with Jack and Hugh in half an hour."

"Is Jack still piloting planes?" Zev asked.

"Yes. That man will never slow down."

"Would you mind texting me his number? I want to talk with him about flying me back to Silver Island Sunday. The inn has a private landing strip. It'd be a hell of a lot easier than hitting the airport."

"Sure, I'll do that now." Noah took out his phone, and as he thumbed out the text, he said, "I've got everything set up for you guys. It's great to meet you, Carly. If you ever want company when this guy's out at sea, you know where to find me."

"Dude, I'm right *here*," Zev protested. "You know the *family knows no boundaries* stuff applies to love *and* war, right? I'm not afraid to take a cousin down to protect my woman."

Noah splayed his hands and said, "I meant *platonically*." He headed down the hall, and Bandit bounded after him. Noah turned, walking backward as he said, "Or *did* I?"

"Get out of here, you fool." Zev laughed. "Bandit! Come here, buddy."

Bandit circled back to them, tail wagging.

"When did you get so possessive?" Carly asked.

"When I realized what a dummy I was for leaving the only woman I'd ever love open to being hit on by guys like him."

She couldn't resist pushing his buttons. "Noah's *cute*. Does he live around here?"

"For now," Zev said with narrowing eyes. A slow grin spread across his face, and he hiked a thumb in the direction Noah had gone. "I hear he's got a micropenis. If you're into that sort of thing, I can probably catch him in the parking lot for you."

She burst into laughter. "You're *terrible!*"

"I was kidding." He hauled her into his arms and said, "I've seen the dude naked, and *you*, my sexy little kitten, are *never* going to get an eyeful of *that*."

"The only man I want an eyeful of is holding me captive and refuses to tell me why we're here. What did Noah mean that he had everything set up for us?"

"You'll see."

"He sounded serious about you joining them. Is that something you're considering?"

"Nah. That was just talk." He pulled open one of the double doors and waved her through. "After you, beautiful."

Carly walked through the door, surprised to find herself in a sparkling-clean laboratory. Her eyes swept over marine tanks and workstations, microscopes and shelves full of equipment. On the far wall were two large chalkboards. One was covered with notes and equations. It had been ages since she'd set foot in any sort of lab, and the sight of it brought a wave of memories, of hopes and dreams that she'd tabled when her life had spiraled out of control. "Is this Noah's lab?"

"Yes." Zev took her hand, leading her through the laboratory.

Bandit sprawled out in a splash of sunlight pouring through a window.

Zev stopped beside two workstations, each set up with a concretion, pneumatic air scribes, and other tools. Carly's pulse quickened. Between the workstations was a table with two computer monitors, each displaying several X-rays. It took only a second for her to realize they were X-rays of the concretions, showing what looked like coins, a spike or a handle to a tool, something rounded that was hard to make out, and—*holy cow*—she spun toward Zev, so excited she could barely speak. "Zevy! Are these from...? Is that...?" She saw the answer in his eyes before he said a word.

"The concretions are from the wreckage I found off Silver Island. I'm hoping something in them will tie them to the *Pride*. I shipped them here right before the wedding. I was going to tell you about them when we were at Silk Hollow, but I decided to surprise you instead. It's been killing me to hold it in." He pointed to an X-ray and said, "I don't know what that coiled thing is. A decorative item, maybe?" He pointed at another X-ray and said, "I'm ninety-nine percent sure that's the trigger guard on a pistol, but it's deep. There's no way I can get anywhere near it this week, but I wanted you to see it. I thought you might want to help extract the artifacts that are closer to the surface of the smaller concretions."

Her jaw dropped. The full weight of what he was offering nearly brought her to tears. "You want me to *help*? You trust me? I haven't done anything like this in years."

"I trust you, babe, and if you can't remember how to do it, I'll show you."

"Oh my gosh. *Zevy*? You want *me* to....Yes. *Yes!* Oh *no*. What if I screw up? This is big. *Huge*. This is the *mother* of all things. Our childhood dreams coming true!" She was rambling, laughing, shaking, and unable to hold back her excitement. She threw her arms around his neck and kissed him *hard*. "*Thank you!* But I can't. I don't want to mess up your chance at fame."

He laughed as he kissed her. "You won't screw up. Remember the club digs we went on? You were overly cautious around artifacts then, and you've only gotten more careful. Carly, this isn't about fame or fortune. These last few days I kept thinking there was more than just luck behind my finding the concretions when I did. *This* has got to be the reason, Carls. They were always meant for *us*, so I could see that magnificent light in your eyes."

"You're *crazy*, Zevy."

"Only about you, babe. I want to share this with you because it's *our* dream, not just mine. You were the driving force that kept me searching, and as horrible as it sounds, if something gets screwed up, then it does, because nothing we find in these concretions will mean more to me than finding them with you."

Ohgodohgodohgod. She was so overwhelmed with emotions, she felt like she might pass out. He *loved* her. Truly, deeply, and probably a little *madly.* He *believed* in her. Maybe it was time to unleash that hope she'd been holding back. Maybe it was time *she* believed in *him.*

"Okay," she said breathlessly, shaking her hands out as if they were wet, but they were just tingling with excitement. "I'll do it."

"Yes!" he shouted, and wrapped her in his arms, causing Bandit to run over.

They kissed a dozen times, and she tried to calm herself down, but it was useless. She had never been more excited in her life, and not just because she was getting a chance to work on concretions from what she truly believed to be *their* ship, which was *insane* in and of itself. But she was doing it with *Zev*! Checking off one of their most anticipated *one-day* items from a list she never thought they'd have a chance to complete.

"Can we do it now?" she asked, bouncing on her toes.

He chuckled and hauled her in for another kiss. "I wouldn't have it any other way."

As Zev went over the equipment and the process, it all came back to her as clear as if she'd done that type of work yesterday. They suited up with lab coats, gloves, surgical masks to prevent the inhalation of concretion dust, headgear with face shields to protect their eyes from flying concretion fragments, and ear protection for the noise. For now, they left the ear protection off.

"How is it possible that you can be covered in protective gear and still be the hottest woman on the planet?"

"This is called *laboratory chic*." She turned in a circle and struck a pose, hip jutting out, arms up. He couldn't see that she was smiling behind the mask, but his smile reached all the way up to his eyes. "I'm thinking of wearing this every day from now on."

"Maybe we'll bring the lab coats home with us. You can prance around with nothing on underneath and see how long it takes before it's on my floor."

"I just might do that." She mentally added *lab coat* to her fantasy list.

"How am I supposed to concentrate on concretions with *that* image in my head?" He gritted his teeth and turned away for a second. He cleared his throat, and when he turned back, he looked at the workstations instead of at her and said, "These face shields need blinders."

He was impossibly cute.

"Err on the side of caution," he said, all business as they took their seats at their workstations. "Be gentle, yet precise. Use the magnifiers when you need them."

When she picked up the air scribe, her hand shook a little. Even though she'd taken a different career path, she'd studied and dreamed about this type of work since second grade. If the artifacts were proven to be from the *Pride*, what they found would be documented in history books. She knew how delicate artifacts could be when encased in concretions. If she screwed any of them up, she would never forgive herself.

No pressure or anything.

As if Zev had heard her thoughts, he nodded reassuringly and said, "You've got this, Carly."

She turned on the air scribe, which was like a mini jack-hammer, and took a moment to get comfortable with the buzzing sound and the vibration. It reminded her of her early days at the shop and of her chocolatier schooling. She turned the scribe off and said, "I just realized that in some ways I've been preparing for this for years. I make chocolate towers that require a gentle touch and a steady hand, and I bet you didn't know there was a science to making chocolate. It takes a great deal of precision and attention." She wondered if Zev could tell that while she was praising her abilities to him, she was also giving herself a little pep talk. "I also took a class to learn how to carve chocolate to create things like animals and designs, which also takes great patience and a light touch. And even though I haven't done this in a while, I never stopped studying the art of conservation through documentaries and books."

He reached over and wrapped his hand around her forearm. "Babe, I believe in you, or you wouldn't be sitting there."

"Thank you," she said as he moved his hand from her arm. She was a little calmer, but acutely aware of Zev watching her.

No, that was wrong.

Admiring her, which made her even more nervous, though it was a good kind of nervous. This was his career, his turn to shine, and he was sharing it with her. He should be watching her every move.

She was *not* going to let him down.

She pushed all thoughts aside, becoming laser focused as she touched the air scribe to the concretion. She'd experienced few things as memorable as this moment, and as the scribe and her gentle, precise touch worked their magic, she knew she'd remember every second of it for the rest of her life.

HOURS PASSED LIKE minutes as they worked on the concretions. It was a meticulous, time-consuming process that required intense focus and left little time for small talk. The vibration of the tool in his hand had nothing on the excitement vibrating around them like a cable binding them together. Their shared energy was everything he remembered and more. His mother used to say that the strength of a relationship could be heard in the silence they shared. He finally understood what that meant. He was stronger, happier, and probably more interesting with Carly by his side.

He turned off the air scribe and stole a glance at Carly, hunkered down over the concretion, completely focused on scraping an area with a small pick. Noah had asked him what it was about her that had kept him hooked for all the years they'd spent apart, and he'd had a hard time putting into words the reasons he'd never felt whole or truly happy without her. He could have listed the obvious: she was beautiful, smart, funny, and they had common interests. But the things that had stayed with him were not that tangible. He'd finally said that when he was with her, he breathed deeper, felt everything more intensely, and loved harder.

He felt that way now as he watched her work. Her lab coat was filthy, but she'd never minded getting dirty. Her hair partially blocked his view of her face, but that beautiful sight was etched in his mind. He knew her brow was furrowed, her lips slightly pursed. Could this have been their lives if he hadn't taken off? Could they have worked through their devastation? Would they have lasted through college, through their growing-up years? They'd never know, but they'd always lived in the *now*, enjoying every minute they'd had together.

This was their new *now*, and he was grabbing that brass ring with both hands.

"*Zev!*" she shouted, startling him from his thoughts. Her eyes were wide as saucers as she waved him over. "I found something!"

He went to check it out, his pulse ratcheting up at her excitement.

"*Look!* That's iron, isn't it?" She used the tip of the pick to show him an area of dark metal about as big around as a dime. "It is, *right*? That's the spike? Or whatever that thing is in the X-ray?"

He grabbed the magnifying glass and inspected the area. "Holy shit, babe. I think you just uncovered the first visible piece of an artifact!"

She shrieked and jumped into his arms. Their protective face masks banged together. Bandit ran over, barking as their voices escalated.

"I can't believe it!" she said as he set her on her feet. "A piece of the wreckage of our ship is *really* in there! I saw the X-rays, but this makes it *real*."

"This is just the beginning, Carls. This discovery is going to be *huge*. I can feel it in my bones."

"Me too! My heart is beating so fast. Whatever this is, it goes straight down. It could take weeks to get it out. Oh, *Zevy*. Thank you for letting me be part of this." Her words flew too fast for him to respond. "I can't believe you're standing here right now and not out there using the metal detector to see if there's more treasure buried deeper. Not that I want you to leave, but I'd give my left arm to get out there and look for more, and it's not even my discovery."

Part of him couldn't believe he was there, either, while more treasures awaited discovery, but not one part of him wanted to leave. He wouldn't trade a second of their time together for anything. Carly might have found a home in the world of chocolate, but this was proof that she also belonged in the world she'd left behind—the world he lived in, where days were spent teetering on the precarious point between adventure and discovery. And he was determined to show her *more* of what she'd been missing.

"If these artifacts *are* from the *Pride*, what will you do with them?" she asked.

"If I gain the rights to the wreckage, my plan is to do the same thing we always talked about doing. Keep history intact and put them in museums for the world to enjoy."

"No *ifs*," she said adamantly, reminding him of the way she'd looked as a younger girl when she'd refused to allow anyone to tell her what to do. "You *have* to gain the rights. How long until your attorney gets the vessel arrested?"

"He's working on it. Hopefully this week. Listen, you know not to talk about all of this to anyone, right? I know you're bursting at the seams, but until the vessel is arrested, which should be taken care of this week, we have to keep this hush-hush or every would-be treasure hunter will be searching the water off Silver Island."

"I know. Don't worry. Will you tell me when the attorney gets it done?" she asked eagerly.

Her question gave him pause. "You'll be the *first* person I tell. Don't you know that?"

"I don't know. That's a lot to hope for when we've only just reconnected. You must have so much on your mind with all of this."

"I do have a lot on my mind, but *you're* at the top of that list, Carly. That's what I've been trying to tell you and show you. There was a world of time and space between us, but you were *always* on my mind. We might not have been together when I discovered these concretions, but in my mind, this has always been *ours*."

She was quiet for a moment, looking at him gratefully through the face shield. "You can't imagine how much that means to me. When I read about your discovery with Luis, I wondered if the notoriety or money had changed you. You've changed in some ways, of course. I mean, you're a grown-up, sexy man," she said cheekily. "But the person you are inside hasn't changed at all. You shared this once-in-a-lifetime experience with me. That was a huge risk for you to take. You really are still the same person you used to be."

"No, Carly. Don't fool yourself into thinking that. I'm smarter now. I'm the same guy who believes it's all about the adventure, but when it comes to you, I'm a much better man."

"I know that. I believe that."

Thank God. "This is pretty cool, huh?"

"More than cool. It's…"

"What?"

She sighed, looking a little bashful. "I had forgotten the feeling of wanting to explore and the thrill of discovering the undiscoverable. You know what I mean?"

"Yeah, I do."

"Can you take a picture for me?" she asked. "I want to always remember this moment. Every last detail."

"Of course I will." He pulled out his phone and said, "I need to get a picture to send to my attorney and my dive team, too. Come here. You hold the concretion." He removed their headgear and face masks and took a picture of Carly holding the concretion and pointing to the element she'd uncovered. Her smile was brighter than the sun. He took a selfie of the two of them with it, and when he took a third, he was kissing Carly's cheek and Bandit was sniffing the concretion.

Carly set the concretion on the table, and as Zev took a few close-ups, she said, "How many people are on your dive team?"

"Just two full time, and two others as needed," he said as he thumbed out a text. "Ford Kincaid and Randi Remington are my full timers. We've worked together for a few years now, and we've done some traveling together in the winters. We call ourselves the Fearless Threesome. You'll like them. Ford is a lot like Graham. He thinks everything through before making a move and he's got strong opinions. He drives Randi crazy sometimes. But it's reciprocated. She can be bossy and just as opinionated." He pocketed his phone. "But we make a great team."

"Oh," she said uneasily.

"What's the matter?"

"Nothing," she said unconvincingly.

"Carls, I know that look in your eyes."

She winced. "I got a little jealous. I'm sorry. I know what you did before we got together is none of my business."

"Jealous of *Randi*?"

She nodded, embarrassment rising in her eyes.

"I'm flattered, but don't be jealous. She's a cool chick, a marine archaeologist, and a vital part of my team. But there's *never* been anything between us. Besides, I'm pretty sure she and Ford could light the ocean on fire if they ever stopped bickering long enough to notice."

Relief eased the tension in her features, but she said, "I will probably hate myself for asking this, but I have to. You said you haven't *clicked* with anyone in your travels and you haven't had a real girlfriend. But clicking and girlfriend or boyfriend can mean different things to different people. Have you traveled with a woman as a…*partner?*"

Holding her gaze, he said, "I was honest about never having a meaningful intimate connection with any other woman. If I was hanging out in one place for a few days, I might hook up with someone a time or two, but that was just, you know, hooking up. There was a woman I surfed with one summer, and we road-tripped up the coast, surfed there for a few days with a group of people we met up with. But she wasn't my *adventure partner*. She was just some chick out having fun."

Carly swallowed hard, and he recognized the hurt in her eyes.

He took off his gloves and cradled her face in his hands, wanting her full attention. "Listen to me, Carly. If I didn't make it clear before, let me make it clear now. I tried to forget what I felt for you at first just to save my sanity. But it was impossible, so I stopped trying. But I *never* tried to replace you. Even at nineteen I knew you were irreplaceable. My heart has always been yours."

"Okay," she said softly.

"You can ask me anything, Carly, and I'll always be honest."

"You can ask me anything, too."

"I didn't hold back this afternoon, did I?"

"No," she said with a smile. "And I loved that."

"If we each try to figure out what the other did for every minute we were apart, we'd lose our minds. You're mine now, and that's what I'm focusing on. But you know me. When we're at the bar tonight, if I have a question about any of the guys, I'll ask. Speaking of which, what time do you want to meet your friends?" He glanced at the clock. It was seven, and they still needed to clean up the lab, take Bandit back to the inn, and get themselves cleaned up.

"Oh my gosh, I forgot. I *really* want to keep working, but I also want you to meet everyone." She glanced at the concretion, clearly torn. "I want to get that artifact out *so* bad, or at least get closer to figuring out exactly what it is. We only have until *Sunday*. That's not that much time for this type of work. Can we come back tomorrow? Do you have time? Is that okay? *Wait*...I'm totally inviting myself to do more work on this. I'm sorry. Was this a one-time thing?" she asked apologetically. "If so, that's okay. I had such an amazing time. I can't thank you enough for reminding me how much I love this type of work. And doing it with you..."

She was talking so fast, he had to laugh. "This wasn't a one-time thing. We can meet any time you want. What time do you get off work tomorrow?"

"Four. But Quinn only works at the bank until noon tomorrow. She's supposed to come in later in the afternoon, but I'll ask her to come in early. There is no way I'm passing up my chance to work on this with you. Can I meet you here around noon?"

"Is that your sneaky way of hinting for a *nooner*?" He stepped closer, enjoying the flush on her cheeks. "If so, we should probably meet at the inn. I don't want to give Noah a show."

"For a guy I had to push into giving up his virginity, you sure think about sex a lot."

"I think a lot about sex with *you*. But hey, I can stop."

He turned to walk away, and she grabbed the sleeve of his lab coat, tugging him back to her with a fierce and somehow also playful expression.

"Don't stop, Zevy. Don't *ever* stop."

Chapter Thirteen

"ONE LAST HANDFUL," Carly said as she buried her arm in the half-empty box of Cap'n Crunch they'd brought to eat on the way to the bar.

They'd been so sidetracked getting *dirty* in the shower, they'd ended up running too late to eat anything real before leaving to meet her friends at the bar. Carly shoved a handful of cereal into her mouth as Zev climbed out of the truck, taking in the parking lot full of motorcycles and pickup trucks. The building looked like a rustic version of Cracker Barrel, with a long front porch and enormous windows. A neon ROADHOUSE sign glowed bright orange above the front doors. Several tough-looking bearded and tattooed guys sporting black leather vests with Dark Knights motorcycle club patches were talking by the front door. Zev couldn't imagine Carly going near a biker hangout, and as he helped her from the truck, he wondered if he was being pranked.

"This is going to be so fun," she said, straightening her cleavage-baring top.

As she ran her hand over the hip of her flouncy miniskirt, looking too damn sexy for a dive like this, Zev looked at the guys by the door. One of them had his eyes locked on Carly.

Zev rolled his shoulders back and stepped into his line of vision, staring him down as he put an arm around Carly.

"Is this some kind of joke?" he asked.

She made a face. "A joke? No. Why?"

"I can't see you in a biker bar."

"Neither could I until I met the Whiskeys. Come on," she said, heading for the entrance. "You'll love them."

He wasn't so sure.

The men turned as they approached, and several pairs of scrutinizing eyes hit Zev at once. *This should be fun.* He tightened his hold on Carly, lifting his chin in greeting. "How's it going?"

The men all answered at once with a round of *goods, fines,* and *not bads.*

"Hi," Carly said cheerily, earning much more enthusiastic greetings from the men.

The big, bearded guy who had been eyeing her stepped forward. He was a good two or three inches taller than Zev and probably thirty pounds heavier. *What is it with the men out here? Do they eat cows for lunch and work out for fun?* His brown hair was short, his beard thick. Tattoos snaked down his arms, and several piercings decorated his ears, septum, and nostril. He locked his eyes on Carly and said, "How about some sugar, princess?"

Zev stepped between them, readying to fuck him up, and said, "Her *sugar* is spoken for."

"Says who?" the guy countered, looming over him. More guys wearing the leather vests with Dark Knights patches stepped beside him, arms crossed, steely scowls offering fair warnings.

Unaffected by the show of force, Zev said, "Your *worst*

nightmare," and stepped closer with his *own* warning. "You show my lady respect. Got it?"

"Oh my gosh, you two, *stop!*" Carly put a hand on each of their chests and pushed them back, earning chuckles from the other guys. "What is it with men and pissing contests? Zev, this is my friend Dare Whiskey. Dare is one of Birdie's brothers. Dare, this is my..." She looked perplexed for a second, then quickly said, "My *Zev*. Zev Braden. He's in town for the week."

My Zev? He guessed that was a hell of a lot better than *friend*. He extended his hand and said, "You talk to all your female friends that way?"

"Only the ones I give a shit about." Dare shook his hand. "You're a Braden? You related to Hal and Rex? They own a ranch in Weston."

"Yeah, I am. Hal is my father's cousin."

Dare gave him another serious once-over and said, "They're good people."

"So am *I*." Zev returned the scrutinizing glance. "You're a Whiskey? Any relation to the Whiskeys in Peaceful Harbor, Maryland?"

"Cousins," Dare answered gruffly.

Zev nodded curtly, and with a smirk, he said, "They're good people."

"Are you two done sizing each other up yet?" Carly asked. "Think you can play nice tonight?"

Zev draped his arm around her and said, "I'm not looking for trouble, babe, but if your friends bring it, I'll give it right back."

A slow smile crept across Dare's face, and he nodded. "See you inside, Braden."

"Looking forward to it, Whiskey. You can buy me a beer."

As they stepped into the loud and fairly crowded bar, Zev did a visual sweep of the room, taking note of the large number of black vests sporting Dark Knights patches. A few dozen tables separated them from the bar across the back wall, behind which two female bartenders—a blonde and a brunette—were serving drinks. A crowd of people to their right cheered on a young guy riding a mechanical bull. To their left were pool tables and a dance floor, where couples were dancing to music that sounded like a cross between country and pop.

Zev led Carly away from the door and into his arms. "Your *Zev...*?"

"I was put on the spot. I didn't know what to say, but I wanted him to know I was *with* you."

"Babe, you claim me any way you want." He kissed her jaw and said, "Your *Zev.*" He brushed his lips beside her ear and whispered, "Your sex slave," earning a press of her body against his. He kissed her cheek and said, "Your boyfriend." Holding her gaze, he said, "Any way you cut it, I'm still yours."

"*Hm.* I kind of like sex slave."

"Carly! Zev!" Birdie waved from a stool at the far end of the bar, where she sat beside a brunette wearing glasses who was chatting with Cutter.

"There's Birdie," Carly said, and they made their way toward the bar. "Sorry about Dare."

"Is he always like that?"

"*No.* I don't know what that was about."

"If the Whiskeys are anything like my family, he was just watching out for you." He had a feeling there would be a lot of that going on tonight. The guy standing beside Cutter turned as they approached. *Cowboy.*

Birdie slipped off her chair, wearing another interesting

outfit—high-waisted polka-dot shorts with a matching crop top and cowgirl boots. She threw her arms around Carly. "I'm so glad you made it!" She greeted Zev with the same enthusiastic embrace. "Remember me? I'm Birdie." Before he could answer, she pulled the other brunette off her stool and said, "And this is Quinn. She works with me and Carly and she's been dying to meet you."

He recognized Quinn, wearing the same tight skirt and cleavage-baring blouse she'd had on earlier in the day when he'd gone to see Carly at work. "Hi, Quinn. I think I passed you leaving the chocolate shop when I was going in to see Carly."

"That was me," Quinn said. "You two are all anyone in here is talking about. It's like someone put out a notice that Carly was bringing a date tonight."

"*What?* Why?" Carly asked.

Birdie swatted the air and said, "Don't worry about it. Let's have fun."

"Hey, darlin'," Cowboy said, embracing Carly. "This guy treating you right?"

Carly rolled her eyes. "*Yes*, Cowboy. Dare just did the whole Neanderthal thing out front. What is up with you guys?"

As she and Cowboy talked, Cutter shook Zev's hand and said, "Glad you made it."

"Thanks, man." Zev put a hand on Carly's back and lowered his voice to say, "Do you still like Sex on the Beach?"

She turned with daggers in her eyes, cheeks flaming. "*Shh.* Yes, but someone will hear you."

"I heard him!" Birdie chimed in as she climbed onto a stool. "And my answer is most definitely *yes!*"

Cowboy glowered at her.

"I meant the *drink*," Zev said to Carly. "That's what you

drank in college." He leaned closer and lowered his voice. "But it's good to know you still like doing it on the beach."

She half scowled, half smiled.

"Now who has sex on the brain?" he whispered in her ear.

"You'd think after our naughty shower I could *stop* thinking about it," she said for his ears only. "You'd better just get me a Blue Moon, or else all I'll think about is the name of the drink."

He winked and said, "One Sex on the Beach it is."

Carly shook her head, and Quinn pulled her into a conversation with Birdie. Zev leaned on the bar to get the bartender's attention.

The tall brunette bartender sauntered over, eyeing Zev curiously. "I haven't seen you before," she said, giving off a tough vibe. "You new in town?"

"Billie," Cutter interrupted. "This is Zev. He's with Carly."

Billie's brown eyes looked between Zev and Carly, who was chatting with Quinn and Birdie. Billie nodded and said, "That makes sense. Carly deserves a man as pretty as she is. What are you, some kind of model?"

"Hardly." Zev chuckled. "I do a little of this and that, but no modeling."

"He's a big-time treasure hunter," Cutter clarified.

Billie scoffed. "People don't really make a living doing that shit."

"You're probably right. Maybe I'm just a model after all. Can I get a Blue Moon and a Guinness, please?"

"Coming right up." Billie went to fill the drinks order.

"Did I just hear that you're a *model*?" Cowboy asked as he sidled up to Zev.

"Underwear model. Calvin Klein mostly, but some Ralph Lauren, Polo, you know, the ones with extra room in the crotch," Zev said as Billie set the drinks in front of him.

"Lucky Carly," Billie said, openly checking out his body as he pulled out his wallet and tossed cash on the bar.

"I'm the lucky one," Zev said. He handed Carly her beer as Dare walked into the bar, heading directly for them. "Here you go, babe."

"Thanks." She flashed a hell of a sexy smile at Zev, then a softer one at Dare, and said, "Hi. You finally made it in."

"Hey, sugar. You good?" Dare asked.

"Always," she said, and turned back to her conversation with the girls.

Cowboy took a swig of his beer, his steely gaze fixed on Zev as he said, "What makes you think you're man enough for her?"

Dare arched a brow, eyeing Zev with amusement in his eyes.

Carly spun around, glowered at Cowboy. "Did you seriously just ask him if he's man enough for me?"

"Damn right I did," Cowboy said. "Models aren't known for being rugged, and we need to know he can protect you."

Carly looked curiously at Zev. "*Models?*"

Zev held her gaze, and a second later he saw the spark of understanding light up her features. *That's right, sweetheart, it's story time.*

"You're a model *and* a treasure hunter?" Quinn asked excitedly. "I bet that's *so* fun. No wonder you're so fit."

"I bet he knows tons of hot guys," Birdie chimed in, earning scowls from her brothers.

"Modeling is a rough gig," Zev said, enjoying the smirk on Carly's beautiful face. "You know, posing for long periods, staying in shape, and all that. But it has its benefits, and yeah, I know most of the A-listers."

"He modeled with the *Sports Illustrated* models in Tanzania last winter, right, Zev?" Carly said, falling right into their old storytelling days.

"I sure did, and not one of them was as hot as you." He pulled her into his arms and kissed her.

"She's so lucky," Quinn said.

Cowboy made a disgruntled noise and said, "I'm still waiting for my answer."

"Trust me, Cowboy, Zev is *all* man," Carly said arrogantly.

"I'm with Carly," Birdie said. "Just *look* at him."

"It's okay, girls. I get it. These guys are boot-wearing, hat-tipping, hardworking men. They just want to make sure this *pretty boy* can handle anything that comes my way. I respect that." Zev cocked a grin and said, "Try to keep up, boys, because I'm only going to say this once. I free dive, deep-sea dive, base jump, skydive, and I've climbed the Andes. *Twice.* I dove off the cliffs at Devil's Canyon, trekked through deserts, sailed through the stormiest of seas, and surfed forty-foot waves." He took a drink and said, "Oh yeah, I also revived a guy who had drowned in Portugal. I'm *pretty sure* I'm man enough for Carly."

Cutter and Cowboy exchanged a look that clearly said *damn...*

"Pretty impressive. I didn't know models did those things." Cowboy took another swig of his beer.

Zev stifled a laugh and said, "There's usually more to people than meets the eye."

"A *lot* more," Carly added. "Especially below the waist."

Birdie and Quinn burst into laughter. Zev drew Carly into a long, slow *claim* of a kiss. *Eat it up, Cowboy, because she's all mine.*

"Lucky is right," Birdie said, earning an "Mm-hm" from

Quinn.

Cowboy cleared his throat. "You ever ridden a bull?" he asked gruffly.

"Aw, *shit*. Here we go," Dare said.

Zev shook his head. "Can't say that I have, but I'm up for anything."

"Cowboy, what are you doing?" Carly demanded. "Did Billie put testosterone in all your drinks tonight? Zev, you do *not* have to prove anything to him."

"I've got this, babe," Zev said with a wink.

"Around these parts, there's only one measure of manliness. And right now, my baby *sister* holds the record."

"Uh-oh." Birdie glanced at Carly and said, "I think you'd better prepare him for a black-and-blue butt."

Zev pointed his beer bottle at Cowboy and said, "I was wondering why my gorgeous girl was still single with all you big cowboys around. But if a cute little thing like Birdie holds the *manliest* record in town, that pretty much explains it all, doesn't it?"

Cowboy glowered, Dare and Cutter chuckled, and the girls had a freaking laughfest.

Zev sucked down his beer and said, "Bring. It. *On*."

CARLY ADMIRED ZEV'S ability to stand up to any challenge, but she'd seen bigger men than him fall off the mechanical bull. The last thing she wanted was for him to get hurt and not be able to dive next week, or to get humiliated in front of Cowboy, who she was ready to *throttle*. "Zev, please don't do this. You could get hurt," she pleaded as they made their way through the crowd.

"Have faith, babe," Zev said, watching a guy ride the bull. "There's nothing I can't do."

"I want to believe that, but you have no idea how hard it is to ride that thing." She turned to Birdie and said, "*Tell him,* Birdie."

"She's right, Zev. It's an ass-kicker for sure. I've been riding since I was a little girl, but it definitely takes finesse. You need to move *with* it, like you're making love to it. Like this." Birdie started undulating her pelvis.

"Damn it, Birdie!" Dare growled, turning a dark stare toward the guys ogling his younger sister. He turned that stare on Birdie, who was still undulating, and said, "*Stop. Now.*"

Birdie huffed and put her hands on her hips. "I'm just showing Zev how to finesse the bull."

"Sure you are, Bird," Dare said with a shake of his head. "You keep it up and I'm going to have to *finesse* the fuck out of a few of the guys in here."

"Dare," Carly interrupted, "*please* tell Zev not to do it."

"I've got this, Carls," Zev reassured her again, still studying the guy on the bull. "Piece of cake."

"You're my kind of guy, Braden. Good luck, man," Dare said, giving Zev a fist bump.

"What is *wrong* with everyone tonight?" Carly complained as the rider left the ring, and Cowboy strode into it.

Cowboy held his hands up and said, "We have a special guest here today. You might recognize him from *Sports Illustrated.* He's a hotshot model."

"*Ohmygod,*" Carly said, leaning defeatedly against Zev. "You should probably clear that up."

Zev gave her a quick kiss and said, "But it's so fun seeing him buying into it."

"Let's hear it for Zev Braden!" Cowboy shouted.

The crowd whooped and applauded as Zev stepped into the ring waving both hands, totally hamming it up as he took a bow. He set his eyes on Carly and hollered, "This one's for you, babe!" He put his fingers to his mouth and tossed her a kiss just like he used to.

Despite her worries about Zev getting hurt, Carly couldn't stop grinning as she reached up and pretended to catch the kiss midair.

"God, I love him," Quinn said.

Me too.

Dare and Cutter flanked Carly. She scowled at them. "What the hell, you guys? You could have stopped this." Cowboy didn't know about Zev and Carly's past, and for the life of her, she had no idea why Cowboy was being so hard on him.

"There's no stopping this," Cutter said. "You know how Cowboy is. Once he starts, he doesn't back down until he *wins* or someone puts him in his place."

"So do it," Carly said. "Put him in his place."

Cutter held his hands up in surrender. "Hey, I told Cowboy that I had a long talk with Zev and that I like him. I respect him. He obviously has your best interests at heart. But Cowboy had a thing for you when you first got into town. He's not going to let just anyone win your heart without making sure the guy can handle anything."

"Cowboy had a thing for me?" How had she missed that? She glanced at Zev, who was checking out the mechanical bull.

"A heck of a crush for a while when you first moved here," Cutter explained. "But you showed no interest. He's over it, but he'll always watch out for you."

"Great," she said sarcastically.

"Your new man can handle himself," Dare said gruffly. "Check it out. He's about to climb on."

Cowboy walked out of the ring, and Zev took *off* his boots and socks. He stripped off his shirt, making a show of churning his hips and flexing his abs, causing a cacophony of howls, cheers, and *take it all off*s.

What the heck are you doing?

As if Zev's ears were burning, his eyes found hers and he winked. He stretched his neck to the left and right, shook out his arms and legs, and rolled his shoulders back, as women screamed for him to take off his pants. Jealousy prickled Carly's limbs, but his eyes were still locked on her, turning her jealousy into something much hotter and more welcome.

"What the hell is he doing?" Cutter asked as Cowboy joined them.

"Fuck if I know," Dare said. "But he's got all the girls going wild."

Carly rolled her eyes.

"Guess all he knows how to do is take off his clothes." Cowboy chuckled.

"If he gets hurt, Cowboy, I'm going to *kill* you," Carly said as Zev mounted the mechanical bull *backward*. "Oh *no*. Cowboy! Help him!"

The crowd laughed and called out for Zev to turn around.

"Jesus, Carly. Could you have picked more of a pansy?" Cowboy headed for the ring.

Zev pointed his finger like a gun at Cowboy and said, "I've got this, tough guy. Turn this kitten on."

"You've got to turn around," Cowboy shouted.

"Nah, let's have some fun!" Zev made a whirling sign with his finger, and the mechanical bull began moving.

Carly watched with her heart in her throat as Zev balanced on the bull as it jerked forward and back, as if he were getting used to the motion. After a few seconds, the butt of the bull tipped up, and Zev pushed off with his hands and kicked his feet up behind him all at once, landing on the bull like he was riding a surfboard.

The crowd went wild—and so did Carly. Women jumped up and down screaming and cheering, men shouted and whistled, and Zev hammed it up. He jumped up as the bull jerked and spun, and he landed on his feet facing the other direction, moving in sync with every jolt of the bull. His abs flexed enticingly, turning Carly's worries to white-hot lust. The bull spun, and Zev jumped, landing on his ass straddling the bull. He feigned a hurt expression, which made the crowd whoop even louder. Carly laughed, cheering him on as he popped to his feet again and shimmied with his arms out to his sides. He crouched with the spin of the bull, balancing like a surfer, and continued his shenanigans until every person in the bar was gathered around the ring, enthralled by Zev.

Carly nudged Cowboy and said, "What do you think of my *pansy* man now?"

"He's not really a model, is he?" Cowboy asked.

Carly looked at Zev riding that mechanical bull and her heart swelled. "Today he's a model. Tomorrow who knows what he'll be?" *I don't really care what he is, as long as he's with me.* As Zev showed off his skills, she turned to Cowboy and said, "I know you worry about me, and I appreciate it more than you can imagine."

"I just don't want you to get hurt, darlin'."

"Neither do I. But no relationship comes without risks." As she said it, she realized how true it was. Their risks might be bigger than some, but that didn't mean they had to be show-stoppers.

"You've got a point, and the guy must really care about you to put up with my shit and lay himself out there like this." Cowboy's expression turned serious, and he said, "You've never brought a date on a Wednesday night before. You obviously really dig this dude. How long have you known him?"

"We grew up together, and we dated for a really long time. You once told me that a person found their horse when they looked into its eyes and saw a piece of themselves looking back. The first time I experienced anything like that was in Zev's eyes when we were in second grade, and I still see it, stronger than ever. He's a good man, Cowboy, and so are you. I hope you guys can be friends." Carly could hardly hear herself think over the cheers of the crowd as the bull slowed to a stop.

Zev's eyes collided with hers, and all that noise faded away, except for the sizzle and pop of the inferno blazing between them.

Chapter Fourteen

ZEV STOOD AT the bar watching Carly and her friends sitting around the table as he waited for Billie, who was busy wiping down the other end of the bar, to make her way down to him. They'd closed the place down. The Roadhouse was empty save for Carly's friends, and Zev was in no hurry to leave. He'd gotten to know each of her friends, and their protective scrutiny had quickly changed to good-natured ribbing. Her friends had been sharing stories about *life with Carly* all evening, stories about fun times they'd had and the different ways they'd taken care of each other. Though they'd described the same warm, caring person Zev had always loved, the woman they had embraced as one of their own was a careful homebody, not the adventure seeker he knew her to be. It was clear that they adored her just as she was, but Zev had no doubt that as Carly's old self rose to the surface, her friends would love those parts, too.

"What can I get you, pretty boy?" Billie asked teasingly.

Zev had learned that Billie and her sister, Bobbie, ran the bar, which was owned by their father, Manny, another Dark Knight. "Two ice waters, please." He and Carly had been furtively touching and taunting each other under the table, and it had been hell trying to keep a straight face. He hoped the ice water would help cool him down.

Billie set the glasses on the bar and said, "That was quite a show you put on. Not many men will stand up to Cowboy."

"Then they're not really men, are they?" He glanced at Carly and said, "I've learned not to let fear stand in my way, especially when it comes to that woman right there. I've learned to fight demons, and they are a hell of a lot tougher than a mechanical bull." He picked up the glasses and said, "Thanks for these."

As Zev made his way back to the table, another round of laughter rang out. He liked Carly's friends, and he fit in with them despite their rocky start. He had been alone for so many years he'd forgotten what it was like to *belong* with a group of people other than his family and his dive crew. But in the same way that he had never connected with another woman, he'd also never found his place among bigger groups of would-be friends. Something had always been missing. And that *something* was currently joking around with the others, her sweet, unforgettable laughter drawing him in.

He set the glasses down and sat beside Carly, trying not to disrupt Quinn while she told a story about her brother, who was away visiting friends for the next several weeks.

Carly leaned closer and whispered, "I missed you."

Those three words hit him right in the center of his chest. "I'll fill up all your lonely parts later, when we're alone." Her cheeks pinked up, and he pressed his lips to hers.

"Are you ever going to tell me what your powwow with Birdie and Cutter was about when I was dancing with Quinn?" she asked quietly.

"Shh." He pointed to his ear, then to Quinn, as if he want-

231

ed to hear what she was saying. But in truth, he didn't want to tell Carly that Birdie and Cutter were helping him with a little surprise.

"That spells *freedom* to me, Quinny," Birdie said. "I can't get rid of my brothers for a week, much less several. Zev, you said you only go home a couple times a year. Don't you miss your family?"

"Sure, but we keep in touch by phone and video chat. And if they're traveling and the timing works out, sometimes we meet up wherever they are." He had become adept at explaining himself without going into detail about how painful it was to go back to Pleasant Hill. He wondered if it would be easier to go home now that he and Carly had reconnected. He imagined it would, since everything seemed better with her by his side. But he knew he was getting ahead of himself. Even though he believed they'd figure out a way to make things work, he knew careful Carly needed more time to trust him not to take off again.

"Gosh, I don't think I could do that." A shimmer of mischief rose in Birdie's eyes, and she said, "I mean, my brothers are a pain sometimes, but I don't think *they* could live without me."

"*You*, we'd miss." Cowboy pointed at Dare and said, "But this guy? Him, we can spare."

Dare chuckled. "You'd be lost without me."

"Like hell we would," Cowboy said.

"The women around here sure would be," Quinn chimed in. "Dare's the best dancer around."

Cowboy scoffed. "*Hardly.* I've got moves. I just like to show them off in the bedroom." He fist-bumped Zev and they both laughed.

Quinn rolled her eyes. "*No one* dances as well as Dare."

Zev looked at Dare, who was eating up Quinn's praise, and said, "You're that good, huh?"

"A wise man once said there's usually more to people than meets the eye." Dare nodded and took a drink of his beer.

"He doesn't just dance," Quinn said. "He dances *on* the bar."

"The last time Dare pulled a *Coyote Ugly*, an out-of-towner stuck a twenty-dollar bill in his pants." Cowboy laughed and said, "It was a *dude!*"

"And what'd this guy do?" Cutter hiked a thumb at Dare and said, "Gave him an *encore.*"

They all cracked up. Zev couldn't *stop* laughing as he tried to picture the badass biker dancing, much less dancing *on* a bar.

"What're you laughing at, Braden?" Dare asked.

"I can't get over the fact that you actually danced *on* the bar."

"I can't get over the fact that you don't," Dare said, and high-fived Cowboy.

Zev smirked. "Who says I don't?"

"You tell 'em, man." Cutter fist-bumped Zev.

"Forget telling us. *Show* us!" Birdie dug into her purse and whipped out a twenty-dollar bill, waving it in the air.

"Yes!" Quinn cheered, jumping to her feet. "Cowboy and Cutter, too! Me, Birdie, and Carly will be the judges to see who's got the hottest moves!"

"*Not* happening, girlie." Cutter put a hand on her shoulder, pulling her back down to her seat beside him.

"*Fine,*" Quinn said sharply. "Then you can sit this one out and just the *real* men will dance."

"That's right, darlin'." Cowboy winked at Quinn; then he

looked at Dare and Zev and said, "What do you think? Dance off on the bar?"

Birdie started chanting, *"Dance off! Dance off!"*

"No way, Birdie," Carly said. "You've ogled my man enough. And, Cowboy, didn't you learn your lesson with the mechanical bull? Zev's moves will light that bar on fire." She pushed to her feet and pulled Zev up to his. "The only dancing Zev is doing is with *me*. Right now, on the dance floor."

"Now, there's an offer I can't refuse." Zev put his arm around Carly and they headed for the dance floor.

"Are you sick of being here yet?" Carly asked.

"Not at all. I've had a great time, and I'm glad we came. I've learned so much about you, your life here, and your friends."

"They can be a lot to take in."

"I like them, Carls, and I'm glad they're watching out for you." He gathered her in his arms and began swaying to a slow country song. He brushed his cheek along hers and said, "It's been so long since we've danced together, I forgot how good it feels."

"Senior prom," she said softly. "That was our last slow dance."

"I've missed this, babe. I've missed out on doing so many things with you," he said, thinking of her friends' stories. "I wish I had been there for the sled-riding fiascos and the horseback trail rides your friends told me about." They'd told him so many stories, he couldn't list them all, though he remembered every word about pie-eating contests at fall festivals and breakfasts with the Whiskeys.

"You *can* be there for sled riding if you want to, since you can't dive in New England in the winter," she said.

"Trust me, I *will* be." But for how long? And would it be

enough? Could he really calm the restless nomad inside him and be happy staying in one place for a while if that was what Carly needed? He didn't know if he could, but he sure as hell wanted to try. "When Cutter told that story about the time you were sick and the Whiskeys took turns helping Birdie run the shop and nursing you back to health, all I could think about was that I wish I had been there then, too."

"That was an awful virus. It was before I hired Quinn, or else I wouldn't have had to bother them. They saved me."

"From what they said, you've been there for them just as often. It's obvious that you're as important to your friends as they are to you."

"I had no idea they were such blabbermouths," she said with an endearing lilt to her voice.

"They love you." He kissed her softly and said, "I like knowing that you don't take catering gigs that would disrupt your Wednesday-night get-togethers and that you go to Redemption Ranch Friendsgivings with other people the ranch has helped. They filled in a lot of gaps for me. I didn't know that you went home to Pleasant Hill for all the big holidays, or that you celebrate with the Whiskeys before leaving town. I'm glad I learned those things about you. I'd love to check out the ranch sometime and meet the other people who helped you."

"You would? You can't imagine how much that means to me."

"Yes, I can. It's probably about half as much as you mean to me." The song ended and a faster one began, but Carly and Zev continued slow dancing.

Quinn and Birdie breezed onto the dance floor, and Birdie said, "Hey, snuggle bunnies. We convinced the guys to dance with us."

Dare gyrated his hips and rocked his shoulders, dirty dancing his way over to the girls, showing off his awesome dance moves. "Come on, Braden. You've got to keep up."

"Told you he had moves," Quinn said.

Cutter looked quizzically at Carly and Zev slow dancing and said, "Dude, can you even *hear* the beat?"

"At least do the country two-step," Cowboy added.

"It's called *romance*, you goofs. You should be taking notes." Quinn grabbed them both by the wrists and dragged them away.

Zev chuckled as the others began dancing in sync with some kind of fancy footwork. The guys would probably always harass him, but they had essentially given him their blessing earlier in the night. Not that Zev needed it, but for Carly's sake he was glad they approved.

As he gazed into her eyes, other things became crystal clear. "Remember when I said that the universe chose now to bring us back together?" She nodded, and he said, "I think I figured out why I needed you so badly."

"Why?" Her eyes glittered with anticipation.

"Because I'm the guy who isn't afraid to die but is terrified of losing the people I love. I thought if I put distance between us, and between me and my family, I could disconnect enough that if something terrible were to happen to any of you, it would be easier to deal with."

"Zevy," she said, full of emotion. "That's the saddest thing I've heard in a long time. We were so close, and you and your family were, too. You gave up so much."

"I see that now. I needed to see you, Carls, to *feel* the thunder in my chest and the intensity of my love for you in order to realize that love doesn't work that way. If we hadn't reconnected and something had happened, it *still* would have killed me. And I think I needed to spend time with you and your friends to remember that I enjoy connecting with people as much as I enjoy disappearing into adventures. I've been so busy running from our past, from the hurt I caused you and my family, I'd forgotten how *valuable* love and friendships are. I needed you to teach me what you learned years ago—that I should be spending time with the people I care about before it's too late."

"Oh, Zev," she said softly. "I think you might be right."

"I *know* I am. I always thought I was brave for the risks I took, but you're the brave one, Carls. You never let Tory's death stop you from forming relationships with other people. You've forged on, put down roots, and built a life, while I've lost out on years with everyone I care about."

"You've built a life, too, Zev. You've done things most men could never do."

"Professionally, *yes*. But I've done everything I could *not* to put down roots." He slid his hand to the nape of her neck, brushing his thumb over her warm skin, and said, "I am so lucky you're willing to give me a second chance."

"After the way I left you in Mexico, I'm just as lucky."

He lowered his lips to hers, and from the moment their mouths connected, he sensed a difference. She had kissed him eagerly every time since they'd reconnected, but this was more purposeful, *possessive*. Like she was opening up to *them* even more, *believing* in them. He crushed her to him, taking the kiss deeper, wanting to live in that moment until they reached the next level, the one where she let go of *all* her doubts.

"Now, that's a kiss!" Birdie cheered.

"Dude, let her up for air," Cutter hollered.

"Jealous, Cutter?" Quinn said. "Let them have their fun."

As their lips parted, lust simmered in Carly's eyes. Zev pressed a kiss beside her ear and said, "How about I take you back to the inn and show you just how grateful I am?"

Chapter Fifteen

CARLY'S BODY WAS on *fire* as they stumbled through the front door of the inn, kissing and groping. She was vaguely aware of Bandit darting past them to get outside. Zev had started to show her how *grateful* he was at every red light as they drove through town on their way back to the inn. And on the ride up the mountain *she'd* shown *him* how grateful she was with her hands *and* mouth. He hadn't bothered to button or zip his jeans when they'd gotten out of the truck.

"Should we wait for Bandit?" she panted out between kisses. She was desperate to get her mouth on Zev, tempted to get down on her knees right there in the foyer if he said they should wait. It was the best kind of torture watching him ride the bull, shirtless and sexy as sin and holding his own with her friends. Never in her life did she think *that* would be an aphrodisiac, but it was.

"Baby, you're lucky I didn't pull the truck over on the side of the road and take my fill. He can come when he's ready—and so can *we*." He lifted her into his arms, leaving the front door open as he carried her deeper into the inn and crushed his mouth to hers.

"What if a raccoon comes in?" she asked against his lips.

"That's what Bandit is for." He stepped over a canteen as they passed the stairs, heading for the kitchen, and said, "That and stealing my shit."

"Where are you going?"

His lips curved up in a devilish grin and he said, "I believe we have a little treasure hunting to do."

"In the kitche—" *The chocolate!* How could she have forgotten? Butterflies took flight in her belly.

The kitchen was dark, save for the moonlight spilling in through the windows and door. Zev set her on the edge of the large kitchen table. As he took the treasure chest out of the refrigerator and set it beside her, he said, "I've been thinking about doing this with you all evening."

She licked her lips, and the muscles in his jaw twitched, turning her on even more.

He held her gaze as he took off her sandals and ran his hands down her calves pressing a kiss above one knee. Her body vibrated with anticipation as he peered intently into the treasure chest, picking up a chocolate beaded necklace. A wolfish grin spread across his face as he placed it next to her. He studied the contents of the chest, carefully selecting two gold bars, one jewel, and one gold-dusted truffle. Without a word, he returned the chest to the fridge and retrieved a plate, moving quickly as he put the bars on the plate and into the microwave for several seconds, softening them.

Holy hotness.

The thought of him planning this out, eagerly waiting to touch her, to *take* her, made her even more nervous. He set the plate beside her, and their gazes collided. He took off his boots and stripped off his clothes, his eyes drilling into her. She tried to keep her eyes trained on his, but desire sent them lower, to his formidable erection straining behind his black boxer briefs. She bit her lower lip, trying to silence the hungry sounds coming out of her mouth as he wedged his beautiful body between her legs. He threaded both hands into her hair, bringing her mouth to his, swallowing her needy sounds with a savagely intense kiss. He tasted of beer, seduction, and everything she'd been missing for so long. His tongue swept demandingly over hers, his whiskers scratching her cheeks. His aggression was enticing, the feel of him, addicting. She wrapped her legs around him, pouring everything she had into their connection. He sank deeper into the kiss. She wanted this moment to last forever, and at the same time she was eager to explore this uncharted territory with him.

His hot mouth worked its way down her neck, nipping and kissing. He lifted the hem of her shirt and said, "This pretty top needs to go." He stripped it off and set it on a chair, his eyes brimming with desire, moving leisurely over her lace bra. "You know I love you in lace." He traced the swell of her breasts with his fingers and said, "You're so beautiful, Carly. I want to memorize every inch of you."

The love in his voice, and his words, tunneled beneath her skin, taking root beside her heart.

He dragged one finger down the center of her chest and unhooked her bra. Dark, greedy eyes flicked up to hers as he slid it off her shoulders, like he needed to see the inferno he caused. She could barely breathe, slave to the desire pulsing through her. Her fingers curled around the edges of the table. He picked up a gold chocolate bar, bringing it to her mouth, and said, "Lick it, baby," masterfully coaxing her into submission.

Lust pooled in her core as she licked the length of the sweet candy.

"*Fuck*," he rasped. "We're definitely doing more of this."

He dragged the wet chocolate down her chest, across one breast, circling her nipple, and slowly painted a trail to the other side, where he went over and around the taut peak. He lifted the bar to her lips again, and when she opened her mouth, he said, "Lick it like it's my cock."

His dirty demand made her ache for his touch. He moved the chocolate in and out of her mouth as if he were fucking it, watching so intently as she teased it with her tongue, she dug her nails into the wooden table. When he took the candy out of her mouth, his other hand dove into her hair, and he crushed his mouth to hers, agonizingly and deliciously *fierce*, alighting every nerve in her body. She arched into him, grabbing his hair, holding his mouth to hers as he ground against her center. Passion pounded through her as they devoured each other. He made a guttural, masculine noise, and she felt the chocolate moving up and down her belly and over her ribs.

He broke their kiss, both of them panting, their noses touching as he said, "I want to stay right here, kissing you forever."

She never knew words could feel so big, but his words dripped with as much sincerity as desire.

He drew back slowly, his eyes searing a path down her body, and that seductive, hungry grin returned. She loved that grin and the dirty promises it held. He put the remainder of the chocolate in his mouth and brought his chocolate-covered fingers to hers. She had barely begun licking them, when he kissed her again, slower this time, but every bit as potent. "Carly," he said against her lips. "*God...*"

He guided her hands to the table and curled his around her hips, holding tight as he lowered his mouth to the center of her chest, licking and kissing his way down the chocolate path. Every slick of his tongue sent scintillating pleasures through her. She pressed her shoulders back, thrusting her chest forward as he dragged his tongue around her nipple, following the chocolate path. His eyes met hers and he lowered his mouth over one taut peak, sucking *hard*. Heat skated along her flesh. He teased her with his tongue, licking and flicking, and she swore she felt it between her legs. He tasted his way to her other breast, giving it the same exquisite treatment. The room spun as pleasure consumed her, moans and whimpers escaped, and she didn't care how loud she was. Let him *hear* what he did to her and bask in the glory of his talents.

As he feasted his way down her belly and ribs, it tickled and delighted her in all the best ways. She was so needy, so *greedy* for him, demands kept slipping out.

"*There…Yes…Don't stop…Suck harder…Lick me again…*"

He granted her every wish. When he lifted his mouth from her belly, cool air washed over the wetness he left, causing her to shiver. He pushed his hands up her legs, taking her miniskirt with them, and squeezed her thighs. His thumbs brushed over her panties between her legs, and he made a growling noise. His eyes narrowed, and those muscles in his jaw bunched repeatedly. He looked like he was going to tear off her panties with his teeth and bury his face between her legs right then. Her sex clenched with anticipation, and the wickedness in his eyes told her how much he enjoyed having that effect on her.

"Soon, baby," he said gruffly, and reached around her to unzip her skirt.

His fingers lingered there, moving up and down between her ass and the bottom of her spine. She closed her eyes at the tantalizing tease.

He continued in slow strokes, dipping a little lower between her cheeks with each one, and said, "That's going to be my tongue later."

Yes, please.

"Lift up, sexy girl. We don't want to ruin your skirt."

Using his shoulders for leverage, she lifted her bottom off the table, and he stripped the skirt down her legs, dropping it on the chair with her other clothes. He placed several sweet kisses over her tattoo, his eyes flicking up to hers. And then he picked up the chocolate necklace and dangled it from his finger as he licked up the string of beads.

Good Lord. Everything he did made her want him even more desperately.

He dragged the necklace over her breasts, down her belly, and over her thighs. Every touch of the sticky chocolate made her ache for more. He moved the necklace over her foot and up her leg like a garter, wrapped his hands around her hips, and bent at the waist to kiss the crest of each thigh. She clutched his forearms as he dragged his tongue along her inner thigh and over the chocolates, where he sealed his mouth, licking and sucking, working all sorts of exhilarating magic. He was relentless, drenching her thighs with attention. He stopped just short of her panties, lingering there, his hot breath coasting over her center. She tried to squeeze her legs together to lessen her trembling, but he quickly lowered his chin, his whiskers chafing her inner thighs, and slicked his tongue along her damp panties.

"*Zevy*—" she pleaded, rocking her hips.

He brushed his chin over her panties. His whiskers poked through the material, sending prickles of pleasure coursing through her. She whimpered, and he grinned as she dug her fingernails into his skin. He made a gruff, appreciative noise and kissed each of her thighs so tenderly, the conflicting emotions were torturous.

He rose to his full height, his eyes blazing as he pushed her hand into his underwear and demanded, "*Stroke me.*" He crushed his mouth to hers.

No demand necessary. She wanted this more than she wanted her next breath. His demand made it all the more titillating. He sucked her tongue, and she stroked him tighter. He moaned into their kisses, his hips thrusting, fucking her hand as he ate at her mouth. She stroked faster—he kissed deeper. She squeezed tighter—he thrust harder. He leaned into the kiss, opening his mouth wider, his tongue plunging over hers. He was a little rough, and she *loved* it. A long, rumbling groan flew from his lungs as he tore his mouth away and pulled her hand from his underwear, his face a mask of restraint as he said, "I fucking love your mouth, and your hands."

"I fucking love your cock," she countered boldly. "I want to *suck* it."

"Oh, you *will*," he promised.

He hauled her to the edge of the table, pushed his hands into the sides of her panties, palming her ass. He ground against her center, taking her in another punishingly intense kiss. Angling his hips, he created exquisite friction on her most sensitive nerves. Lust pooled inside her, pounding through her chest. Her nipples burned, the tease of an orgasm tugging at her periphery. She kissed him harder, willing it to take hold. He shifted his hands lower, lifting and angling her forward so she was rubbing against the head of his cock. She wrapped her arms tighter around him, her thighs flexing as his fingers moved through her wetness. Tingling sensations consumed her, stealing her breath. He intensified his efforts, applying pressure in all the right places, sending her spiraling into ecstasy. She tore her mouth away, gasping for air as her body pulsed and bucked. He sealed his mouth over her neck, setting her off like a volcano.

"*Don't stop!*" she pleaded as her climax, and her *man*, ravaged her.

When she finally collapsed, boneless and dizzy, in his arms, he whispered in her ear, "I've got you, babe."

He showered her with kisses, whispering sweetnesses between each press of his lips. When her breathing finally calmed, he drew back with a predatory look in his eyes, reviving all of her tired parts, as he said, "Now, to enjoy the *rest* of my *treasure*." He eyed the rest of the chocolates he'd set out, and then those hungry eyes hit hers. He took her face between his hands and said, "I'm a greedy bastard for you. I don't want anything changing your perfect taste."

His lips covered hers so tenderly, she went soft in his arms. He continued kissing her as he guided her hands to the table behind her hips. When their lips parted, he stripped off her panties and the necklace. The ravenous look in his eyes did her in.

"*Hurry*," she pleaded.

"That's one demand I will *not* follow," he said as he spread her legs wider.

He sank down and proceeded to drive her out of her mind with his hands and mouth. He licked and flicked, fucked and sucked, pleasuring her so thoroughly, streams of indiscernible noises spilled from her lungs. She clawed at the table, pleasure building inside her until she was hanging on to reality by a fast-fraying thread. His rough hands moved up her torso, fondling her breasts as he devoured her. He did something wicked with his tongue, and she fell back on the table, surrendering to his masterful touch. She arched into his hands and he squeezed her nipples, sending fire through her core. The graze of his teeth between her legs catapulted her into a dizzying world. She writhed and bucked with the endless pleasure, but he was ruthless, feasting and touching in all the right places to keep her flying higher, screaming louder, until she cried out his name, shattering into a million jagged pieces.

She collapsed to her back, panting as her vision started to clear. He eased his efforts to slow slicks of his tongue and pressed tender kisses beside her center. For a few split seconds, his mouth and hands left her, and she whimpered.

"I need you, baby," he said huskily, his voice a wave of lust washing over her.

She realized he was stripping off his underwear, and he loved his way up her body. She felt his bare hard length against her as he perched naked above her, taking her in a kiss so deep, she felt transported once again. He tasted of her, but she didn't care. She wanted *everything* he had to give.

"I need your mouth on me, baby," he panted out. "Suck me while I feast on you."

"Oh *God* yes," she said in one long breath.

He turned around, straddling her shoulders. As she took him in her mouth, he let out a long, sensual moan and lowered his mouth to the very heart of her. She'd missed his touch, his *taste*, their sexual freedom. He fucked her mouth like he owned her, touched her body like he loved her. She wanted to fill up on him and give it back in equal measure. She tried to focus on pleasuring him, but her concentration waned as he played her body like a fiddle, sending her right up to the clouds again. She moaned around his cock, and he reached down and squeezed the base of it like he used to do when he didn't want to come.

She took advantage of his slower moves, licking the broad head. He groaned, his hips thrusting once again.

In a blur of movement, he turned around, kissing her shoulders and neck, and perched above her on the table, gazing deeply into her eyes. "I need to be inside you."

He pushed his hands beneath her, cradling her as their bodies came together slowly and oh so good. When he was buried to the hilt, his head dipped beside hers, and in a low voice dripping with emotion, he said, "This is where we belong, as close as two people can be. And it's still not close enough."

Her heart was so full, she couldn't find her voice. When he lifted his face, neither one of them said a word. His mouth covered hers in a kiss as deep and as meaningful as the moment. As they found the slow, sensual rhythm that bound them together, breathing air into each other's lungs and love into each other's hearts, Zev rose up with an entrancing, hopeful look in his eyes. She was right there with him, and she didn't even try to hold back.

"I feel it, too," she confessed.

"The power of us, baby. It's stronger than ever."

With their confession, everything intensified. The weight of his body, the tickling of his whiskers, the lust and love igniting between them. Her hips rose to meet his every thrust as he buried himself deep time and time again, lighting her up until she was sure she glowed from the inside out. She reveled in the feel of his muscles flexing as he loved her, taking her higher with every sensual kiss, every powerful piston of his hips, until they both cried out, clinging together through the very last pulse.

When they collapsed, breathless and sated, to the hard wooden table, their bodies covered with a sheen of sweat, hearts beating as one, Zev showered her in kisses.

"You slay me, baby," he whispered, and rolled off her. He gathered her in his arms, bringing them nose to nose. "I forgot we were on the table. I should have carried you upstairs to the bed."

"No, this was perfect. This was us."

He kissed her slowly and sweetly. A loud *thump* sounded in the living room, startling them out of their kiss.

"Shit. The door is still open." He gave her a quick kiss and climbed off the table, helping her off, too, and pulled her against him. He ran his hands down her back and over her bottom. "Now I get to pamper you."

"*Pamper* me? How about you go make sure there's no serial killer in the living room while I get cleaned up?"

"If anyone tries to get near our cereal, I'll kill *them*." He smacked her butt, and she giggled as she headed for the bathroom off the kitchen.

She cleaned herself up and was bent over in the kitchen, pulling on her underwear when the sound of leather cracking made her jump and shriek. She spun around and found Zev holding a leather whip covered with dirt. Bandit stood beside him, panting like he was due a good petting.

"One leather whip. I'd say it's worth about a hundred bucks," he said. "But that view of your gorgeous ass? *Priceless*."

"My heart is racing! You scared the heck out of me. *Where* did you get that thing?"

"Our resident thief dragged it into the house." He looked down at Bandit, and the dog *woof*ed. "I don't want to know what my brother and Char are into, but I think Beau has trained his wingman pretty damn well. Now, get that pretty little ass upstairs so I can pamper you." He cracked the whip again, and she squealed and ran out of the kitchen.

"Get that thing away from me!" she shouted through her laughter as he and Bandit chased after her. "Whips are *not* pampering!"

Zev dropped the whip and took the steps two at a time, catching her around the waist, making her laugh even harder.

"Zevy!"

He hauled her over his shoulder like a sack of grain and smacked her ass as he carried her down the hall. "You're mine, lover girl. *All* mine."

She wasn't about to argue with that.

Bandit ran around them, nearly tripping Zev as he followed them into the bathroom.

"Give it up, thief." He set Carly down and said, "Dude, didn't you hear me? She's mine. *I'm* the lucky one." He turned on the water to fill the tub.

"Aw, that's so mean," she said as he poured bubble bath into the water.

Zev drew her into his arms. "The day that dog can make you come with your clothes on is the day I'll relinquish my claim."

"Guess I'm stuck with you." She went up on her toes and touched her lips to his.

"Be right back, beautiful." He disappeared out the door, returning a few minutes later with his phone, candles, a lighter, and fresh towels. He set them all on the counter, queued music on his phone, and placed candles along the ceramic shelf next to the tub, the windowsill, and the sink.

"You know you don't have to pamper me," she said as he lit the candles.

He turned out the lights and said, "I've got to show my girl that I'm more than just a good lay."

She wiggled out of her underwear, and he reached for her hand, pulling her into a toe-curling kiss. When the tub was ready, he helped her in and climbed in behind her so she was sitting between his legs. She settled back against his chest and said, "I recognize these songs. They're from one of the CDs you made for me."

"I've got them all on playlists." He used his hands to bathe her arms and shoulders. "They kept me company when we were apart."

Every little thing he said brought them closer together. "It's been years since I've taken a bubble bath. It feels luxurious."

He gently massaged her arms and kissed her shoulder. "I've been looking forward to doing this ever since we left the lab. In all the years we were together, I never had the chance to pamper you."

She'd never thought of herself as someone who needed pampering. But as he rubbed her sore muscles, she realized that maybe it wasn't about *need*, but about accepting the love he had to give in all the ways he wanted to give it. "And you want to?" She glanced over her shoulder, and the look of contentment on his face made her feel good all over.

He pressed his lips to hers and said, "More than you could know. I want to do so much for you, *with* you…*to* you."

He began massaging her fingers, and she closed her eyes, sinking into him.

"I can't erase the hurt I caused, but I can show you how much you mean to me, and hopefully one day you'll trust that when I say I never want to hurt you again, I really mean it."

She believed him with her whole heart, and the more pieces of himself he shared with her, the quieter the whispers in her head became.

"I was so lost in you downstairs, I should have asked if your hand was too sore from working with the air scribe to touch me. Does it hurt?"

"Not really," she said, loving that he'd thought to ask.

He kissed her palm and said, "I want to do right by you, Carls, in every way. But I definitely get lost in us."

"If you did any righter by me, I'd be in big trouble. This was the most incredible day I've ever had." She smiled to herself, cheekily adding, "Well, it's right up there with Silk Hollow."

"For me, too." He kissed her shoulder, massaging her palm and wrist, and then he took her other hand, giving it the same attention. "I love this, Carls, taking care of you. Being close."

"I didn't think there were many intimate *firsts* left for us."

"Then you thought wrong. We've never kissed at the top of the Empire State Building, or made love on my boat at sunrise, or caught fish off an exotic island and eaten it under the stars."

"Mm. Sounds dreamy," she said, enjoying his touch as he rubbed the soreness from her forearm. "That feels good."

He gathered her hair over her other shoulder and kissed the skin he'd bared. "Did you have a chance to ask Quinn to cover for you tomorrow so you could work at the lab with me again?"

"Yes. I'll meet you there at noon. I'm excited to see what else we can discover."

"How about I meet you at your place, and we'll take one truck?"

Her chest constricted. She should be comfortable letting him into her house, but she wasn't quite there yet, even if she was already in too deep to think she could walk away unscathed if this week was all they'd have. Once he was in her house, in her bed, she'd have *no* safe haven, no place to hide from the hurt. But what if they *could* find a way to color outside the lines and blend their lives together? She reminded herself not to go down that tenuous path. The trouble was, no matter where she went, every path led to Zev.

He pressed another kiss to her shoulder and said, "I forgot about the no-Zev zone you're pretending to have. Why don't you meet me *here*, and we'll take Beau's truck."

"Okay," she said, comforted by the thought that he could still read her worries so accurately.

"Close your eyes and relax," he coaxed as he moved warm water over her shoulders and breasts.

She wanted to share in *this* discovery, too. To explore their new, mature and enlightened coupledom and show him how much she cared about him. She might not be ready to cut her safety net free, or to say those three magical, scary words that were eagerly perched on the tip of her tongue, but that didn't mean she didn't feel them with every ounce of herself.

Bandit lumbered into the bathroom and dropped a pair of fuzzy pink handcuffs by the tub; then he trotted out the door.

"Um…?" Carly laughed.

Zev picked up the handcuffs and dangled them from his finger. "Kind of makes you wonder what Char and Beau do in the bathtub."

"How about instead, you think about what *we* can do in this bathtub?" She ran her hands down his thighs and said, "I'm not into handcuffs, but as I recall, you wanted me to ride you like a stallion." His cock hardened against her back, and she *loved* earning that reaction.

"That dirty mouth of yours is going to do me in."

She turned on her knees between his legs, facing him. The cool air bristled her wet skin. "Did I say something *dirty*?" she asked as innocently as she could. "If I said I wanted to suck your cock, *that* would be dirty. Or if I said I wanted you to fuck me from behind, that's *kind of* dirty."

His cock twitched between them. "*Kind of* dirty? Baby, look what the thought of you bent over, or on your hands and knees, does to me."

His hungry gaze was a powerful lure, and she debated turning around and letting him do just that. But then *he'd* be in control, and she wanted that pleasure. He palmed her breasts, brushing his thumbs over her nipples as she straddled his thighs. His touch was distracting. It took a moment for her to remember she was supposed to be seducing him.

Determined to make him lose his mind, she guided his hand between her legs and said, "When I think of *dirty* talk, I think of something like this…" She practically purred, "I *loved* when you fucked my mouth with your big, *thick* cock."

"*Fucking hell*. I need you *now*, Carly."

She shook her head, trying her best to remain in control, but his fingers pushed inside her, wreaking havoc with her ability to think. She was *this close* to forgetting the dirty talk and mounting him. But she focused on his mouth and the pleasures it brought her, trying to block out the mind-numbing sensations he was doling out between her legs, and forced herself to continue taunting him. "It's *kind of* dirty when I tell you that I loved the way you made me come on your tongue."

"*So fucking* dirty," he said through gritted teeth, his every muscle tight.

His entire body flexed in restraint, and he grabbed her ass with both hands. The roughness of his grip shredded her resolve. She rose up on her knees and grabbed his cock, aligning it with her body. Hovering over him, she felt in control and powerful, and at the same time she felt utterly *powerless*, a willing slave to their love. It was gloriously addicting.

"You planted a *very* dirty thought in my mind about riding my *stallion*," she said heatedly. "I've been thinking about how good that would feel. Do you want that, Zevy? Do you want *me?*"

"*Only* you. Every minute of every single day." His voice was laden with desire, his fingers pressing into her flesh so hard, she'd probably bruise.

She sank down on his shaft, taking in every inch of him, and a loud, lustful moan rumbled from his lips. The greedy sound unleashed the animal in her, and she went a little wild. Zev crushed his mouth to hers, loving her like he never wanted to let her go, and Lord knew she didn't want him to. He was the *only* man who made her feel that way, and as they spiraled into ecstasy, crying out each other's names in the throes of passion, she knew he was the only man who ever would.

Chapter Sixteen

ZEV WOKE WITH the alarm at six thirty Thursday morning with Carly snuggled into the curve of his body. His sweet *little spoon* still fit perfectly. He reached behind him slowly, giving her a last minute of sleep as he turned off his alarm. *Three more mornings.* The thought was accompanied by a pang of regret. He tried not to think about how little time they had left before he had to leave, but it was hard not to when *this* was how he wanted to wake up every morning.

Bandit ambled onto the sleeping porch and rested his chin on the side of the bed, waiting for his morning pets. Zev had to hand it to Beau. His dog might be a thief, but he was a well-trained thief.

Carly made a sleepy sound, wiggling her butt deeper into the crook of his hips. She pulled his arm tighter around her and said, "Just a few more minutes?"

"The last time I made you late for work, you weren't very happy." He trailed kisses along her shoulder. "I don't want to end up in the doghouse."

She turned around with a glimmer of mischief in her eyes and said, "Where's college-boy Zev? The guy who coaxed me into staying in bed and missing my lab twice in one week."

"He took off and made a mess of both of us." He kissed her softly. "Now you get grown-up Zev, the guy who makes sure you don't miss out on a damn thing, including work." He ran his hand down her hip, soaking in the feel of her for a few more seconds. If he allowed himself any more than that, she'd be late for sure. He gave her a quick kiss and said, "While you're showering, I'll take Bandit out and feed the chickens, and clean up the evidence of last night's debauchery."

"You're not showering with me?" she asked with an adorable pout.

"If I shower with you, or if we stay in this bed much longer, you're definitely going to be late." He kissed the tip of her nose and forced himself to sit up. "I want to go with you this morning and see my girl in action."

She sat up, bright eyed and grinning. "You're coming with me to the shop? That's great! Birdie can't come in until ten. She's helping our friend Karma with inventory at her boutique. But don't you have things to do? Aren't you anxious to get back to the lab?"

"I am, but I'll be there later with you. I'm meeting Jack at ten thirty for a quick visit, and I have a few errands to run. But I want to spend as much time with you as I can."

"Yay for me!" She straddled him, naked, and said, "Is Jack going to fly you out on Sunday?"

"Yes, at noon, but if you don't climb off me right now, you're going down on your back, and I'm going to be buried eight inches deep in less than ten seconds."

She giggled and stepped off the bed, looking mouthwateringly delicious.

He gritted his teeth. "You'd better get in the shower."

"I'd better, *huh*?" She sauntered slowly and sexily toward the bedroom.

She was his goddess, his fantasy, and he wanted everything she had to give: heart, body, and soul. His love for her was so all-consuming, he wanted to shout it from the rooftops. He loved her teasing ways, her sweet and seductive smiles, and her careful new approaches. He loved watching her adventurous spirit reawaken and seeing the surprise and elation on her face as it did. And he loved the way she was taunting him at that very second.

"You're evil," he said, and lunged for her. She squealed, slipping through his fingers. He tried again, catching her around the waist, and tossed her onto the bed on her stomach, coming down over her. She smelled so good, like vanilla bubble bath and their lovemaking. Her laughter was as enticing as the feel of her soft body beneath him.

"You like torturing me, Carls?"

"Maybe." She lifted her hips, rubbing against his cock. "We can be *fast*."

"We don't *do* fast, baby." He eased off her back, kissing down her spine. "But maybe this morning…" He eased off the bed and caressed her ass, kissing each gorgeous globe, and said, "We could try to be quick."

She rose on her knees, looking at him over her shoulder with a challenge in her eyes as she said, "I *dare* you to make me come twice in five minutes or less."

"Fuck, babe. I want to devour you *and* make love to you."

She grinned. "Okay. *Six* minutes."

"You're killing me." He dipped lower, kissing the curve of her ass and then licking her sweetest spot. She was already wet, and she tasted like heaven. The clock was ticking. He tapped her ass and said, "Scooch forward."

She crawled forward on hands and knees, and he lay on his back between her legs. He guided her center to his mouth and took his fill, teasing her with his hand, making her tremble and pant, taking her right up to the edge.

"There, *there!*" she pleaded as if he didn't know her body better than his own.

He gave her what she needed, and she came hard, crying out as he took his fill. He changed positions, moving behind her on his knees, and drove into her with one hard thrust. She went down on her elbows with a loud mewl.

He pulled back. "Too hard?"

"No," she panted out. "*Perfect.* Take me like I'm yours, Zevy."

With those magical words, words he hoped were going to prove true, he grabbed her hips and pounded into her with everything he had.

Minutes later they collapsed to the mattress on their backs. Carly gazed dreamily at him and said, "Best six minutes of my life."

He chuckled. "I have no self-control with you."

"*Really?* I couldn't tell," she teased.

He leaned over her, kissing her freckled nose, and said, "Did we make you late?"

"If we did, I think my boss will be okay with it just this once."

THE MORNING FLEW by in a whirlwind of baking and happiness. Carly had thought Zev would be a major distraction while she was trying to prepare for her day. Not that she'd mind, especially after last night when he'd proven how *talented* he could be in the kitchen. But he'd been an incredible help and an inspiration. Not only had they made trifle, peanut butter cups, brownies, truffles, chocolate cupcakes, and marshmallows dipped in chocolate, but they'd come up with another new creation—Treasure Hunter Fudge. They'd hidden all sorts of goodies inside pieces of fudge, like coconut, nuts, candies, and marshmallows, but the contents of each piece were a mystery.

"I can't believe you do this every morning. It's a lot of work," Zev said as he dipped the last marshmallow in chocolate and then rolled it in coconut shavings. "Do you ever get tired of the demand?"

She added chocolate shavings to the top of the trifle and said, "I'm sure we all have days when we don't feel like working, but it passes." Her eyes moved over the plethora of treats they'd made together. "Wow, we got a lot done, didn't we? You were a huge help. Thank you. I know my customers will love the Treasure Hunter Fudge."

"How about the treasure *hunter?*" he asked as he took off his gloves and wrapped his arms around her.

"I'm pretty sure he could charm the panties off a nun."

He kissed her, chuckling. "How about off a chocolatier?"

"I can say with good authority that he's an *expert* at that."

"And I can say with good authority that he has no interest in charming the panties off anyone else." He kissed her again and said, "Are we done with the dipping chocolate?"

He'd been asking for tastes of *everything*, like a kid in a candy store. "Yes. You can stick your finger in the bowl now."

"How did you know I wanted to do that?" he asked as he scooped chocolate onto his finger.

She leaned over and sucked it off. "Because I know you, and *I* was waiting to do *that*."

"And I've been waiting to do *this*." He swept her into his arms, taking her in a tantalizingly slow kiss, as if he were savoring every second.

"Again," she whispered, and he rewarded her with another spine-tingling kiss.

"I thought I saw—"

Their lips parted at the sound of Birdie's voice. She stood at the entrance to the kitchen wearing a glittery gold tank minidress with black Converse sneakers, hands on her hips and a cheesy grin on her pretty face.

"Don't let me interrupt. I get as much out of watching you kiss as you get out of doing it." Birdie motioned with her hand and said, "Carry on."

Zev lowered his mouth to Carly's, but she laughed and pushed him away. "We are *not* giving her a show."

"Aw, come on," Zev teased. "She got all dressed up and everything."

Birdie twirled around and said, "Karma just got in a truckload of new dresses, and she let me rifle through it. I bought *three* outfits. Isn't this one awesome?"

"Gorgeous," Zev said.

Birdie curtsied. "Thank you. I need a favor from you, Zev. I have something in my trunk that's *really* heavy and needs to go in the dumpster. Would you mind carrying it for me?"

"Sure." Zev gave Carly a quick peck on the cheek. "Be right back."

Birdie dropped the keys in his hand and he left the kitchen.

"What's in your trunk?" Carly asked.

"*Junk*. Heavy junk. Trust me, I need his muscles." She

flapped her arms and said, "Look at these spaghetti arms." As soon as the bells above the front door signaled Zev had left the shop, she said, "Tell me everything before he gets back! You guys were so hot together last night. *Everyone* loves him! I wish Sasha and Doc could have met him. But they will one day. *So...?* What's the deal with you two? You look so happy, you're *glowing.* Is he staying longer? Are you going with him if he leaves?"

"I don't know. We haven't gotten that far. We're just enjoying each other while he's here." Carly was trying to play it cool, even though she was nervous about how they could ever blend their lives together, but at the same time, she wanted to jump out of her skin and sing his praises.

"Please tell me that by *enjoying* you mean doing the dirty, riding the hog, slipping along that heavenly highway."

Carly laughed. "Birdie!"

"I'm just hoping someone's getting it, because I'm sure not. So...?"

"*Yes,* we're enjoying each other a lot, like *all* the time. I can't keep my hands off him," she said with a giggle. "I'm a total nympho, like we're eighteen again. It's insane."

"I knew it! It's not insane. It's meant to be. He looks like the kind of guy who knows his way around a bedroom."

"And a bathtub, a shower, the porch..." She lowered her voice and whispered, "The kitchen table."

Birdie squealed and hugged her. "I'm *so* happy for you!" She walked around the kitchen looking at the treats and talking a mile a minute. "I knew you two were in love! The way he looks at you is just *so*...I want that one day. You're a whole different person with him. You light up when you see him, and you take time off. You're *always* happy. Not that you weren't before, but this is different. It's like you're drenched in love for that man, and *wow*, Carly. It's such a great thing. Have you told him yet?"

Carly was struck mute, trying to figure out how Birdie could see all of that so quickly.

"Oh my God." Birdie looked appalled as she closed the gap between them. "Do *not* tell me you don't love him. It practically drips off you two. I'm your best friend—you can't lie to me. Look me in the eyes and tell me. Am I off base? That would be weird. I'm never off base. I'm like a love ninja. A love *guru*. I can smell love a mile away." She made a hurry-up motion with her hand. "Well? I'm dying here. Do you love him?"

"Yes!" The word burst from Carly's lips like it had been trapped for years. "I *love* him! I love his *face*. I love the way he holds me, the way he *talks* to me. I love his long hair when we're making love and it tickles my cheeks. I love the way he holds my freaking hand like it's his greatest pleasure." She looked at her best friend melting with her every word, both of them tearing up, and said, "I even love the way he mumbles in his sleep. He's always done it. Like he can't turn his brain off. I *love* him, Birdie. I love him with everything I am and everything I have." She realized she was shaking. "But I can't tell him. It'll make it *real*, and I know it *is* real, and this sounds crazy, but it's like my house. If I say it, and we realize we can't make this work, it'll crush me."

"That man won't *ever* crush you again. I believe that with everything *I* am and everything *I* have." Birdie's brows slanted, and she said, "Granted, I don't have much, but I *am* a lot to handle, so that counts twice."

"You've only just met him, Birdie. You can't know that any more than I can."

The bells above the door chimed. Birdie grabbed her hand,

and with the most serious expression Carly had ever seen on her, she said, "You're allowed to be terrified. But you have to trust me. You can tell him how you feel. He will *not* hurt you again."

Zev walked into the kitchen, looking curiously at them.

Carly was still processing her confession and Birdie's declaration. Birdie must have realized Carly was tongue-tied, because she lifted Carly's hand higher, pretending to inspect it, and said, "Yes, peach is the perfect nail color for you. Or red, if you're feeling saucy." She dropped Carly's hand and strutted across the room to Zev. "Thank you for taking care of that junk."

He handed her the keys. "That was quite a lot of stuff."

"I got a little carried away when I was cleaning out my place. Cleaning up is like opening a blank canvas and a dozen cans of paint. I got caught up in the excitement of all the things I could do with the space and just kept going." She looked over her shoulder at Carly and said, "I'm going to open the register and let you two make out some more."

"She's a trip," Zev said when she left the room, and pulled Carly into his arms. "Are you okay? You seem a little rattled."

I just poured my heart out to Birdie, when I should be pouring it out to you, so yeah, I'm little rattled. "I'm fine, just thinking about all the things I need to get done. I'm excited to meet you later and work on the concretions."

"It's going to be a great day, babe. I loved spending this morning with you, working side by side, and seeing you in action."

"You've been seeing me in action a lot lately," she teased.

"That makes me the luckiest guy on the planet." He embraced her and said, "Since luck seems to be our thing, maybe you should think about making Lucky Charms bars, like Rice Krispies Treats, but with Lucky Charms. I'm always around to taste test."

Not always. The pit of her stomach sank with that reality, and by the look in Zev's eyes, he was thinking the same thing.

"I know, babe," he said, holding her tighter. "But whether you believe it or not, I'm *not* going to disappear on you. Not ever again."

She wanted to believe him, and deep down, she did believe him. So why was she so nervous?

"You okay?"

"Yeah, I'm good."

He gave her a scrutinizing look. "That's a nervous *good*. I'm supposed to meet Jack, but I can put it off if you want to talk."

"No, don't be silly. I'm fine."

"Okay." He kissed her and said, "I'll see you around noon at the inn?"

"Yes. I'm looking forward to it."

As she watched him walk out the door, she realized she'd *needed* to share her feelings with Birdie first in order to see things more clearly. Zev was *here*, and he was saying and doing all the right things. If she wanted their relationship to work out, she couldn't keep holding back. He wanted her to color outside the lines, and she wanted to. *Desperately.* But before she could do that, she needed to be able to see beyond those lines, to see what their future might look like. She'd been waiting for the answer to become clear, but how could they find *any* answers if she wasn't telling him the questions?

Chapter Seventeen

THE BUZZ OF the tools in Zev's and Carly's hands did nothing to quiet his thoughts. He'd spoken to his dive team and his attorney. His team was itching to get back on the water, and his attorney had hit a snag with another case but was going to court tomorrow for Zev. Zev focused on clearing concretion away from the artifacts he'd been working to expose instead of the million worries zipping through his mind about the legal process and the aftermath. When the area was fairly clear, he set down his tools and glanced at Carly working diligently beside him. She'd shown up half an hour early at the inn, bursting with excitement to work on the concretions. He couldn't wait to surprise her. He wanted to give her everything she'd missed out on and so much more. But he wasn't sure how to do that, because those experiences would mean nothing if she had to give up any of the things she'd worked so hard for.

Carly glanced over, and a smile curved her beautiful lips, sending his emotions spinning. He pointed to her tool and said, "Turn it off."

She set the tool down, anticipation brimming in her eyes. "Did you find something?"

This was the reason he hadn't told her how close he'd come to exposing the artifacts yesterday. He wanted to experience this moment and not take away from yesterday's discovery and the excitement that had come with it.

"Come over here and take a look," he said, pushing to his feet.

She leaned over his workstation and peered at the concretion. "Holy crap, Zev! That's *gold!* You uncovered the coins!"

"That's right, and *you're* going to extract them." He pulled out the chair for her.

"What? *No!* This is *your* discovery."

"It's *our* discovery, and it would mean more to me if you would finish extracting them."

Her eyes filled with disbelief. "*Zevy...?* You can't mean that. You've worked so hard for so many years to find them."

"Do it for me, Carly. You're the reason I was so focused on the *Pride* in the first place. Two treasure hunters, one ship, remember?"

She looked longingly at him. "Are you sure? This is such a huge moment for you to give up."

He wanted to take off their protective masks, take her in his arms, and kiss her until she agreed. But that would delay the extraction and her excitement. Instead, he took her gloved hands in his, gazed into her eyes through their clear protective face shields, and said, "I'm not giving it up, babe. I'm making it even more memorable. This is what I've been hoping for since we first heard about the ship. This is your time to shine, babe." He guided her into the chair, giving her shoulder a reassuring squeeze. "Let's do this."

"Thank you!" She shook out her hands and said, "I'm so nervous."

She got to work, and Zev sat at her workstation, taking over where she'd left off on the other concretion. Witnessing her excitement over the next several hours as she extracted each of five Peruvian gold cobs—hand-hammered coins—made the discovery even more memorable. He'd never forget the sight of her mile-wide smile and the sound of her thrilling *Look! Look! Look!* as she'd freed each one.

"I don't see any more," she said, poking at the concretion with the tip of a pick. "But we can keep going! The X-ray shows two more, and they don't look that much deeper." She stretched her neck from side to side and arched her back, rolling her shoulders.

He took off his protective headgear and said, "It's seven o'clock, and we've been at it for hours. I think we should clean up and go celebrate." He reached for her hand, helping her to her feet, and took off her headgear, kissing her softly. "Look at what you've done." He placed the coins in her hand. "Once the loot is tied to the *Pride*, you'll have made history for the second time this week."

"What *we* did," she corrected him, and ran her gloved finger over the coins. "Look how beautiful and clear the lions and castles are in the cross quadrants, and the dates—1710 and 1712!" Her eyes glittered with delight. "Based on the historical maps, and the dates, these have to be from the *Pride*."

"I'm sure of it, but you know how this works. Once the vessel is arrested and people hear about the discovery, it'll be disputed until we have irrefutable proof."

"I know, but, *Zev*, these are more than *three hundred* years old, and *you* dredged them up from the sea. That's amazing in and of itself! I don't care what anyone says."

"And you extracted them from the concretion. We make a good team."

"We always did," she said, holding his gaze for an extra beat. Her eyes widened. "We have to take pictures! Don't you need to send a picture to your attorney and your dive team?"

He chuckled. Her excitement was contagious. "Absolutely."

They took pictures of only the coins, then of them holding the coins. Then they took a number of selfies kissing, laughing, and making funny faces—and just like that, Zev did the impossible. He fell even deeper in love with her.

"Thank you for letting me be such a big part of this," Carly said as they began cleaning up. "I can't even begin to tell you how much this means to me."

"You don't have to. I already *know*."

She looked at the concretions, the coins, and then she tipped her beautiful face up to him and said, "It's surreal, isn't it?"

"What's surreal is that a week ago I was trying to figure out which of my siblings I could coerce into taking care of Beau's animals. Now here I am making history with you"—*my love*—"the person I have the most history with. You and me together again, diving, hanging out, making chocolates"—he lowered his voice—"making love." He kissed her and said, "And doing all of this, just like we always dreamed. *That's* what's surreal to me."

She swallowed hard, as if she were considering her words carefully, and said, "It really is."

"Let's finish cleaning up. I want to celebrate with my girl. How does dinner and a bonfire at the inn sound?"

"Beyond perfect. What should we do with the coins? I feel like you need a vault."

"I have one, actually. I'm renting one, along with a secure warehouse, on Silver Island."

"That's not going to help while you're here. Does Beau have

a safe at the inn? I suddenly feel paranoid that someone might steal them. Is that normal? Did you feel that way when you and Luis found all that treasure? Nobody knows about this but your family, right? Gosh, *what* is wrong with me?"

God, I love you. He laughed at her rambling and leaned in for a kiss. "Beau has a safe, and yes, it's totally normal. As for what's wrong with you, not a damn thing, other than I think you've caught the treasure-hunting bug."

A spark of heat rose in her eyes and she said, "I blame your one-eyed snake."

CARLY WAS STILL on cloud nine as they made their way up the mountain after cleaning the lab. But she was also in a quandary. Ever since she'd confessed her love for Zev to Birdie, she hadn't been able to tamp down those feelings. She'd almost blurted out *I love you* when Zev had said that letting her extract the coins would make it even more memorable, and *again* when she'd pulled out the first coin. She'd literally had to clench her teeth to keep from saying it when he'd said they made a great team. She knew she *needed* to figure out how to start a conversation about their future, but they'd had such an incredible day, she didn't want to take anything away from it.

She gazed out the window pondering those thoughts as they approached—and passed—the road to the inn. Was he just as lost in the excitement as she was? "You must be on cloud nine, too. You passed the road to the inn."

"Did I?" He shrugged. "It's a nice night for a drive. Let's go a little farther."

"What about Bandit? He's been inside a long time."

He glanced at her with a coy smile and said, "I closed the bedroom door. If he steals anything, it's not going to be our stuff."

"I meant that he might have to go out."

"We won't be long," he said casually.

He turned onto a narrow, winding road and continued up the mountain. Two turns later they came to a clearing, and up ahead was a landing strip and a small airplane.

"What are we doing here?" Carly asked.

Zev cut the engine, winked, and hopped out of the truck without answering. As he walked around the truck, he waved in the direction of the plane. She followed his gaze to a man she hadn't noticed standing beside it.

She opened her door and took his hand as she hopped out. "Is that Jack? Didn't you guys meet earlier?"

"That is Jack Remington, Treat's sister Savannah's husband." He put his arms around her and said, "We're taking a little trip to Silver Island, and tomorrow we're going out on my boat for a dive at the site of the wreckage."

Her jaw dropped as she tried to process what he'd said. "I…We're *going*…" came out as a stunned, breathless whisper, and the emotions she'd been tamping down bubbled to the surface. She squealed and leapt into his arms. "Zevy! Silver Island? Your boat? The *Pride*? I don't have clothes, or a bathing suit, but I don't care! This is the *most* romantic, amazing thing anyone has *ever* done for me!" As she gushed with excitement, reality hit her, and she reluctantly took a step back, her heart shattering. "It sounds brilliant. *Perfect*, actually. *Crazy*, but so very *us*. But I can't just leave, Zev. I have a business to run. It's not like I can just call in sick and expect Birdie to figure things out. And what about the Chickendales and Band—"

He silenced her with a firm press of his lips and drew her into his arms. "I would never expect you to leave your business unattended. I talked with Birdie and Quinn when we were at the bar. They're covering the shop, and Cutter's at the inn right now. He's staying there, caring for the animals."

"They are? He is?" she asked, tearing up, unable to believe what he'd done.

"Yes, and you know that heavy stuff in Birdie's trunk and the inventory she was doing at Karma's boutique? She was actually doing a favor for me. She was buying you clothes and a bathing suit, and she was pretty damn excited. She said something about it being even better than your hair-down days, whatever that means, which she said you'd had plenty of since we reconnected."

She laughed, tears slipping down her cheeks as Birdie's voice whispered through her mind. *You're allowed to be terrified. But you have to trust me. He will not hurt you again.* "She knew all along," she said more to herself than to him. Her head was spinning at all he'd done, and her heart could barely keep up it was so full.

"You know I was never good at slowing down or taking time to plan. I'm more of a get up and go guy. But not this time, Carls. This time I tried to think of everything so you wouldn't be stressed. I packed your toiletries from the inn, and all the things Birdie bought are waiting for us in the plane. There's one hitch, and I can't figure out a way around it. You know we can't fly for twenty-four hours after we dive, which means we can only do *one* dive, and it has to be very early. We won't be able to fly back until Saturday morning, and you won't get to work until midafternoon. Birdie said she could handle it and take care of preparing for the baby shower, but I know you like doing that. And you probably have other things to do. So if you would rather not go, that's okay."

The man who didn't plan had thought of everything. "Are you kidding? Not go? I trust Birdie, and I don't care if it's only *one* dive. That's one dive and a trip to Silver Island I never thought we'd get," she said, as fresh tears fell.

"I was hoping you'd say that. I talked to Cowboy and Dare, who said if the girls run into any trouble, they'd help them out. You have really good friends, Carly. I couldn't have done this without them."

"I can't believe you did all of this for me."

"For *you* and for *us*." He touched his forehead to hers, wrapping his arms tighter around her like the sweetest, most perfect ribbon, and said, "I love you so damn much, Carls. There's nothing I wouldn't do for you." He gazed into her teary eyes, and a world of emotion stared back at her as he said, "I know you don't need private planes or extravagant trips, but we have three nights until I leave, and I want to give you a chance to experience everything you've dreamed of and everything I do. I don't want *any* Carly-free zones in my life."

She had a fleeting thought about how they would make things work and protecting her heart, but there was no protecting it from itself. Their love had survived all these years like artifacts in the sea, cocooned away in heartache and unresolved questions. *Time, touch,* and *truth* had scraped away those hurtful layers, giving them a second chance. She didn't know exactly what their second chance would look like beyond that moment, and it might take a while to figure out the logistics. But she didn't care if it took years, because when she gazed into his loving eyes, she wanted to hang on to their love with both hands and never let it go.

"I love you, too, Zevy. I was afraid to say it, but I've never stopped loving you."

And I know I never will.

Chapter Eighteen

THE GENTLE ROCKING of the boat and Zev's warm body were *almost* enough to keep Carly in bed, but the thought of what he had planned for them and the urge to look at the pictures of them plastering the wall by his desk one more time were too strong. She slipped silently out from his arms and padded naked across the cabin to the window. She peered out at the dusky predawn sky and the inky water, unable to believe she was really on Zev's boat, docked at a marina on Silver Island. She glanced at him, sleeping soundly on his back, one arm arced above his head, the other on his abs, a small smile on his lips. The sheet was bunched around his waist, one leg straight, the other knee bent. Love billowed inside her. He must have said he loved her a hundred times on the long plane ride to the island, and she was right there with him, setting free the words that she'd held captive for what she knew would seem like not much time at all to anyone else. They'd only see the few days she and Zev had spent together. But love like theirs didn't fade away. It grew roots, spreading deeper, farther, and faster than anyone could imagine.

She went to his desk, admiring their remember-when pictures hanging beside it. There were a few of Luis and Zev, and he was right. Luis looked like an aging pirate with wild hair and the same shimmer of life Zev had. There were so many photos of her and Zev, they overlapped, their edges frayed, creases streaking a few. She couldn't believe he'd had them hanging there for all this time. When she'd asked him about them last night, he'd said, *I told you that you were always with me.* There were pictures of them as kids decked out in hiking gear with backpacks on their shoulders. One had been taken in sixth grade, another in tenth, and another in college. There were silly pictures of Carly making faces and blowing kisses and one of her standing on his parents' lawn in a black bikini, water from a sprinkler raining down on her. Her wet hair hung in her face, her cheeks pink with sunburn. She had one hand perched on her jutted-out hip, a scowl masking her unstoppable smile. There were pictures of them in dive gear sitting on the side of his uncle Ace's boat in Peaceful Harbor, Maryland. She had fond memories of those visits.

Her gaze moved to a picture of a school trip to a museum they'd taken in seventh grade, the day after he'd asked her to be his girlfriend. They stood side by side, fingertips touching, goofy smiles on their faces. She remembered wanting to tell everyone she was Zev's girlfriend, and at the same time, feeling embarrassed because none of her friends were boy crazy like she was for him. He had pictures of them kissing, swimming, dancing. Pictures at his mother's family winery after high school graduation, both of them dressed up. She remembered feeling like they were finally *almost* free to live out their traveling dreams. *Just four more years.* They'd been so close to having it all.

Her favorite picture was taken in ninth grade. They were holding their passports in their teeth and making funny faces.

Zev's hair was long like it was now, with sun-kissed highlights. They'd been preparing for an archaeological club trip to Spain that summer.

Zev's arms circled her from behind at the same second she became aware of his body heat on her back. "Morning," she said.

"I like waking up to you naked in my cabin." He kissed her shoulder. "Did you have trouble sleeping?"

She turned in his arms and said, "I slept great. But I was too excited to go back to sleep. I still can't believe you have all these pictures hanging up. Didn't it hinder your sex life?"

"I told you I didn't hook up with women on my boat."

"I know, but…" She shrugged.

"No *buts*. I've never lied to you. I'm not about to start. When I bought my own boat and knew the pictures would be safe, I put them up. They've been there ever since." He kissed her again and said, "No Carly-free zones, remember? Come on, I want to show you something."

He took her hand and headed out the cabin door. "Wait. I'm *naked*."

"The sun's not even up yet. No one will see you."

"Zevy…"

He snagged the shirt he'd worn last night from the chair and slipped it over her head, kissed the bridge of her nose, and started to lead her out of the cabin.

"Zev, *you're* naked. Put some shorts on."

He looked appalled. "You want me to cover up my first mate?"

She laughed and tossed him his shorts. He put them on and led her up to the deck. She shivered against the brisk morning air, inhaling the scents of the sea. She hadn't realized how much she missed the carefree feeling of being on a boat. She followed him into the control room, and there on the wall was their *Goonies*-style map showing where they believed the *Pride* had gone down. Beside it was a picture of the two of them hunkered over his parents' kitchen table with his father. Carly had a pencil in her hand, and she was biting her lower lip as she drew on the map. Zev was watching her with the same look on his face, the same love in his eyes she'd seen so many times over the last several days, she knew it by heart.

Her pulse quickened, and she turned to look at him. Sure as the sea was deep, that look was staring back at her. "You took our map with you when you left?"

"I figured it was a fair trade, since I left my heart in your hands."

"Zev," she said softly.

He took her hand, drawing her into his arms. "You're my destiny, babe. I love you. Always have, always will." He kissed her and said, "I want to start a new one-day list with you, Carly, and I want everything on it to become our reality."

"I want that, too. But shouldn't we figure out how we're going to work as a couple before we jump into making one-day lists? How can we have a real relationship without one of us giving up everything?"

"I don't have all the answers. I'll dive for a while; then I'll come see you. You'll do your thing, and when you can take a break, you'll come see me. We've gone years without each other, and our love hasn't lessened. We can make this work, Carly. We just have to be creative."

She swallowed hard, fighting against the planner she'd become.

"Can that be enough until we see what other challenges

we're facing?" he asked. "You know how diving is. I'm dependent on the weather and on what I find when I'm down there. I'm sure I can take a few days every couple of weeks to head to Colorado. I know it's not ideal. I'd rather you were by my side every day. But I know how much your friends and your business mean to you. I won't make you choose between me and any of that. And as much as I'd like to say I could go to Colorado and stay there—"

"Don't even say it. You'd be like a caged animal, and I'd never forgive myself for that. I'd never let you give up everything, either."

"We won't have to. The future is in *our* hands. It'll be up to us to make time to be together. We'll just have to plan a little."

In the past, their *plans* were whims and ideas of things they wanted to do. Even the trip they'd so-called planned to Silver Island in college hadn't included anything more specific than renting a cottage and a boat and searching for the *Pride*. And yet meticulously planning her life had been a critical part of what had pulled her through her heartache. Could she live without solid plans? She wasn't foolish enough to ask for more, when he was already giving all he had *and* respecting her need to remain in Colorado.

"By *plan* I assume you mean make a call a few days before and say, *Hey, I'm coming into town*?" she teased, loving that he was really trying and thinking things through as best he could, given their situation.

His face went serious, and he said, "*Shit. Yes*, probably." He sighed and pushed a hand through his hair, turning away. "That's not enough for you, is it?" He looked at her and said, "You're a planner now. I'll plan. Dates, times, everything."

She loved him even more for offering to do the impossible.

When he opened his mouth to speak, she silenced him with a press of her lips.

"It's enough for now, Zev. I want *us*, so I'll learn to color outside the lines again. You don't have to do all the work in this relationship. We're a team, remember? Besides, what's the worst that can happen?" She walked backward toward the door, crooking her finger.

He followed her out of the control room, past the equipment room, which was filled with tanks, wet suits, and other supplies, to the dive deck.

"That I'll end up naked on a boat with the man of my dreams?" She walked to the edge of the deck and said, "Or that I'll forget my careful ways and dare you to join me in something ridiculously irresponsible, like this—" She whipped off her shirt and jumped in the water.

When she broke the surface, Zev was flying through the air naked as a jaybird. He plunged into the water a few feet away. He popped up beside her and pulled her into his arms, kissing her *hard*.

"God, I love you," he said, their legs bumping as they kicked to keep afloat. Their laughter filled the air between steamy kisses.

"It's freezing!" she said through chattering teeth.

"I'll keep you warm." He grabbed her butt.

"You bring out the naughty girl in me, Mr. Braden."

"If you're looking for an apology, you're not going to get one."

"I was going to say *thank you*. I've missed her." She wrapped her legs around his waist, making him do all the kicking, which he did without hesitation.

"Oh, babe. I've missed *all* of you, but you need to know

that I love you when you're careful." *Kiss, kiss.* "I love you when you're wild." *Kiss, kiss.* "Most of all, I love you when you're naked in my arms."

"Braden! That you?" a raspy voice called out.

Carly scrambled around Zev, hiding behind his back and peering over his shoulder at the man standing on the dock. He looked like a younger, sun-kissed Jeff Bridges with gray-brown hair that brushed the collar of his Hawaiian-print shirt, which was opened three buttons deep.

"Who is *that?*" Carly asked urgently. "You said no one would see me!"

"Roddy Remington—Randi's father. He owns the marina." Zev waved and said, "How's it going, Roddy?"

"Fair to middling, you know," Roddy said, casually slipping a hand into the pocket of his worn jeans, like he had all day to stand there.

Carly clung to Zev's shoulders, shivering.

"Randi said you were coming in for the day," Roddy shouted. "But I didn't expect you quite so early. Who's your friend?"

"This is Carly," Zev hollered. "My girlfriend."

Small talk? Really? Although she loved hearing Zev call her his girlfriend.

"Well, now, I guess there's a first for everything." Roddy laughed heartily and waved, calling out, "Hello there, darlin'. I'm Roddy, master of this marina and friend to all."

I'd like you to be a little less of a friend right now. Carly lifted one hand, wiggling her fingers in a tentative wave. "Hi."

"Bring that pretty little lady in here so I can meet her." Roddy motioned with his hand for them to come in.

"*Nononono,*" Carly whispered. "I'm naked over here…"

"Hold tight, babe. I'll get us out of this," Zev reassured her.

"Roddy, what the heck, man?" A big, brawny guy walked out of the cabin on the boat beside Roddy. He had a small tattoo on his neck, muscles upon muscles, and a scowl on his handsome face. "It's the ass crack of dawn and you're out here hollerin'."

"*Ohmygod!*" Carly sank lower into the water, and Zev angled himself toward the guy so he couldn't see her body. "Who is *that?*"

"He's a buddy of mine, Archer Steele," Zev said. "He's a good guy with a big chip on his shoulder."

"Sorry, Archer." Roddy nodded toward the water and said, "I saw Braden out there and wanted to say hello."

"Zev's back?" Archer squinted out toward the water.

Carly ducked a little lower. *Nothing to see over here. Please go away!*

"Hey, dude. Sorry to wake you," Zev hollered. "We were just…taking a morning swim."

Carly imagined him smirking.

"I bet you are." Archer chuckled and shook his head. "Hey, Roddy, give these two some privacy, will ya?"

"What?" Roddy scratched his head. He looked at Carly and Zev again and said, "Aw, *Jiminy Cricket.* Been there myself a few dozen times with the missus. Nice to meet you, Carly. You kids have fun. I'll just be on my way." He turned and walked down the dock toward shore.

Archer hollered, "You're welcome!" and headed into the cabin of his boat.

Carly let out a breath she hadn't realized she was holding as Zev turned around with the biggest grin she'd seen in a long time. When she opened her mouth to complain, all that came out was laughter.

"Sorry, babe," Zev said through his laughs. "I forgot that Roddy comes out here so early."

"Like I said…" She wound her arms around his neck and said, "What's the worst that can happen?"

"You know I'm too possessive to let anyone see you naked," he said, and pressed his lips to hers.

"Zev!" another male voice called out. "Get your naked ass out of that water! We brought breakfast."

"What'd you do, sell tickets?" Carly said, scrambling behind Zev again.

A tall, fit guy with short light brown hair was walking down the dock carrying a to-go tray of coffee cups. He wore a long-sleeved shirt, shorts, and a cocky smirk. Behind him, a slim brunette in a sweatshirt and shorts was talking with Roddy.

Zev chuckled. "It's just Ford. That's Randi behind him."

"Great," she said and hollered, "Anyone else want to see me naked?"

Zev looked over his shoulder, flashing a wolfish grin.

Carly shook her head and said, "You had better find a way to get me out of here without my coochie being seen, or it'll be a long time before *you* see it again."

"FAIR WARNING," ZEV hollered as he climbed into the boat. "Sea snake on board." He grabbed one of the towels Ford had tossed on the deck and toweled off.

"Cover up those raisins before you embarrass all of us," Ford called from the equipment room, where he and Randi were looking over their supplies.

Zev pulled on his shorts. Chuckling, he held up a towel as Carly climbed out of the water, blocking her from Ford's view, and wrapped it around her.

"Thanks." She secured the top of the towel with a quick tuck.

"Want to put my shirt on?"

"No, this is fine. I'll get dressed after I say hello to your friends." Her gaze moved over his shoulder, and a smile lit up her eyes. "The island is even more beautiful in person than it is in pictures. Look at all of those pretty houses overlooking the water, and that restaurant built right on the marina. There's the ferry! And *look*. I can see Silver Monument." She pointed to the monument in the distance. "Will we have time to see Fortune's Landing or the wildlife sanctuary while we're here?"

"I think we can fit those in. But if we don't, we'll put them on the top of our one-day list."

"Sounds perfect." She took his hand and said, "I still can't believe I'm here with you. I feel like I'm dreaming."

He pulled her closer and said, "I'm going to make all your dreams come true." He lowered his lips to hers in a sweet kiss.

"*Ahem*," Randi said as she and Ford walked out on the deck.

Carly blushed, holding tight to Zev's hand, and said, "Hi. I'm Carly. You must be the other two members of the Fearless Threesome."

"That's right. I'm Alex Pettyfer," Ford said with a British accent and a big-ass grin. "Nice to meet you."

Randi rolled her eyes. Zev chuckled. Ford did that a lot. He looked just like a younger version of the actor, and women ate it up.

"*C'mon*. You know I look just like him, only better." Ford lifted his shirt and flexed his abs.

Randi smacked his stomach. "How many times do I have to tell you that nobody wants to see your abs?"

"Twelve, fifteen...*hundred*," Ford said without the accent, dodging another swat.

Randi, who was petite with friendly eyes despite her no-bullshit swats, flashed a warm smile and said, "That's big-headed *Ford*, and I'm Randi. It's nice to finally meet the elusive *Goonie* girl."

"*Goonie girl?*" Carly looked curiously at Zev.

"Don't look at me. I never called you that," Zev said.

"He never called you *anything*," Randi clarified. "When we asked about the girl in the pictures, he said she was his *first and only love*, his *lost treasure*. But if we pried for more, he shut us down."

Carly looked adoringly at Zev and said, "I think we were both lost treasures for a while."

He couldn't imagine loving her more than he did right then.

"To be honest," Ford said, "I figured you dumped his ass and broke his heart, and that was why he refused to talk about you. But that map you two made looked like it came right out of *The Goonies*. That thing is awesome."

"Hence *Goonie girl*," Randi explained. "Personally, I like *Carly* better. Congrats on extracting the gold coins. Zev sent us pictures. That kind of makes you a real-life Goonie."

"That makes us all Goonies," Carly said.

"I put the coins in the safe in my cabin. We'll have to take them to the vault after we dive, but I knew you and Ford would want to get your hands on them," Zev said. "I took loads of pictures of the extraction process and captured the very moment Carls pulled out the first coin. Hers were the first hands to hold it."

"Holy shit." Ford smacked his own forehead and said, "She's 'This one's for you, Carls!'"

"Yes, she is." Zev pulled her closer, drinking in the adoring look in Carly's eyes, and said, "My first adventure partner, my first love, and my most valuable treasure. She's pretty much *everything*, so don't be a dick, Ford. Got it?"

Ford held up his hands. "Never, man."

"I'll keep him in line." Randi waggled her finger at Ford.

Ford leaned on her shoulder and said, "You couldn't keep a fly in line with a pest strip."

"Watch it, buddy," Randi said, stepping out of his reach. "I might have to line your wet suit with chum."

"On that note, we're going to change so we can get out on the water." Zev draped an arm over Carly's shoulder and headed for the cabin.

"Don't get lost down there, you two lovebirds. Your coffee will get cold," Ford said as he put an arm around Randi.

Randi smacked his arm.

Carly giggled, and looking over her shoulder, she said, "Good thing I like my coffee *iced*."

Chapter Nineteen

"RANDI, CAN YOU grab the spear gun?" Zev asked. They were anchored at the site where Zev had found the concretions, checking equipment and getting ready for their dive.

"You've got it, boss." Randi headed into the equipment room.

Carly gazed at the water, thinking about how much her life had changed. Before Tory had been killed and she and Zev had broken up, she'd spent time indoors for obligations only, like school and dinners. Now, other than her weekly horseback rides, her life had become bound by walls and guided by indoor tasks. She'd forgotten the freeing feeling of spending time in the fresh air. The way it magnified every sensation. Zev's touches were more potent, his every look less restrained, and *she* felt sexier and more invigorated with the sun warming her skin and her hair whipping in the salty sea air.

She zipped her wet suit and said, "I still can't believe we're here, where Garrick 'One-Leg' Clegg's ship went down." She could hardly contain her excitement. "Did you guys know the *Pride* was used as a passenger, cargo, and slave ship before it was overtaken by Clegg? They say it was carrying more than two *tons* of silver, gold, and jewelry. Then there are the cannons and other weapons, tools, and the *people*..." She turned around and found all three of them looking at her with amused expressions. She wrinkled her nose and said, "Of course you know all that. Sorry for geeking out."

"You're sexy when you geek out," Zev said with a wink, and went back to checking the equipment with Ford.

Zev had practically salivated over her in the light blue string bikini Birdie had bought for her, rekindling delicious memories of Zev kissing her entire body earlier as she'd put it on. If Randi and Ford hadn't been waiting, they wouldn't have made it out of the cabin for hours.

"Do you ever wonder what Clegg was thinking when the nor'easter hit?" Randi asked as she carried a spear gun out of the equipment room.

"Probably something like, 'I should've gotten laid last night,'" Zev said.

"That and, 'Holy shit, I'm gonna die,'" Ford added.

They all laughed.

Ford loomed over Randi's shoulder as she checked the spear gun. Randi glared at him. Ford leaned closer, his chest brushing Randi's back, and said, "Was I too far away?"

Randi scoffed. "Like that's even possible? Maybe you should go join Luis's team."

"And miss out on all this fun?" Ford pointed to something on the spear gun and said, "You've got to tighten the—"

"I *did*," Randi said sternly.

"Let me try." Ford reached for it, and Randi looked like she was going to kill him.

They went head-to-head a lot, as Zev had mentioned, but there was a definite sizzle factor between them. Carly wondered if there was a secret attraction there—or if they had already hooked up and didn't want anyone to know. She really liked them both. They clearly respected Zev, but they also teased him like siblings, and they treated her like an old friend, rather than someone who was riding the coattails on their expedition. They'd asked her dozens of questions about her business and had seemed genuinely interested in who she was and in her life in Colorado, which she appreciated.

As Ford and Randi bickered, Zev meticulously checked an oxygen tank, brows knitted, jaw tight. Carly had forgotten how serious he became when he was doing safety checks, so different from the easygoing guy he was otherwise. On the trip out to the dive site, he'd given her a complete safety lesson, including a lecture on shark behavior. She'd listened to every word, even if she'd been staring at his lips and wanting to kiss them.

He must have felt her staring now, because he looked up, and the *zing* that always accompanied their connection brought goose bumps. She loved being on the water with him, sharing another adventure. Memories of their adventurous dreams had been rising to the surface all morning. Being with Zev in Colorado had made her feel more alive than ever, and now she knew that was just the tip of the iceberg. She hadn't realized how *desperately* she'd missed him and their shared love of the thrill of the unknown.

Zev blew her a kiss, pulling her from her reverie. She swore she felt that kiss land on her lips.

"Where's mine?" Ford said with a waggle of his brows.

Zev shook his head and finished checking the tank. Carly went to join him.

"Better have peroxide on hand if you kiss Ford," Randi said. "Lord knows where his lips have been."

Zev rose to his feet as Carly approached. "Are you ready,

babe?" he asked, putting a hand on her back.

She inhaled deeply. "As ready as I'll ever be."

"I'll be by your side the whole time." He drew her closer, gazing deeply into her eyes, and said, "Promise me if anything feels off, if you get rattled, or just need to surface, you'll let me know. Okay?"

"Of course." He'd been worried that the dive might be overwhelming for her, since she didn't dive very often. But she was confident in her skills, and she was too excited to get rattled.

Zev had gone over every detail of the dive. Randi was going to stay on board in case anything went wrong, Carly and Zev were going to use the magnetometer, a large tubular underwater metal detector that was about three feet long and weighed about thirty-five pounds, and Ford was going to carry a spear gun and keep an eye out for sharks. Apparently they'd had to evacuate the water a few times in the past because of sharks. That worried Carly, but not enough to keep her from diving. It was funny how meticulous Zev was about safety and dangerous adventures, like diving, and how casual the rest of his life was. She had a feeling another woman might think he should be able to plan time to see her as intricately as he'd planned this trip. But Carly knew the nature of treasure hunting, and she didn't resent Zev for his days and schedules changing like the wind. She hoped he'd find every artifact from the *Pride*, even if that meant she'd have less time with him and the time they'd get together had to be at the spur of the moment. Wasn't that another part of loving someone? Wanting them to have everything they'd ever dreamed of?

Her hair whipped across her face, and Zev slid his hand along her forehead, threading his fingers into her hair along her scalp, pushing it away from her face and holding it there. He stepped closer, his eyes holding hers as he said, "I *love* you, Carls." He said it so passionately, it almost sounded like it held more of a message.

"I love you, too. Are you okay? I know you're nervous about me getting overwhelmed, but I'm going to be fine."

"I'm better than I've ever been. I know you'll be okay." His grip on her hair tightened as he brought his face closer to hers and lowered his voice to say, "It's just that you're *here*, and we're about to dive for *our* treasure. How many stars had to align for us to come together again? For us to be in this moment? I feel so damn lucky I want to shout it out to the world."

He pressed his lips to hers, and she thought, *I want to shout it, too.*

"Are we going to dive or make out?" Ford asked.

"I'm starting to think you're jealous," Randi said.

"Give us a sec." Zev grabbed his phone and said, "Remember-when picture?"

Her heart leapt. "Yes!" As he lifted the phone to take a selfie, she knew it wouldn't matter if they'd taken a picture or not. Like all the other things they'd ever done together, she'd never forget a second of this trip, because every minute with Zev was unforgettable. After he took the picture, she said, "I just want you to know that this has already been an unforgettable experience, and even if we don't find anything down there, this has already been the best adventure of my life."

"Every day with you is the best adventure of my life," Zev said. "It always has been."

Ford gave them a hurry-up look, but he was smiling. Carly knew he was happy for his friend. She put her face next to Zev's, both of them grinning as he took a selfie.

"Get in here, you two," Zev said, waving Randi and Ford over.

"Maybe we'll get a place on the sacred *Goonies* collage!" Randi said as she put her arm around Carly and Ford put his arm around Zev.

Zev took the picture and said, "Let the hunting begin!"

They put on their equipment and went in search of treasure.

ZEV HELD ON to the handles on either side of the magnetometer, while keeping his eye on Carly to make sure she was okay as they made their way toward the ocean floor. Ford was on her other side. He'd given Ford strict instruction that if they got into trouble, Carly's safety came first. Zev had always worried about her, but nothing compared to what he felt now that he knew what it was like to be without her.

Carly gave him a thumbs-up as she descended into the cold, dark depths of the sea. He'd purposefully taken her down a good distance from where they'd blasted the seafloor so she would have a few minutes to explore areas that hadn't been affected by the blast. He was glad he'd thought ahead, because as excited as she was to get to the site, watching her explore was *his* best adventure yet. He reached for his underwater camera clipped to his equipment, capturing her beauty as she touched rocks, crustaceans, and everything else she could get her pretty little hands on. She picked up a starfish, eyes wide as she pointed to it, posing for the picture. Even underwater excitement radiated off her.

Behind her Ford was keeping watch in the murky water.

Zev was acutely aware of their time limit, but after a minute or two, Ford mimed tapping his foot. He was ready to get moving. Zev was anxious to see what they'd find, too, even though he'd already found his *real* treasure. He gave Carly another few seconds before getting her attention and pointing in the direction of the site. As they swam across the ocean floor, he took great pleasure in how his thoughts had changed from *I*, *my*, and *alone* to *we*, *our*, and *together*.

The seabed surrounding the crater looked like a whole different world with the natural ocean floor covered by the sand they'd blown. Zev indicated that he was ready to give Carly the magnetometer. She'd spent time getting used to the feel and weight of it on the boat, and he'd taught her how to read the LED panel. Excited, confident eyes smiled back at him from behind her mask as they transferred the heavy equipment. She nodded when she was ready. The magnetometer was buoyant, but it was still a lot to manage. Zev stayed close, just in case she needed him to take it.

While she watched the LED readout displaying the gamma count, anxiously awaiting a spike, Zev watched her and *everything* around them. He trusted Ford, but Carly was *his* to protect, and her safety came before everything and anything else.

He motioned with his hand, indicating they should work their way along one side of the crater and circle down toward the bottom, then inspect the other side. Ford hovered above them, keeping guard as they made their way deeper. Time ticked by with heart-palpitating anticipation. He silently prayed they'd pick up something, though as she'd said, she'd be thrilled with the experience either way.

When they reached the bottom of the crater and were

swimming along the perimeter, Carly's head swung in his direction. She pointed to the LED, showing him that it was picking up something. They swam in a grid-like fashion, crossing the crater to determine how big the area of metal was, but the reading faded fast. They gave the equipment time to clear, then swam back for another read of the area to see if it had been an error, but they got the same results. Whatever the metal detector had picked up was small. They were running out of time, and Zev wanted to cover as much ground as possible. He pointed to the other side of the crater, and they swam in that direction. As they approached the farthest point, the LED lit up, sending chills through him. Carly raised a fist, shaking it with excitement, and they continued swimming, watching the readout, their disbelieving eyes connecting every few seconds as the reading got stronger, covering a massive area.

They swam away, giving the LED time to settle back down, and then they retraced their paths, double-checking the readout. Confirmation sent them into high-five excitement. They swam up to Ford, and Zev relayed the discovery as best he could, which must have been pretty damn well, because Ford did a fist pump and an underwater happy dance.

Zev took the metal detector, and they swam toward the surface, taking necessary decompression stops. When they began the last part of their ascent, Carly grabbed Zev's arm, pointing frantically down and to the right, where a shark appeared in the murky water. Zev's protective instincts surged. He indicated for her to swim toward the surface and moved between her and the predator. As she ascended, Ford took his place beside Zev, spear gun at the ready. They swam slowly toward the surface, eyes locked on the enormous shark. As it neared, Zev got a better look at its fins and realized it was a basking shark and of no threat to them. Relief swamped him.

They made quick work of getting out of the water and shucking their flippers and masks. They all spoke at once as they took off the rest of their equipment.

"We found the motherload!" Ford said.

"Randi...?" Zev tapped his wrist. He wanted to be sure Carly had twenty-four hours before their flight, which was leaving at nine the next morning.

"I was sure we were going to be eaten before we had a chance to celebrate," Carly said, panting heavily.

"It was a basking shark." Zev leaned closer, speaking directly into her ear as he said, "But you're not out of danger. I'm looking forward to a celebratory *feast* later."

Carly blushed a red streak.

"Zev, it's eight forty. You're good," Randi said. "And Jeremy called while you were in the water."

Zev spun around. "What'd he say?"

"I didn't answer it," Randi said. "I just saw his name on your phone screen."

Zev grabbed his phone, his mind whirling from their new discovery. Everyone went silent as he made the call. He paced the deck, waiting for the receptionist to patch him through, and tossed a silent prayer out to the universe in hopes of gaining the rights to the vessel.

"Zev." Jeremy Ryder's deep voice traveled through the lines. "I've got good news. We have the order appointing your company as the substitute custodian and the signed warrant of arrest..."

Zev pumped his fist, locking eyes with Carly, who had tears in hers. Ford and Randi cheered and hugged, pulling Carly into their celebration as Zev listened to Jeremy talk about legalities and next steps. Zev told him about their dive and his hopes that they'd find something significant that tied to the *Pride*. "I'll see you Monday morning, and, Jeremy, thank you again for everything."

When he ended the call, Carly leapt into his arms. "You did it!" She kissed him and said, "You gained the rights to whatever is down there, which we both know is from the *Pride*. You made our childhood dreams come true. I love you, Captain Zev!"

Ford was arguing with Randi about something and stopped midsentence to say, "Does that name carry into the bedroom?"

Zev glowered at him as he set Carly on her feet, but they all cracked up. As they talked over one another, their voices escalating with excitement, the full weight of it all hit Zev. The vessel was *his*, and there was something big down there just waiting to be unearthed. He looked at Carly, bouncing on her toes, smiling brighter than the sun as she described to Randi what it had been like to see the LED illuminate on the magnetometer. When Ford began telling Randi that he and Zev had saved Carly from a great white shark, Carly's eyes found Zev's. She might not have been there for the first discovery, but she was here now, celebrating the part that mattered most. He'd worried about Carly being overwhelmed by the dive, but he'd never expected to be the one who would become swamped with too much emotion to think straight.

He strode across the deck, reaching for her hand. "Excuse me," he said, pulling her away from the others and into his embrace. He held her tight, their wet suits still hanging off their hips, and said, "God, baby. We did it. We really did it. The *Pride* is ours."

"*You* did it!"

"No. You've always been with me." He gazed into her eyes and said, "You're my lucky charm, Carls." He lowered his lips to hers, wishing he could kiss her for hours.

"Hey, *smoochers*," Ford interrupted, waving his phone at them. "Remember-when picture?"

"Oh, man, you're an ass," Zev teased, and hauled Ford and Randi into a picture. They took several, and then they stripped off their wet suits and switched into work mode.

Zev grabbed a pad and pen while the others took care of the equipment and talked about what the magnetometer might have picked up. He sat down and said, "All right, guys, let's focus. We need to get our arms around our plans for next week. Then Ford and Randi can dive, and later we'll take the coins to the vault, shower, change, and meet at Rock Bottom for a celebration dinner."

They all cheered.

"We've got a lot of plans to make for next week. I'm meeting Jeremy Monday morning in Boston to finalize all the paperwork. We'll need extra hands to do this quickly. Ford, you want to see if Cliff and Tanner are available?" Cliff and Tanner were two divers Zev trusted and had worked with a number of times. Zev would have them sign nondisclosure agreements to ensure the dive location and other details would be kept confidential, but they knew the routine.

"I'm on it," Ford said.

"Randi, is Brant around? I want to put him on standby with the crane." Brant was Randi's oldest brother. He was a shipwright, and he owned a marine equipment company and a host of fishing boats.

"Yeah, he's around. I'll let him know," Randi said.

"Great. Whatever pinged the system spans at least ten or

twelve feet in length, and it isn't far beneath the surface. We'll see if we can get to it with the dredge engine and pump. Wait until you use that equipment, Carly. It moves six hundred gallons of water a minute and sucks the sediment like a vacuum cleaner, blowing it out onto a twelve-foot floating screen deck covered in fine mesh, so we can sift through the debris without losing any artifacts."

He was talking fast, and Carly was crouched beside an oxygen tank, looking at him forlornly. Reality hit him like a slap to the face.

This wasn't their real life. This was a trip, a jaunt into *his* life. Carly wouldn't get her hands on that equipment or *him* next week. She'd be two thousand miles away, handling crowds at the festival.

"Babe," he said as they both rose to their feet, and he reached for her.

Ford and Randi fell silent, watching them.

"We'll FaceTime," she said quickly, the disappointment in her eyes palpable. "You can fill me in on how it goes."

"Right." He swallowed hard against the crushing feeling in his chest. How the hell was he going to survive being apart from her? "I know you can't be here, and you can't miss the festival, but *damn it*, baby…" He gathered her in his arms and said, "I wish you could."

Chapter Twenty

CARLY DIDN'T KNOW if she should slaughter Birdie or praise her for the clothes she'd bought on Zev's dime. In addition to the barely there string bikini, she'd purchased a white lace thong, a ridiculously small miniskirt, a gold tank top, and a gauzy, see-through and backless cream-colored minidress. She opted to wear the flowy dress to dinner with Ford and Randi, even though it was far more provocative than anything she'd ever choose for herself. The front panel of the dress had a swatch of lace down the center, baring a path of skin between her breasts all the way down to her waist, and lace strings attached to the sides of the panel that tied across her bare back. Two more laces tied around her neck, like a halter. There would be no hiding *anything* tonight.

Zev stepped behind her as she slipped her feet into the cute strappy sandals Birdie had chosen, which went perfectly with the dress. He moved her hair to one side, pressing a kiss to the skin he'd bared, and said, "I think Birdie should be your personal shopper."

"It is pretty, isn't it?"

"The dress is sexy as sin, but *you're* stunning." He turned her in his arms, looking incredibly handsome in a gray button-down short-sleeved shirt and jeans.

"Thank you. I just wish she'd chosen something other than a thong."

"You still hate them, huh?" He reached beneath her skirt, hooked his fingers in the sides of the thong, and said, "I dare you not to wear it."

She inhaled a ragged breath, the feel of his fingers on her hips sending heat to all the right places. "If I accept your challenge, then I dare you not to touch my naked parts while we're out tonight."

His eyes narrowed. "That's asking for a lot." He kissed her neck and said, "I can last through dinner. No promises afterward."

"You're *so* wrong. Your voice holds the dirtiest type of promises. Too bad Jack's plane doesn't have a private cabin for our trip home tomorrow."

"Jack's not flying us back. Randi's sister, Tessa, is. She lives on the island." He dragged the thong down to the floor and said, "It offers a bit more privacy."

She stepped out of the thong, and he ran his hands up her legs, dropping a kiss on each of her thighs before rising to his feet, leaving her wanting more. She glanced at the clock, wondering if they had time for a quickie before meeting Ford and Randi. When they'd come back to the marina, Ford and Randi had taken the coins to the vault and Zev and Carly walked to the wildlife sanctuary. She'd been wanting to see it since she was a teenager, and being there with Zev was even better than she'd imagined. They held hands, enjoying the sights. There were long grasses with trails snaking through them, patches of pine woodlands, and a sandy barrier beach. They saw turtles, egrets, herons, swallows, and sandpipers. Carly could have walked for hours, but they'd needed to get back to the boat to shower and get ready for dinner. They were meeting Randi and Ford in half an hour.

Zev's phone rang, and they both glanced at it on his desk. *Dad* flashed on the screen with a FaceTime call, and she remembered that he'd left a message for his parents to share his news. She wanted to say, *Ignore it*, but that wasn't fair. Her sexual desires didn't trump sharing his incredible news with his family.

"Better answer it before you fail your dare." She was only half-teasing.

He kissed her and said, "Grab your sweater. It'll be chilly soon." He reached for the phone as she got her sweater, and then he took her hand, leading her up to the deck.

A gentle breeze washed over Carly's skin. She went to the railing to give him privacy. As his parents told him about their day, she gazed out at the other boats in the marina and the cute cottages and buildings on Silver Island. She still felt like she was living someone else's life.

The life she'd once dreamed of.

"How are you, honey?" she heard his mother ask.

Carly couldn't see the phone screen, but hearing his parents' voices and being together with Zev again made her long for the connection with them. She loved his parents. Seeing them at the wedding had reminded her of how much she missed them. Distancing herself from his close-knit family had been one of the hardest things she'd ever done, but it had been necessary because she couldn't have spent time with them without thinking of Zev.

"I'm better than I've been in years. I have news to share," Zev said.

"*Wait!* I want to hear!" Jillian's voice rang out. "Hi, Zev. Come on, you guys. Hurry! He has *news!*"

Carly wondered who Jillian was talking to. Three deep voices greeting Zev gave her the answer. Graham, Jax, and Nick had easily discernible voices.

"Hi, Zev," said a sweet female voice Carly didn't recognize.

"Hi, Morgyn," Zev said.

Ah, Graham's wife.

"How's Bandit?" Graham asked. "Did he steal all your stuff?"

"What do you think?" Zev laughed. "What's everyone doing there?"

"Having dinner, of course," Jillian said. "If you were around more often, you'd know that. But that's enough chitchat. What's your news?"

"Which do you want first—the *good* news or the *best* news?" Zev asked.

Carly wondered which was the best news—today's discovery or the vessel being arrested.

"Gosh, honey. I don't know," his mother said.

"Then I'm going with the *best* news," Zev said. "I found my *treasure.*"

He sounded proud and happy, like he had been bursting to tell them. Everyone congratulated him in an uproar of excitement. Carly was thrilled for Zev, right along with them.

Zev stepped beside her, bringing her into the frame, and he gazed into her eyes as he said, "The funny thing is, she was in Colorado the whole time."

Carly's heart stumbled. *She* was his *best* news, his *treasure*?

"Oh, honey! *Carly!*" his mother exclaimed. "You two are back together?"

"Yes, we are." Zev hugged her, kissing her temple.

Jillian and Morgyn cheered and hugged as everyone congratulated them. It felt wonderful to be swept into the Bradens' inner circle again and welcomed so eagerly after all the time that had passed.

"I have to call Char and let her know it worked!" Jillian shouted.

Morgyn gasped, and Jillian froze like a deer caught in headlights. Jax and Nick shot her angry glares. Graham scrubbed a hand down his face, chuckling.

"*What* worked?" Zev asked, looking as confused and curious as Carly.

"*Um...*" Jillian said, looking apologetically at Morgyn and her brothers, who were all scowling, except Morgyn, whose guilt-filled eyes were wide as saucers.

Zev narrowed his eyes. "*Wait* a second," he said angrily. "Graham, I thought you and Morgyn were going to Seattle, and Jilly and Jax were supposed to be out of town for a fashion show. Nick? Weren't you going to Virginia to pick up horses or something?"

"Seattle? Fashion show? Virginia?" His mother looked at her other children and said, "What the devil are you kids up to?"

"Don't look at me. I just did what I was told," Graham said, earning a blush and shrug from Morgyn.

"Me too," Nick and Jax said in unison.

Their father laughed. "Oh boy. I think we've got a conspiracy on our hands."

"*Jilly?*" Zev asked in a deathly serious tone.

Jillian threw up her hands and said, "It was *all* Char's idea! Ever since Morgyn told her that Zev was gray, she's wanted to fix him!"

"Is that a *Fifty Shades* reference?" Nick asked with a snicker.

Jillian rolled her eyes. "Tell them, Morgyn!"

"Yes, please enlighten us, Sunshine," Zev urged.

Morgyn looked at Graham, and he nodded encouragingly. She sighed and said, "You guys know I see auras, the energy people give off. The first time I met Zev and Graham, Zev's aura was muddy. Like dirty gray, which doesn't mean anything sexual. It means he was overly guarded, blocking energies, despite his carefree, outgoing personality. That's why I called him *Foreplay*—"

Nick and Jax chuckled. Zev shot them a warning stare.

"Really, boys?" their mother said. "Let Morgyn finish her story."

"That's why I *used to* call him Foreplay," Morgyn corrected herself. "Because I could see that it wouldn't matter who he was with; he simply wasn't open to long-term energy. I'm sorry, Zev, but it was true. All that energy you threw out felt like a cover-up. But now I can see it's changed. I see the full spectrum of the rainbow around both of you."

Carly wondered what her colors had looked like before she and Zev had reconnected.

"See?" Jillian exclaimed. "Char said Zev and Carly just needed a little nudge in the right direction and that the inn would work its magic. And I *knew* the only way to make Zev stay in Colorado long enough to test her theory was if nobody else offered to help Beau with the animals."

His mother covered her face, laughing. "Oh, Jilly…"

Zev was looking at Jillian like she'd lost her mind, but when his loving eyes hit Carly's, looking at her the way he had so often, like she was his whole world, the air around them didn't sizzle and pop this time. It warmed with the comfort of a best friend and embraced like the strong, safe arms of a lover. In that moment two things became clear. She had no doubt that she would have looked muddy before, too, and she and Zev were the ones who had lost their minds—over each other.

Thank you, Char and Jilly.

"That could have backfired so badly, Jilly," their father said.

"But it didn't!" Jillian exclaimed. "Look at them!"

Zev was still gazing at Carly as he said, "Yeah, look at us." He slid his hand to the nape of her neck and drew her mouth to his in a long, slow kiss.

"Damn, bro." Graham whistled as Zev's and Carly's lips parted, both of them smiling.

"See?" Jillian said snarkily. "What do you have to say about Char's plan *now*?"

Carly bit her lower lip, embarrassed and blissfully happy. Zev leaned in and pressed his lips to hers again in a sweet peck.

"I think we should use Char's romantic savant abilities to find you, Jax, and Nick significant others," their mother said.

Nick shook his head and said, "No thanks. I'm good."

"Me too," Jax agreed. "My life is way too busy for that kind of commitment."

"I'm already on Char's list, thank you very much," Jillian said with a fluff of her hair.

Carly looked at his family, overwhelmed with the trip, the welcome, and all that Zev turned out to be. But even that couldn't slow her words from tumbling out. "Well, I'd like to say thank you for Char's plan, and to each of you for caring enough after all these years to go to so much trouble to pull the wool over Zev's eyes. You opened a door that we couldn't help but plow through." She looked at Zev and said, "I didn't realize how much I was missing until you *pushed* your way back into my life."

"I love you," he said softly, and kissed her again.

"Now I'm going to cry," his mother said, making them all laugh.

"Zev, you said there was good news and best news. We all love the best news, but what's the *good* news?" his father asked.

"Is Carly knocked up?" Nick asked.

"No," Zev and Carly said in unison.

As Zev shared the rest of his news and his family praised his efforts, Carly said a silent *thank you* to Char for believing in true love, second chances, and happily ever afters when she and Zev had believed their story had already ended.

THE ROCK BOTTOM Bar and Grill was built along the marina and offered a casual, rustic atmosphere where patrons could eat inside the restaurant or outside on the large open deck overlooking the water, as Carly, Zev, Randi, and Ford were doing now. Boaters also docked beside the deck, ordered dinner from one of the dock waitstaff, and ate on their boats. As Carly listened to Randi and Ford tell stories about trips they'd taken with and without Zev, she imagined a future of summer evenings just like this one, with a cool breeze at her back, sharing a slice of key lime pie with Zev, so in love she was sure everyone around them could feel it.

"And then there was the trip we took in the fall two years ago, when we went to the Canary Islands to surf and Ford told everyone he was Alex Pettyfer." Randi paused to take a sip of her drink. She looked beautiful in a colorful peasant blouse and miniskirt.

"That was last year, and it was *winter*," Ford insisted. "We were in *Panama* for a festival, remember?"

Randi rolled her eyes. "You're wrong. It was definitely *fall*."

"I'm always right," Ford said, and lounged back in his chair, appearing far too sure of himself. He cleaned up nicely and looked handsome in a black T-shirt and jeans.

"You're always *arrogant*." Randi whipped out her phone and said, "I'll show you."

Ford peered over Randi's shoulder at her cleavage. A minute later his eyes flicked up to Zev and Carly, and he said, "I pulled off Alex brilliantly."

"Your British accent wasn't all that great," Randi said flatly.

Ford scoffed. "My accent rocked. I got loads of phone numbers that night."

Zev leaned closer to Carly for a kiss, and then he whispered in her ear, "Told you…"

"They need one of Char's plans," she said softly, catching his hand as it slid across her thigh beneath her skirt. She pressed her thighs together, as she'd been doing all night, and gave him a warning glare. But it just made the wickedness in his eyes *hotter*, which made her want him even more. "You're going to lose the dare."

He rubbed his whiskers along her cheek, his hand sneaking between her thighs again, as he whispered, "I don't care."

"*Hello?*" Randi said in a singsong voice. "We lost them again. They're in some sort of lovers' trance."

Carly jerked Zev's hand away and said, "Sorry." Geez, she really was in a lover's trance.

"I'm not," Zev said smugly.

That look got under Carly's skin, turning her on even more.

She needed a distraction from her *biggest* distraction and said, "Who was right about the timing of your trip?"

Randi grinned and pointed at herself with both hands. "*Me*, of course. I knew it wasn't last fall because Zev met up with Graham in Belize last fall, and it wasn't the winter in Panama, because Zev wasn't even there with us. He'd gone home to see his parents for the weekend and then he went to see Luis."

"None of that matters anyway," Ford said. "The only thing that matters is that you, Carly, missed Zev doing a *Magic Mike* dance that night."

"Yes!" Randi clapped. "When all the ladies begged *Alex Pettyfer* to get up and do a *Magic Mike* dance, Ford chickened out. Have you ever seen a harem of angry, drunken females? I thought Ford was going to get his butt kicked, but Zev rescued him. He dragged Ford's lame ass up to the stage, and they both did a *horrible* rendition of Magic Mike's sexy dancing. Ford was the better of the two, in case you're wondering."

"But Zev was the *best* dancer in our high school, and he won a dance contest when we were in college." She looked quizzically at him and said, "Zevy, have you lost all your sexy moves? Because I might have to rethink this relationship."

"No, but I wasn't going to outdance my buddy."

"What?" Ford pointed at Zev and said, "I'm not *that* bad of a dancer."

"*That's* debatable," Randi chimed in.

Zev put an arm around Carly and said, "Besides, I didn't want any of those crazy women jumping my bones."

They had a good laugh over that, but Carly knew from the look in Zev's eyes that he was telling the truth.

As they finished dessert, Randi said, "I'm bummed that you're going back to Colorado tomorrow. It was so fun having another woman on board."

"And this guy has never seemed happier," Ford said, motioning to Zev. "You're not going to dump his ass and leave us with a weepy Braden, are you?"

"No way. I just got him back," Carly said. "Believe me, going home is the last thing I want to do. I've had more fun today than I've had in a long time." Her heart hurt thinking about being away from Zev, but this was their reality. When Zev returned to his boat Sunday evening, he would be embarking on a life-changing adventure, and who knew how long it would be before they saw each other again. She was honored to have been part of working on the concretions and to have taken part in today's expedition, and she wasn't going to let the fact that they'd be apart for a few—*several?*—weeks get her down. So she said, "I'm beyond thrilled for you guys. You're going to make *history*, and I want to hear *all* about it. Every detail."

"I'm going to buy stock in video-chat software," Ford said. "I have a feeling its use is about to spike. Don't worry about Zev, Carly. I'll keep him warm when you're gone."

Zev shook his head, chuckling.

"Ford had a few too much to drink one night and wandered into Zev's cabin thinking it was his," Randi explained.

"Sounds juicy." Carly bumped Zev's shoulder and said, "Is there a side of you I don't know about?"

"Hardly," he said.

"That was the night we found out that Ford is *very* handsy when he's drunk and Zev likes to sleep in the nude," Randi said with a giggle.

"I happen to love that he sleeps in the nude." Carly pointed at Ford and said, "But I'm a fearsome force when it comes to protecting what's mine, so keep you paws off my man, buddy."

They all chuckled. Randi flagged down a waiter and ordered three rounds of shots. When he brought them to the table, she lifted her glass and said, "To Zev, for finally getting his ass in gear and going after his *Goonie girl*."

"Hear, hear!" Ford said, clinking glasses with Randi.

Zev and Carly tapped glasses, and Zev said, "Amen to that!"

They each picked up another shot glass, and Carly said, "To the Fearless Threesome. May next week bring you fame, fortune, and *no* shark bites." She held her glass out, waiting for them to tap it with theirs, but they were exchanging glances she couldn't read.

"I think you got the tagline wrong, babe," Zev said.

"What do you mean? You told me you were the Fearless Threesome."

"*Were* is the operative word," Randi said.

"Now that Zev has a better half, I think it's time we change our name to the Fearless Foursome," Ford said with a wink, and they *all* clinked glasses with Carly.

There had been about a million times since she and Zev had reconnected when Carly hadn't thought she could feel any happier, but as they cheered and drank, she realized she was wrong *again*. Being part of Zev's circle of friends, his *family on the sea*, brought a whole new level of joy.

They entertained Carly with more stories until nearly eleven o'clock, when Zev took her hand and said, "If you guys don't mind, I'd like to take Carly down to the beach for a walk."

"That's code for 'get you naked,'" Ford teased.

They paid the bill and said their goodbyes in the parking lot. Carly hated leaving, but Randi and Ford made it easier. Ford hugged her and reiterated how happy he was that she and Zev were together. He promised, with a wink this time, to keep

Zev warm and hoped she'd be back soon. She and Randi exchanged phone numbers, and Randi promised to keep Ford out of Zev's bed in exchange for Carly bringing chocolates the next time she visited. They both wished her luck with the festival, and before parting ways, Zev took a last-time-we picture of the four of them for Carly.

She loved that the most.

It was a beautiful, clear night, and as they made their way down to the beach, the sounds of the waves crashing against the shore brought a heightened sense of peace. They took off their shoes and carried them as they walked along the beach. Carly was a little tipsy, and blissfully happy. She wanted the night to go on forever. But despite the alcohol warming her, she shivered against the breeze billowing off the ocean.

"Let me help you with your sweater." Zev helped her put it on and said, "So, you said you're from Colorado?"

She recognized the playful look in his eyes. It was story time. "No. *Coronado*. It's a city in California. I traveled all this way in my dingy."

He arched a brow. "In your *dingy*."

"That's right. I didn't want to attract attention, given how famous I am."

"Ah, right. I almost forgot. You're an Olympic yodeler."

She laughed. "You couldn't go with pop star?"

"Way too easy." He stole a kiss and said, "I'm a model."

"Well, isn't that fancy?"

He nuzzled against her neck as they walked and said, "If you yodel for me, I'll let you touch my ten-million-dollar abs."

"Ten million?" she said dramatically. "Is that all abs are worth these days? Sheesh. You should have been a yodeler. I've got seventeen houses and a kangaroo."

They both laughed.

"You *are* living the high life," he said. "I had a house once, but I got in a fight with the mailman who refused to deliver my mail just because I like to answer the door naked. The bastard burned down my house."

She'd missed disappearing into the secret world of Carly and Zev. She looked out at the moonlight glistening off the water and said, "Ten-million-dollar abs and you only had one house?"

"*I* think my abs are worth ten mill, but all I was able to book were cheesy commercials. The casting directors said something about my penis being too big and inappropriate for movies."

She giggled and said, "That must have been *hard* to take."

"You have no idea. They were like, 'Dude, you can do porn,' and I was like, *Screw that.* I took the insurance money from my house, bought and renovated a van, and now I travel and live in it."

"You live in a *van?*"

He hiked a thumb toward the marina parking lot. "Sure do. I've got it right up there. Do you want to see it?"

"I don't know," she said coyly. "My daddy taught me not to let cute guys with big *you know what*s lure me into their vans."

"Oh, right. That's probably smart. Well, we could drive out to Fortune's Landing and see the sights there."

"Really?" She slipped right back into Carly mode, forgetting her ruse.

He hauled her into his arms, hugging her tight, and said, "What do you say, yodeler? Want to drive up to the cliffs with a cheesy commercial model and show me what you can do with your vocal cords? I'll show you what I can do with my rock-hard...*abs?*"

"Yes! I love this! I love *us!*" She threw her arms around his neck and plastered her lips to his.

They ran hand in hand back to the marina, laughing and kissing every few steps, and continued frolicking all the way to the parking lot.

"Here's my other girl," Zev said, leading Carly to an orange Volkswagen van with a white roof.

"She's quite pretty. Does she have a name?" Carly asked.

"Sunrise. Because the orange reminds me of the sunrises you and I used to watch."

Carly reached up and pretended to brush something off his ear. "Sorry, you had bullshit coming out of it."

He laughed and swept her into his arms. "You think so?"

"I know so."

"Would you bet your chance to see my *abs* on it?"

She thought about that for a second. "No, but I don't believe you."

He went to the side of the van, unlocked the door, and slid it open, waving her in. "After you, beautiful."

She brushed the sand off her feet and peered inside. Across from the doors was a narrow counter with a camping stove on top and drawers beneath it. A double bed took up the back of the long van, with shelves full of clothes on one side.

"Climb in," he urged.

They placed their shoes just inside the door and she climbed in. There was a surfboard hanging on the other side of the van, and on the ceiling above the bed was an eight-by-ten photograph of Carly sitting with her knees pulled up, arms crossed over them, and her cheek resting on her arms. She was sitting on a hill, and the sun was rising in the background, spreading layers of orange and yellow across the sky.

"Zevy" slipped out full of disbelief, memories flooding her. "That was the summer your family drove cross-country."

"Three weeks without you nearly killed me. I begged my parents not to stop overnight on the last leg of our trip because I couldn't take another day without you."

"I remember. You came to my window at three in the morning and said, 'Carls, come with me on an adventure.'" Her body tingled with memories of how much she'd missed him, too. It had always been that way. Hours apart had seemed like days, weeks like months, and each year after they'd lost Tory and he'd left—she only just realized—had felt like a lifetime.

"I brought a blanket, and we rode our bikes to our spot on the overlook and just held each other for hours."

"And watched the sunrise," she said softly. He was standing outside the van, and he felt too far away. She went up on her knees, putting her arms around his neck. "I'll never doubt your word again."

"Then I guess I'd better start working on my abs."

She began unbuttoning his shirt and brushed her lips over his warm skin. "Nah, they're already worth more than ten mill." She kissed his stomach and up his sternum, enjoying the way his body flexed to her touch. "But it might be nice to see the sunrise from Fortune's Landing. I bet it's romantic this time of night, and I do want to see if you were telling the truth about your *gigantic* porn-worthy penis." She pressed herself against him, his hard length as enticing as the love in his eyes as she kissed his cheek and whispered, "Friendly reminder...I'm not wearing any underwear."

"I'd say *fuck* Fortune's Landing, but I will *not* let you down." His eyes blazed as he handed her the keys and said, "You drive. Use the GPS. I'm going to be a little busy."

And busy he was.

Zev might have been a safety warrior about diving, but there wasn't a seat belt in sight for him as she drove at a snail's pace to Fortune's Landing. It was hard to concentrate when the boy-turned-man with whom she'd fumbled through discovering the glories of sex and love had his talented mouth on her neck and magical hands between her legs.

By the time they reached Fortune's Landing, she could barely see straight. The second she cut the engine, Zev pulled her off the seat and into his arms. His mouth was hot and demanding as they fumbled and crawled onto the bed in the back of the van. She pushed at his shirt and tore open his jeans. His hands were everywhere at once, trying to get her dress off, quickly growing frustrated with the strings in the back.

"I'm going to shred the fucking thing," he growled.

"There's *one* bow!" She sat up, breathless and needy. As she reached behind her back, she said, "You do you. I'll do me. *Hurry.*"

"Fuck that. I'm doing *you.*"

She giggled. "I meant getting naked."

As he made quick work of stripping off his clothes, she shifted off the bed, bending over a little so she didn't bump her head, and the flimsy dress sailed down her body and puddled at her feet.

Zev's eyes turned volcanic. His hands circled her waist, and he tossed her on the bed, burying himself to the root in one hard thrust. Their mouths crashed together. There was no finesse, no holding back. Every piston of his hips caused an explosion of sparks along her heated flesh. She clawed at his back, trying to meet his pace, but she had no control as their bodies took over, and too many divine sensations engulfed her.

Her head fell back, and she cried out his name, but he tugged her mouth back to his, loving her through her climax. Her inner muscles had never pulsed so tight. His cock had never filled her so perfectly. He pushed his hands beneath her, curling his fingers around her shoulders and locking on like a vise, driving deeper into her with every feverish thrust. The world spun away again, and he was right there with her, tearing his mouth away to grunt out her name as ecstasy consumed them.

When he collapsed against her, their hearts thundering to the same frantic beat, her muscles were too weak to move. They murmured their love between kisses, and Zev shifted beside her, gathering her in his arms. She snuggled into him and closed her eyes, his sweet whispers carrying her off to sleep.

Chapter Twenty-One

SATURDAY MORNING CARLY and Zev lay with their bodies intertwined beneath a thick blanket, the cool ocean air drifting over the cliffs and into the open doors in the back of the van. They didn't have long before their flight, but neither was in a hurry to move. Carly nuzzled closer, and he kissed her softly. He wanted to keep her there forever, so they could love each other and dive for treasures together, and at the same time, he wanted to share her life in Colorado, hang with her friends, and help her business thrive.

He knew she worried about how they'd make a long-distance relationship work, and having her all to himself made his mind skip ahead, too—to visions of a future he wanted, and *needed*, to figure out. A future with the only woman he'd ever loved. The person with whom he'd grown from a silly boy to a possessive, horny teenager, eventually giving Carly her very first orgasm when he'd made it his mission to find the elusive G-spot they'd heard about.

Carly moved her hand over his chest and said, "What's that smile for?"

"You don't want to know," he said, kissing her forehead.

She leaned up on one elbow, her beautiful eyes imploring

316

him. "Now I *really* want to know."

"I was thinking about when we first tried to find your G-spot."

"Oh my God!" She buried her face in his chest, laughing.

He threaded his fingers through her hair and said, "We had so much fun."

She lifted smiling eyes and said, "Remember when you helped me learn how not to gag when I was…?"

"Heck yeah. I remember letting you get the hang of it and then thrusting hard to make you gag, just so you'd want to keep practicing."

"You *ass*." She smacked his stomach.

"I think it was a brilliant plan." He hugged her and said, "I'll never forget when you told me my come tasted gross."

She flopped onto her back, cracking up. "You were so offended!"

"What'd you expect? The girl I loved hated something about me."

Her brows knitted. "Was that why you were so upset? I thought it was because you wanted blow jobs in your future."

"Well, yeah, that too," he said honestly.

"I figured as much."

He leaned over her and said, "I could have lived without blow jobs, but it felt like something that could drive us apart. I hated knowing there was something about me you didn't like."

"Aw. I'm sorry." She ran her fingers over his lips and said, "But you found a solution."

He'd read everything he could to try to figure out how to change the taste, and he'd eaten cinnamon, peppermint, pineapple, cranberries, and celery on the daily. "Yeah, but my poor mother thought I must have had some sort of vitamin deficiency to crave all those foods every day."

"At least it worked," she said playfully.

"Yeah, and then Nick turned me on to pineapple juice."

Her eyes widened with shock. "Please tell me you did *not* tell him."

"I didn't have to. He used my computer and found it in my browser history."

"That is *so* embarrassing." She was quiet for a second, and then she said, "I definitely owe him a thank-you card."

"*I'm* the one who sought out the answer," he said, feigning jealousy.

"And as I recall, you were rewarded *often* for that research. Would you have rather had a card?"

"Hell no."

"Well, if I didn't thank you appropriately back then, thank you for going the extra mile, and thank you for this trip. I've loved every second of it. I love your friends—"

"*Our* friends now," he corrected her, kissing her neck. He was going to kiss her so many times over the next twenty-four hours, he could stock up and draw on the memories when they were apart.

"I love being on your boat and here in your van. I love sharing your world, Zevy."

He fought the urge to say, *Then stay in it with me.* He didn't want to put her in the position of having to choose between the two lives she loved. Instead, he said, "I love sharing it with you. I told you, I don't want any Carly-free zones."

She rocked against his erection with a seductive glimmer in her eyes and said, "I have a particular *zone* that needs a little— *big*—dose of you right now."

As he lowered his lips to hers, their phone alarms went off.

Zev uttered a curse and Carly groaned. They'd set their alarms for the very last minute, allowing them just enough time to get to the boat for a quick shower and then to the airport.

"Think we can turn our six-minute record into three?" she asked.

He shook his head. "I want you more than I want to link our treasure to the *Pride*, but I am *not* going to earn a three-minute crown that'll leave us both unsatisfied." He gave her a chaste kiss and said, "I promise to make it up to you so fantastically you'll *never* want to do it quick again."

LESS THAN AN hour later they were seated in Tessa Remington's luxurious small plane. Going home was bittersweet for Carly. She had Zev for *only* one more day, but at the same time, she *had Zev for one more day*! One more day to sit with him, hold his hand, and kiss his lips. She'd already relived their dive, the dinner with Ford and Randi, their walk through the sanctuary, and every moment of last night so many times, she could recall it all like a movie. And now, as she added this morning's memories to her stockpile, she realized she'd never even set her eyes on Fortune's Landing. She'd only seen the sky. But what a glorious time they'd had!

She glanced at Zev and saw deep affection gazing back at her. She was trying to go with the flow, but as their time together neared an end, it wasn't easy not to think about how their relationship would work in the long run.

As if he'd read her mind, he took her hand and kissed her cheek, soothing the rough edges of her worries. How could they have only found each other a week ago? It felt like the wedding had taken place ages ago. But Zev had always had that effect on her. She leaned closer, their shoulders touching, and said, "You always make me feel like I've lived a month in just a few days."

"It's not me, Carls. It's *us*. We've always lived more than anyone else."

It was true. When they were younger, they had experienced many of the same outings as their friends, but somehow they'd always gotten more out of them and came away feeling higher and more in love than ever. She realized that not only hadn't she thought about her to-do lists even once, but she hadn't *made* a to-do list since Zev had come back into her life. She wasn't sure if that was good or bad, but the fact that she wasn't stressed over it had her leaning toward pretty damn good.

Tessa stepped from her seat in the cockpit and stood at the front of the plane. She was taller than Randi, with dark blond hair and serious but friendly brown eyes. "We've got a long flight ahead, so make the best of it," she said with a wink.

She slid the partition between the cockpit and the seats closed, and Zev and Carly's eyes collided with the heat of a torch. Zev put his hand on her leg, brushing his fingers over her upper thigh, and her breathing quickened as the plane moved down the runway. She thought of a litany of dirty things they could do now that they were alone.

Zev held her gaze, squeezing her thigh as the plane took off and leveled out.

She didn't want to level out.

She wanted to rock his world.

They took off their seat belts, and he lifted the armrest between them, leaning closer. They were so in sync: one heart, two bodies.

"Please tell me you haven't joined the mile-high club in Tessa's plane before."

"I haven't *ever* joined the mile-high club," he said firmly. "But I sure as hell hope to with you."

He slid his hand beneath her miniskirt, under which she wasn't wearing any panties. He growled with the surprise. All of the filthy promises she'd seen in his eyes that morning were nothing compared to the hunger looking back at her now.

She grabbed his shirt, pulling him into a deep, penetrating kiss, and over the next several hours, he fulfilled every last one of those promises.

Twice.

Chapter Twenty-Two

THE DAY HAD started out *perfect*, waking up in Zev's arms on Fortune's Landing, joining the mile-high club, getting lost in fits of laughter and long, steamy kisses. But after their beautiful morning together, Carly had gone into the shop and thanked Birdie and Quinn profusely for holding down the fort and making the treats for the baby shower so she could go away with Zev. They asked Carly so many questions her head spun, and she poured her nervous energy into preparing inventory for the festival and making a dozen truffles to give Cutter as a thank-you for watching the animals. She gushed about the incredible time she'd had, telling them about Zev's boat, their run-in with Roddy and Archer, what it was like to spend time with Randi and Ford, and how much she loved being part of Zev's world again. She couldn't stop thinking about the freedom of being on the water, the thrill of not knowing what their dive would turn up, and her elation at diving with Zev again. She told them about their discovery, the shark, the arresting of the vessel, and his call with his family. But as she relayed Zev's plans for next week and the exciting possibilities of what he might find, reality crept in.

Zev was leaving *tomorrow*, and she wouldn't be taking part

in more dives anytime soon. She had a chocolate shop to run. She couldn't have been more grateful for the constant flow of customers and the festival preparations, both of which helped to keep her mind off the longing that was burrowing deep inside her.

Carly carried a stack of gift bags out of the supply room, thinking about the million things she still had to do for the festival. "We need to package the pretzels for the festival," she said as she caught up to Quinn, who was carrying a tray of brownies out to the front display. "I have to package the truffles, too, and price them." She wondered what else she'd forgotten to do.

"You know you told me both of those things already, right?" Quinn said. She looked chic in a pair of skinny jeans, a cute pink top, and high heels, which she zipped around in like roller skates. "Are you okay? You've been a bit scattered today."

"Huh? Yeah. Fine." *I just feel like my entire life is swirling above my head and I don't know which pieces to hold on to.*

Birdie was standing on a ladder behind the counter in her pretty yellow minidress, hanging up a Divine Intervention T-shirt with the festival logo and the year printed underneath it. They'd sold out of them so fast the last two years, Carly had doubled her order this year.

Carly set the gift bags on the counter and said, "I could have done that. You're wearing a dress, for goodness' sake."

"I came prepared." Birdie lifted up her dress, showing off spandex shorts with eggplants printed all over them.

"*Eggplants?* Really?"

"I said the same thing," Quinn said as she slid the tray of brownies into the display cabinet.

"That's about as close to the real thing as my hoo-ha is

getting these days," Birdie said. "I'm living vicariously through you and Zev."

"Me too," Quinn said. "Not the hoo-ha thing, just living vicariously through you and your hot treasure hunter."

They sure were having enough sex to go around!

As Birdie came down the ladder, Carly said, "I guess I should be glad you're not wearing a thong."

"Speaking of *thongs*, you can thank me now for picking out such a sexy one for you." Birdie waggled her brows.

Carly gave her a deadpan look. "You know I hate them."

"I'm sure Zev *loved* it," Quinn chimed in.

"I wouldn't know. I took it off before dinner, remember? Commando was *way* better than having a string up my butt all night." Carly reached for a package of price tags, realized what she'd revealed, and froze. How had she let that slip?

"*What?*" Birdie exclaimed. "No-thong Carly went *commando?*"

Thinking fast, Carly said, "Did I say that? That's not what I meant. Of course I didn't go commando." She slapped the price tags on the counter. "You know me better than that."

Birdie covered Carly's hand with hers and said, "I *thought* I knew you, but, *girl*, that man *does* bring out your adventurous side. And apparently the secretive side, too, which I am *not* okay with. I bought you all those sexy clothes. I deserve *all* the dirty details."

Carly pulled her hand free and said, "Sorry, but *no*."

"*Aha!* You *did* go commando!" Quinn said.

"Where are all the customers that were bombarding us?" Carly grabbed the tags and said, "Focus on work, you guys. I feel like we're forgetting a hundred things. Oh no! We forgot to make the coconut clusters!"

"Coconut clusters are Friday's specials, Carly," Birdie said. "Today is Saturday. We made the specials—don't worry."

"Right. Sorry. Missing yesterday totally threw me off."

"Another good reason for you to hire me full time," Quinn said. "So you can take a day off every now and again and not feel like it's the end of the world."

"That's not a bad idea, Quinn," she said, mulling over the idea of having those potential days off with Zev. But now was not the time to get lost in possibilities. They had too much to do. "But don't worry. I've got this. I just need to reorganize my brain. Did I remember to tell you guys that we need to double the amount of fudge we make for samples? We always run out so fast."

"Yes," Birdie and Quinn said in unison.

"Good." Carly tried to recall what had been on her to-do lists, which she'd misplaced. "Did we get the cereals to make the special treats we talked about?"

"I told you we did the last two times you asked. *What* is wrong with you? Did Zev literally screw you senseless?" Birdie exchanged a worried glance with Quinn. "Where are your lists?"

"I don't know—about the lists, not the screwing. They're in the back somewhere, I think." Why *was* she so scatterbrained?

Birdie studied Carly's face. "Your lists are *missing*? You don't even usually need the lists for the festival prep. You have it all ingrained in your brain."

"Maybe the sea air or all the traveling wore me out more than I realized." Carly sighed and leaned on the counter. "I don't *feel* tired, but I can't focus. Do you think there's something wrong with me?"

"Yes, but I think it has more to do with a certain sexy man whisking you across the country and romancing you all night long than anything else," Quinn said.

Birdie grabbed a legal pad from the counter and said, "Lucky for you, I was trained by the best chocolatier in Colorado, and I *always* have your back." She rattled off a list of things Carly had mentioned needed to get done. "Carly, why don't you take a breather? Rest in your office for half an hour. Maybe you're jet-lagged. Let me and Quinn find your lists and make sure we're checking off all the to-dos. I'm sure they're around here somewhere, or in the kitchen. I saw you carry them out of your office a little while ago."

"*Rest?* I have too much to do to rest. I'm fine." *Or at least I'm trying to be.* Ugh.

"Is your earring bothering you?" Quinn asked. "You keep touching it."

Carly dropped her hand. Okay, maybe she wasn't fine.

"We're a team, and we kicked ass while you were gone," Birdie reminded her. "The baby shower order is filled and ready to be picked up tomorrow morning, and we're right on schedule with inventory for the festival. You *know* I can handle keeping us all on schedule."

As Birdie urged her to take a breather, Carly suddenly realized what was wrong. She was trying so hard *not* to think about Zev leaving tomorrow, or missing out on all the things she wanted to do with him, it was *impossible* for her to think clearly about anything at all. If she couldn't ignore her emotions without her entire life becoming upended, then maybe she really wasn't very good at being a fly-by-the-seat-of-her-pants person anymore.

That thought brought a wave of regret. Could she have lost her ability to do things on a whim and bounce right back on track? Did that mean she would never be okay not knowing when they'd see each other again? Flying loosey-goosey?

Oh boy. This wasn't good.

She needed to wrap her head around this. "I need a plan," she said under her breath.

"You *have* a very good, detailed plan," Quinn reminded her. "We just need to find your lists so you feel better about it. Give yourself a break, Carly. You don't have to be Wonder Woman. It's okay to be tired or a little off-kilter after flying across the country."

"And being screwed senseless," Birdie added.

"You're right," she said absently. It *was* okay to feel off-kilter. She had a chance at a future she never saw coming, and the man she loved was leaving.

"See? She did have awesome island sex," Birdie said.

"I meant about needing a break," Carly said, but her mind was three steps ahead, drowning in anxiety about Zev leaving. "I'll be in my office."

She strode through the kitchen and closed her office door behind her, steeling herself against the out-of-control feeling gnawing away at her. She thought she'd prepared for this. She'd known Zev was leaving and that they would have no idea when they'd see each other again. A lump formed in her throat, but she refused to let it take hold. They'd had a wonderful time together, a new beginning. They'd been given a second chance at forever, which should be celebrated, not mourned by a layover. She thought about her independent aunt, who would never let a man derail her, and Wynnie, and all the things she'd learned from her about staying grounded and seeing things clearly even in the toughest of times.

Wynnie's voice played in her mind. *Don't expect change to be easy. You have to honor the difficulty, experience the pain, and deal with it as it comes.* Marie's familiar voice chased Wynnie's. *Change starts with attitude. Acknowledge every positive attribute about yourself. Seeing yourself as capable is a good first step.*

Attitude might not be everything, but it was a start.

She knew she was capable and needed to allow herself space to be sad, but she was no longer a lost young girl. She was determined to think through this situation without falling apart. She could do this. She just needed a plan. That's why she felt so off-balance. What was really bothering her?

He was leaving. But she wanted him near. She needed to feel his presence even in his absence. She looked around her Zev-free office.

This she could fix.

Next!

Timing. She needed to get a handle on when she and Zev would see each other again. She made a mental note to talk with him about it tonight, to see if they could nail down something solid for her to look forward to. Once those things were in line, she could focus on her business.

With those two pieces of her plan in place, she pushed to her feet and retrieved her secret stash of pictures. She sat down in the chair behind her desk with the box in her lap. She whipped off the top of the box and began sifting through the pictures. She'd spent so much energy repressing their memories, she'd forgotten the sweetness of them. The way the pictures filled her with happiness and hope. The painful memories felt like they happened a lifetime ago. And they *had.* Not just for her, but for him, too. They'd grown up in their time apart. They'd spent the last week talking and healing, allowing their love to bloom again, and all of that allowed her to see the good memories without experiencing the pain of the past. In the pictures, she saw two kids who were madly in love and believed the world was theirs for the taking. She felt that way now, too, only like a grown, competent and confident woman. She was a businesswoman, and, she realized, *he* was a businessman. Even if his business wasn't conventional, he had a job to do, and just as her job relied on science, customers, and marketing, his relied on weather, research, and a good bit of luck. Sure, they'd have to piece their time together for a while like a long-loved quilt spun of desires, hopes, and dreams. But it was *their* future to build, theirs to *discover*, and *theirs* to make last forever. Only they could mess it up, and she knew he was as determined not to as she was.

Maybe she didn't need a solid plan after all.

She just needed to believe in *them*.

Which she did, with every iota of her being. He wasn't going to take off and disappear this time, and she wasn't going to leave without a trace, either.

Feeling more grounded, she selected several of her favorite pictures of Zev and several more of the two of them. She hung a few on the message board behind her, and she tacked up a few others around the room—securing two with magnets to the side of the file cabinet, and she wedged another in the corner of the picture of the mountains hanging across from her desk. She placed the framed pictures of them with their passports in their mouths and of them holding the *Goonies*-style map on her desk, and felt a lot better.

She'd take the rest of the pictures home and hang them up there. Her stomach knotted at the thought of going home. She hadn't slept there all week, but it felt more like *months*. But even as she thought about hanging pictures up in her house, she knew it wouldn't be enough. With her heart in her throat, she scrambled for her phone and called Zev.

"Hey there, sexy girl. I just ate a few of the chocolates from the treasure chest you made me." His tone turned seductive, and he said, "I have a few ideas about what we could do with the remaining chocolate."

"Zevy," she said urgently. "I've made a horrible mistake."

ZEV SHOT TO his feet at the inn's dining room table where he was working, his protective urges surging at the desperation in Carly's voice. "What's wrong? Where are you?"

"I thought I needed Zev-free zones, but I *don't*. I *need* your scent on my sheets and to feel you in my house. I need to remember what you looked like in every room and what it feels like to have you there with me. You were right—you were always with me and part of me. But having you just in my heart and on my mind is no longer enough. I'm sorry I waited so long to come to my senses, but if you leave tomorrow and I go back to a Zev-free house, I'll be a mess. Can you bring Bandit and stay at my house tonight? *Please?* We can get up at the crack of dawn to take care of the chickens."

"*Babe…*" Zev bowed his head, relieved she wasn't in danger. "Do you have any idea how much that means to me? How much I *love* you?"

"Hopefully enough to say *yes*."

"*Yes*, of course. I know how big a deal this decision was for you, and I appreciate the trust you've put in me. I'll sleep anywhere you want, and we don't have to get up early. The chickens will be okay until we get there."

She exhaled loudly, her relief palpable.

"Are you okay, babe? Do you want me to come to the shop? I was just lining up shipping to get the concretions back to the island and doing laundry."

"No, I'm fine. I'm glad you'll come over tonight, though." She gave him her home address and said, "I was putting up pictures of us in my office when it hit me that you haven't even been to my house yet, and it knocked my legs out from under me. I've slept without you for a decade, and suddenly the idea of it feels awful. How did that happen so fast?"

"It wasn't fast, Carly. You set your sights on me in second grade."

"Oh, this is all one-sided now? Is that how you're going to play it?"

He heard the smile in her voice and said, "It feels fast because we've opened the floodgates, and now all we can do is ride the tide, baby."

"You make it sound so easy. It's going to feel weird being in a house where you haven't spent time in every room."

"Then we'll make it our mission to get *our* scent in every room, on every surface, so there are no Zev-free areas left. You sure you don't want me to stop by the shop so we can make sure there are no Zev-free surfaces there, too?"

"As much as I want to say *yes*, I think Birdie and Quinn would pull up front-row seats for that show."

The lightness in her voice told him she was feeling better. "That's just fine by me, gorgeous. My *first mate* is only for *your* eyes, mouth, hands, and body."

Chapter Twenty-Three

ZEV COULD HAVE picked out Carly's cedar-sided bungalow even without having been given the address. It was as unique as she was, with one story in the front, a two-story A-frame in the back, surrounded by lush lawns, full trees, and gardens overflowing with leafy plants and colorful blooms. The other houses on her street had perfectly manicured lawns and organized gardens, while hers looked like it had been dropped in the middle of the wild.

Zev shouldered his backpack, thinking about the call he'd received from Carly's father earlier. He grabbed the box with the chocolate treasure chest in it and the bouquet of roses he'd bought for her. He knew he had to tell her about the call and hoped the right time would present itself.

He headed up the slate walkway with Bandit by his side. Bandit veered off with his nose to the ground.

"Come on, boy." He waited for Bandit to amble over before climbing the stone steps to the spacious front deck, which had forest-green balusters and natural railings. While Bandit sniffed along the edge of the deck, Zev admired the picture windows on either side of the yellow front door and the maroon trim around the porch roof, all of which underscored Carly's natural style.

He had no idea how something like a house could make him love her even more, but he had a feeling it was because it proved once again that she'd never completely silenced the creative nature girl with a flair all her own that he'd fallen in love with when he was just a boy. The girl who had challenged him to a race just to prove she wouldn't be outdone. She'd outdone him by miles in the years they'd been apart.

Then again, she'd always outshone him.

Bandit leaned against Zev's leg, and Zev crouched to love him up. "I get why Beau takes you everywhere, buddy. I mean, besides your klepto habits. You're a good companion, and I like having you around. But this is a special night, and I need you to remember our talk."

As if on cue, Bandit barked.

"That's right. You promised to behave, and I'm holding you to it. I'll hold up my end of the bargain, too, and help Beau build you that doghouse we talked about." Just in case, he'd bought two new chew toys, which he hoped would keep Bandit out of trouble.

Bandit barked again.

"Yeah, I know he doesn't need my help, but you don't have to rub it in."

Bandit pushed his snout against the crook of Zev's neck, and Zev hugged him with one arm. "Attaboy. Now, let's go see our girl."

Zev pushed to his feet to knock, but the door swung open, and there before him, wearing denim shorts with floral patches and a Journey T-shirt, her hair tousled and beautiful, was his *heart*, his *home*, his *future*.

He was ninety-nine percent sure she was wearing *his* shirt, which they'd bought together at a concert their senior year of high school. He doubted there were two Journey concert shirts with a hole in the right shoulder that had been stitched up with red thread. That made him feel pretty damn good.

"Hey, baby." His heart thudded even harder as he leaned in for a kiss and Carly's summery scent enveloped him. He wished he could bottle it up and take it with him. "Did you steal my T-shirt?"

She looked down at the shirt. "No. I thought you put it in my backpack." Bandit barreled into her, and she stroked his head.

Zev chuckled. "I have a feeling Char has taught Bandit a bit of matchmaking magic. When I was doing laundry, Bandit brought me the clothes he'd stolen. After I washed them, I put yours beside my duffel bag and left the room to get a drink. When I came back, he was lying on my bag and your clothes were gone. I thought Bandit had absconded with them again, but when I went to zip my bag, I found them stuffed inside it. I'm holding your clothes hostage by the way, so you have a reason to make time to see me."

She smiled and said, "Then we're even, because that was my plan, too, only I have no intention of giving your shirt back even *after* we see each other again."

"You can have everything of mine, as long as I have you." He leaned in for another kiss and handed her the bouquet. "I know you didn't use to love getting flowers, but while cereal says I've never forgotten anything about you—us—or stopped loving you, red roses say *I love you* in a universal language, and I want you to know I love you in every way possible."

"*Zevy.* They're gorgeous, but you didn't have to buy me anything. I know you love me."

"That's great, but I'm not leaving any room for miscommunication."

"I love them. Thank you." She lifted them to her nose and said, "They smell beautiful. I've actually never gotten roses before. I think I *like* it."

"Good, because I intend to discover all of your undiscovered likes."

Her eyes heated. "I look forward to that." She motioned with her hand, and said, "Come inside."

"You sure you're ready for that?" he teased. "Once I'm in the Zev-free zone, there's no going back."

"Oh my gosh, get *in* here." She grabbed him by the collar, dragging him into the house. A savory scent hung in the air.

"Something smells delicious." He slid his backpack off his shoulder and set it by the door. Bandit's nails tapped along the hardwood floors as they followed Carly through the living room, passing a coral love seat and two yellow chairs that formed an inviting nook by the fireplace. In the far-right corner of the living room was a spiral staircase, and just beyond was a sunroom with a small round table set for two. A half wall lined with pretty plants separated the living room from a cozy kitchen.

"Grown-up Carly knows how to cook," she said as they walked through the sunroom. She opened a cabinet, pulled out a vase, and began filling it with water. "You've done so much for me, I wanted to do something special for you. I know your mom's whiskey crab soup and herb butter lobster tails and your dad's cheddar biscuits used to be your favorites, so I called your mom and got your parents' recipes."

She lifted the top of a pot sitting on the stove, and the delicious, spicy scent of whiskey crab soup billowed out with the steam.

"Wow. That brings back memories," he said, setting the bakery box on the counter. "You called my mom? Was she surprised to hear from you?"

"*Mm-hm.*" She set the vase on the counter and hooked her fingers into the belt loops on his jeans, stepping closer. "I thought it might be a little awkward, even after how great your family was during the video chat on the boat. But your mom was just as warm and friendly as she used to be. We ended up talking for a *long* time. She asked me all sorts of questions about us, even the hard ones, like was I sure I trusted you and did I still love you."

"*Ouch.* Way to throw me under the bus, Mom."

Carly laughed softly. "It wasn't like that. You know she was always like a second mom to me. I think she wanted me to know that I could still tell her anything. She said it had been hard for her, letting you wander the world for all these years, when what she really wanted to do was send your father and brothers after you and—*I'm quoting here*—drag your butt back and make you see that you couldn't run from grief or from what we had."

"Now, *that* sounds like my mom."

"She loves you so much, Zevy. She said true love was rarely a straight and narrow path and that some people got lost along the way, but love always brought them back."

"It sounds like we need to start calling Char and Jilly *Love*, since this was all part of their master plan."

"Right? It might get confusing if they both have the same nickname." She pressed her lips to his, and then she withdrew bowls and plates from a cabinet. "I told your mom all about Redemption Ranch, but I guess my mom had already filled her in on everything that I'd gone through back then." As she ladled soup into the bowls, she said, "Sometimes I forget how quickly word spreads back home."

"Faster than a shark in the sea."

"Definitely. Your mom really is happy for us. I called *my* mother right after that. So much has happened so fast, I haven't had a chance to call her or my aunt. But as it turned out, *your* mom had called *my* mom after our video chat, and mine had called Aunt Marie. Which reminds me, I should really call my aunt, too, or she'll feel left out." She took the biscuits and lobster out of the oven and transferred them to plates.

"This looks incredible. Thanks for going to all this trouble." He kissed her neck, earning a sweet peck on his lips. "Carls, there's another call you need to know about." She was reaching for wineglasses. He waited until she looked at him, then said, "Your father called me today."

"My dad?" she asked as she poured the wine. "Are you kidding? Why?"

"Would I kid about that?" Morris Dylan was the chief of police in Pleasant Hill. While he'd always been a loving father to Carly, he was stern and had high standards. In order for Carly to take part in adventures with Zev, she'd always had to first do her homework and tell her parents where they were going. He'd never caught them sneaking out, but Zev had always been terrified that if he had, he would have tried to stop them from seeing each other. Before Tory's death, *nothing* could have stopped him, not even Carly's father.

Carly picked up their glasses. "Help me carry?" As she carried them to the table, she said, "What did he say?"

Zev carried the bowls to the table. She'd set their places close together, which he loved. Sitting across from her would feel too far away. They went back for the biscuits and lobster, and he said, "He actually had a lot to say. I wrote a letter to your parents a few months after I left town, before I saw you in Mexic—"

"You *wrote* to them? Why would you write to them and not to me?"

The hurt in her voice sliced through him. He moved from his chair, kneeling in front of her, and took her hand, hoping to waylay the look of betrayal in her eyes. "I couldn't have written to you knowing you would have no way to write back. I didn't know where I was going—"

"But Graham wrote to you."

"Not until two years after I left home, when I had a better sense of where I was going. I couldn't have done that to you right after I left. It would have just made things worse."

"It would have been worse, but *still*," she said sadly.

"No *but stills*, babe. I'd done enough hurting for one lifetime. There was no way in hell I would have done anything to hurt you more. You can be mad at me, but that's the truth."

She closed her eyes for a second, breathing deeply. When she opened them, the betrayal he'd seen was gone, but the sadness lingered. "I'm not *mad*. I know you're right. It wouldn't have done any good. I just wanted to hear from you so badly back then, it kind of hurts knowing that they did."

"I'm sorry, Carls. It seems like all the hurt I tried to avoid happened anyway." He held her hand between both of his and bowed his head, resting his forehead against their joined hands as he tried to push the ache down deep. She ran her fingers through his hair, and when he lifted his face, the forgiveness in her eyes slayed him anew.

"I'm sorry," she said softly. "But we said we'd always be honest with each other. I'm not mad at you now, and that hurt wasn't the kind of hurt that clings to your bones. It's already almost gone." A small smile curved her lips, and she said, "But why didn't *they* tell me you wrote to them? What did the letter say?"

"I always assumed they told you, but today your dad explained why they didn't. He said when they received my letter, you were still getting over Tory's death and my leaving, but you were in a much better place than when it had all first gone down. They didn't want to disrupt your healing."

She swallowed hard. "I guess that was probably smart, because it definitely would have made things harder."

"They love you so much, babe." He pulled his chair over and sat in it so they were eye to eye. "I loved your parents, and I knew by hurting you I had also hurt them. The reason I wrote to them was to apologize for leaving the way I did, and for hurting you, and to explain myself. I wrote about all the things I said to you in the park Monday night. I told them how messed up I was and how much I loved you, and that I knew that would never change, but if I stayed, you'd end up hating me. I said I worried that being with me when I was so messed up would change you and that I didn't want that. I wanted them to hear from me that I knew my weaknesses, and I needed them to know how much I adored their daughter."

"Enough to let me go," she said softly.

"As cliché as it sounds, yes. Only now you know, and they know, that I was never truly able to let you go."

She leaned in and pressed her lips to his. She didn't say a word, but she didn't have to. He knew that forgiving kiss was her way of saying the past was the past.

"When your father called today, he'd already spoken to your mom and to my parents. You know your dad—there was no small talk. He said that I was a boy when I left, and that he can forgive a boy, because making mistakes is how boys learn to be men. Then he said that now that I was a man, he expected that I understood that a man's word was as good as gold. I told him I did, and he said that was good, because I was a *Braden*, and he also expected that I live up to that name." Zev paused, remembering the crushing blow of those words. "When he said that to me, Carls, it was like he knew my deepest secret. I watched my brothers make my parents proud, and I know that my family is proud of all that I've accomplished, but that doesn't negate the way I let them down. Right then and there I made a promise to myself to fix that, the same way I had vowed to be the best man I can for you. I want to be the guy who goes the extra mile for family and friends, for all the people I care about. The guy who goes home over the holidays and stays until everyone is sick of me. I want your father to look me in the eyes years from now and say that I never let him down again. I want to be that guy because your father was right. I'm proud to be a Braden, and it's about time I live up to the name on all fronts."

"YOU LIVE UP to the Braden name, Zevy, but I love that you want to do more and be around more, and I know everyone else will, too." This was Carly's chance to talk about their plans, but she was a little nervous to bring it up. She got up to light the candles and tried to sound playful. "So…at least I know I'll see you at Christmas."

"Christmas? That's months away. We'd better see each other before then." He smacked her butt as she went back to her seat.

"Do you have any thoughts on when that might happen?" She sipped her drink, looking at him over the rim of the glass and hoping he couldn't tell that she felt like she had a swarm of bees nesting in her stomach.

"I don't know, babe, hopefully pretty quickly." He set down his fork, his expression serious, and said, "More specifically, I guess when I get my arms around things or when you get a break and can steal away for a few days. Isn't that what we agreed on?" He rubbed his nose along her cheek, an intimate move she'd come to love. "You know I won't be able to stay away for long. I'll seize every opportunity to fly back and see you."

"I know you will," she said, believing him. "I will, too."

She realized that trying to nail down dates wasn't a feasible option for either of them just yet. She had no idea what events would come up or how much time Quinn could take off from the bank if she needed her to cover for her while she went to see Zev. Maybe her plan to come up with a plan was wrong, too, and what she really needed was to change the way she was thinking. They might not have dates on the calendar, but they had a plan in their hearts and they were both committed to making it work. That should be enough for now.

He ate a spoonful of soup and said, "This is delicious, even better than my mom's."

"Really? Thank you."

They ate in silence for a few minutes, but something felt off. She didn't think it was the lack of a plan. Their commitment had settled that worry for now. It wasn't the food or Zev, and Bandit was sitting by the patio door, not off stealing her stuff.

"What's wrong?" Zev asked.

"Does something feel weird to you?"

"Everything you made tastes amazing, and the candles are romantic." He cocked a brow and said, "So please don't take offense to this, but all we need is a Kenny G song playing and we could be our parents."

"Oh my gosh!" She laughed. "*That's* what it is."

"Yeah, this is great, but it's a bit too *adult* for us."

"I totally agree. I have an idea." She pushed to her feet, and Bandit jumped up, too, following her into the living room. She dragged the coffee table to the middle of the room and tossed two pillows from the couch on the floor. "How's this?"

"Perfect," he said, carrying their plates to the coffee table. They went back for the rest of their meal and the candles. "Remember how we used to sit in my parents' living room and plan our adventures?"

"Yes. I have a picture of that! Hold on." She ran into the dining room and grabbed the box of pictures she'd brought home. Zev was sitting on a pillow, and Bandit was lying beside him with his chin on Zev's lap when she returned. She sat on the pillow beside them and opened the box.

"I told you your house wasn't Zev-free," he said cockily.

"These were in the closet in my office, smarty pants. But now that I have pictures of us in my office, I wanted to put some of these up here."

"Hear that, Bandit? Told you she loved me." He hooked an arm around Carly's neck, tugging her into a kiss. "It's about damn time."

"You're a brat. You knew I loved you when you saw me at the wedding."

He smirked. "How could you not?"

She blew out the candles and pushed the coffee table a few

feet away so they would have room to go through the pictures.

"What do you think, Bandit?" he said conspiratorially. "Is she moving furniture to get naked, or is this a bad sign?"

"Would you stop? Bandit's going to think I really don't like you."

"I think you give him too much credit."

"Really? He stuffed my clothes in your bag. I'm pretty sure that dog is part human." She eyed Bandit, who lifted his head and then rested his chin on Zev again with a sigh. "I was just making room so we can look through the pictures."

"Damn. I was hoping for naked."

She gave him a deadpan look.

He chuckled. "Let's see what you've got."

"A lot of the pictures are the same as yours," she said as they started going through them. "This is the one I was talking about." She handed him a picture of the two of them sitting on pillows leaning over his parents' coffee table, writing in notebooks. They couldn't have been more than nine or ten years old. Their hair curtained their faces and their feet were bare. Beside them were two plates, each with an untouched sandwich and potato chips.

Zev ran his finger over the picture and said, "Even *then* you were trying to get my attention."

"Why do you say that?" She studied the picture. "I was working."

"Look at those skimpy shorts. See your arm pressed against mine? You were *always* after me." He stole another kiss, and then he studied the picture for a minute. "We were so young."

"I know." She pulled out a few more pictures of them fishing, hiking, and playing Monopoly with Beau and Nick. "Look at the scowl on Nick's face."

"Ornery bastard." Zev snickered and fished out a picture of him and Carly riding their bikes in front of his parents' house. Jillian and Jax were sitting on the hood of their mother's car, Beau and Nick were playing catch with their father on the grass, and Graham was pulling his bike out of the garage. "Remember how Graham used to try to follow us?"

"Yes, and half the time you tricked him into staying behind as the lookout with the walkie-talkie."

Zev flashed a cocky grin. "Because I wanted to be alone with you."

"We were *ten*."

"What can I say? I fell in love with you the day I first asked you to be my adventure partner when we were in second grade."

"You did not."

"You're right. It was before that. But that was a major day for me. When I went home that afternoon, my dad and I had a man-to-man talk."

"I think you mean a man-to-boy talk."

"Don't dis my manliness. I might have been little, but I knew what I wanted. My father gave me a lecture about being careful when we went out on adventures. He said to remember that you were a girl and that it was my job to protect you."

"I was pretty tough," she said, loving his father even more for having had that talk with Zev.

"I told him that. I said you were tougher than all the boys in my class. But he said it was still my responsibility to make sure you were safe."

"He's a good dad."

Zev set the picture down and said, "Want to know what else he said?"

"What?" She reached into the box for more pictures.

"He said if I got any funky feelings, like if I wanted to kiss you or if you tried to kiss me, that we should probably wait until we were older so it didn't ruin our friendship."

"Really? But we were so young."

"I know. I was kind of floored. My father never said much. Even back then I knew that when he spoke, whatever he was saying was worth listening to. Why do you think you had to be the one to push us toward every base?" He held her gaze and said, "It wasn't that I didn't want you. I was supposed to be *protecting* you, and I was always walking a fine line that I didn't fully understand. I had all these hormones pulling me toward doing things, but the last thing I wanted to risk was our friendship or do the wrong thing."

He sounded so heartfelt and honest, her words came unbidden. "You've never stopped protecting me. As much as it hurt us both, you left because you thought you were protecting me, and you didn't go after me when I left Mexico because you thought you were doing what I wanted. You were *still* protecting me."

"And then when I saw you at the wedding, all that protecting went to shit."

She pressed her shoulder against his. "Dream on, Braden. You'll always protect me."

"Oh, I'm dreamin' all right, *Dylan*. Dreaming of you naked in my arms again."

They reminisced, kissed, and kidded around as they went through more pictures of the two of them on field trips and archaeological digs, sled riding with his siblings, and bundled up in a tepee they'd built on Zev's bed. There were holiday pictures with funny Santa hats and Fourth of July celebrations where they were running around with sparklers. There was a picture of

Carly and Zev at fifteen asleep on the Bradens' couch, fully clothed, with Zev lying behind her, his arm around her middle. Nick was standing over them, arms crossed, a scowl on his young face. Carly remembered that night well. She and Zev had asked their parents if she could stay over to watch a Freddy Kruger marathon. It was all fairly innocent, although they'd made out and gone to second base when they were alone. They'd woken up to that scowl and to Jillian claiming she had *blackmail material* on her digital camera—including the picture they were now looking at and one of Zev and Carly kissing. Zev had confiscated her camera, keeping the evidence.

"Babe, look at this one." Zev leaned closer, showing her a picture of them with Beau and Tory at a Pleasant Hill Spring Festival.

"That picture was taken a few months before the accident."

"She was so young," he said sadly. "It's hard to believe so much time has passed. I wonder how her parents are doing."

"I visit them when I'm home. They've never been the same, but I don't think anyone who knew Tory was ever the same after she was gone."

"Yeah," he said, sounding choked up. "You should hang that up, keep her spirit alive. We had a lot of fun with her and Beau."

"You're right. Those were really good times." She reached into the box and pulled out a picture of her and Zev taken the night of the Maroon 5 concert. He was holding her from behind, kissing her cheek, and she was smiling from ear to ear, reaching over her shoulders and holding his face. She set the picture on his lap and said, "I'm definitely hanging this one up."

"The concert. That was a fantastic night."

"You just liked making out in the car afterward."

"Damn right, I did. And as I remember, so did you." He looked at the pictures they'd set aside to hang up and said, "I guess you need to buy some frames."

"I stopped at the craft store on the way home. They had frames on sale, so I bought about twenty of them."

"Great, let's hang some of these up," he said, pushing to his feet.

"You don't mind? It's our last night together. You sure you want to waste time putting up pictures?"

He helped her to her feet and held her against him. "It's not our last night together. It's our last night *for now*, and bringing our memories into your home is not wasting time. It's honoring our relationship."

"You always know just what to say."

"No I don't. Most of the time I'm just hoping I don't mess things up. But some things come easily, like being honest with you. I want to be here with you, Carly, and it doesn't matter if we're making out, making love, or hanging pictures. I want you to have happy memories of us that make you feel good when I'm not here with you. Memories of going through these pictures and of the way we suck at doing normal adult things like sitting at a regular table." He glanced at the coffee table and said, "You worked hard to make a special dinner, and we haven't even finished it yet. Some guys would feel guilty about that, but I know that *you* know how much I appreciate your efforts and that this is who we are. We follow our hearts wherever they take us, and sometimes that means we forget to eat. Right now your heart needs pictures on the walls. Later, we'll heat up dinner, and we'll enjoy every last bite."

She kissed the center of his chest and said, "See? I told you. You know just what to say to make me happy. Come on, let's get the hammer and nails."

"I'll wield your hammer if you wield mine," he said, following her into the dining room.

"Okay, *Thor.*" She pulled a pink-handled hammer out of the hutch, set it on the table, and began taking the frames she'd bought out of the shopping bags.

"It's pink," he said. "And tiny."

"You said it, not me," she said with a giggle, earning a scowl. "If you can't handle the pink handle, maybe you can't handle the girl who owns it."

He pulled her into his arms and said, "There's nothing about you I can't handle, Carly Dylan, except maybe that smart mouth of yours."

"But your *massive hammer* loves my smart mouth." She wiggled out of his arms and said, "Come on, Thor. Let's frame the pictures and see how well you bang nails. Then maybe later you can bang *me.*"

"Now who knows just what to say?"

She flashed a cheesy grin. "You're lucky I'm not making you do it wearing nothing but a tool belt."

"You think I'd complain?" He started to unbutton his jeans.

"I'm kidding!" She fell into his arms, laughing. "I love that you would do that for me."

"I'd do anything for you, and *to* you."

He squeezed her bottom and went to let Bandit out to play in the fenced backyard, leaving her to mull over all the naughty possibilities.

"I'll be right there. I bought Bandit a few new chew toys. I'm just going to throw them outside for him."

She watched him as she paired frames with pictures. When she'd been cooking dinner, she'd wondered how it would feel to have Zev in her home after all the years she'd spent denying her feelings for him. But it felt as natural as everything else had, like he really had been there with her the whole time.

After they chose frames for the pictures, they placed a few of them on the mantel and the half wall between the kitchen and the living room. They hung pictures on the wall beside the spiral staircase, and Zev stole kisses after every nail he hammered. He nibbled on Carly's neck as she assessed the angles and groped her every time she walked by. She was far from an innocent victim, egging him on by rubbing against him and brushing against his back as he hammered. She loved teasing him, earning greedy sounds and feeling his muscles taut with restraint. She took it a little farther every time, running her hands over his chest, and when he moved to the next spot, groping him in places that made him moan. He followed her up the spiral staircase, stopping her midway as he felt her up, kissing her so deeply, her knees weakened.

"What's next, sexy girl?" he whispered in her ear.

Your mouth on my naked body. "Office," she said breathily, and made her way up the rest of the way on shaky legs. Her office was the only room on the second floor. It had a peaked ceiling with a skylight so she could see the stars, an antique couch on its last legs, which she'd bought at a secondhand store, a matching end table, and a chic green desk that had been her aunt's.

"*Mm.* I *like* this room," Zev said heatedly, eyes locked on her as he dragged his fingers along the length of the desk.

She set the pictures on the desk, swamped by titillating memories of what he'd done to her on the kitchen table at the inn. She leaned both hands on the desk and closed her eyes, trying to remember how to breathe as a montage of dirty images hit her like a hurricane.

Zev pressed his body to her back, his hands circling her middle. "What's the matter, Carls?" he said huskily. He sucked her earlobe into his mouth as he unbuttoned her shorts and pushed his hand into her panties. They both moaned as his fingers slid through her wetness and he pressed his hard length against her ass.

"*Yes*" came out hot and needy.

She arched back, rubbing her ass against him, and grabbed his wrist, pushing his hand deeper. His fingers dove inside her as his teeth grazed her neck, sending bolts of lust to her core. He teased her, sucking her neck and stroking the secret spot inside her, until she went up on her toes, pleading for more. His thumb hit the sensitive bundle of nerves that made her thoughts fracture. She closed her eyes, grinding, chasing the explosion she craved. But he was holding back, she could feel it, ruthlessly keeping her on the verge of madness. He sealed his mouth over her neck, sucking harder.

"Zev...*please!*"

"Shirt off," he gritted out as he stripped her bare from the waist down. "Hands on the desk."

She'd hang from a chandelier if he asked her to. She leaned forward, spreading her legs wider. He claimed her breast with one hand, driving her wild between her legs with his other. His hot mouth blazed across her shoulders, licking, kissing, and biting *just* hard enough. Every stroke of his hand took her closer to the edge. He tasted his way down her back and over her ass, slowing to lavish her with openmouthed kisses at the top of her hamstrings. She lost her breath at the feel of his tongue sliding deliciously along her flesh. Her head fell between her shoulders, and she clawed at the desk. He pushed his fingers inside her, and she arched back, moaning as she thrust her ass out, giving him all the green lights he needed. But while her world was careening away, he was in total control, taking his time, feasting painfully close to her sex but not nearly close enough.

His hands left her for an instant as he stripped off his clothes. Then he grabbed her hips, pressing his hot, hard length between her legs, resting against her wetness as he dragged his tongue along her shoulder, practically growling, "You're so fucking sexy. Touch yourself for me, baby."

She put her hand between her legs, her fingertips brushing over the broad head of his cock as he pumped his hips.

"Where you need it most," he demanded.

She moved her fingers to her clit, his cock moving quicker along her wetness. The friction was delicious, his commands addicting.

"Squeeze your thighs together." His voice was low and greedy as he palmed her breasts. She obeyed, and he ground out, "*Fuuuck*," pumping quicker, rolling her nipples between his fingers and thumbs. She was barely breathing, at the mercy of his pleasure. He gritted out, "Come on my dick," and squeezed her nipples hard, sinking his teeth into her neck. She cried out, her body bucking and clenching. "That's it, baby, come good and hard." The mix of demand and gratitude in his voice made it even more thrilling as he coaxed her through the very last pulse of her climax.

He turned her roughly in his arms, taking her in a deep, penetrating kiss. She was shaking, barely able to think or see. He put his hand between her legs, drenching it with her arousal, and fisted his cock. His dark eyes bored into her as he said, "Watch me," and dropped to his knees, stroking himself as he feasted on her.

Holy freaking hell. His talented mouth was a force all on its own, but seeing him stroke himself as he pleasured her was too much to bear. Her eyes slammed shut and she spiraled over the edge again, coming so hard her legs gave out. But Zev was there to catch her.

He carried her to the couch and laid her on her back, coming down over her, and said, "How am I going to leave you tomorrow?"

The love in his eyes and the torture in his voice pulled her from her lust-drunk haze. His love was an aphrodisiac, giving her a second wind. She didn't want to think about him leaving and tugged his mouth to hers. His hips thrust slowly, entering her one inch at a time until he filled her completely. "*Car-ly*" came out with awe, as if she felt *too* good.

She was right there with him, swept up and wanting to remain lost in them, running from the reality tomorrow would bring. When he moved, she moved with him, hips rising, thrusting, grinding, fingers pressing into his skin, as if they could imprint each other's bodies on their own. Their mouths connected, tongues battling, probing, *consuming*. He held her tighter, thrust harder, *faster*, the couch shook and rattled with their forceful efforts. He drove deeper, so *incredibly* good, she loved him harder than she ever had, squeezed her inner muscles tighter, sending them both into an agonizing world of raw, explosive pleasure. He ground out her name, his hips shooting forward as his release gripped him. Suddenly there was a loud *crack*. Carly shrieked as the couch pitched at an angle to the floor, sending them hurling as one wooden leg shot across the room. Zev clung to her, his body weight crushing her chest. Silence engulfed them, their bodies still connected, lying at an angle on the broken couch. In the next second laughter burst from their lungs.

"We..." She snort-laughed, making him laugh harder. "We *broke* it!"

He buried his face in her neck, his scruff tickling her skin as he laughed out, "I'll buy you a new couch." He lifted his face, his unstoppable grin making her laugh even more. He kissed her through her giggles and said, "I bet you're regretting letting me come over tonight."

"No way. Better a broken couch than a broken heart," she choked out, hardly able to breathe between his weight bearing down on her and her laughter.

His eyes turned serious, his laughter silencing. "I'll never break your heart again."

"I want to believe you," she teased, believing him with everything she had. "But if you keep lying on top of me, you're going to crush *all* of my organs."

He rolled off her and *plunked* onto his back on the floor, sending them back into hysterics. She tumbled off the couch on top of him. His eyes flamed, and he said, "It's still early. Have any other furniture that needs replacing?"

Chapter Twenty-Four

CARLY WATCHED THE numbers ticking by on the digital clock beside her bed, wishing she could stop time. Their quasi plan had temporarily settled her worries, but she'd woken in a panic forty minutes ago, and her brain wouldn't shut off. She was warm and safe in Zev's arms as he spooned her, his heart beating sure and steady against her back. She *shouldn't* feel panicked. But she had a feeling nineteen-year-old Carly was digging her heels in, making sure grown-up Carly never forgot how much it had hurt to be left behind. She'd never forget, the same way she was sure he'd never forget how it had felt when she'd taken off in Mexico. But they had both forgiven, and they weren't those scared kids anymore. They were smarter, more careful with themselves and with each other's hearts.

Bandit made a whimpering noise in his sleep. Carly wondered if he was feeling off-kilter, too. He was curled up behind Zev's knees. He'd never climbed on the bed at Beau's. Carly had been awake when Bandit had snuck onto the bed like a ninja, but she hadn't had the heart to move him. She had a feeling Bandit sensed something was about to change, and he needed to be close to Zev, too.

Her gaze drifted to the pictures they'd hung on the wall of

her and Zev, cliff diving back home in Maryland and bundled up in the snow holding snowboards on a trip they'd taken their first year in college. A picture of them with Tory and Beau dressed up for a middle school dance sat on the dresser across from her bed. Zev and Beau were decked out in button-down shirts, ties, and slacks. Beau wore dress shoes, his hair neatly brushed. Zev wore hiking boots. His tie was crooked, and his hair hung in his eyes. Carly still got tingles in her belly at the sight of her younger boyfriend just as she had back then. She looked at Tory, her childhood best friend, pink cheeked and glowing in a peach dress with a matching corsage and heels. Carly remembered them getting ready for that dance together. She and Tory had been all giggles and giddiness as they'd dressed. Carly had paired a royal-blue dress with flats, because Zev hadn't yet hit his growth spurt and he'd been only an inch or two taller than she was. He had made her a corsage using fishing line to string together all her favorite cereals. He'd looped and tied, creating funky flowers and bulky stems. Her friends had thought it was weird, but she'd thought it was the most magnificent thing she'd ever been given. She'd thought *he* was the most magnificent boy to ever walk the earth.

He pressed a kiss to the back of her neck, his warm lips drawing her from her memories as he whispered, "Morning, gorgeous."

She swore she felt her heart smile. That old adage about time healing wounds wasn't as true as she'd once believed. She'd had years to heal from her heartbreak, and she'd thought she had. But now she knew that she'd still had wounds that had needed tending and could only be healed by her and Zev working through pain and tears together, talking, loving, accusing, and accepting. Now, on the other side of all that, she saw parts of her future so clearly. She and Zev might not be perfect by other people's standards, but they were honest, and their love was truer and deeper than any she'd ever known.

As she turned in his arms, knowing all of his faults and weaknesses as well as she knew her own, his sleepy eyes met hers, and she still thought he was the most magnificent creature to ever walk this earth.

"I have a surprise for you," he said softly, holding her close. "I arranged for two horses at the ranch this morning so you wouldn't miss your Sunday horseback ride. I know you have a huge day of festival prep planned and need to be at the shop early, so they'll have the horses ready by six."

Her Sunday-morning horseback ride was the last thing on her mind. How could it be in the forefront of his? "Were you always this thoughtful?"

"I don't know, but I promised to add to your life here, not take away from it, and I meant it."

She loved him so much. How was she supposed to go back to her life without him by her side and maintain her sanity when she didn't know how long they'd be apart? The void his presence and his *love* would leave behind felt like a villain waiting in the wings.

"It means the world to me that you thought ahead and arranged all of that, but would you mind if we skipped riding?" she asked. "I really want to just be alone with you until you have to leave. I don't care if we go to the inn to feed the chickens, stay in bed, or take a walk. I just want to be selfish a little longer."

"Is that why you've been up for the last hour?" He kissed the bridge of her nose. "I'm going to miss those freckles."

I'm going to miss the sweet things you do and say, like seeing all the hidden pieces of me when so few people ever try to look past the person I show them.

"You were awake?" she asked.

"Of course. If you're up, I'm up. I could feel you worrying. Are you still anxious about the *how*s and *when*s of our plans?"

"A little."

His brow furrowed, and she knew he didn't believe her.

"Okay, more than a little," she confessed. "I thought I was okay without having solid plans, but it's kind of driving me batty."

"That's okay, babe. The new Carly plans much more specifically than the old Carly did. I respect all the changes you've gone through. Look how far they've gotten you. I'm not sure I can give you all the answers you want, but don't stress in silence. Let's talk about it and see how far we get."

"I'm just wondering what you're thinking about when we'll see each other again. Two weeks? A month? Longer? Sooner?"

"Considering that it's going to suck being apart, my hope is that we'll be able to find whatever the magnetometer detected and get it on dry land quickly. Once I know what we're dealing with and have everything in order, when I see a chance to take a break, I'll steal a few days and come back. Hopefully within the next two weeks. But I don't have any idea how things will pan out. You know how this kind of thing goes. It could take weeks just to dig up and locate whatever's beneath the ocean floor, or we could find out that it isn't even part of the wreckage, in which case we'll have to start over. But I'll be in touch every day, and I'll head back as soon as I can, for as long as I can. I'm working with a small window of time here, and once the colder weather comes, that window closes."

"I know. I'm not asking for exact dates. I just wanted to get a better idea of your plans."

"*Our* plans," he corrected her. "What about your shop? Do you have any slow periods coming up?"

"Not really. Summer and fall are pretty busy with the town festivals, and then we're into the holidays. But it might be easier for me to plan time off than it will be for you."

"This isn't all going to fall on your shoulders. I won't let that happen." He trailed his fingers down her back and said, "We'll figure it out together. We're pretty creative. I'm sure we'll find ways to make it work. I didn't have a chance to tell you last night, but when I called Noah to make arrangements to ship the concretions back to the island, he brought up the idea again of holding a special shipwreck exhibition at the discovery park for a few weeks over the winter, and changing it up each year. I thought it might be worth discussing, since I can't dive at the *Pride* site in the colder months, and you'll want to be here taking care of your shop."

"You would consider spending a few weeks at a time here?" Her hopes soared. "I thought you'd lose your mind if you weren't always on the move."

"I honestly have no idea how I'll adjust to staying in one place, or on dry land, for long stretches of time without a project to keep me busy. But I want to be with *you*, and having an exhibition to run would give me something to focus on. Noah's talking about offering hands-on areas for kids and having me give talks about diving, shipwrecks, and treasure hunting. It could be fun."

"But you travel in the winters, and it sounded like sometimes you travel with Randi and Ford."

"True, but now that we're together, I want to travel with *you*, with or without the team. Trips won't mean anything without you by my side, which brings up another thing I think we should talk about. The *Pride* is *ours*, babe. I hope at some point you'll have time to dive with me again."

"You've really been thinking about all of this, too? I thought you were giving me off-the-cuff answers about coloring outside the lines."

"They weren't off-the-cuff answers. I just meant that we'll have to be creative."

"It sounds like we have a lot to think about now," she said, feeling much better even though they still didn't have solid plans. "I love the idea of you hosting exhibitions and working with your cousins. That sounds right up your alley, but only you know if you can handle being trapped inside in the winter."

"This is Colorado, babe. You still ski, right? Snowboard?"

"Yes," she said happily. "I see where you're going with this. We could have a lot of fun. I've been wanting to go cross-country skiing."

"That's definitely going on our one-day list. My cousin Ty and his wife, Aiyla, love to cross-country ski. We'll hook up with them. What about diving for the *Pride*?"

"I haven't stopped thinking about it since we left the island. I'm dying to get back there, so *yes*. I'll make time for sure. I assumed if I went there, we'd dive and do whatever else you wanted or needed to do, and if you came here, I'd probably still have to work at least a modified schedule, but we would fit in other things, too."

"Then it sounds like we're on the same page, but you still don't have any clearer idea of a timeline than you did last night."

"I know, but I do feel better knowing you might be willing to spend time here in the winters."

He looked at her skeptically. "That's great, but I still see questions in your eyes that weren't there last night. What is it, Carly? What's really bugging you?"

"I don't *know*," she said in a pained, frustrated voice.

Concern riddled his features. "Are you worried about how a long-distance relationship will work when we're apart, or are you afraid I'll disappear again if there's a crisis?"

"I'm not worried about either anymore," she said too quickly, not wanting to try to sort out the difficult questions.

"Good, but it would be understandable if you have doubts about my commitment, and I don't want to be one of those couples who harbor secret worries. I lost a decade with you because of that mistake. There's no way I'm letting it happen again."

She snuggled closer. "Me either. I *don't* have secret doubts about your commitment, or your love for me. I don't think you would do that to me again, or to us. Not after everything we've been through."

"I *know* I wouldn't," he said emphatically. "But that doesn't mean you have to take my word for it. I know I handled things wrong, and I'll never stop proving to you that I am the right man for you and that you can count on me."

"You don't have to keep proving anything, Zevy. I believe you and I believe *in* you."

He pressed his lips to her forehead and said, "Thank you, babe, because I love you with all that I am and all that I have, and I want you to know that."

"*Wait.*" Her heart raced. "What did you say?"

"That I love you?"

"No. The rest."

"That I love you with all that I am and all that I have?"

She couldn't stop grinning. "*Yes.* I said that same thing to Birdie about you, word for word. At the wedding Jilly said we're two sides of the same coin."

"Guess that solidifies it. You're stuck with me." He kissed her and said, "I was going to let you find this on your own timetable, but I think you need to see it now."

"See what?"

He went up on his knees, bare assed and beautiful, and Bandit leapt to the floor. Zev opened the curtains behind the bed, revealing an envelope with *Carls* written across it taped to the inside of the window.

She couldn't stop grinning. "What is *that?* When did you put it there?"

As she went up on her knees and snagged the envelope, he said, "I was going to tape it to the outside of the window after you fell asleep last night, but I was afraid Bandit might bark and wake you up, so I had to do it this way. Open it."

Her pulse quickened as she tore open the envelope and withdrew two legal documents for Two Treasure Hunters, One Ship, LLC, a deep-ocean exploration and shipwreck recovery business. One document named Zev and Carly as the sole members of the company; the other appointed the LLC as the substitute custodian for the *Pride.*

Her gaze shot to his. "Zev…? What is this?"

"I want to add you as an owner of my company. I opened it years ago, but I'm the sole member right now."

"You named your company Two Treasure Hunters, One Ship?" *Holy cow.*

"What else would I call it?" he asked with a grin. "Adding you would make it *our* company. That is, if you want to be my partner. I wanted to make you the substitute custodian of the

Pride to alleviate any concerns you might have about my commitment to our relationship. But I also wanted to protect you legally, and this is the best way to do it. I'm not going anywhere, babe, and I hope this proves it to you."

"Are you *serious?*" She sat back on her heels, her emotions reeling. "You want to be my *business* partner? What does this mean? I don't have money to invest…"

"I don't want your money, Carly, and make no mistake, I want to be much more than your business partner. But I know you need time to believe in me before you're ready for that. This is a *start*, a *promise* that what's mine is yours, including the *Pride*. You don't have to *do* anything other than sign the papers in the presence of a notary, making you part of the business. I'll never take a penny of your money. But, babe, you're smarter than I am, and I wouldn't ask you to be my business partner if I didn't want you to be my partner in every sense. I would *love* to teach you about the custodial process and all that's involved with the business so you understand the commitment. I'm taking care of insurance, making sure you're not risking anything…except maybe your heart," he said with that devastating smile that did her in. "And if this is too much, or too overwhelming, just say the word."

Emotions clogged her throat, but she pushed past them to say, "Oh, it's *definitely* overwhelming, but…You're really serious? What about Randi and Ford?"

He took the papers from her hands and put them on the nightstand. "They work for me, Carly. They're my dive partners, not my business partners."

"But you've been working with them for years."

He guided her down to her back and moved over her, gazing into her eyes as he said, "And I've been in love with you since I was seven years old. What do *you* want, Carly?"

You! I want you! Her heart couldn't take any more. "I *know* you're committed to us. I don't have doubts about that, and I want this so badly. But I don't know how I can be a supportive, contributing partner if I'm two thousand miles away. I just need a little time to get comfortable with the logistics before I can say yes. This is *big*, Zevy. This is your life's work. This is your *everything*."

He was quiet for a moment, and her mind raced, wondering if he thought she was talking about them or his business offer. But then he shifted, aligning their bodies as he cradled her face between his hands, and in his eyes, she saw that she was wrong.

That ship wasn't his everything.

She was.

"You're right, Carly. The *Pride* is my life's work."

Oh no. Had she misread him? Was she only seeing what she wanted to see?

"Before the wedding it *had* been my everything, but only because it had been *our* everything, and it *was* my life's work because I didn't know I'd have a shot at us." He brushed his lips over hers and said, "You're my world, Carly, my one true *love*, and you always have been. You don't have to be a legal part of the company, but you'll always be part of me."

His mouth came coaxingly down over hers, kissing her thoroughly as their bodies joined together, obliterating the shock of his offer and allowing her to think more clearly.

She knew what she wanted. What she'd *always* wanted.

And he was lying above her, loving her like she was the most precious thing on earth.

WHEN CARLY WAS in his arms, Zev truly believed the strength of their love would pull him through their time apart. But after making slow, passionate love, after holding each other in the shower hoping they could stop time if they held on tight enough, after sitting outside as their breakfasts got cold because knowing he was leaving made everything taste wrong, Zev realized he was in denial. He tossed his backpack on the seat of Beau's truck, and Bandit looked up at him accusatorially. He was sure the dog was wondering what the hell made him think leaving was a good idea.

"Don't look at me like that," Zev said to Bandit as they headed back up the walk.

Carly was sitting on the stairs to the deck putting on a brave face. Every step felt like quicksand weighing him down, sucking him under, far too reminiscent of when he'd left Pleasant Hill all those years ago. Back then he'd been so fucking scared taking off into the world without anyone to lean on but himself, he'd poured all of those emotions into forcing himself to focus on the next mile, the next country, the next adventure, which had all seemed more like a jail sentence. He'd made a life of moving around, no attachments, no goodbyes. He'd gone wherever the wind had taken him because he'd thought he'd lost Carly forever, and if she wasn't waiting for him, then who the hell cared what was?

Carly rose to her feet as he neared the deck, a forced smile sliding into place on her beautiful face. "Guess this is it," she said far too cheerily. "Back to the kitchen for me and the sea for you."

They'd been readying themselves for this moment, but there was no hiding the longing in her eyes or the sadness wafting off her like a gale-force wind as she reluctantly pushed him to leave. The trouble was, he no longer wanted to be carried by the wind. He wanted to *be* her wind, to sweep her up and carry her with him.

"Let's not do that," he said, taking her hand.

She lifted her chin, her lower lip trembling as she said, "Do what?"

He gathered her in his arms and buried his face in her neck, breathing her in. "Pretend this doesn't hurt. You're not alone in this, Carls."

"It's too hard," she choked out, burrowing closer.

He felt her trembling and put one hand on the back of her head, his other arm around her middle, and squeezed his eyes tightly closed, willing his strength to become hers. "Nothing is too hard for us. Life is our highway, baby. We walked through our darkened doors. Our blues can't haunt us anymore."

She made a half-laughing, half-crying sound. He pressed his lips to her cheek, wishing he had the magic words to take her pain away. Hell, he wished he could take his own pain away, too. He drew back, gazing into her glassy eyes, and his chest constricted. He needed to find a way to get her into a better place before he left so she wasn't a wreck when he was gone.

"You're going to make a killing at the festival, and with any luck I'll find something amazing this week." He kissed her softly and said, "We'll talk every night. The time will fly by—you'll see."

She nodded, blinking rapidly, struggling to keep her tears at bay, which made it that much harder for him to keep his own emotions in check. He framed her face between his hands, brushing his thumbs over her cheeks. He hated not knowing when he'd be with her again, but he had to be strong for her.

"I love you, Carls. Always have, always will."

Tears pooled in her eyes. "I know. I love you, too," she said just above a whisper. "But you have to leave."

"Sick of me already?"

She shook her head. "But if you don't leave now, I might drag you inside, tie you to my bed, and never let you go."

"Baby, that is *not* the way to get me to leave." He pulled out his phone, put one arm around her, touching the side of his head to hers, and said, "Last-time-we or remember- when pic?"

"How about if we call this one *until next time*?"

"Sounds perfect." He took the picture, and then he took another while kissing her cheek, then another kissing her lips. Bandit went paws-up on his legs, and they took a picture with him, too. Zev pocketed his phone and embraced Carly one last time. "Love you, baby."

"I love you so much, Zevy. But *please* leave," she said, fanning her teary eyes. "Get out of here before I cry a river and you need a boat to get away."

How could he leave when she was on the verge of breaking down? "Don't cry, babe. We've got our second chance."

"I *know*," she said, shoving him toward the truck with shaky hands. "But go, please, just *go*."

Bandit jumped into the truck, and as Zev followed him in, he tried to get Carly to smile, saying, "A guy could get a complex being pushed away like this." She waved him off, crossing her arms, jaw tight, the edges of her lips drawn down. He blew her a kiss through the open window and said, "See you soon, beautiful. I love you."

He pulled away slowly, watching her in the rearview mirror

as the truck crawled down the street. Her arms hung limply by her sides, as if her heart were shredding into a million razor-sharp pieces, too. Her shoulders slumped, knotting up his insides even more. She covered her face with her hands, her shoulders heaving, and he felt like he was destroying them all over again.

Fuck. This.

He slammed on the brakes, threw the truck into park, and *flew* out the door, leaving it wide open in the middle of the road as he sprinted toward her with Bandit on his heels. She dropped her hands, revealing red-rimmed eyes as he wrapped her in his arms, lifting her feet off the ground, and kissed her. Her salty tears slipped between their lips, making him teary-eyed, too.

"I *just* got you back," he said between urgent kisses. "How can I leave you?"

She choked out, "You have to."

"*Baby…*" Kiss. Kiss. "Not like this…" *Kiss. Kiss.*

"I *want* you to stay." She drew back, tears streaming down her cheeks, and said, "But you have to go, Zevy. You have a crew waiting for you. I'll be *fine*." She swiped at her tears as he set her feet on the ground, but they kept coming. "I'm sorry for crying. It's not fair."

"Don't be sorry. Don't ever be sorry for loving me enough to be sad. This is killing me, too." He embraced her again, wishing he could take her with him, wishing he could stay, wishing he'd never left all those years ago. Carly's words came back to him. *If Tory's death taught me one thing, it was the importance of spending time with the people I love.*

He drew back and said, "Come with me. Take a chance, another leap of faith. Let's do this together like we were meant to." He'd get down on his knees and beg if it kept them together. But his plea only brought more tears.

"I *can't*," she said. "You *know* I can't just pick up and leave."

"Okay, I'm sorry. It wasn't fair of me to ask. *Goddamn it,* Carly. I can't leave you. I'll put everything off for a while," he said anxiously, having no idea if that was even possible since he had to finish the legal paperwork tomorrow.

She made a sorrowful, defeated sound and said, "You can't do that, and that wouldn't make it any easier to say—"

He silenced her with a hard press of his lips. "Don't say it, babe. We don't say that word." He touched his forehead to hers, the crushing sensation in his chest making it hard to breathe. "I promised not to hurt you, and look at us."

"But we're not hurting; we're just sad. There's a big difference." She looked down at Bandit, sitting beside them with his tongue hanging out of his mouth. Her gaze moved to the truck. A smile lifted her lips, despite her tears, as she brought her eyes back to his and said, "You left Beau's truck in the middle of the road and ran up here like my own personal superhero."

"I bet I'd look cute in a cape and tights." Their levity didn't make leaving any easier.

"You look even better naked," she said just above a whisper. She inhaled deeply, straightened her spine, and put a hand on his chest. "I love you, Zevy. Now get the heck out of here before I lose it again."

He hauled her into another long, passionate kiss, leaving her a little hazy-eyed, which he adored. He lifted her hand to his lips, pressing a kiss to the back of it, and took a step toward the truck, still holding on as he said, "You sure? Last chance to tie me to your bed."

Her musical laughter lightened the pain in his chest as their fingers slipped apart, and that beautiful sound followed him all the way back to the inn.

Chapter Twenty-Five

BEAU AND CHAR were coming out the front door of the inn as Zev pulled down the driveway. The second he opened his door, Bandit leapt over his lap and sprinted across the grass, nearly tackling Beau. Beau dropped to his knees to love up his dog as Zev climbed out of the truck.

"Beau thought you ran off with his buddy," Charlotte said, looking refreshed and cute in gray shorts, one of Beau's short-sleeved button-downs tied above her belly button, and a pair of knee-high bright red rubber boots.

"That little thief? He's a good dog, but way too sneaky for me." Zev embraced her and said, "How was your honeymoon?"

Charlotte clasped her hands under her chin and lifted her shoulders, smiling brightly. "It was better than a fairy tale! Beau planned a ton of fun outings and romantic dinners and dancing. I showed him all the places my grandfather used to take me, and we visited a real castle. I have bunches of pictures. It couldn't have been more perfect. But I hear *you* had a pretty magical time yourself."

"Congrats on the vessel being arrested," Beau said as he pushed to his feet, looking even happier than he had at his wedding, which Zev hadn't thought possible. He ran an assessing eye over Zev, and as he pulled him into a manly embrace, he said, "You look different. It's good to see you, man. Thanks for watching Bandit and the Chickendales."

"I think we need to have a little talk about that animal-watching arrangement. I heard all about Char's matchmaking plan." Zev eyed Beau and said, "And I hear you were in on it."

Charlotte put her arms around Beau, his big body dwarfing her petite frame. "Don't blame Beau. It was all my idea. He just agreed to go along with it. But in his defense, that's what a good husband does."

"Thanks, babe." Beau stood up a little taller, grinning like a proud peacock. "If you're looking for an apology, Zev, the best I can do is to say I probably shouldn't have blindsided you."

"I can't say I like you doing shit behind my back, but, man, I owe you both heaps of gratitude."

"Yay!" Charlotte hugged Zev. "I'm so happy! I want *all* the details. I'm sure it's a book in the making."

Zev chuckled. As an erotic romance novelist, Charlotte was always looking for new story lines. "Sorry, Char, but you're not getting details from me."

"Then I guess I'll have to pump Carly for information. Where is she, anyway? I thought she'd be here to say goodbye to you."

"She had to go to the chocolate shop to get ready for the festival." Zev wondered how Carly was holding up. He was tempted to text and ask her for a selfie to see if she was still crying, but he worried that would just make it harder for both of them.

"He doesn't do goodbyes, remember?" Beau reminded Char.

"That's right. I forgot about that." Charlotte turned a serious expression to Zev and said, "But you said goodbye to her, right? You're not just sneaking out of town?"

Zev bristled, although it was a fair question given their history. "I'm not sneaking off, Char, and I didn't sneak off last time. I said goodbye. That's why I never say it anymore. I'll *never* hurt Carly like that again."

"You'd better not, or I'll sic my husband on you." She tucked her long dark hair behind her ear and said, "I'm just kidding. I did my research before putting this whole scheme into action. From what your brothers and Jilly said, Carly really *is* your forever love. Everyone agreed that you would never hurt her again, or we wouldn't have tried to reunite the two of you. Now, if you'll excuse me, I'm off to see my Chickendales. I've missed them so much." She kissed Beau, said, "Toodles, *lover boy*," to Zev, and as she ran toward the woods, she twirled around, yelled, "Come on, Bandit!" and skipped down the path, singing at the top of her lungs.

Beau watched her disappear into the woods with a goofy grin on his face.

"She's something else," Zev said.

"And she's all mine. I'm one lucky son of a bitch," Beau said. "Actually, it sounds like you and I are both pretty damn lucky. What time is your flight?"

"Nine. Jack's picking me up at the airstrip. I've got all my stuff in your truck." He looked at his watch and said, "We've got about twenty minutes before we have to leave."

Beau slung an arm over Zev's shoulder and said, "Good. Just enough time to catch up." They went around to the back of the inn and sat on the patio. "You doing okay?"

"Yeah, man. I'm good. You? Married life treating you okay? Was your honeymoon everything you'd hoped?"

Beau's face brightened. "There are no words to describe what it's like to wake up to that woman every day, much less spend time in a place that brings her so much joy. I'm afraid to talk about how happy I am, you know?"

"I know."

"Of course you do. You and I were in the trenches of hell together when Tory died."

"No kidding."

"We were both pretty fucked up. Char saved me from my self-imposed penance for not being sober the night Tory called."

"I'd give anything not to have dragged you to that party."

"Don't say that, man. We've both drowned in guilt over something that might not have made a difference. It could have been me instead of the cabdriver. We'll never know. But Tory knew I loved her, and she called a number of people that night. We need to let that go. Remember *her*, of course, but live our lives, you know?"

Zev scrubbed a hand down his face and said, "I sure do."

"I've got to tell you, I wasn't one hundred percent sure how you'd react to seeing Carly again. I knew you might deck me when you found out about Char's plan. But Char changed my world, man. I have a fuller life than I ever thought possible, and I just couldn't stand back watching you run from yours any longer." Beau paused, studying Zev's face for a beat. "You look happier, but something's *off*. What's going on? Did we fuck up?"

"What do you think is going on?" Zev didn't mean to snap, but he was beyond frustrated. "Carly's back in my life, Beau. *Carly*. I'm *still* wrapping my head around it. I never thought I could love anyone more than I loved Carly when we were teenagers, but I was wrong. I love *this* Carly—grown-up, careful thinking, chocolatier Carly—ten times more than I loved her when we were kids." He told Beau everything about their time together, save for the intimate details. He told him about their heartfelt confessions, the accusations, the pain they'd dredged up, and the healing that came with it. He also told him about taking her to the dive site, sleeping in the van, and his expedition plans for the upcoming week.

Zev leaned his elbows on his knees, worrying with his hands as he confided in the brother who had suffered an even greater loss than any of them, and he told Beau about their time in Mexico. He wanted to ask Beau how to handle the guilt he felt about Carly going through the miscarriage alone, but that wasn't his story to tell. He would never breach her confidence like that. He needed to figure out a way to find peace around the guilt, and he didn't want to make Carly relive it again. He trusted Beau, and he hoped he could offer a little advice.

"Carly went through a lot of shit after seeing me in Mexico. It really messed her up. That's why she quit school and ended up here. I feel so guilty, and I don't know what to do with that."

"Damn, Zev. I'm sorry."

"I keep thinking that if I had gone after her, she wouldn't have suffered so much."

"You can't think like that. Even if you had gotten back together, you don't know if you would have stayed together for any length of time. You don't have a crystal ball."

"How did you stop thinking about all the things you've lost?" Zev realized he was talking about more than the miscarriage.

Beau shook his head. "I haven't stopped thinking about losing Tory, if that's what you're asking, or the time that I lost with our family, and I'm pretty sure I never will. Char taught me that it was okay to honor those feelings and that the only way to move forward was to let them exist and to deal with them. Did you apologize to Carly? Tell her how you felt? Did you tell her everything you told me?"

"Yes. She's moved on from it. *I* just don't know what to do with all the guilt."

"It's okay to feel guilty, but for the love of God, Zev, don't fool yourself into thinking you could have somehow changed the outcome of you two if you'd gone after her in Mexico. You made that mistake when Tory died. You've *always* wanted to take the burden of pain off Carly. That's your thing, bro. But this is *after* the fact. You can't fix whatever she went through. There's no going back in time. We both know that all too well. I don't know what she went through, but in any situation, the best you can do is to let the pain exist, be there to help if she needs to talk about it, hold her, love her, and let her do the same for you. You don't forget it. You learn from it. Then you can let the guilt go, because it'll only eat away at all the goodness you two have to look forward to. You have a chance at a real future together, and *that's* what you should be focused on."

"You're absolutely right, and I am learning from all of my mistakes. It's time to set them on a shelf and move on more carefully. Thanks for listening, Beau. I appreciate it."

"Hey, I've been there. I get it, and I'm here any time you want to talk." Beau leaned back, clasped his hands behind his head, and said. "What else can I fix for you?"

"Settle that ego down, unless you have some answers about how to blend our lives together. I offered her a partnership in my company, but she said she needed to think about it."

Disbelief rose in his brother's eyes. "You asked her to be your *business* partner?"

"It's a commitment to *us*."

"How'd she react?"

"She needs time to get comfortable with logistics. I get it. It's a huge commitment, but that was the point. To show her I'm committed." He gritted his teeth. "Leaving her this morning sucked the life out of me. I asked her to come with me, and *here's a shocker*," he said sarcastically. "She said no."

"Aw, man." Beau looked shocked. "I'm sorry."

"It wasn't a fair position to put her in, but I just couldn't hold back. I know she needs more, but I'm not going to give her empty promises. I offered all I can for now. And, man, I get where she's coming from. I know how much her business and her friends mean to her. I can't expect her to uproot her life. She's not that same whimsical girl she was, and that's okay. I adore the person she's become. But I definitely need to learn how to navigate calmer waters. Her life has become as steady and stable as the mountains, and my life ebbs and flows like the fucking tide. She needs concrete plans, and I've got nothing but good intentions."

"I wondered when you were going to get around to that. She probably feels like you put her life in a blender."

"No shit, man."

"I'd say slow down, but that's not who you are. What I can tell you is that I changed my entire life for Char, and I've never regretted it for a second."

"I can't exactly walk away from the *Pride*. That was *our* dream. Knowing how badly she wanted to find it is what has driven me to search for it for all these years. But on the flip side, how the hell am I supposed to walk away from *her* for weeks at a time?"

Beau shrugged. "I guess I'm better at fixing houses than relationships, because I've got nothing. Our lives are so different, I can't even begin to imagine how you two can coordinate schedules. I think those answers have to come from you and Carly." He stood up and walked off the patio without saying anything. He rubbed the back of his neck, pacing, and then he set a serious stare on Zev and said, "Can I ask you a hard question?"

"Might as well."

"Given your propensity for traveling on a whim, are you *sure* you can be the man she needs? Are you sure you're not setting both of you up for broken hearts?"

Zev pushed to his feet, eating up the space between them, his hands fisting. "I *am* the man she needs. There's no *can I be* in the equation."

Beau held up his hands and took a step back. "I'm just asking, man. You're about to get on a plane and leave her again."

"Are you trying to fuck with my head?" Zev seethed through gritted teeth. "You don't think I've been battling those demons every damn second since I drove away from her?"

"I'm just trying to understand where you're heading."

"That's what I'm *telling* you," Zev seethed. "I'm heading for forever with Carly, but we're not carefree kids anymore and I don't have the answers we need. It's fucking killing me that I don't, but I'm not running away or abandoning her. We just need to figure shit out."

Beau cocked a grin.

"What's that shit-eating grin for?"

"Because I was testing you, and you passed."

"You're an asshole." Zev shoved him away with an incredulous laugh.

"I'm the asshole who told my brilliant wife that we needed to get you and Carly back together."

Zev stood stock-still, processing his words. "I thought that was *Char's* idea."

Beau motioned for Zev to walk with him, and they headed around the side of the house toward the front yard. "I dropped hints, and my beautiful wife ran with them. The way I see it, you owe me big-time." He clapped a hand on Zev's shoulder and said, "Tell me it doesn't feel fucking fantastic to love someone so much you hate leaving them."

"I'm done telling you anything. You're either full of shit or…" He looked at his brother's playful grin and said, "*Nah*, you're *definitely* full of shit."

Beau laughed loudly.

"*Prick*," Zev muttered with a chuckle as they rounded the front of the house.

Bandit bounded toward them.

"Hey, you guys!" Charlotte waved from the hood of Beau's truck, where she sat with her legs outstretched. "I'm working on my tan!"

"Do you think she realizes she's wearing knee-high rubber boots?" Zev asked.

"Of course. Absolutely *nothing* gets by my girl. She just beats to her own drum, and I love her for it. Come on, we have to get to the airstrip." Beau jogged toward Char, and she slid off the truck and into his arms, kissing him. "I have to run Zev up to the airstrip to meet Jack. Want to come?"

"I would love to, but I can't," Char said. "I'm giving myself fifteen minutes in the sun, and then I have to tackle emails."

"Then get in here and give me a hug." Zev pulled her into

his arms. "I'm glad you had a great honeymoon. I want to see the pictures, so hook me up with them, okay?"

"Of course," she said sweetly. "I'll email you a link to them. When will we see you again?"

"Hopefully in the next couple of weeks. We're still figuring that out, but it looks like I'll be around more this winter."

"Really?" Beau asked.

"Carly's here, so yeah, *really*. Noah and I are bouncing around the idea of partnering for a shipwreck exhibition at the Real DEAL. I can't believe I forgot to mention that to you. Nothing's set in stone, but it's one of the things we're considering. Carls and I are also thinking about heading home for a couple of weeks over the holidays."

Beau looked at him skeptically.

"A couple of *weeks*? That's *great!*" Charlotte exclaimed. "Forget the inn working its magic. Carly must have her own brand of wizardry."

Zev smirked. *Hell yes, she does.*

A mischievous glimmer rose in Charlotte's eyes. "I need to call Carly and see if she'll share some of those tricks for my next book."

Zev laughed. "Speaking of those kinds of *tricks*, your thief dragged your leather whip in from outdoors. It was pretty dirty, so I cleaned it up and put it in Char's office."

"I told you Bandit stole it," Charlotte said to Beau. "I've been looking all over for that thing so we could—"

"Whoa, stop right there," Zev said, waving his hand. "I don't want to know the kinky shit you and my brother do."

Beau gave him a deadpan look. "She uses it to work out the mechanics for the erotic scenes in her books."

"I bet she does. The fuzzy handcuffs, too? Bandit dropped a

pair beside the tub when we were in it. You've trained that dog well, bro."

Charlotte blushed, and Beau pulled her into his arms. She buried her face in his chest and said, "Caught!"

"Don't worry, Char. Your secret is safe with me." Zev whipped out his phone and said, "Last-time-we pic?"

"Yes!" Charlotte said.

As Beau draped his arms around Charlotte and Zev, Zev held up his phone and said, "By the way, you're out of multisurface cleaner. I didn't have time to replace it, but at least the inn's kitchen table is sanitary." He took the picture, capturing Beau's scowl and Charlotte's happy eyes.

"Tell me you *didn't*," Beau said as Zev pocketed his phone.

"No can do, bro. I just dropped the hints, then *I* ran with it."

ZEV STOOD ON the bluff overlooking Fortune's Cove on Silver Island Sunday evening, taking his first break since he'd stepped off the plane. He was wound so tight, even the sights and smells of the sea, his go-to tension relievers, didn't ease the strain in his corded muscles. When he'd landed on the island, he'd gone straight to his boat to review the legal documents Jeremy had sent for their meeting tomorrow, as well as the nondisclosure agreements for Cliff and Tanner. That had brought his mind back to Carly and what she'd said about the offer she hadn't yet accepted. *I don't know how I can be a supportive, contributing partner if I'm two thousand miles away.* Her words had plagued him throughout the afternoon as he'd met with his team to prepare for the week, as well as during his meeting with Brant Remington about using the marine crane to exhume the concretion.

He *finally* had time to take a break. He pulled out his phone, and with the brisk sea air stinging his cheeks and the world at his back, he placed a video call to Carly. When her smiling face appeared on the screen, her entrancing baby blues cut right through his tension.

"Hi, Zev!" Her hair was in a ponytail, a few blond tendrils framing her face.

"Hi, beautiful. How are you?"

Before Carly could answer, Birdie's voice rang out. "She misses you!"

Birdie's face appeared over Carly's shoulder, and Quinn's face popped up over her other shoulder. Quinn waved. It was after hours there, but he knew they were working late.

"Hi, Birdie. Hi Quinn." He was glad Carly wasn't alone, but he wished he was the one keeping her company. "I miss you, too, Carls."

Birdie leaned on Carly's shoulder and said, "Don't worry. We're taking her out to dinner so she won't be too lonely."

"She's going to eat all the white chocolate if we don't," Quinn chimed in.

"You guys," Carly said excitedly, "I had the best idea. We've been trapped in here all day. Why don't we pick up dinner from the Wicked Spur and take it out to the lake to eat? I can swing by home and pick up a picnic blanket."

"A *picnic?*" Birdie asked with a hint of distaste.

A picnic. He knew exactly what Carly was thinking.

Quinn wrinkled her nose. "Why would we sit outside with the bugs when we could eat at the Wicked Spur and listen to a band?"

Zev eyed Carly. He hadn't realized his heart could get any fuller. He knew exactly what Carly was feeling. She'd dipped her toes back into nature and adventures. She'd had a taste of the freedoms she used to love, and now she was restless after being confined inside all day. He knew this because he felt the same about—and without—*her*.

"Who *are* you?" Birdie asked with a quizzical look. "If you suggested eating at your place so you could watch one of your boring documentaries, I'd understand. But a picnic?" She pointed at Zev and said, "This is *your* fault. You broke her."

A smile lifted Carly's lips, and she said, "No, he didn't. He fixed me."

That made him feel all kinds of awesome. "You were never broken, baby. There's just a lot more to you than meets most people's eyes."

"Okay, then," Quinn said. "A picnic it is. But for the record, there's not more to me than meets the eye. I like nice restaurants where my heels won't get stuck in the dirt."

"I think a picnic with a *guy* is romantic." Birdie patted Carly's shoulder and said, "Just so you know, I'm not making out with either of you under the stars."

"Okay, *peanut gallery*, can we have some privacy now, please?" Carly shooed them out of Zev's view, though he could still hear them.

"I bet they want to talk dirty," Quinn said.

"Then let's stay!" Birdie exclaimed.

Carly glowered at them.

"We're going," Birdie said, and then she yelled, "Bye, Zev! We miss you, too!"

"I miss you, too," he said with a shake of his head.

"Sorry," Carly said softly. "They're out of the kitchen now."

"It's okay. I'm glad you're not alone. How was your day?"

"Let's see, my morning started out great, then you left, and I cried a river, kayaked into work, and poured all of my energy into getting ready for the festival." As she relayed her busy day, she sounded a little flat, so different from the first time she'd told him about what her job entailed.

"Are you okay?" he asked, worrying that he'd exhausted her. The last thing he wanted was to hinder her business. "I know we had a crazy week. I'm sorry if I wore you out."

"No, I'm good. Why?"

Her words sounded too easy for the knotted gut he'd been towing around all day. "You don't sound as enthusiastic as you had about the festival preparations."

She shrugged one shoulder. "I've done the festival for years. Prep is never very exciting."

"What else is bugging you, babe?"

She lowered her eyes, and when she lifted them, he saw trouble brewing.

"I'm sorry I didn't go with you when you asked."

"Don't be sorry. I was caught up in the moment. I know you can't leave, and I shouldn't have put you in that position. We'll figure this out. It's just going to take some time and some getting used to."

"I know. How was your day?"

He filled her in on the things he'd done, and the more he shared about his plans for the week, the more excited she became.

"How are Randi and Ford? I bet they're on pins and needles, too."

"They're pretty stoked. We're diving as soon as I get back

from meeting with my attorney in Boston."

"I hope you find something amazing! I can't wait to hear all about it." Her brows knitted, and she said, "Wait a sec. Are you on the waterfront in Boston? It looks like you're on the island."

"I am on the island."

"I don't know why, but I thought you'd fly into Boston and stay there for your morning meeting."

"I'm taking off first thing in the morning. But if I'd stayed in Boston, I couldn't have shown you this." He turned the phone, showing her the view of the water, and said, "Welcome to the cliffs at Fortune's Landing."

She gasped, beaming at him. "*Zevy!*"

"Since we ended up horizontal in my van and you never got to see it, I thought I'd give you a private tour." He walked closer to the edge of the cliff, speaking in his best tour-guide voice. "As you know, Silver Island was founded in 1601 by Bartholomew Silver. Legend has it that good ol' Bart landed his boat, the *Fortune*, right down there." He angled the phone, showing her the long way down to the base of the cliffs, where a slim sandy beach met the crashing waves. "I heard Bart was drunk and actually crashed into the cliffs. Rumor has it that he was found naked with a harem of drunken women, but you know how gossip changes the truth."

"I believe the gossip," Carly said. "This is amazing! What else can you see from there? Can you see Bellamy Island? The marina? Where we had dinner?"

He'd never tire of her enthusiasm. She asked a hundred questions and he answered every one of them as he walked along the rocky ridge, showing her everything he saw and describing the things he couldn't from memory.

As the sun began to set, she said, "I feel like I'm right there with you. I can't believe you did this for me."

He turned the phone so he could see her and said, "You didn't think I'd forget that you wanted to see it, did you?"

"I just thought you would be in Boston preparing for your meeting. But to be honest, when we were apart for all those years, I wondered if you remembered *anything* about me. But after last week, I think it's impossible for you to ever *forget* anything about me."

"Nothing could be truer."

"Then you remember how we used to dream about discovering our own island," she said excitedly.

"Right after we watched *The Blue Lagoon* with that blond guy you said I looked like—"

"Chris Atkins. I said you were cuter than him. You reminded me of him because he and Brooke Shields were so close, and they fumbled through their firsts like we did. I used to fantasize about us alone on an island like they were, finding ways to make it through each day, watching out for each other."

"Right there lies the difference between girls and boys, because after watching that movie, I fantasized about you walking around topless on our island. I still fantasize about that."

They both laughed. But in the moment of silence that followed, sadness rose in Carly's eyes and disappeared as quickly as it had come, leaving a heaviness in his heart.

"Hey, babe, what's wrong?"

"Nothing is *wrong*. I just wish I was there with you on that bluff. I could go topless and you could wear a loincloth, and we could pretend it was our island and fall asleep under the stars."

"I wish I could reach through the phone, hold you, and help you take your top off." He was glad to see her smile again. "We've got this, babe. We'll make all our dreams come true."

"Are you guys done yet?"

Zev heard Birdie's voice but couldn't see her.

"Almost," Carly said, looking away from the phone.

Birdie's face popped into the screen, and she said, "She's not blushing. Do you want me to call my brothers to give you lessons in dirty talk?"

"*Birdie!*" Carly complained. "Zev could talk your brothers under the table."

"I didn't want to get Carly hot and bothered before going out with you and Quinn," Zev said, but it was a fib. If he thought it wouldn't make him and Carly lonelier, he would have gotten her all revved up, and it would have made it even more thrilling knowing that she'd have to play it cool when Birdie and Quinn walked in—which he knew they would.

"Quinny," Birdie hollered. "Chalk up a few gentleman points for Zev."

"Got 'em!" Quinn said from somewhere in the room.

"Sorry," Carly said, nudging Birdie out of the way. "I'd better go. I loved my tour, and I love you more than you can imagine."

"Right back at you, babe. Good luck at the festival. Send me some pictures. I'd love to see what it's like."

"I'll take some of *her!*" Birdie called out.

"Thanks, Birdie," he said, enjoying the hint of embarrassment on Carly's face. He blew her a kiss. "Until tomorrow, sexy girl."

She mimed catching the kiss and touched two fingers to her lips. "Until tomorrow."

Birdie and Quinn made kissing noises in the background, and Carly rolled her eyes as she ended the video call.

Zev looked at Carly's picture on the lock screen on his phone. He hadn't even been gone for a day, and he felt her absence like a missing limb. *What have you done to me, baby?*

Eleven hours down, too many more to go.

Chapter Twenty-Six

CARLY PULLED A tray of brownies from the oven Monday morning, moving to the beat of "Rock Your Body," from a CD Zev had made her in high school. She'd had to put on music at home, too. The quiet had felt too quiet, making her miss Zev even more. After she'd had dinner with the girls—which they'd eaten *at* the restaurant because Carly had been outvoted—she and Zev had texted for hours. And after they'd finally said good night, she'd stayed up agonizing over his offer to be his business partner, saying she couldn't go with him, and wanting to be in two places at once. She should be exhausted this morning, but she had woken up ready to take on the world. Her hair was up in a ponytail, her white Divine Intervention T-shirt was knotted at the waist of her denim shorts—a chocolate-shop-festival tradition—and she had on her most comfortable sneakers.

Unfortunately, the world she really wanted to take on was two thousand miles away.

Between missing Zev and the excitement over what his dive might turn up later today, she could barely think of anything else. But she was trying. She couldn't wait to tell her aunt all of her news. She'd tried to reach her yesterday, but the call had gone straight to voicemail and she hadn't left a message. She set the tray of brownies on the counter and glanced at the clock, glad to see it was finally six o'clock. Nassau was two hours ahead of Colorado, and she knew her aunt took a walk on the beach every morning at eight.

She put in her earphones and placed the call.

"I've been wondering when you'd get around to calling me," Marie said when she answered.

"Sorry. Life has been a whirlwind this week. I've been prepping for the festival since five, but I didn't want to call you too early. How are you?"

"I've never been better. More importantly, how are *you*? Your mama told me that your first love is back in your life. How do *we* feel about this?"

There was no missing the concern in her aunt's voice. Marie only used *we* when she was concerned about things that she thought Carly either should be, or was, stewing over. Carly knew Marie would be overly cautious about Zev coming back into her life. Marie knew the Bradens who lived in Weston, and she'd met Zev's parents once when she'd been in Maryland visiting Carly's family when she was young. But her aunt didn't believe in judging a family as a unit, because as she'd told Carly a million times, good people can raise bad children and vice versa.

"*We* feel incredible," Carly said, even if a bit confused and lonely. She didn't want to worry her.

"Mm-hm. Forgive me for withholding judgment until I hear all the facts, sweetheart, but my auntie claws are extended and ready."

Carly began mixing the frosting for the brownies and said, "Aunt Marie…"

"Save it, sugar. Tell me what I need to know. You know

these claws retract as easily as they come out."

That was true. Carly had seen Marie go head-to-head with a man who stood at the counter eating nearly all of their fudge samples, then tell his girlfriend she should skip a taste because she was getting a little thick in the hips. Marie had given him a verbal lashing. Carly had also seen her aunt eye a teenage boy who she thought was going to shoplift, only to find out after his father came into the shop that the boy was skittish because of anxiety issues, not because he was getting ready to steal. Marie had told the father about Redemption Ranch, and she'd given the boy a chocolate lollipop and a Divine Intervention journal because she believed everyone should have a private place to get things out of their head.

"What did my mom tell you?" Carly asked.

"Enough to make me think I need to hear it all myself. Start at the beginning."

Carly told her everything, from the heart palpitations she'd had when she'd first seen Zev, to the tears she'd shed when they'd talked, and the love she felt all the way through. She set down the bowl of frosting and paced the kitchen, too excited to stand still as she shared the details of their time together, reliving it all as she told her aunt about every conversation, every unspoken worry, and how Zev noticed and addressed each of the worries she'd tried to hide. She gushed about cliff diving, sleeping on the porch at the inn, the surprise trip to Silver Island, and their deep-sea exploration.

"I wish you could have been there when we went cliff diving. It was exhilarating and terrifying, and when I jumped…" She paused to inhale deeply, as she had at the top of the cliff, remembering how good it had felt. "Aunt Marie, it was the most freeing, wonderful feeling. I had forgotten how much I *loved* doing it, how much I loved being outdoors and allowing myself to *feel* everything. I hadn't realized how much *life* I'd put away, and I know I needed to, but it was...it was like finding parts of myself that I had lost. And when we went in search of the wreckage from the *Pride*? There are no words to explain how incredible that felt."

Although apparently there *were*, because she went on to rave about it for fifteen minutes.

"That was the shipwreck you two were always going on about as kids, right?"

"*Yes*. He searched for years, and he *found* it. And then he *took* me there. It was one of the biggest thrills of my entire life."

"I can hear that. I don't think I've heard *this* Carly since...gosh...forever ago."

"I know—that's how I feel, too! I forgot to tell you about the concretions!"

Twenty-five minutes later, as Carly finished telling her story, Birdie flitted into the kitchen with a wave. Carly mouthed, *Aunt Marie*, and Birdie gave her a thumbs-up, and picked up with the festival preparations where Carly had left off.

"Let me retract my claws a little," Marie said carefully. "I don't know anything about treasure hunting, but from what you've told me, it sounds like extracting those coins and finding the other thing—"

"We think it's a tool of some sort."

"Right. They sound like very big deals."

"*Huge*, history-making deals, and that's not all. He offered to make me a partner in his company, which he named after our senior project—Two Treasure Hunters, One Ship—years ago. By making me a partner, I'd become a legal custodian for the *Pride*."

389

"I have no idea what that means."

"It's complicated, but basically it makes me responsible for ensuring that the ship and any artifacts that are found are protected. It's a *huge* deal. He's offering to legally make me part of the *Pride* expedition—*our* ship, *our* dream—in the only capacity that he can, since I'm here and the team and the ship are there." Her heart raced just talking about it. "He's giving me the chance to get my name in history books. But more importantly, he's showing me how dedicated he is to *me*, and to *us*."

"Okay, slow down, sweetheart. That sounds like a *lot* of legal responsibility for someone who's not around the things that need protecting."

"I know," she said a little too sharply. "He asked me to go with him, but don't worry, I turned him down." She felt a pang of regret. *Come with me! Take a chance, a leap of faith. Let's do this together, like we were meant to.* She forced Zev's voice away and said, "He knows I can't just up and leave on a whim. I haven't accepted the partnership yet because I'm struggling with exactly what you brought up. You know how I am. I need to have my finger on the pulse of everything I'm responsible for. How can I do that if I'm not there?"

How can we be partners in anything if we're this far apart?

"That was smart, sweetheart. But what do you want?" her aunt asked.

She wanted the partnership almost as much as she wanted the man offering it, but she kept that to herself. While she wanted Zev and to be part of the expedition, she also loved her business, and her life, even if it now seemed to pale in comparison to the life she'd left behind.

No. Scratch that.

It paled in comparison to the life, and the woman, she'd only just begun to rediscover.

"I want it all," she said honestly, wondering how she could have ever let herself stop dreaming of anything beyond her small, safe world. "The shop, my life here, Zev. But that's too big a discussion to have right now. But if I decide to accept the partnership, Zev made sure I was covered legally. He has the required insurance, and he has a secure warehouse, a lab, everything he needs to keep the artifacts safe and get them evaluated."

She got Birdie's attention and indicated she was going into her office, and as she headed in, she said, "And I'll be there sometimes. I'm not sure how often or for how long, but I *want* to be there with him and experience the thrill of it *with* him. I'm sure I can figure out a way to get there once a month while the weather's warm enough to dive." But would that ever be enough? And what if they wanted to have a family one day? How would that work?

"I'm sure you will. You're a very determined woman," Marie said.

Carly realized she was going on about being someplace else when her aunt had taken her in, helped her survive the hardest of times, and given her a life *and* a career. Marie had trusted Carly with her own dream—the chocolate shop. She quickly said, "And he'll come here, too. Zev knows how important the shop is to me. I can't wait for you to see the new merchandise we've brought in and taste all the new desserts we've created."

"I look forward to it," her aunt said distractedly, as if she were still mulling over what Carly had said.

"I know you're worried about Zev hurting me again."

"Yes, that's part of it, although from what you've said, it

sounds like he's doing everything he can to show you he's not going to hurt you again, and it sounds like he's tortured himself over the years for hurting you. It takes a big man to admit to his faults."

Carly's eyes stung at the truth of her aunt's words. "He *has* tortured himself, and I *love* him, Aunt Marie. I love him with all that I am and all that I have."

"Oh, Carly," Birdie said softly.

Carly turned around.

Birdie lifted the tray she was holding, indicating she was just walking by when she'd heard her, and mouthed, *I'm so happy for you*, and continued walking to the freezer.

"I trust your judgment, honey. If I didn't, I wouldn't have given you the chocolate shop," her aunt said, and Carly realized she'd missed whatever Marie had said when she was focused on Birdie. "I just need to say something, because I love you too much not to. Your mama and I were so worried about you the summer Tory was killed and Zev left. But by the end of that summer, when you went back to school, you were on a healing path. We knew you had a long way to go, but you'd found a way to pick yourself up and carry on. When I saw you that Christmas, you were definitely stronger. You didn't fool us, though, we knew Tory and Zev had both taken a big part of you with them. But that was to be expected, and we thought time would heal you even more. But the next summer…honey, your mama and I never knew what led to your spiraling back into a depression, and I'm not asking you to tell me. That's your business. But if it had anything to do with Zev, please be sure that you're not just brushing anything under the carpet."

Carly closed her office door. She owed her aunt the truth. "Zev wasn't the only one guilty of abandoning someone. Over spring break the year after he left, I ran into him in Mexico, and we spent the night together. I still loved him with every part of me, and I felt so much love from him when I was in his arms that night. But I didn't trust my instincts." Tears slipped down her cheeks, and she sank to the edge of her desk with the weight of her confession. "I was afraid I was misreading his emotions, or it just was wishful thinking. I don't really know what I was thinking. I just knew I wouldn't survive if he walked away again, so while he lay sleeping, I took off without a word. I didn't leave a note or *anything*." She swiped at her tears, accepting the crushing feeling in her chest as her due. "As cruel as it was, and as embarrassing as it is to admit, I think part of me was still so hurt, I wanted him to feel the pain I had felt when he'd left me."

"Oh, *honey*."

"There's more," she said, steeling herself against the sobs vying for release. "I didn't know it then, but that night while I was realizing I couldn't survive getting hurt again, he'd realized he'd made a mistake by leaving the way he had, and he'd wanted to try to work things out. But I never gave him the chance to tell me. He woke up to an empty bed, and he assumed *I* was *done*."

"And maybe in that moment of self-protection, you *were* done. And that's okay, sweetheart. But if a man loves you, he doesn't back off because you tell him to. He keeps trying."

"Maybe some men in some situations would. But Zevy knew how much he'd already hurt me, and he gave me what my leaving told him I wanted. He loved me enough to walk away. I thought I needed to walk away because I *had* to be done with us to protect myself." One day Carly would tell her aunt and her mother about the miscarriage, but for now she kept that to herself, because she didn't want her aunt to mistake the miscarriage as the reason for what she said next. "But it didn't take long for me to realize that I wasn't *done* with him. I looked for him online, but there was nothing. I could have asked his family, but I figured he didn't want me to find him, and then, well, I ended up here. But until I came face-to-face with him at Char's wedding, until I *felt* his presence, *truly* felt the *pull* of our hearts and the electric, all-consuming energy between us, I couldn't have known I was repressing so much of myself. And without that realization, there's no *way* I could have realized the bigger truth. I'll *never* be done with Zevy, and I don't want to be. He's my other half, too big a part of me to ever be overshadowed again. We're two sides of the same coin. He loved me too much to stay after Tory died, and I loved him too much to stay in Mexico. Now we've grown up, and we're finally in a place in our lives where we love each other too much to ever let go again."

Marie was quiet for so long, Carly wondered if her aunt thought she was making a mistake.

"Pain is never a one-way street, Carly. You two were so young when you found each other, the odds of staying together were against you. I guess some love defies the odds."

"You don't think I'm crazy?" she asked nervously.

"Oh, you're definitely crazy at the moment, honey," her aunt said lightly. "Love is *supposed* to make you crazy."

A relieved laugh bubbled out, and Carly wiped her tears.

"But this makes me wonder if Colorado was just a pit stop for you."

"What? *No.* Are you kidding?" Carly's heart sank. "You and Wynnie saved my life, and I *love* my life. I love and appreciate *you*, and this chocolate shop."

"Maybe the guy is her pit stop."

Carly froze at the male voice coming through the phone. "Was that a *man*? Is he listening to our conversation? Where *are* you?"

"Yes, that was a man, and if you must know, I'm still in bed."

"*What?* You're in bed with a man and you're talking to me like nothing is going on? Aunt Marie!"

Marie laughed. "Well, we were *done* when you called."

"*Ew!* Stop! I don't want to hear that. Tell whoever he is that Zev is *not* a pit stop, and—"

"I call him *Tiger*," Marie said.

"I'm hanging up now," Carly said, smiling. "I love you. Thank you for listening."

"Wait! You don't want to say hello to my Latin lover? My Antonio Banderas lookalike?"

"*Goodbye*, Auntie…" She ended the call, cutting off her aunt's laughter, and looked at the pictures on her desk of her and Zev with their passports in their mouths and holding their treasure map. She was filled with longing.

Her phone vibrated with a text, and Zev's name appeared in the bubble, as if he'd sensed her thinking about him. She opened the message, and a selfie of him on the boat popped up. He was shirtless, his hair blowing in the wind. His right arm was outstretched, his elbow slightly bent, his hand cupped. In his left hand he held a piece of cardboard on which he'd written *I wish you were here* and drawn an arrow to the right. Elation bubbled up inside her. She grabbed a sticky note and wrote *I am* on it and stuck it to the picture of them holding the map. She held the picture beside her face, puckered up to blow a kiss, and took a selfie, sending it off to Zev with a heart emoji.

There was a knock at the door, and Birdie poked her head in. "Are you still raving about your endless love or can you help me with something?"

Carly leaned back in her chair and kicked her feet up onto the desk. "He's just *so* hot and *so sexy*," she said dramatically. "I think I need a few more minutes to rave, or maybe an hour or two."

Birdie stomped over in her white cowgirl boots and booty shorts. Her red Divine Intervention tank top was knotted above her waist, showing about an inch of tanned, toned stomach. "Let's go, Madam Sexpot." She took Carly's hand and yanked her to her feet, dragging her toward the door. "This business won't run itself."

BY LATE AFTERNOON, the sidewalks were packed with festivalgoers. Balloons danced from long strings tied to children's wrists, and music from the park at the end of the block lingered in the air. Carly stood behind the table on the sidewalk in front of the shop, helping customers, while Quinn and Birdie helped customers inside. This was usually her favorite part of the festival, but as she made small talk and enticed customers into checking out their new offerings inside the shop, she was too distracted to enjoy it. She was usually an avid listener, sincerely interested in everyone's stories and questions, but today the only thing she was eager to do was to be part of the expedition going on off Silver Island.

"You can pay for the cake pop inside. You'll find the peppermint bars and Treasure Hunter Fudge in the glass display to the right of the register," Carly said to the older couple she was helping.

The silver-haired man said, "Very wise marketing, getting your customers to pay *inside*, where they can't resist buying more chocolate."

"That's the hope," Carly said, the eager lilt in her voice forced. Guilt and frustration bubbled up inside her. She loved this business and working with Birdie and Quinn. She loved the noise and the goings-on of the festival, so why did she suddenly feel like she was standing in a gully, buffered from the rest of the world by the surrounding mountains that had once brought her peace?

"Is this white chocolate?" a young mother asked, pulling Carly from her thoughts. Two little redheaded girls stared up her, anxiously awaiting an answer.

"Yes. I'm sorry, my flavor chart seems to have gone missing." Carly peered over the tray looking for the chart she'd made and felt her phone vibrate in her pocket. Zev had texted hours ago after his meeting with the attorney to say it had gone well and he was heading back to the island to meet up with his team. Randi had sent texts on and off throughout the day with messages about what they were doing and funny comments about *the boys*. Her last text had included a picture of Zev leaning over a table with Ford, Cliff, and Tanner, with the caption *Predive strategy meeting*. Anxious to see the latest text, Carly quickly pointed to each of the samples as she named them. "These are white chocolate, vanilla, mint-chocolate swirl, milk chocolate, chocolate cherry, maple walnut, and our newest special, Treasure Hunter Fudge." She went on to describe what could be found inside the special fudge.

The girls' eyes flicked excitedly up at their mother.

"Thank you." Their mother put a hand on each of their pretty little heads and said, "You can each choose one sample."

As the girls begged for more, Carly bit her tongue and helped two other customers. She'd learned her lesson early on. When she'd first started working for her aunt, she'd made the mistake of telling children they could take *two*, only to get the stink eye from their parents.

She spotted the flavor chart on the ground beside the table as she was giving the girls their samples, but before she could pick it up, another wave of customers arrived.

Forty minutes later, she was finishing up with the last customer—at least for the moment—and said, "We're open seven days a week. I hope to see you again soon." She quickly put the flavor chart where it belonged, then pulled out her phone and navigated to the text from Randi. It was a picture of Zev and the guys in their wet suits with the caption *Dive #2!* Carly's attention was riveted to Zev's athletic body trapped beneath the wet suit, leaving no room for imagination, and his mesmerizing eyes glittering at the camera. She could practically feel his heart thundering with anticipation. She remembered the thrill that had shot through her when she'd gotten her first look at him underwater.

A hand shot between her phone and her face, and she startled. "Sorry, I—"

Cutter stood beside her with a cocky smile and said, "What happened? Did you fall down the rabbit hole on a dirty-diver site?"

She hadn't seen him since she'd dropped off the truffles as a thank-you gift for watching the animals. She looked around, relieved to see there were no customers in earshot. "Of course not. I don't look at those sites. Is that even a thing? Dirty divers?"

"I don't know. There are dirty cowboy sites, so I assume so."

"How do you know that? Are *you* on them?" She thought better of it and said, "Don't answer that."

He laughed. "Well, something had your attention. I said your name three times."

"Sorry. It's Zev. He's diving today and I'm anxious to hear from him."

"I bet. How are you holding up now that he's gone?"

She sighed. "How do you think?"

"I can't imagine," he said empathetically.

"Trust me, you don't want to try. It's like having the door to a new world open and you see all of its bright, shiny pieces, and then someone pushes the door so it's *almost* closed, leaving just enough space for you to get a peek of the other side. Then they hang a sign that says 'Coming Soon,' and they push a giant block of lead against the door so you can't open it, making all that special goodness that lit you up inside just out of reach. And you know you'll get to see it again, but you don't know when."

Cutter's brows slanted. "You mean Miss Organization doesn't have dates and times for her next tryst?"

"Nope, and it's not a tryst. But I'm okay with it. I'm here and I'm focusing on the festival." She saw another group of people coming down the street. *Is it just me, or is this day taking forever?* She straightened the table to distract herself and said, "I'm cool. I don't need solid plans."

"Uh-huh," he said with a heavy dose of disbelief.

"You're not helping," she said in a singsong voice.

"Maybe this will help. I wanted to mention it the other day, but you were in a hurry. Zev went to a *lot* of trouble to get that trip set up for you. I don't know how he pulled it off so fast, but it was obviously important to him that *you* didn't miss out on going diving. If Beau hadn't already told me about all the deep-sea diving, cliff diving, hang gliding, freediving, and other crazy shit you and Zev did growing up, I would've told Zev he was crazy to plan a diving trip for you."

"Wait. What was that about Beau?" She pocketed her phone and crossed her arms, staring him down.

He cleared his throat.

"*Cutter?* Ohmygod. You stinker!" She swatted him. "You were in on Char's matchmaking scheme, weren't you? What if Zev had been a jerk?"

"Do you really think I'd let the guy near you if I had concerns? Beau assured me that Zev wasn't going to be a dick."

Beau. He'd been as lost as Zev had been after Tory was killed, and look where he was now. Where they both were.

Thank you, Beau.

"So you had concerns before you went to Beau?" she asked.

"Yes and no." Cutter glanced at the shop and said, "How many times did I walk in on you and Birdie role-playing so you could be calm, cool, and collected when you saw your old flame?"

"Dozens. It didn't work," she said with a smile. "I got so flustered that I told him you and I were dating, until you started dirty dancing with Sable, and that lie went to crap."

"No shit? I wish I could have heard you trying to get out of that." He shook his head and said, "I knew all that planning and role-playing wouldn't work. I don't know much about love, but I do know this. You told me Zev had broken your heart, but every time you talked about him, you got this look in your eyes, like…" He shrugged. "I don't know what that look was exactly, but it told me you weren't over him. So when Char said she and Beau were getting married, I went to see Beau. I told him that if he had any inclination that Zev would cause an ounce of trouble for you, I needed to know. I would have found a way to make sure you didn't go to that wedding. But I trust Beau, and he told me where *he* thought Zev's head had been all these years, which put my mind at ease."

"You did that for me?"

"I'd do anything for you, darlin'. You're family."

"Aw, I love knowing that. Thank you. What did Beau say to you?" she asked as a group of pretty women approached the table.

"Guy code. Can't talk about it. All that matters is that he was *right*." Cutter winked and picked up the sample tray, turning his attention to the women who were ogling him in his tight jeans and cowboy hat. "Howdy, ladies. What's your pleasure?"

If only Beau had the answers *she* needed right *now*.

THE TABLE WAS three customers deep for the rest of Carly's shift, giving her little time to think about anything but the people peppering her with questions. She was thankful for Cutter's help with the customers, even if he did seem to be using her confections like a dating app. Women had offered him their phone numbers, Tinder account names, and one even offered to *be* his dessert. She had no idea there were so many forthright, horny women in their small town, and she was thankful when the crowds finally died down.

"That's fascinating," Carly said to a middle-aged man who was going on about his great-aunt who owned a chocolate shop in Paris. She was trying not to think about her phone vibrating in her pocket. It had been vibrating on and off like she was a drug dealer for the last couple of hours.

Quinn came out of the shop carrying a tray of fudge samples, and her expression brightened when she saw Cutter. She stood up a little taller, walked a little slinkier in her tight black Divine Intervention tank top, which was knotted a good two inches above the waist of her soft gray miniskirt. "Cutter? I didn't know you were helping," she said as she set the tray on the table.

Cutter dragged his eyes appreciatively down her body, all the way to the leather straps wound around her calves from her high-heeled sandals.

"This is when you speak," Carly said, nudging Cutter as the long-winded customer headed inside to check out the rest of their treats.

Cutter half coughed, half cleared his throat and said, "I was just helping Carly."

Quinn was too smart for that. She looked at the women standing on Cutter's side of the table and said, "Everyone comes out for the hot cowboy. Just don't try to take my job. I'm next in line for more hours."

"I'll hire you," a buxom blonde said as she eyed Cutter.

Quinn put her hand on her hip, flashing the sweetest of smiles, the one that brought men to their knees, and said, "What kind of work do you have in mind for him?"

"Oh, I'm sure I can think of *something*," the blonde said. "I have a few items that need fixing around my house."

"That's good, because he's *great* with his hands. But if you need a man who can work *long* hours, his staying power leaves a little to be desired." Quinn picked up the sample tray and held it out to her. "Taste?"

The blonde turned on her heel and strutted away, mumbling something about it *always being the hot ones.*

"Quinn, that skirted a very thin line," Carly said as she reached for her phone, then thought better of it and began reorganizing the table. Reading the texts would be her reward after the table was organized.

"I'm sorry, but she looked like she was ready to give him a *handy* right here at the table," Quinn said.

Cutter scoffed. "And you screwed that up for me, didn't you?"

"I probably saved you from an STD." Quinn set the sample tray down and said, "Have some scruples."

Carly retrieved a package of napkins from beneath the table, chuckling to herself. She should probably stop this line of banter, but there were no customers in earshot, and she was having too much fun watching the show.

Cutter looked like he was chewing on nails as he said, "I have more scruples than *you* can imagine."

"I said *scruples*, not Oodles of Noodles." Quinn giggled and popped a piece of fudge into her mouth.

He scowled. "Paybacks are hell, tater tot."

"*Tater tot?*" Carly arched a brow.

He eyed Quinn and said, "You know, a little crunchy on the outside, succulent on the inside."

Quinn's eyes narrowed despite the crimson staining her cheeks.

Whoa. They put Randi and Ford to shame. "Thanks for the

help, Cutter," Carly said. "Are you taking off?"

His gaze never left Quinn's as he said, "I think I'll stick around for a while."

"Great. How about you two harness all that pent-up energy and see who can sell more chocolate? I'm heading inside to help Birdie." *Reward time!* She pulled her phone from her pocket on the way inside.

"Carly?" Birdie called out from behind the counter. "Would you mind grabbing another tray of Treasure Hunter Fudge?"

"Sure." She was thrilled that their new creation was selling so well. The cereal bars were doing well, too. She'd dipped them in different flavors of chocolate, and she'd eaten one dipped in white chocolate for breakfast.

She headed into the kitchen as she opened Zev's texts and stopped cold, riveted to the image of Zev underwater, eyes dancing with joy. He was holding a number of horseshoe-shaped metal bracelets with enlarged finial ends. Her pulse skyrocketed as she looked through the pictures he'd texted. There was one of him pointing to the ocean floor, which was littered with more bracelets, and several others of only the bracelets. She wondered if they were manillas, horseshoe-shaped bracelets and armlets used as a form of currency for bartering in West Africa. They were usually made from bronze or copper and sometimes used in the slave trade, as they would have been with Clegg's ship.

She scoured the pictures, zooming in to see the treasures more clearly, taking in their pitted surfaces and the underwater identification tags placed in the artifacts. She mentally ran through the process of identifying and recording artifacts and locations, which were captured on film and on a grid of the site to help with the recovery efforts and so future generations could see exactly where each of the artifacts were found. Oh, how she wished she were there! Happy tears welled in her eyes, and she reached for the counter to combat her shaky legs.

Her phone rang, startling her. Zev's picture appeared with the FaceTime call. She answered quickly. "Are they manillas?" she asked at the same time Zev said, "Baby!"

Zev laughed and flicked his chin, sending his wet hair out of his eyes. "They've got to be, and there are *hundreds* of them down here. Aw, Carls! I wish you were here. We were using the dredge pump, about eight inches down when we hit them…"

He described every detail, and once again she felt like she'd been right there with him when he'd found them.

Only she hadn't been.

Sadness pooled inside her, but she forced her happiness for Zev to rise above it.

His wet hair fell forward again, and he pushed it out of his face in the same fashion he had when he was a kid, as if his hair had some nerve getting in his way. "We still don't have anything positively identifying what we've found as coming from the *Pride*, but—"

"Zev! They've found something!" Randi hollered.

"I've got to go, babe. I love y—*wait!* How's the festival?"

"Zev!" Randi shouted again.

Zev looked perched to bolt, and yet he still waited for her to answer. This man was *not* a pit stop in her life. She wanted all of *his* dreams to come true, just as she knew he wanted hers to. "The festival is *fine*. I love you! Go find our treasure!"

When he ended the call, she was still clinging to the counter. Her phone vibrated, and a text popped up from Birdie. *Treasure hunter fudge???*

Shoot. She needed to get her head on straight. She had a

business to run.

She forced herself to move, and carried the tray of fudge into the shop, greeting customers and trying to push thoughts of Zev and the expedition to the side. But her mind sprinted down that path. What else did they find? What was happening with the concretions they'd worked on? Had he made arrangements for the coins to be evaluated?

Carly put the fudge into the display cabinet, catching a curious look from Birdie. She felt like a *fraud* with her forced smile and thoughts that refused to fall into line.

But she *wasn't* a fraud. She'd grown this business, nurtured relationships with customers and vendors. She'd colored within the lines for almost a decade, building a safe, predictable life that had been instrumental in her healing. It was *okay* to want to color outside them sometimes, wasn't it? That wouldn't mean she was throwing in the towel at the chocolate shop; she just wanted more.

She wanted *Zev* and their adventures. Couldn't she be two people at once—chocolate-shop Carly and adventure-girl Carls?

Birdie touched Carly's shoulder, startling her.

"I can color outside the lines if I want to!" came out before Carly could stop it.

"You can color any way you want to," Birdie said with an amused expression. "But are you sure you want to eat all that fudge?"

Carly realized she was still bent over the tray, which was sticking halfway off the shelf, and there were two glaringly empty spots where fudge should be. Her fingers were coated with the sticky sweets...and so was her *mouth*.

As she rose to her feet, Birdie lowered her voice and said, "Are you okay?"

Not even close. Carly looked at the customers milling about, none of whom were ready to pay, and she said, "I'm okay. Marie said something this morning that's got me overthinking things. Do you ever feel like this is a pit stop for you?"

"Why? Did Quinn tell you I was flirting with the hippie guy who came in?" She crossed her arms and said, "You can't fire me for giving him my number, can you?"

"No, of course not. I'm just curious," she said lightly.

"Well, it's a ridiculous question. I mean, I guess it wouldn't be if I had other aspirations, but you know how much I love this business. Ever since the first day I worked here, it's all I've wanted to do."

"So you never feel like you're missing out on something bigger or better?"

"Like what? Working in a clothing shop? As much as I love clothes…*boring.* Or a bank like Quinn? I'd shoot myself in the foot if I had to do that. College is out for me, because you know, my brain is *way* too busy for that nonsense. I'm a creative person, and in case you haven't noticed, I need to be doing ten different things at once. Case in point." She picked up her phone and showed Carly the Divine Intervention Instagram feed, and then she flipped to three other social media sites, all of which had pictures of the beautifully displayed chocolates, the Divine Intervention shirts and sweatshirts, the shop filled with customers, and the sidewalk bustling with festivalgoers. Each had a different enticing post with hundreds of comments. "What other job would allow me to make delicious confections, handle marketing, deal with customers, flirt with cute guys, maintain killer social media profiles, *and* work with my two best friends? You're stuck with me, boss. I love my job, and when I'm not dreaming of the hot bikers my brothers won't let me near, I'm coming up with new ideas for us here at DI." She lowered her voice and said, "Although tonight, Hippie Dude is going to be front and center in my mind. If you catch my drift."

A customer flagged them from across the room, and another came to the register with a basketful of merchandise.

Birdie whispered, "My X-rated drift."

The next few hours passed in a blur of dealing with customers, restocking displays, and overthinking. When they finally closed for the evening, Carly went with Birdie, Quinn, and Cutter to watch Kaylie Crew's last show. They met up with Birdie's family at the park, which was packed with people sitting on blankets and gathered in small groups. Kaylie stood center stage, belting out the lyrics to one of her latest singles. But even surrounded by her friends, listening to her favorite singer, with hundreds of people milling about, Carly couldn't stop thinking about how Birdie's passion for the business was vastly different from her own. Carly had never seen chocolatiering as her life's dream, though she'd never seen it as a pit stop, either. It had been one of her saving graces.

But she no longer needed saving.

Her phone vibrated with another text from Zev, and her pulse quickened. *We found a huge concretion. Hoping it's a cannon. The size is right, but who knows. I've got a meeting tonight to coordinate equipment and schedules, but I'll call you later. How was your day? Wish you were here.*

She was reading it for a third time when Dare sat beside her on the grass.

"Hey," he said, studying her face.

"Hi. How'd you guys do with your booth today?"

"Great. We had a lot of inquiries and collected a good number of donations." He leaned into her side and said, "You okay, darlin'?"

"Why is everyone asking me that?"

"Maybe because you look like someone stole your favorite teddy bear." He cocked a grin. "You miss him, huh?"

She nodded. "But I'm good."

"Yeah, and I'm a virgin." He leaned into her again and said, "It's okay to be bummed when your old man is gone."

"Is it okay to feel like my heart is in two places at once?"

"It's better to have a full heart in two places than an empty heart with no place at all." He pushed to his feet, pulling her up beside him. "Come on, dance with me and make all the ladies jealous." As he led her down by the stage, he said, "We'll take a selfie for you to send to your other half. Maybe he'll come running back to stake his claim and try to kick my ass."

"He trusts me, and I'm pretty sure he trusts you, too."

Dare swept her into his arms and said, "How do you expect to keep a man if he's not afraid of losing you?"

"Wanting your partner to be insecure isn't healthy, Dare. I think you need a few sessions with your mom," she teased.

"Says you and about half this county. You didn't answer my question."

"It was a dumb question." She smiled at his scowl.

"Okay, new question. Want me to go drag his ass back here?"

She rested her cheek on his chest as they slow danced and said, "More than you can imagine."

Chapter Twenty-Seven

ZEV SAT ON the deck of his boat admiring Carly over FaceTime as she gazed up at the sky from her perch at a table outside the café a few doors down from the chocolate shop. They'd watched the sunrise over Allure more than an hour ago. Birdie had already shown up to help prepare for their busy day, and Ford and Randi were expected to arrive soon, but neither Zev nor Carly were ready to end the call. It had been four treacherously long days since he'd held her in his arms, four excruciatingly lonely nights since he'd kissed her lips, held her hand, or made love to her. Four days since he'd felt her hair tickling his skin or caught the scent of her perfume. He had no idea how he'd made it through a day, much less all the years they'd lost. The miles between them had never felt so vast, despite their ongoing texts and video chats.

Zev had noticed a difference in Carly in the days they'd been apart, as if she were holding something back. He wondered if it was exhaustion, stress, or their lack of concrete plans already taking a toll. Although last night she'd surprised him when their video chat had gone from talking about how much they missed each other to volleying sexy innuendos, which had led to Carly teasing him with a sensual, hip-swaying, seductive striptease.

She'd taunted him into joining her in a striptease of his own, and they'd ended up naked and sating their desires by their own hands. After, Carly had lain breathless and beautiful, gazing longingly at him, frustratingly *untouchable*, which had only made him miss her even more. In truth, he'd sensed a difference in himself, too. After salvaging more than two hundred manillas, they'd finally finished unearthing the enormous concretion they'd located Monday afternoon. Today they were going to lift it out of the seafloor with the crane and tow it back to shore. It appeared to be a cannon, another significant find, but there was only one thing he was chomping at the bit to get his hands on—and he was looking at her, two thousand miles away.

"This was such a good idea," she said, drawing him from his thoughts. "The perfect way to welcome the morning together."

As glad as he was for video-chat software, it was a poor substitute for the real thing. "I wish I were sitting beside you so you could feel my lips on your skin."

"Don't be silly. You're doing important things. And today you have your first television interview. I'm so proud of you. Besides, you'd be bored if you were here. It's just a festival. It doesn't compare to what's going on out there."

He'd been dodging reporters all week. Roddy had increased marina security, and Zev had tried to stay in the background, which had been easier when Luis was running the expedition. Now it was all on his shoulders. He'd finally given in and agreed to do *one* interview with the World Exploration Network, an LWW Enterprises channel, for their *Discovery Hour* show, and it was taking place in half an hour and airing later in the afternoon. He'd only agreed to the interview because his cousin Flynn worked for the network and the reporter was a friend of

Randi's who had grown up on Silver Island. He should be thrilled, but it didn't mean much when he was missing out on all the little things with Carly. He wanted to be the one helping her hand out samples and dancing under the stars. As much as he loved that her friends were taking her out to dinner and keeping her busy, he hated that they needed to.

"I don't know what you've done to me, Carls, but I don't think it's possible for me to be bored when I'm with you," he said honestly, the love in her eyes tugging at him. "I hate not being able to hold your hand or surprise you at work. When you were at the Roadhouse last night with your friends and I was on the boat planning for today, all I could think about was being there with you."

Sadness rose in her eyes, but she sat up a little straighter, putting on that beautiful brave face she'd mastered this week, and said, "We knew it was going to be hard."

"Yeah, well…" He shrugged. "This is harder than I ever imagined it would be. Babe, I was *jealous* of Dare dancing with you, not because he's a threat but because he got to hold you in his arms and be there to see the starlight reflecting in your eyes. What the hell…? How can this be our lives if some other guy gets all the good parts?"

Her warm smile reached all the way up to her eyes. "You think seeing a reflection in my eyes is a good part?"

"I see everything in your eyes. When you're sad, when you're happy, when you want me. I couldn't go a day without seeing them."

"That's because you love me."

"I've always loved you."

"But you love me *more* now," she said braggingly.

Damn right he did.

"I'm doing the same thing," she said softly. "When I'm supposed to be paying attention to customers, I'm daydreaming about being there with you. Birdie says I'm suffering from boyfriend withdrawal."

"I'm dying to come see you. I went over the schedule last night after our call, but then I realized I can't make any commitments until we get this cannon out and see if there's more under there. But trust me, I'm trying to make it happen."

"I looked at my schedule, too, and I don't know when I'll get a break."

He turned at the sound of voices and saw Ford and Randi heading down the dock. He and Carly had so little time to talk, he didn't want to share her with anyone. But Carly had mentioned several times that she and Randi had been texting, and he knew she'd want to see her. "Ford and Randi are here. Want to say hello?"

"Yes," she said, nodding eagerly, but her smile appeared strained again.

"If you'd rather not, it's—"

"I want to. I miss them, and Randi has been so nice sending me all those pictures."

Zev pushed to his feet and waved them over as Randi stepped onto the boat.

"Hey, boss." Randi handed him a bag from the bakery. "I brought you a muffin."

"Thanks. And I brought you Carly."

He turned the phone, and Carly said, "Good morning!"

"Hey, girlfriend! How's the festival?" Randi asked.

"It's great," Carly said. "Busy, but fun."

"Hi, Carly. Think you can get here by this afternoon?" Ford put a hand on Zev's shoulder and said, "This guy's been an ornery pain in my ass all week, and I have a feeling it's because he's missing you."

"I can't even imagine Zev being ornery," she said with a sweet smile. "Arrogant, yes. Cocky, definitely. But *ornery?*" She shook her head. "I don't believe it."

Ford scoffed. "Hear that, Randi? Take a few videos of Zev today and send them to Carly. Show her what we're dealing with."

"Don't believe a word he says." Zev put his face in front of the phone, blocking Ford, and said, "He's just trying to get you to bring out more fudge."

"The bastard ate most of the box you sent," Randi complained.

"I did not. She's the culprit. Just check out the evidence." Ford smacked Randi's ass.

"Hey!" Randi turned and socked him in the arm, and he ran after her.

As they chased each other around—Randi complaining about spilling her coffee and Ford telling her to run faster and work off the fudge—Zev got Carly all to himself again and climbed to the upper deck.

"They're so much fun," she said. "Where are Cliff and Tanner?"

"They'll be here after the interview."

Birdie appeared behind Carly and put her hands on Carly's shoulders. She grinned into the camera and said, "Hey there, heart stealer."

"Hi, Birdie. How are you?" Zev said as Randi darted past threatening Ford, who was right behind her.

"If you'd asked me ten minutes ago, I would have said *fan-tabulous*," Birdie said. "But there was a little *snafu* in the kitchen, and I need to steal Carly for a minute."

Carly looked up at her. "Snafu?"

Birdie lowered her voice and said, "A little...*fire*..."

Carly's face blanched and she shot to her feet, panicked. "What?" She looked at Zev and said, "I've got to—"

"Go!" *Shit.* He fucking hated being this far away.

"*I put it out!*" Birdie hollered as she ran after Carly.

This was the last thing Carly needed when she was already overloaded with the festival and he was two thousand miles away. He heard a shriek, a *splash*, and turned to see Ford and Randi grappling in the water.

"Zev Braden?"

He whipped around at the sound of an unfamiliar woman's voice and found an attractive blonde standing on the dock alongside a beefy guy. "Yes?"

"Hi. I'm Sutton Steele from the World Exploration Network, and this is my cameraman, Ted."

Fuck. He'd forgotten about the interview. "Yes, hi," he said distractedly as Ford and Randi bickered and splashed in the water. "I'm sorry, but can you give me just one minute, please?"

"Sure," she said. She touched Ted's arm, and they both turned around, as if to give him privacy.

Zev walked a few feet away and called Beau. "Hey, I'm sorry to call so early, but I need a favor."

"You okay?"

"Yeah, but Carly had a fire at the chocolate shop. It didn't sound bad, but can you please go over there and check on her? See if she needs any help? Let me know what's going on?"

"Absolutely."

"I hate doing this to you. Thanks, man. I've got to run." He ended the call and strode over to the side of the boat. Ford had

Randi trapped with her back against his chest, and she was cursing at him. Zev hollered, "Hey!" They both looked over, and he said, "The reporter is here. Any chance you guys can look like a real dive team?"

Chapter Twenty-Eight

THE BEAUTIFUL SUNRISE Carly had watched with Zev led to a warm morning that brought out the crowds. Music from the bluegrass band playing in the park drifted in as customers came and went from the chocolate shop. Gossip spread quickly in the small town, and it seemed like everyone had heard about the fire. Answering a million questions was the last thing Carly needed after a lonely week spent dodging her own thoughts and pretending to be okay. At least the fire hadn't caused any major damage. Birdie had accidentally bumped a towel into the flame on the stove as she'd gone to get something from the stockroom and had gotten sidetracked while posting on Instagram. The fire had spread to a plastic container on the counter. She had quickly put the fire out, but the alarm had brought a firetruck and an ambulance. Carly had been frazzled by the chaos in her kitchen and then Beau and Charlotte had come barreling in, adding to the confusion—and stirring up a zillion more worries in Carly's mind. While it was thoughtful of Zev to send his brother to check on her, Beau wasn't *Zev*. Her thoughts had taken hold of that fact and run with it. This was what their lives would be like for years to come, at least over the summers. Anything could happen. What if they decided to have children?

How would that work? What if one of them got hurt or sick and Zev was thousands of miles away? What if *Zev* got sick or was bitten by a shark, and she was far away? Her heart raced as an even scarier thought trampled through her mind. What if there was a storm and Zev got lost at sea?

Holy crap. Anything could happen.

She was drowning in worry and struggling to keep her head above water, but at least Birdie and Quinn hadn't seemed to notice.

By midafternoon the scent of smoke and melted plastic had dissipated and the flow of customers had eased, giving Carly a moment to catch her breath. If only her mind would stop aggravating her with new concerns about her and Zev's future.

Quinn peeked in the front door and looked around the empty shop. "Can I please just put up a sign that says the fire wasn't bad, nobody was hurt, and we'll be open as usual? I feel like I'm spending all my time talking about the fire instead of chocolate."

"Sorry," Birdie said for the hundredth time.

She had been apologizing all day for the fire, but Carly blamed herself. She *knew* Birdie's mind was on seventeen things at once, especially during the festival. If she'd been working instead of selfishly wanting to eke out every minute she could with Zev, maybe the fire could have been avoided.

"Birdie, please stop apologizing. It could have happened to any of us, and I should have been here with you," Carly said. "But that's a good idea about the sign."

"I'll make something pretty and fun and print it out," Birdie offered. "Just give me fifteen minutes so I can finish restocking the chocolate-covered coffee beans first."

"Great!" Quinn headed back outside.

"Carly, I have a great idea!" Birdie exclaimed. "We should have a fire sale. Retailers do it all the time."

"I think they do that when they're going bankrupt," Carly said, making room in the display cabinet for another tray of brownies.

"Oh…" Birdie's shoulders slumped, and in the next second her eyes lit up and she said, "Well, here's another idea I've been thinking about. Next year we should hire college kids to give out samples down by the stage." She set three bags of beans on the shelf and reached for more. "We're hitting customers on the sidewalk, but there are *tons* of people who are at the festival just to listen to music and hang out on the green. They might not even know about the shop, and I have the perfect way to spread the word. You know how in the olden days candy girls walked around movie theaters with trays that hung from neck straps?"

"Do you mean at sporting events?"

"It's pretty much the same thing. Maybe they were called cigarette girls back then, not candy girls. Anyway, if we get four or five people to sell our chocolates down by the green, we could probably make money and gain new customers. And as a bonus, we'd have a few young hotties to ogle."

"I love your brain, Birdie. We would need trays that keep the chocolate cool." Carly made a mental note to add the concept to her future ideas list for more serious consideration, which brought her mind to her and Zev's one-day list. While they were watching the sunrise, they'd added a few things to the list, like attending a concert, cliff diving at Mahana Point, and snowboarding in Allure.

"I'll look into it," Birdie said as she went around the counter and pulled the company laptop out from under the register. "I'll get started on the sign for Quinn."

Carly closed the display cabinet thinking about that one-day list. If summer plans were so hard to figure out, how would she and Zev ever get to the rest of the things on their lists? They both wanted to spend time in Pleasant Hill for the holidays, and she couldn't just take off a month from the shop to travel.

"You know, even if you paid fifteen dollars an hour, that's only like two small sales," Birdie said as she typed.

It took Carly a second to realize Birdie was talking about the college kids she'd mentioned and not the sign she was making for Quinn.

"Yeah, okay," Carly said absently, wondering why her dreams with Zev had seemed realistic when they were together. *We can make this work, Carly. We just have to be creative.* Everything had always seemed possible when they were together. They'd taken advantage of every second they'd had while Zev was in town, living every moment to the fullest, and when they were younger, everything *had* not only seemed possible, but the dreams that were within reach had come to fruition. Had it been easier then? *No. It couldn't have been.* They'd had the demands of school, homework, and their parents' rules to follow.

Was she just overthinking? Putting limits on their limitless adventures?

"And if we hired more people, you might be able to get time off to see that man of yours. Or maybe you could hook up with those college guys."

"Uh-huh," Carly said absently.

"*Carly!*" Birdie clapped her hands, startling her. "You aren't even listening to me."

"What?" *Shoot.* What *was* she talking about? "Yes I was."

"*Bullhockey*, and what's that look on your face?"

"There's no look on my face." There was definitely a look; she could feel it. But she didn't want to talk about it.

"You look like you're trying to solve world peace again."

Again? She didn't have the patience for an inquisition. "Maybe I *am*," she snapped, and stormed off toward the kitchen. Hating herself for being short with Birdie, she turned around and said, "Sorry, Bird. Long day. I'm going to get more brownies."

She had to pull herself together. Zev had been gone only four days, and she was acting like he'd been gone a year with no hope in sight of her ever seeing him again. So what if they didn't see each other for a few more weeks? A person couldn't die from missing someone—even if it felt like she might.

She ducked into her office, calmed by the sight of the pictures of her and Zev. She wondered how the interview had gone. Zev had said he would have Randi send the link as soon as they had it, since he'd most likely be in the water. She touched the postcard he'd mailed to her from Silver Island, reliving the thrill that she'd felt when she'd seen it in the mailbox yesterday. It was hanging on the corkboard behind her desk, the picture of the Silver Island monument smiling back at her. She'd read the note on the back so many times, she knew it by heart.

Remember the time when we were miles apart and our love got stronger? Yours then, yours now, yours forever, Zev

How was he getting through this without losing his mind? She knew how much he missed her. He'd told her dozens of times, but was he as tortured as she was? She hoped not, because this anguish was horrible.

She glanced at the calendar on her desk. The highlighted

events that had once proven how far she'd come now felt like weights dragging her down, and she hated that feeling.

Her phone vibrated, and she pulled it from her back pocket and saw a message from Birdie. *You have a visitor.*

For a split second, Carly hoped it was Zev. But he was pulling the cannon out of the sea today. She drew in a few rejuvenating breaths and headed into the shop.

Birdie was straightening a display near the entrance to the kitchen. She looked at Carly funny and said, "Brownies?"

"*Shoot.* I forgot." Carly took a quick glance around the shop and said, "I thought someone was here to see me."

Birdie pointed behind a display near the far corner of the store, where someone was bent over looking at gift baskets. "I'll get the brownies."

Carly approached the customer and said, "Hi, I'm Carly Dy—" The woman turned around, and Carly's heart leapt at the warm brown eyes looking back at her from behind mahogany cat-eye frames. "Aunt Marie!" She practically launched herself into her loving arms. Marie held her tight against her tall, thin frame. She smelled like hope and healing and all the good things she'd brought into Carly's life.

"What are you doing here?" Carly asked, stepping back, unable to stop grinning as she took stock of how happy her aunt looked. Her eyes had a shimmer to them, and her auburn hair had grown out from the pixie cut she'd worn for as long as Carly could remember. It had a Meg Ryan look to it, shaggy and a little jagged at the edges, like a cute, side-parted layered razor cut. Her new hairdo, and the casual white linen pants and loose beige tank top she wore with a single brown beaded necklace, gave her a softer, chic, youthful appearance.

Marie glanced at Birdie, carrying the tray of brownies to the counter, and said, "A little *bird* told me that you might need your auntie."

Carly eyed her bestie. In all the years they'd worked together, Birdie had *never* gone behind her back like that—except when she'd helped Zev plan the surprise trip to the island. But that was different. "I don't know what Birdie told you, but I'm *fine.*"

Birdie rolled her eyes. "Oh *please.* You can't fool me with that fake smile, Carly Dylan." She strutted over to them, crossed her arms, and jutted her hip. "You're flighty as a jaybird, you've got dark circles under your eyes, which tells me you're not sleeping, and this morning you put caramel in the cherry truffles. You're the farthest thing from *fine* in here."

"I'm just tired, Birdie." Carly realized she was playing with her earring and quickly dropped her hand. "I'm *fine*, Aunt Marie. I'm sorry she dragged you all the way out here, *especially* when you finally had a man in your bed."

"Marie had a man in her bed?" Birdie asked with wide eyes.

"A very *fine* man with strong principles who I could actually talk to without feeling like I needed to inject him with brain cells," Marie said. "Was it nice to have found a man that I actually enjoyed? One who knows the G-spot isn't just a location in a parking garage? Hell *yes*. But the timing of Birdie's call was perfect. I was done traipsing around the world searching for Lord knows what. This is my home, and I miss having my own bed to return to every night. And you both know that I don't need a man to make me happy."

"But Carly does." Birdie touched Carly's arm, her expression softening. "When Zev was here you were a different person. You had more zest for life than I'd ever seen, and I know it wasn't just all those fantastic orgasms working their magic. Carly, I think he found a part of you that *I* didn't even know existed. A good part. Maybe even the best part. I think he took it with him when he left, and I think you need it."

Tears burned Carly's eyes, and she forced them to remain at bay, unwilling to worry her aunt or Birdie any further. "That's what love is, Birdie. You miss the person when they're away. That's not unusual. Just because I'm waiting with bated breath to see him again and I'm anxious to hear about the cannon he's pulling out of the ocean and see what else he'll find doesn't mean I can't do my job." She mustered all of her confidence and said, "Don't worry, Aunt Marie. I miss him, but I'll get over it. The shop is doing better than ever, and—"

"Except our truffles have the wrong fillings," Birdie interrupted. "And yesterday I caught Carly eating her weight in white chocolate."

"Uh-oh," Marie said with a wrinkled brow. "Sounds like our girl is a bit more than a *little* sidetracked."

"That wasn't the first time," Birdie said. "The other day it was fudge, and I'm not bringing it up because she might gain weight. I think she could gain a hundred pounds and turn green and Zev would still be gaga over her. But have you ever worked with *Carly* when she's hyped up on sugar *and* sad? It's a wicked combination. After the sugar high comes the flopping in her chair and staring at pictures of her and Zev in her office. It's breaking *my* heart."

"Would you stop—" The bells above the door jangled, and Carly bit her tongue as a young couple walked in. She feigned a smile and said, "Hi. Welcome to Divine Intervention."

"Hi. The woman outside said you have white-chocolate nonpareils and chocolate-coated cereal bars," the woman said.

"We sure do," Birdie said.

Birdie led them to the display cabinet, and Marie took Carly by the arm, walking her toward the rear of the shop, speaking in hushed tone. "Do you want to go into your office and talk?"

As badly as Carly wanted to cry on her aunt's shoulder, she wasn't a broken girl anymore and she didn't want to worry her aunt. "I appreciate your concern, and coming all this way, but I'm really fine. We're just trying to figure out when we'll see each other again. You know how busy summers are here, and he's making the biggest discovery of his life, and—"

"And you miss him," Marie said empathetically.

Carly tried to swallow past the lump in her throat and managed, "Very much."

"You know, sweetheart, I've gone my whole life not knowing what it feels like to miss a man. But I think I understand it now."

"You and...*Tiger*?"

Marie shrugged. "What can I say? He was pretty great."

"Then go *back* and be with him. I'm a big girl. I can cry myself to sleep and still function the next day."

"I chase dreams, honey, not men," she said adamantly.

Carly found it funny that her own *dream* and *man* went hand in hand. Her phone vibrated. She pulled it from her pocket and opened the text from Randi. "It's a link to Zev's interview. He was on *Discovery Hour* today." She knew how much Zev hated the limelight, and she was excited to see how he'd handled the interview.

"Well, click the link, honey. Let's see this man of yours in action."

Carly glanced up front, wondering if they should go into the office, but she didn't want to leave Birdie alone in the shop. They may be having a lull now, but she knew it wouldn't last.

"Goodness, Carly," Marie said with exasperation. "This is a chocolate shop, not a house of worship. You're allowed to make noise."

"I was just thinking about Birdie." Carly had almost forgotten how pushy her aunt could be. There was something comforting about it.

"Then let's go up front so she can watch it, too. Birdie was right. You're not your quick-thinking self. I'm glad I'm here." On their way up front, Marie called out, "Gather around, people. Carly's boyfriend is on *Discovery Hour*."

"*Marie*," Carly chided her.

"Be proud, sweetheart. It's a big accomplishment and deserves to be celebrated."

"Perfect timing. We just finished." Birdie handed the couple she was helping their bag and receipt and said, "Come back and let us know how you liked them."

"We will," the woman said.

Birdie hurried around the counter to join Marie and Carly and said, "The link finally came?"

"Sure did." Marie motioned to the couple and said, "Have you ever seen a real treasure hunter?"

"Can't say we have," the guy said.

"Then you're in for a real treat." Marie waved them over.

"Why don't we watch it on the laptop?" Birdie suggested.

Carly sent Birdie the link, and Birdie navigated to the site on the laptop and turned it so everyone could see.

"This is Carly's favorite channel," Birdie said. "Most weeks she's glued to it three or four nights, but not when Zev's in town."

"*Birdie*," Carly said with a shake of her head.

"I'm just saying that you like the show," Birdie said as the

Discovery Hour logo appeared on the screen. "Okay, *shh*."

Carly and Marie exchanged an amused glance at Birdie shushing herself.

Sutton Steele, a porcelain-skinned blonde with dainty features, appeared on the screen. "Sutton is my favorite reporter," Carly said excitedly. "She's not hard-nosed like some of the reporters are, and she always seems genuinely intrigued by the guests."

"I'm Sutton Steele, and I'm coming to you from Silver Island, Massachusetts, with treasure hunter Zev Braden on his boat, the *Lucky Charm*."

Carly's heart squeezed. How had she not known he'd named his boat the *Lucky Charm*? He hadn't mentioned it, and the trip had been such a whirlwind, she hadn't noticed.

"There he is!" Birdie exclaimed.

The camera zoomed out, and Zev appeared beside Sutton, wearing a white T-shirt and shorts, his leather bracelets circling his wrist and looking as rugged and handsome as he had that morning. He raked a hand through his hair, lowering his eyes for a split second. That was *his* tell. He'd done it the night they'd met at the park and talked. He was nervous, and that endeared him to Carly even more. His gaze moved from the camera to Sutton and back again, as if he wasn't sure where he should look.

"Oh, honey," Marie said quietly. "He's grown up to be one gorgeous man."

"Inside and out," Carly said. She was so proud of him, her heart beat triple time.

Sutton gave a brief history of Zev's background, and then she said, "Zev believes he has found the wreckage from the *Pride*, a ship that sank during a nor'easter in 1716." She went on to describe the ship, talk about One-Leg Clegg, and explain the circumstances surrounding the ship's disappearance. Then she asked Zev, "How long have you been searching for this treasure?"

Zev looked into the camera, and Carly swore he was looking right at her as he said, "I've been searching for so long, it feels like forever."

"Why this ship? What was it about the *Pride* that brought you out here?" Sutton asked.

Eyes still locked on the camera, he said, "My love for the girl I gave my heart to in second grade. Finding the *Pride* was *our* dream."

Tears welled in Carly's eyes. Had he really said that? Was she dreaming?

Birdie squeezed her arm and whispered, "I'm in love!"

"Oh, baby girl. He's a good egg," Marie said.

Carly blinked through her tears, riveted to Zev as he answered a litany of questions about the mystery girl, who he refused to name.

"She knows who she is," Zev said, and winked at the camera.

Carly remembered what he'd said when she'd mentioned not being able to find any pictures of him after he and Luis had discovered the other shipwreck. *I'd rather be the grungy-looking guy with the backpack people give space to than the rich guy who found the sunken ship who becomes the target of every scam out there.* He was protecting her. She inhaled a shaky breath as Sutton moved on, asking about what they'd found so far and what he planned to do with the artifacts if they were definitively linked to the Pride.

"Carly went diving with him right there at the site," Birdie said. "She should be on the show, too. Did you know—"

"*Shh*," Marie said. "Let him shine, sweetie."

Zev answered dozens of questions, and as the show neared the end, Sutton asked, "How many stars had to align for you to find this wreckage?"

Zev cocked a grin and said, "I think the stars had a little matchmaking help to bring us together."

Carly could barely breathe. He was talking about *them*. Sutton asked more questions, but Carly had trouble focusing past the sound of her racing heart.

"He's doing so well," Marie whispered.

As the interview came to a close, Sutton said, "What's next for Zev Braden? Where does a treasure hunter go after making a find like this?"

"I'll spend the rest of my life discovering *everything* I can about her," Zev answered.

A tear slid down Carly's cheek.

Sutton smiled into the camera and said, "There you have it, folks. A man and his vessel, a match made in the stars…with a little dose of magic."

As the closing credits rolled, everyone clapped and spoke at once, except Carly. She was frozen in thought, knee-deep in love.

"That was incredible," Marie said.

"I felt like he was talking about Carly," Birdie said.

"What did you thi—" Marie turned to Carly, worry chasing her smile away as she took Carly's hand. "Honey? Why are you crying?"

"Carly? What's wrong?" Birdie's voice was laden with concern.

Carly opened her mouth to speak, but nothing came out.

Her thoughts spun, her heart ached, and guilt consumed her.

"Talk to me, sweetheart," Marie pleaded.

"I can't...It's like..." *My words are stuck in my throat.*

"What's it like, honey?" Marie asked. "What is it?"

Marie's eyes implored her to speak, and the words burst from Carly's lungs. "It's like eating Lucky Charms your whole life, and then suddenly Lucky Charms goes off the market and you try other things—Froot Loops, Cocoa Krispies, granola. And sure, they're fruity, chocolaty, crunchy. They're not your *favorite*, but they're pretty good. So you make do, and year after year you shovel substitutes into your mouth because Lucky Charms just *isn't* available." Words flew like daggers, and Carly was powerless to slow them down. "Then one day you walk into a wedding and they're serving Lucky Charms, but only for a limited time. And you *know*"—*know* came out like a curse—"that after that they're only going to be offered across the country. You won't be able to order them online, and you have *no* idea when they'll be back." She paced, her hands flailing as she spewed her heart all over the shop. "And you *try* to resist them even though you don't want to. You're terrified that after that limited time, you not only won't be able to go back to the substitutes, but you won't *be* the person you were before you took that first bite. But you're *salivating* over the marshmallows, craving the unique taste of the oats, and the cereal is *beckoning* you, looking at you like your mouth is the *only* place it wants to be, and you just can't take it anymore. So you take the plunge, and that first bite is out of this world! The more you eat, the more you remember how everything was *better* with Lucky Charms. The air was lighter, the world was brighter, *you* were more alive, happier, *whole*. You feel like you're floating in a never-ending bowl of Lucky Charms even though you *know* they're going away soon." Her hands fisted, arms rigid as she wore a path in the floor. "You tell yourself you can do it. You can hoard enough Lucky Charms to hold you over until they come back. But you *can't*! And then they're *gone*, and nothing feels right anymore. You wake up at night craving the sugar, aching for the high they bring. You *want* the thrills of cliff diving and treasure hunting. You want to be part of the dream you helped create! You want to live moment to moment, because that's what makes you *breathe*. You want to get on a plane and find Zev no matter *what* the cost!" She realized what she'd said and clamped her mouth shut before more hurtful truths tumbled out. She spun around to apologize to Marie, and found her, Birdie, Quinn, and about a dozen gaping-mouthed, wide-eyed customers staring at her.

Beau and Charlotte stepped out from the crowd, and Carly's cheeks flamed with embarrassment.

"Why are you still standing here?" a tall blond woman asked. "Go get your man!"

The crowd cheered.

Tears poured down Carly's cheeks, and she laughed, but then that guilt consumed her again, and she shook her head. "*No*. Marie, I didn't mean that. I *love* this shop. I love you and Birdie and—"

"It's okay, honey." Marie wrapped Carly in her arms and said, "This was never your dream. This was *my* dream, and you've been living in it long enough. Now it's your turn to live your dream with the man you have loved since you were a little girl."

"I can't just leave. I'm not *done* here," Carly said, feeling like she was being torn in half.

"You don't have to be done," Marie said. "I'm here to help,

not to take over."

Carly gasped for air, her chest aching.

"And I'm here," Birdie said. "I promise no more fires!"

"Don't forget me!" Quinn said with a bounce in her step. "Just say the word, Carly. I'll quit the bank and work here full time, extra hours, whatever you need. I love this business!"

Carly crossed her arms over her middle, tears flooding her cheeks as gratitude swelled inside her.

"Sweetheart, you don't have to make any final decisions right now," Marie reassured her. "Just go be with Zev for a few weeks, for a month, however long you need, and *then* decide. We can hold down the fort."

Carly looked at the woman who had welcomed her into her home, nurtured her until she was strong and brave again, and gave her a life and a business, and now she was offering her a chance at the future she'd always wanted. But she wanted time at the shop, too. Was that even possible?

"A few weeks…?" Carly choked out. A few weeks would be enough to figure things out, or at least fill her up to hold her over a few more.

"It's okay, sweetheart. I love you, and you love him. That's all that matters."

"Okay, I'll go," Carly said, swiping at her tears with a shaky hand.

Cheers rang out, and Charlotte said, "Treat is at the festival! If anyone can get you on a plane fast, it's him. Beau! Call Treat!"

Beau pulled out his phone and made the call.

Carly gasped, swiping at her eyes. "Thank you," she said as Marie, Birdie, and Quinn enveloped her in a group hug.

"Hey, I'm getting in on this!" Charlotte threw her arms

around them.

"Thank you all *so* much," Carly said through laughter and tears.

"Let's go, Carly." Beau put a hand on Carly's back, leading her toward the door, and said, "Treat is on his way up the block."

He opened the door and Carly hurried out, smacking right into a hard chest.

CARLY LOOKED UP with tear-streaked cheeks. "Zevy" slipped from her lips as "Carls" fell from his. He panted for air, short of breath from sprinting through town.

"What are you doing here?" she asked, her whole body shaking.

"I broke a promise and I had to fix it." His nerves were fried from the long, stressful trip, but he was finally there, and he wasn't going to waste a second. "I said I'd never hurt you again, but this morning when we FaceTimed I saw how hard you were trying to put on a brave face, but I know you, Carls. You miss me as much as I miss you."

She choked out a sob.

"Babe, if treasure hunting means being away from you, then I never want to look for another treasure in my life. *Nothing* feels as good as when we do it together. You're my adventure partner, my best friend. Carls, you *are* the love of my life. Hell, baby, you *are* my life. You need stability and you have a full life here. I don't want to screw that up. I want to go cliff diving and deep-sea diving *with* you, or not at all. I want to see that spark in your eyes when we find a concretion or pull a cannon from the sea, but we can fit those things in on vacations, when you have time off. They don't have to rule my life. I want to be *here* with you, inspiring new chocolates and by your side to taste test them. *I* want to be the man dancing with you under the stars and handing out samples at the festival. I want to be at the Roadhouse Wednesday nights to give Cowboy and Dare a hard time and to make you hot and bothered under the table."

Chuckles rose around them, and Carly smiled despite her tears.

"Can we clone *him*?" Quinn said, earning a *"Shh"* from Charlotte.

"You *can't* give up your life. I won't let you," Carly said, looking beautifully stubborn. "You're living *our* dream. I was just coming to you to tell you that I want to be *there* with you, but I also want to be here."

His heart beat so hard, he was sure his chest would break open. "Then let's figure it out, write it down, do whatever we need to do. I don't care about the details as long as I get to spend every day with you. You're the only treasure I need."

He dropped to one knee, vaguely aware of a collective gasp as he opened his hand, revealing a yellow plastic treasure chest.

More tears spilled down Carly's cheeks. She lifted a shaky hand over her mouth, laughing softly as she said, *"Zevy...?* Is that *my* treasure chest?"

"It *was*, until you left it on my windowsill the night you agreed to be my girlfriend. But this *is* your ring." He opened the treasure chest, revealing the pink plastic ring with the star on top he'd taken from her jewelry box before he'd left Pleasant Hill all those years ago.

Sobs bubbled out of her lips, and she collapsed to her knees before him, her eyes glittering with love as she said, "You're a *thief*."

"No. I was just a kid who had made a promise I never intended to break. I figured it was a fair trade. I left you my heart, so I took your engagement ring."

She laugh-cried as he withdrew the ring from the treasure chest and said, "Carly, baby, you are and will always be the very air that I breathe, the *only* treasure to my empty chest. I don't want to spend another day waking up without you in my arms. Will you take another leap of faith and color outside the lines with me, Carls? Marry me so we can begin our greatest adventure yet? You're the only one who can keep up with me. Say yes, and I promise we'll figure out the rest with concrete plans you can count on."

"*Yes!*" she said breathlessly. "*Yes* to everything!"

Cheers and applause rang out as he slid the plastic ring onto her finger. It stopped before her knuckle, and everyone laughed. He took the ring off and slid it on her pinkie.

Gazing deeply into her eyes, he said, "I love you, Carls, and I will spend the rest of my life showing you just how much."

Kneeling on the front steps of the chocolate shop, surrounded by throngs of strangers and a handful of family and friends, Zev lowered his mouth to hers, kissing her with everything he had, which had already become more than he'd ever dreamed possible.

Chapter Twenty-Nine

BY NIGHTFALL EVERYONE Carly knew and all of Zev's Colorado relatives had heard about their storefront proposal, and thanks to Beau, they all got to see it on video. Beau had taken one look at Zev's face when Carly had run into him, and he'd followed his gut feeling of what was to come. Slipping off to the side, he'd captured the whole proposal on video. Carly couldn't be happier. She'd been too stunned to try to memorize every second of their magical moment, and now she could relive it as often as she wanted. She and Zev had sent the video to their families and FaceTimed while they'd watched it. Their families were thrilled for them, though they hadn't appeared surprised by the turn of events, claiming that Carly and Zev had always given off more sparks than Fourth of July fireworks.

Birdie, Marie, Quinn, and Charlotte had thrown together an impromptu engagement party on the festival green. They had champagne toasts, festival food, and goodies from the shop. Kaylie Crew was singing one of her newest hits, and Carly felt like she was living a dream. She gazed at Zev, talking with Dare, Cowboy, Cutter, Treat, and a handful of his other relatives, and her heart swelled. She still couldn't believe Zev put the biggest day of his life on hold to come after her—giving them both the *best* day of their lives.

Zev looked over, his eyes instantly finding hers as if he'd sensed her looking at him. Jillian's words sailed through her mind. *Two sides of the same coin.*

Zev lifted his chin, their connection blazing a path between them, as it had all afternoon while he'd helped her hand out fudge samples and all evening since they'd arrived at their party.

Birdie and Quinn sidled up to her, and Quinn said, "Want me to grab a drool rag?"

"I'm still in shock," Carly said, looking at her perfect plastic engagement ring. "Pinch me so I know it's real."

Birdie pinched Carly's butt.

Carly squealed. "*Birdie*, I meant my arm."

"Your butt's more fun." Birdie giggled. "Are you going to leave me for good? Because I know I said I couldn't move away from my family, but if Zev were *my* man, I'd go wherever he went and I might not ever look back."

"You'd never leave your family," Quinn said. "Heck, *I'd* never leave your family."

"I don't know. Zev and Carly make crazy love look mighty tempting," Birdie said.

"*Crazy love*," Carly said, feeling good all over. "That's pretty much what we have, isn't it?"

"I'll say. All the man has to do is look at you and you get all wild eyed, like you want to rip your clothes off, go live in the forest, and have little Tarzan babies." Birdie gasped and grabbed Carly's arm. "If you have babies, can I be a godparent? *Please?* I'd be such a good godmother. I'd spoil your babies rotten."

"We haven't had time to talk about tomorrow, much less about *babies*," Carly said. "But don't worry, Birdie. If or when we have kids, you'll be a big part of their life. But I'll definitely be back. Marie was right. While I love the chocolate shop, it wasn't *my* dream, at least not like the adventurous life with Zev is. But the shop *is* an important part of me, and so are you guys and everyone else around here I've come to love."

"Good, because I would miss you," Quinn said, eyeing Noah talking with two of his cousins. "By the way, I didn't know Zev had so much family in the area. Are any of *those* guys single? I feel like I'm at a stud buffet, and Mama's hungry."

"Dibs on the single relatives," Birdie said.

"Hey, that's not fair. I'm the one who asked," Quinn complained.

As the girls bickered, Carly spotted Marie and Wynnie heading their way. She wondered what they would think of Birdie and Quinn's conversation. She hadn't had a chance to really talk with Wynnie yet about Zev, although Wynnie had congratulated them, and she was sure Birdie and her brothers had filled their mother in over the past week.

Birdie motioned dramatically around them and said, "Most of the single guys in this town are either related to me or Dark Knights, and Cutter *seriously* wants to throw you on the back of his horse and ride off into the Valley of Cunnilingus with you. He's been ogling your ass in that black leather miniskirt all day. It's only fair that I get dibs on any fresh meat in town."

"Fresh *meat*?" Carly shook her head.

Quinn and Birdie giggled.

"For what it's worth, Noah, the guy with the lighter hair, is single," Carly said as Marie and Wynnie joined them. "But the other two are Treat's brothers Dane and Hugh. They're both taken *and* too old for either of you."

Wynnie gave Birdie a stern motherly look and said, "Much too old. I love you, Birdie, but you're going to give your father a heart attack if you bring home a man that much older than you."

"Who says I'd bring him home to *your* place?" Birdie smirked. "I'm a grown woman, Mom. I have needs."

"*Woo-hoo*," Marie said in a singsong voice. "Birdie has flown the nest."

Wynnie glowered at Marie. "Do *not* encourage her. She's all about ruffling my feathers these days."

"I am not ruffling anything. It would just be nice to see some new faces around here." Birdie tapped Quinn's arm and pointed to a handsome man walking across the green. "*Hello, silver fox.*"

"Birdie!" Wynnie snapped.

Birdie doubled over in laughter. "You should see your face!"

Marie put her hand on Wynnie's shoulder and said, "Sorry, sis, but I miss this."

Wynnie sighed. "I suppose I would, too, if I weren't around it all the time."

"I'm going to miss you guys so much," Carly said. "I really appreciate your support earlier today when I kind of lost my mind."

"If by *support* you mean our *pushiness*," Birdie said. "Then you're welcome." She tapped Quinn's shoulder and pointed at another guy.

"Aunt Marie, Wynnie," Carly said. "You came to my rescue, and now I'm going to marry the man who had been instrumental in my landing here in the first place. Are you okay with this?"

The two women exchanged a familiar matronly glance.

"You didn't need rescuing when you came here," Marie said. "You just needed a new start. Someplace lower key, without all the memories of the two of you, so you could begin to see your past, and your future, more clearly."

"And we're not the ones who need to be okay with your decisions, sweetheart," Wynnie added. "Only you know what's right for you, and you have excellent judgment. You can trust it, Carly. We do."

"*I* know that I want to be with Zevy, but I thought I'd see if you had anything to say."

"Honey," Wynnie said warmly, "You once told me that you gave your heart to Zev when you were kids, and I asked you if you still had enough left to ever love that powerfully again."

Carly remembered that conversation. It had taken place early on in their therapy sessions. "I never answered you."

"I know you didn't, and I think we both know why. Like I said, you have excellent judgment. You must have known then that you weren't the only one who had left their heart behind." Wynnie took Carly's hand and said, "You would be *fine* without Zev, honey. You healed here. You became stronger and more independent. You went through school and took charge of a business you had to learn from the ground up. But *fine* isn't enough for an extraordinary woman like you, Carly. Zev lights the fire that illuminates you, allowing you to shine brighter, to be stronger, and most importantly, he sees *all* of you."

"And he *loves* all of you," Marie said.

Carly got choked up. Even though she hadn't needed their approval, it felt really good knowing they saw the same things in Zev she did. But the overthinker in her had to know one last thing. "How do you know what Zev sees in me?"

"Because while you and the girls were dancing, Zev sought us out, and we had a nice long chat." Wynnie nodded at Zev, heading their way with Treat.

Zev was carrying Treat's toddler, Bryce, who was busy petting Zev's scruff with both hands. Treat's other son, Dylan, grabbed Zev's free hand, gazing up at him from beneath his mop of brown hair. Carly could practically feel her ovaries exploding.

"That man came all this way and offered to give up what he's been searching for his whole adult life just so you wouldn't have to leave your life behind," Wynnie said. "But he *is* your life, Carly, and you are his, which is why neither one of you will ever have to give up a darn thing again."

CARLY WAS LOOKING at Zev in that way that sent heat through his chest like flames. He winked, and she blew him a kiss. Many people had told him that no one could make someone else happy and that happiness had to come from within. But Zev had always known they were wrong. For the first time since he'd left Pleasant Hill, he felt truly, deeply happy, like he was exactly where he was supposed to be. He felt *settled* despite their very unsettled living arrangements, and that was because without Carly he wasn't whole. She was as much a part of him as the blood that pumped through his veins.

"Carly!" Dylan broke away from him and bolted toward Carly, barreling into her legs. He gazed up at her and said, "You're getting married!"

"I know. It's *crazy*, isn't it?" she said, crouching to look him in the eyes.

Zev was hit with images of Carly with *their* children. Little stubborn blond girls and challenging long-haired boys with endless energy and Carly's pretty eyes and gorgeous smile.

"My daddy said he'd marry you," Dylan said to her. "But I think that would make my mommy sad."

"Isn't he precious?" Wynnie said.

Treat mouthed, *Sorry.*

Carly tapped the tip of Dylan's nose and said, "Your daddy loves your mommy *very* much. He would never marry *anyone* other than her. I think he meant he would *officiate* the ceremony, which means he'd say a bunch of important words, and then he'd tell me and Zev that we were husband and wife."

"*Oh!*" Dylan spun around and said, "I'm not mad at you anymore, Daddy."

"That's a relief, buddy." Treat looked at Carly and said, "I was telling Zev about how you and I met. It feels like a lifetime ago. I had no idea Zev was the guy you were talking about when you said there was only one man who could claim your heart. Small world."

Carly glanced at Zev and said, "Very."

"I didn't know Dylan was named after you, either," Zev said, as Bryce stroked his cheeks. He kissed the little guy's hand and said, "What other secrets are you keeping from me?"

Carly stepped closer and said, "Play your cards right and maybe one day you'll find out."

"Daddy! Let's go dance with Mommy!" Dylan grabbed Treat's hand, tugging him toward Max, who was standing about fifty feet away, dancing with her sisters-in-law.

"One sec, buddy." Treat reached for Bryce. "Better give me the little guy, Zev. He'll pitch a fit the minute I walk away."

Zev kissed Bryce's cheek and handed him over, enjoying the dreamy look in Carly's eyes.

"*What* is happening?" Birdie hollered, causing them to look over.

"Oh my gosh!" Carly exclaimed. "Who *is* that?"

Marie was dipped over a man's arm, kissing him with one of her legs up in the air. The man's back was facing them, but Marie certainly didn't appear to be struggling.

Dare and Cowboy barreled into the group, shoulder to shoulder, teeth gritted. Cutter was right behind them.

"Who the hell is that?" Dare growled.

"I don't know!" Birdie said. "He just appeared out of nowhere, swept her into his arms, and kissed her."

Cowboy and Dare stepped toward Marie, but Wynnie grabbed their arms. "Settle down, boys. If she didn't want him kissing her, the guy would have a black eye by now."

They glowered at their mother.

"I must be drinking the wrong water, because everyone else is getting kissed," Quinn said.

The man released Marie from the kiss, rising slowly to his full height, holding her as she found her footing. His back was still facing them, but over his shoulder Zev saw Marie's face was flushed, her eyes a little dazed. Her smile told him that whoever that mystery kisser was, he was important to her.

"I have missed you, *mi amor*," the man said.

The familiar gruff voice struck Zev. "*Luis?*"

"*Luis?*" Carly, Cowboy, and Dare said in unison.

"Who is Luis?" Birdie threw her hands up and said, "I'm so confused!"

The man turned around, and Zev instantly recognized Luis's wise eyes and affable smile, but the rest of him didn't make sense. His long, wild hair was cropped short and slicked back, curling at the edge of his collar. His beard was short and manicured. Gone were the tennis shoes and T-shirts he'd worn

443

for a decade, replaced with soft leather moccasins and a white linen button-down.

"*Mijo!*" Luis opened his arms, hauling Zev into a manly embrace.

"Who the hell are you?" Dare said accusatorily.

"Dare, this is my old buddy and mentor, Luis Rojas," Zev said.

"And why is he kissing our aunt?" Cowboy asked.

"Because I *want* him to," Marie said proudly. "Yes, Aunt Marie is allowed to have a social life once every twenty-five years or so."

"Marie, *Tiger* is Luis?" Carly's gaze moved between her aunt and Luis. "Did you know that he knew Zev?"

"Not until you called the other day when Luis and I were together," Marie explained.

"I'm afraid I am to blame." Luis reached for Marie's hand, his accent as thick as ever. "When I came into my fortune, there were a lot of women who wanted my money and not my heart. I finally got smart and took the advice of your boyfriend—"

"*Fiancé*," Zev corrected, drawing Carly into his arms.

"*Really?*" Luis's eyes sparked with joy, and he laughed heartily. "Congratulations to you both. I'd like to explain why Marie didn't know about my relationship with Zev. As I said, I took Zev's advice, and I have kept a low profile these last few years. Until the other morning when you called, Marie thought I was just a retired archaeologist. She didn't even know my last name. It wasn't until she hung up with you, when I asked about the *pit stop*, and she mentioned Zev, which is an uncommon name, that we started putting two and two together. That's when I put Marie's niece *Carly* together with my Zev and realized that my boy had reunited with his lady love." He put his hand over his heart and said, "My *mijo* has found his Carls, and I could not be happier."

"When Luis told me about his travels with Zev and their close relationship, it became clear just how much Zev loves you and how unhappy he was without you," Marie explained. "But I didn't say anything because you can tell me he's wonderful and Luis can put in all the good words he wants, but this stubborn auntie needed to see your fine young gentleman firsthand to make her own assessment."

Carly looked up at Zev and said, "Don't worry. She approves of you."

Zev kissed her, and then he looked at Luis and said, "So tell me, *Tiger*, what are you doing here *besides* kissing Marie?"

"Treasure hunting," Luis said with a wink.

"Aw," Carly said, and Zev hugged her against his side.

"In all the years I spent listening to you talk about Carly as if she were the very heart of you, I never knew what it felt like to love someone that much." Luis gazed into Marie's eyes and said, "You told me you were done with your adventures and going home to settle down. When you left, I finally understood Zev's pain. My life is empty without you, *mi amor*. I'm an old man, and surely you could do much better, but if you want me, I'm yours."

"Oh, *Tiger*," Marie said softly. "I *definitely* want you."

As Luis lowered his lips to Marie's, Birdie exclaimed, "That's it! Forget the chocolate shop. I'm going treasure hunting. I need a boat and someone to drive it. Quinny, you in?"

Quinn shouted, "Yes!"

"The hell you are, tater tot." Cutter grabbed Quinn's arm, hauling her away. Quinn hollered for Birdie, causing everyone to crack up.

As their friends broke out more champagne, the Whiskeys began interrogating Luis, and Zev took advantage of the chaos. He laced his fingers with Carly's and whispered, "Let's go," leading her away from the others. Her melodic laughter was music to his ears as they ran under the cover of the night to a quiet spot beneath a tree, where he gathered her in his arms and devoured her with kisses, as he'd been dying to do all evening.

Zev kept her close, swaying to the music as he said, "That was pretty wild, wasn't it?"

"I can't believe Marie and Luis are together. It's like the stars are aligning for everyone."

"Except Birdie," he said, and they both chuckled.

"She'll have to find her own treasure hunter, because I'm not sharing mine." Carly wound her arms around his neck, and excitement sparked in her eyes. "When do we go back to Silver Island?"

"Whenever you want to. I left it open ended. I didn't expect to find you coming after *me* when I got here."

"I didn't, either," she said with a soft laugh. "You blew into my life like a hurricane, upending everything I thought I knew about myself and reminding me of who I was and who we were together. I *love* us, Zev, and I cannot wait to color outside the lines with you. Let's go back Sunday night and get on the water on Monday. Marie said we could take a few weeks to decide what we want, but for me there's no decision to be made. I want *you*—here, there, everywhere, always and forever."

He kissed the spray of freckles on her nose, threading his fingers through her hair, gazing into her entrancing eyes. He was so lost in her, feeling so blessed to have this second chance, he was speechless.

"Why are you looking at me like that?" Carly asked.

"Because every time I look into your eyes, I see more of you, more of us. I see a future I thought I'd lost. I see Journey, Scout, and Chance, with freckles across the bridge of their noses and mischief dancing in their eyes. I see us flying to far-off lands with lists and agendas made by you. Lists that you know I'll lose, or we'll simply forget we're supposed to follow, as we explore places with names we can't pronounce and make love under the stars on exotic beaches. I envision afternoons here in Colorado with you working in the chocolate shop and me hosting exhibits at the Real DEAL, and evenings snowboarding, hanging out with my cousins and your friends, or curled up in front of a fire." He pressed a kiss to her cheek and whispered, "Naked beneath the blanket, of course."

"Of course," she agreed.

He kissed her lips, her forehead, and the tip of her exquisitely adorable nose and said, "I look forward to growing old and gray with my favorite girl by my side, spending lazy days on our boat daring each other to do things we're way too old to consider—and doing them." That earned him a cute giggle. "I see our grandkids following us around listening to stories of our adventures, and I see you in my arms every night and waking up with me wrapped around you like an octopus every morning."

"You *are* pretty handsy," she teased. "I guess that means you don't regret putting your biggest discovery yet on hold to come here and sweep me off my feet?"

"Not even a little. The cannon's been under water for hundreds of years. A little longer isn't going to make a difference. You made me realize that nothing is more important than spending time with the people I love, and, Carly Dylan, I am utterly and completely in love with everything about you. I can't wait to start our greatest adventure yet as husband and wife."

As he lowered his lips to hers, Birdie's voice cut through the air. "Found the lovebirds! They're *not* naked!"

Carly and Zev exchanged a heated glance and hollered, "*Yet!*"

Chapter Thirty

CARLY SWAM TOWARD the sunlight glittering like diamonds on the surface of the ocean. It was almost as bright as the engagement ring Zev had given her five weeks ago, when she'd woken up before dawn and found him setting up blankets and breakfast on the deck of the boat. They'd snuggled beneath the blankets and watched the sunrise, and when they'd poured their cereal for breakfast, a tiny gold treasure chest had tumbled out of the Lucky Charms box into Carly's bowl. One look at the love in Zev's eyes had brought tears to hers before she'd even opened the chest and found the gorgeous ring he'd had made to resemble the plastic one he'd given her. A round aquamarine gemstone was set in the center of an eight-point rose-gold star. Between each of the points was a diamond, forming shorter points between the longer ones. It was the most beautiful ring she'd ever seen, and soon she was going to marry the most beautiful man she'd ever known. She'd never forget the way he'd looked at her as he'd slid the ring on her finger and said, *I loved you then, I love you now, and I'll love you long after we leave this earth, because Carly Dylan soon-to-be Braden, our adventures have only just begun.*

Zev reached for her hand, drawing her from her thoughts a

few yards from the surface. Ending their dives holding hands had become just one of their many *things* since they returned to the island eight magical weeks ago. As their fingers interlaced, Zev pulled her closer. Just beyond him Carly saw Ford reaching for Randi's hand. Randi swatted it and swam away. Of course Ford went after her.

Zev and Carly continued ascending, and when they breached the surface, the bright summer sun beamed down on them. Randi and Ford popped up a few yards away, and they all made their way to the boat. As they took off their equipment, Carly listened to their friends chatting, surrounded by the scents of the sea, freedom, and love. She could hardly believe this was *their* life. Well, this and everything else she and Zev had chosen to take on. Within a couple of weeks of being on the water, they knew exactly what they wanted, and it all began with Carly becoming Zev's partner in his—*their*—company, Two Treasure Hunters, One Ship.

"That was such a fun dive," Carly said as she unzipped her wet suit. "I swear this never gets old."

"Neither does this." Zev drew her into his arms and kissed her, as he always did the second she was free from all the diving accessories. He'd had a new shimmer in his eyes since earlier that morning when they'd received the news that a sword grip with Garrick One-Leg Clegg's initials inscribed in it had been extracted from one of the concretions.

"Where's my kiss?" Ford teased.

Zev gave Carly a chaste kiss and reached for Ford. Ford laughed as he dodged Zev's grasp and hid behind Randi, who rolled her eyes.

"Oh, I see how it is," Zev said. "My body was good enough for you to spoon, but you're offended by my lips?"

"You're not as pretty as Randi is." Ford draped an arm over Randi's shoulder.

Randi sighed. "Are you delirious or something?"

"Or *something*," Ford said with a waggle of his brows.

Carly chuckled at their bickering. She'd come to love them as much as she loved her friends in Colorado, who she missed every day and kept up with via FaceTime. But her life had never been more fun or more fulfilling. She and Zev wanted to have it all—the adventure-filled days they'd always dreamed of, a foot in the door of Divine Intervention, time with their families in Pleasant Hill and their friends, who had become family to both of them, in Colorado. Carly had proposed a partnership to Marie and Birdie that enabled her to work in the shop during the winters, and for a few weeks throughout the year, while allowing her schedule to remain flexible so she and Zev could travel and dive. Both Birdie and Marie were thrilled with the suggestion. Last week they'd hired Quinn full time and signed a partnership agreement, making it legal. It was no surprise that Cutter was now an even more regular customer. As for Zev, he agreed to run winter exhibits at the Real DEAL for his cousins and Jack, and the treasure-hunting division was now under development.

"Look at that guy with his scruffy beard. You think I want to kiss that?" Ford said.

"Better him than me," Randi said, ducking free from Ford's arm.

"Zev happens to have the best lips on the planet." Carly crossed the deck toward her very handsome man, put her arms around his neck, and said, "I'll gladly let you *offend* me with them, over"—she kissed him—"and over"—*kiss, kiss*—"again."

Randi said, "Hey, *smoochers*, don't forget that I have to be inland by six." The endearment Ford had coined for them had stuck.

"Oh, that's right. You have a date tonight," Carly said as she stripped off her wet suit, acutely aware of Zev visually devouring her. *That* never got old, either.

Ford was unzipping his wet suit and he stopped midzip, brow furrowed. "You have a date?"

"It's not a date. Brant's friend is in town and I'm taking him to dinner and showing him around," Randi said as she pulled a T-shirt over her head.

"Sounds like a date to me." Ford crossed his arms and said, "Which friend?"

"Charlie," Randi said on her way into the equipment room with Ford on her heels.

One of their phones rang from within the equipment room, where they stored them when they went diving.

"Saved by the bell," Randi said as she walked out and handed the phone to Zev. "FaceTime from your parents."

They'd left messages for their parents earlier, wanting to share their news with both families at once. "I'll patch in whoever's available, Carls. Why don't you get your phone and ring your parents and Marie?" Zev said, and then he answered the call.

Carly went to get her phone. She called her parents first on FaceTime and then added Marie to the call. Marie was at the shop with Birdie and Luis, which made the call even more special.

"We have news!" Carly said as she sidled up to Zev and saw Jillian, Jax, Nick, and their parents on the screen.

"Hi, Carly!" Jillian waved.

"Hey, Jilly. I've got my parents, Marie, Birdie, and Luis on my phone." She turned the phone so his family could see the others.

As they all said hello, Ford peered around Zev and waved. "Hi, folks."

"Hi, Ford," Zev's parents and brothers said.

"*Hey*, Ford," Jillian said flirtatiously.

"Hi, beautiful," Ford said. "When are you coming to visit me so I can take you out?"

Zev glowered at him. "You are *not* taking her out."

"Damn right he's not," Nick agreed.

Randi grabbed Ford's arm, dragging him away, and said, "Leave them alone and you can harass me about Charlie."

"Nick's just jealous because he's going to Oak Falls, and scorching-hot cowgirl Trixie Jericho is off-limits, which means poor Nicky will come home blue balled again." Jillian cracked up.

Nick gritted out a warning, "Enough, Jilly," making her laugh harder.

"Jillian, stop riling the boys up," their mother said.

"And watch the sex talk." Zev's father leaned closer to the screen and said, "How about we all listen to what Zev and Carly have to say?"

"We have good news and best news," Zev said. "Which do—"

"Wait! I have to take this call!" Jillian shouted. "It's Johnny Bad's agent. They want me to make the clothes for his next tour. We're negotiating. I'll call you back!" Johnny Bad was a famous musician known for being difficult.

After she ended her call, Zev said, "Should we wait?"

"No. She might be a while," his mother said.

"Okay." Zev put his arm around Carly and said, "Do you

want our good news or our best news first?"

"This is a no-brainer," Nick said. "Best news. Carly's knocked up—boom. Done."

Their mother gasped. "Really? Is it true? We have a grand-baby on the way?"

"I'm going to be a godparent!" Birdie squealed.

"No, you're not," Carly and Zev said at once. They had talked about having children, and they definitely wanted a family at some point. But for now, they wanted to enjoy as much togetherness and go on as many adventures as they could without the pressures a baby would add to their lives.

Marie chuckled and said, "You guys are like live entertain-ment."

Zev gazed into Carly's eyes and said, "We've decided to get married over the holidays in Pleasant Hill."

Everyone cheered and talked at once.

"Yes!" Birdie exclaimed. "I've always wanted to go there!"

Carly watched Zev and his father exchange the most loving and supportive look, and then the most surprising thing happened. Her father gave Zev an equally supportive look, making her heart even fuller.

"Congratulations, *mijo*," Luis said.

"You and Marie had better make the trip out for the wed-ding," Zev said.

"We wouldn't miss it for the world," Marie assured them.

"This is wonderful news," Carly's mother said. "Where do you want to have the wedding?"

Carly and Zev exchanged knowing smiles, and Carly said, "Byers Brook, where we went on our first adventure." When they were young, they'd called it their secret brook. They'd later learned that it was where teenagers went to make out, which

SEARCHING FOR LOVE

was why they hadn't gone there when they'd first had sex. They hadn't wanted to get caught.

"That's perfect," Zev's mother said with a hand over her heart.

"We thought we'd have the reception at the winery," Zev said, eyeing Carly as if he was remembering the first time they'd had sex, too, lying on blankets beneath the stars on the winery grounds.

Nick snort-laughed. "You guys sure have a thing for *firsts*."

Carly leaned closer to Zev and whispered, "Does he know?"

Zev turned his face away from the camera and whispered, "He's the one who told me to go somewhere nobody would find us. I had to ask his opinion."

Carly couldn't help but smile at the teenager-turned-man who had always put protecting her above all else. Neither of them was perfect, and they'd both made their mistakes, but as far as Carly was concerned, perfection was overrated. Her gaze shifted to Nick, who had also tried to keep her safe. He winked, making her blush anew.

"I think the brook and the winery are lovely ideas," Carly's mother said, and everyone agreed.

"Carly, I'd be honored if you'd allow me to make your gown," Jax offered.

"Oh, Jax, thank you! I was going to ask if you would mind," she said. "I just want something simple, like us."

Jax smiled and said, "I'll make whatever you'd like, but there's nothing *simple* about either one of you. Unique, yes, but never simple."

"I hope you'll let us cater desserts," Marie said, sparking a litany of conversation about wedding preparations.

When the excitement settled, they shared their *good* news

and told them about the sword grip. "It's not indisputable proof that the artifacts are from the *Pride*, but we believe it is, and we've got nothing but time ahead of us to discover something that will."

They talked for a while longer, and when they ended the call, they heard Randi and Ford bickering at the other end of the boat. Zev put his arms around Carly and said, "Think they'll ever figure it out?"

"Probably one day, although knowing Randi, she'll put him through the ringer first."

"And Ford wouldn't want it any other way," Zev said.

"I want to get my engagement ring from the safe." She rubbed her body against his and said, "Want to come?"

His eyes darkened. "That's a loaded question if I've ever heard one."

"It was meant to be." She kissed the center of his chest, and as they headed into the cabin, she said, "We have to be fast."

He'd earned his *three-minute crown* a few times since turning her down on Fortune's Landing, and neither of them was left unsatisfied.

They hurried down the steps and into his cabin, dropping their phones on the desk as they kissed and fondled each other. Oh, how she loved their *love*! He crushed her to him, pushing one hand into her hair, holding her mouth precisely where he wanted it as he took her in a knee-weakening kiss. When his phone rang, they both groaned and glanced at it on the desk. Jillian's image lit up the FaceTime screen.

"Are you freaking kidding me?" Zev snapped. "I'm not getting it, the little cockblocker." He lowered his lips to hers, kissing her harder with every ring of the phone. When it stopped ringing, he said, "Finally," against her lips, making her laugh. He kissed her devouringly, turning her laughter into hungry moans as Carly's phone rang. He ground out a curse. "Jilly again. Persistent little pest." He began taking off Carly's bikini bottom, and a text rolled in from Nick on his phone. "Are you fucking kidding me?" He picked up the phone, reading the text aloud. "Jilly says put your pants on and answer the call. Do it. I'm too busy to answer her texts." He mumbled, "Dick," under his breath.

Carly keeled over with laughter.

Zev pushed a hand through his wet hair as Carly's phone stopped ringing. "Sorry, babe," he said with a sexy, though frustrated, smile. "We need to leave our phones outside the bedroom from now on."

"It's okay. She's just excited to hear the news from *us*. We'll just have to go for double-time tonight."

"Triple time. We have a lot to celebrate." He kissed her and crouched to open the safe.

"Aren't you going to call Jilly?"

"Not before I do this." He rose with the ring in his hand, and as he slid it on her finger, he said, "You know what never gets old?"

Zev said, "Seeing the love in your eyes when I put this ring on your finger," at the same time Carly said, "Seeing the love in your eyes when you put that ring on my finger."

They both laughed and said, "Two sides of the same coin."

Ready for more Bradens & Montgomerys?

Trixie Jericho is on a mission to start her own miniature horse business. She's sick of being told her idea is *cute* and wants nothing more than to be taken seriously. When rancher and sought-after freestyle horse trainer Nick Braden offers an opportunity she can't refuse, Trixie jumps on it. The problem is, she also wants to jump on *him*, but the bullheaded, big-muscled, motorcycle-riding cowboy doesn't mix business with pleasure. Little does he know, Trixie has never backed down from a challenge. Saddle up, big boy, because this boot-stompin', risk-taking, Daisy Duke-wearing cowgirl isn't afraid to play dirty.

Fall in love with the Steeles on Silver Island!

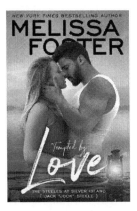

Years ago, bestselling author Jack "Jock" Steele lost his girlfriend and baby in a horrific accident that drove a wedge between Jock and his family, keeping him from sharing a devastating secret. An aging philanthropist saved him from the brink of despair, and for a decade Jock cared for his ailing friend who became his family. Now his friend has passed away and left him a fortune—on the condition that he publishes another book. Jock is floundering, unsure how to rebuild the life he'd walked away from, much less find his muse, have another relationship with a woman, or even think about having a family of his own. But he can't get his sweet, sexy new friend, single-mother Daphne Zablonski out of his head, and her adorable toddler must know something he doesn't, because she wraps her tiny fingers around his heart and won't let go.

Daphne has been through the wringer with her ex-husband and

doesn't believe true love is in the cards for her. Friends she can handle, but letting a man see her mom bod naked? Especially someone as strikingly handsome and unbelievably sexy as Jock? *No, thank you.* Besides, she has a toddler to chase after and enough fictional boyfriends to fill her lonely nights. If only her book boyfriends could make her body tingle the way one look from her mysterious neighbor does.

As Jock and Daphne's friendship turns to something too tempting to deny, their lives take an unexpected turn. Can a man who has lost everything find redemption with a woman who has everything to lose? And then there's that secret…

Have you met The Whiskeys: Dark Knights at Peaceful Harbor?

If you loved reading about Dare, Cowboy, Birdie, and the rest of the Whiskeys at Redemption Ranch, don't worry, they are all going to get their own stories. But first, meet their cousins, the Whiskeys at Peaceful Harbor, and start the series with TRU BLUE.

He wore the skin of a killer and bore the heart of a lover…

There's nothing Truman Gritt won't do to protect his family—including spending years in jail for a crime he didn't commit. When he's finally released, the life he knew is turned upside down by his mother's overdose, and Truman steps in to raise the children she's left behind. Truman's hard, he's secretive, and he's trying to save a brother who's even more broken than he is. He's never needed help in his life, and when beautiful Gemma Wright tries to step in, he's less than accepting. But Gemma has a way of slithering into people's lives, and eventually she pierces through his ironclad heart. When Truman's dark past collides with his future, his loyalties will be tested, and he'll be faced with his toughest decision yet.

New to the Love in Bloom series?

I hope you have enjoyed meeting the Bradens and Montgomerys. If you want to read more of the series, pick up the first book in the series, EMBRACING HER HEART.

If this is your first Love in Bloom book, there are many more love stories featuring loyal, sassy, and sexy heroes and heroines waiting for you. The Bradens & Montgomerys is just one of the series in the Love in Bloom big-family romance collection. Each Love in Bloom book is written to be enjoyed as a stand-alone novel or as part of the larger series. There are no cliffhangers and no unresolved issues. Characters from each series make appearances in future books, so you never miss an engagement, wedding, or birth. You might enjoy my other series within the Love in Bloom big-family romance collection, starting with the very first Braden book, LOVERS AT HEART, REIMAGINED, or the first book in the entire Love in Bloom series, SISTERS IN LOVE.

More Books By Melissa Foster

LOVE IN BLOOM SERIES

SNOW SISTERS
Sisters in Love
Sisters in Bloom
Sisters in White

THE BRADENS at Weston
Lovers at Heart, Reimagined
Destined for Love
Friendship on Fire
Sea of Love
Bursting with Love
Hearts at Play

THE BRADENS at Trusty
Taken by Love
Fated for Love
Romancing My Love
Flirting with Love
Dreaming of Love
Crashing into Love

THE BRADENS at Peaceful Harbor
Healed by Love
Surrender My Love
River of Love
Crushing on Love
Whisper of Love
Thrill of Love

THE BRADENS & MONTGOMERYS at Pleasant Hill – Oak Falls
Embracing Her Heart
Anything For Love

WILD BOYS AFTER DARK
Logan
Heath
Jackson
Cooper

BAD BOYS AFTER DARK
Mick
Dylan
Carson
Brett

<u>HARBORSIDE NIGHTS SERIES</u>
Includes characters from the Love in Bloom series
Catching Cassidy
Discovering Delilah
Tempting Tristan

More Books by Melissa
Chasing Amanda (mystery/suspense)
Come Back to Me (mystery/suspense)
Have No Shame (historical fiction/romance)
Love, Lies & Mystery (3-book bundle)
Megan's Way (literary fiction)
Traces of Kara (psychological thriller)
Where Petals Fall (suspense)

Acknowledgments

I had as much fun writing Zev and Carly's story as I did researching their careers. Now I want to be a treasure hunter and a chocolatier! I am forever grateful for the patience and assistance of admiralty and maritime lawyer Scott Bluestein, of Bluestein Law Firm in South Carolina. Scott answered my endless questions, and though I have yet to find a character to name after him, I will definitely find one. A special thank-you to Lisa Filipe, my friend, employee, and sister from another mother, for talking me off the ledge, researching at a moment's notice, laughing, crying, and fighting me tooth and nail over the little things that matter. I truly appreciate you. As with all of my stories, I have taken fictional liberties; any and all inaccuracies are not a reflection of the people who generously shared their time and knowledge with me.

Thank you to my team and my friends for always having my back, and my fans, who inspire me on a daily basis. If you haven't yet joined my fan club on Facebook, please do. We have a great time chatting about our hunky heroes and sassy heroines. You never know when you'll inspire a story or a character and end up in one of my books, as several fan club members have already discovered.
www.Facebook.com/groups/MelissaFosterFans

Remember to follow my Facebook fan page to stay abreast of

what's going on in our fictional boyfriends' worlds.
www.Facebook.com/MelissaFosterAuthor

Sign up for my newsletter to keep up to date with new releases and special promotions and events and to receive an exclusive short story featuring Jack Remington and Savannah Braden.
www.MelissaFoster.com/Newsletter

And don't forget to download your free reader goodies! For free ebooks, family trees, publication schedules, series checklists, and more, please visit the special Reader Goodies page that I've set up for you!
www.MelissaFoster.com/Reader-Goodies

As always, loads of gratitude to my amazing team of editors and proofreaders: Kristen Weber, Penina Lopez, Elaini Caruso, Juliette Hill, Marlene Engel, Lynn Mullan, and Justinn Harrison. And, of course, I am forever grateful to my family, who allow me to talk about my fictional worlds as if we live in them.

Meet Melissa

www.MelissaFoster.com

Melissa Foster is a *New York Times* and *USA Today* bestselling and award-winning author. Her books have been recommended by *USA Today's* book blog, *Hagerstown* magazine, *The Patriot*, and several other print venues. Melissa has painted and donated several murals to the Hospital for Sick Children in Washington, DC.

Visit Melissa on her website or chat with her on social media. Melissa enjoys discussing her books with book clubs and reader groups and welcomes an invitation to your event. Melissa's books are available through most online retailers in paperback, digital, and audio formats.

Made in the USA
Middletown, DE
28 October 2020